ADI DENNER
THE KISS OF THE NIGHTINGALE

tundra

Tundra Books, an imprint of Tundra Book Group, a division of Penguin Random
House of Canada Limited

Library and Archives Canada Cataloguing in Publication

Title: The kiss of the nightingale / Adi Denner.
Names: Denner, Adi, author.
Identifiers: Canadiana (print) 20230595561 | Canadiana (ebook) 2023059560X |
ISBN 9781774885253 (hardcover) | ISBN 9781774885260 (EPUB)
Subjects: LCGFT: Fantasy fiction. | LCGFT: Romance fiction. | LCGFT: Novels.
Classification: LCC PZ7.1.D46 Kis 2024 | DDC j823/.92—dc23

Published simultaneously in the United States of America by Tundra Books of
Northern New York, an imprint of Tundra Book Group, a division of Penguin
Random House of Canada Limited

Library of Congress Control Number: 2023951959

Edited by Lynne Missen
Jacket designed by Talia Abramson
Typeset by Erin Cooper
The text was set in Bembo Book MT Pro.

Printed in Canada

www.penguinrandomhouse.ca

1 2 3 4 5   28 27 26 25 24

Penguin
Random House

tundra | TUNDRA BOOKS

To those who need the courage to sing.

CHAPTER ONE

Broken Wings

FATHER'S RING SITS barren on my finger—hollow, empty. No jewel sparkles as I gaze at it, no magic singing in my blood. It's as empty as our cash register, with its two silver francs and ten bronze pieces— barely enough to keep my sister and me fed for a fortnight. Our dress shop has definitely seen better days.

I lean on the wooden counter, hands covering my face. I have long learned staring at the door won't magically bring in customers.

A deep cough from the back room makes my throat tighten.

"I'm fine!" Anaella calls with a hoarse voice.

This is the twelfth time my younger sister has coughed in the past five minutes.

I run to the sink and grab a chipped glass from the shelf. The water comes out cloudy, almost gray, but it's the only thing I have to keep her throat from drying up.

"What on earth are you doing out of bed?" I say as soon as I step into the back room, finding my sister crouched at the desk.

"I said I'm fine, Cleo." She rolls her eyes at me before another wave of coughing takes her.

I force the glass into her hand. "No, you're not. You should be resting."

Anaella takes a timid sip, her face contorting at the bitter taste of our water. "I had a new design idea. Look." She points to the desk, which is covered by an array of tiny drawings on thin sheets of paper.

I hold up the nearest one, tracing my fingers over the delicate watercolor strokes that paint a light chiffon ball gown. Like a garden in full bloom, the fabric weaves itself into endless velvety petals, covering the sweeping pink skirt. They circle all the way up to a tight off-the-shoulder corset adorned with golden beads that shimmer like dew in the morning sun. It's everything Anaella and I can never be, contrasting our faded cotton dresses with the luxury and elegance only a fine lady could afford.

The edge of the drawing wrinkles under my grip. My sister has clearly been going over Father's book again—seeing all of our late parents' designs and notes always sparks her creativity. Sure enough, the old leather binding sticks out from under the scattered pages. Just looking at it makes my chest tighten.

"Imagine it in shades of ivory," Anaella says. "I wanted it creamy with touches of gold, but . . . I ran out of paint."

"It's beautiful," I say, pushing down the lump in my throat.

"I was thinking . . . if we can make it and put it in the front window, we could—" Her words are swallowed by another rumbling cough, draining the color from her sunken cheeks. She quiets it with another sip of water. "We could attract more customers."

If Father were here, he'd have agreed at once. But without him our dress shop is nothing but a shadow of its former glory, stacks of shoddy fabrics slowly gathering dust.

"This material isn't cheap, Ann . . . not to mention the beads. Besides, I'm not skilled enough to sew something this complicated."

Her face drops. "Cleo, you might not have inherited Papa's Talent, but you are definitely good enough."

It's my turn to look away, eyes falling again to the ring on my finger. A simple band of gold with no flourishes, and an empty spot where a gem should have been embedded. It is that spot that makes my throat clench. A reminder of the promise our father broke when he died so suddenly, taking his Talent—five generations of honed tailoring skills—to the grave with him. On my sister's finger sits an identical ring, only hers is adorned with a shining opal stone.

She catches me staring and covers her ring with her palm. That tiny gesture proves her words are a lie. Anaella never understood my fate. How could she? Our mother transferred her Design Talent to her before she passed. My sister never had to suffer the emptiness that comes with having none.

"You can't keep the shop open just by doing those minimal alterations for customers. We need new dresses!" Anaella urges.

Her eyes are so full of determination and hope, I cannot bear to tell her that our cash register is empty, or that I don't have any more of Mother's jewels to sell. "Maybe we could buy materials later this month," I lie.

She pushes away from the desk, a dainty hand outstretched, but before she can take a step her legs cave beneath her.

"Ann!" I catch her before she hits the ground.

It takes all my strength to drag her across the tiny room to her corner bed. Back when our parents were alive, we used to own the second floor above the shop, but now this stuffy back room, with its two beds and one desk, is all Anaella and I have to call home.

She groans as I put an extra pillow behind her head. A sickly yellow tint replaces the pink of her cheeks. Her once-flowing hair is dry and brittle, and the glint in her round brown eyes has dimmed. Anaella and I are almost identical, yet I always thought she was the beautiful one. Her wild energy used to light up every room like a fire, sparks luring everyone in. Seeing her broken like this tears my heart.

"You shouldn't be out of bed," I murmur.

"I want to help," Anaella says, before coughing again into her handkerchief. When she pulls her hand away blood splatters her chin, spots covering the old cloth. "I'm sorry . . ."

"There is nothing to apologize for." My lips tremble as I wipe her face. "Just rest for a while. We can talk about dresses when you feel better."

She nods and closes her eyes as I tuck the covers around her and brush the hair from her face. Her forehead is burning.

Sitting on the floor by her side, I rest my head against the wall. She needs a doctor. A good one. One I can't afford. Our cash register mocks me through the open doorway as though echoing the emptiness I feel inside.

Soon Anaella's breathing turns heavier, the sleep taking away some of her pain. There's nothing I wouldn't do to make her better. Nothing I wouldn't give. With a silent groan, I push myself from the floor and slip out of the room, hanging the "Closed" sign on our door, any dreams of customers long gone. I glance back once, my heart wrenching as Anaella coughs in her sleep, before stepping out onto the grim street.

The skies are deep blue with airy cotton clouds floating on the far horizon. Yet in the alley the air is stuffy, gray stone walls soaked with the stench of decay. Back in my childhood, the alley used to buzz with activity. I used to hold Father's hand as we strolled through the maze of streets, listening to the countless stories the old walls of Lutèce kept hidden within: of love, jealousy, and the bravery of those who left a mark on this world. But once he was gone, so were the customers. And soon after the smaller shops closed down or moved, leaving the vacant buildings to rot. No. Father did not leave a mark on this world. Instead, his legacy was stripped down to a faded sign above a broken door and a barren ring—a useless piece of metal that can't help me put food on the table.

Or perhaps . . . it can.

I freeze, trailing my thumb over the gold circle. A second later, I'm kicking the uneven paving stones, turning down another alley toward the main avenue.

Here the storefronts sparkle, the sun reflecting on their enviably spotless surfaces—a promise of the Talented crafts they hold. Customers rush between them like a swarm of bees, pollinating their cash registers from their deep, full pockets. Such glimmering luxury, yet it is merely a tantalizing taste of the riches hidden away in the Elite's secluded domains across the river. After all, they would never live among tradespeople.

To my left, ladies in wide hats sip aromatic coffee over tables spread with crisp white cloths, chattering as they bite into freshly baked, sugar-coated pastries that make my empty stomach churn. To my right, a gentleman helps his laughing daughter into a carriage, handing her a new pair of pink ballet shoes. But straight ahead, the open door to the pawnshop looms in darkness.

I take a deep breath, twisting the ring around my finger. No point in delaying the inevitable.

The pawnshop's familiar musty scent hits me as soon as I cross the threshold. By now I know the stuffed shop well. Like many who lost a Talent to cruel fate, or who never attained one back when the mines still crackled with magic, I, too, quickly discovered that hard labor isn't enough to survive in a world driven by inherited gifts. Upon Father's death, most of our family's possessions ended up on these dusty wooden shelves.

"Can I help you, Miss—? Oh, you again. What can I do for you today?" The broker shoves his glasses up his broken nose with one finger, not bothering to step away from the counter.

I push my shoulders back as I march toward the old man. "I'd like to sell my ring."

The tiny topaz gem atop his eyebrow piercing twitches as he takes a magnifying glass from his pocket. "Wedding ring? Family heirloom?"

"No, but it's solid gold."

He nods, opening a callused palm.

For just a second, my hand closes into a fist, my ring suddenly heavier—imbued with priceless memories and promises that can never be bought back. Am I really ready to say goodbye?

"Well?" The broker eyes me impatiently.

The image of Anaella's sunken cheeks fills my mind. Ready or not—I cannot let her down. Before I can change my mind, I take the ring off.

I bite the inside of my cheek as the broker examines it under his magnifying glass and places it on a bronze scale.

"I can give you one silver franc for it," he says too quickly, even for one with his Analyzing Talent.

"What? It's real gold!"

He sets the ring back on the counter. "Where's the gem? No one wants half a ring."

I clench my jaw against the sudden chatter of my teeth. This can't be the worth of Father's inheritance. This can't be the worth of his memory.

"There has to be a mistake," I mumble. "Check the weight again. Maybe you can melt it. Or—"

"Just because I'm feeling generous, I'll give you a silver franc and a bronze piece. That's the highest I'll go."

I snap the ring from the counter. "No deal."

"You won't get a better offer!" he yells after me, but I'm already rushing out the door.

Blood pumps in my ears, my breath coming short and fast. I shut my eyes and try to block the outside world. This was my last resort, the only thing I had left to give, and it's not enough. Father left me with nothing—just a trinket with sentimental value, memories, and broken promises. The laughter around me rings too loud, the crowd is too thick, the sun too bright. I push between the shoppers, carriages, and horses, not stopping to catch my breath or to apologize for almost knocking a lady over. I need to breathe, to break out of the suffocating crowd.

I only slow down when I reach the bridge crossing the wide river to the other side of town—the *better* side of town. The cruel current lashes at the brick columns as if attempting to wash the sturdy intruders away. The same way it washed Father away so many months ago.

The river took much more than his life that day.

I shake the morbid thoughts from my mind. Green rooftops dot the horizon. Smoke spews out of round chimneys, the light gray wisps disappearing into the clear skies. And just like that, I'm a child again, carrying a wrapped, blue-layered silk dress in my arms, my cheeks flushed with excitement, as Father and I cross the gushing river.

"Remember, mon coeur, this is just one trip of many to come," Father said, his eyes sparkling with pride. "This garment will be worn at the masquerade ball by the great soprano Mirella. In a few years, it will be you who sews her dresses."

It was the first time Father had taken me to a meeting with a client, a reward for managing to make a corset on my own. I blink away the echo of his warm voice in my mind. I haven't even noticed my feet carrying me to the other bank, longing to lose myself in the old memories, to numb the turmoil raging within.

On this side of the city, marble and gold rule the facades. Blossoming trees adorn each housefront, their foliage providing speckled shade over the wide-open street. There are even lazy swans gliding over a canal, full of grace and ease. A dull ache builds in my chest at the beauty of it all; it's a part of a world that will never be mine.

Farther along the bank, a man in a fine black suit checks his pocket watch. "Mon amour, we'll be late," he calls down to a lady standing at the river edge, feeding the swans with a loaf of bread. Even from afar, the golden crust shines, and my mouth waters with the memory of glazed honey.

"Just a moment, dear. The performance doesn't start until sunset." The woman brushes a perfect blond lock from her face, the sheer fabric of her winged sleeves swaying in the light breeze.

"This is the last performance of the season," the man insists. "I'd prefer to get there early to check our seats. You know it'll be a full house."

The lady laughs and throws the rest of the bread into the water. I gasp as the loaf sinks, taking my heart with it as birds attack it from all sides. That could have fed my sister and me for a week.

"It's the same box we've had all season long. I'm sure it'll be fine," she says, but goes to her husband's side nonetheless.

I should turn back, return home and check on Anaella, but I can't help following them. Perhaps it's the grace of the lady's movement, or the adoration in the gentleman's eyes when he looks at his wife, reminding me of my parents. It's as if watching the couple is a mirror to a world I've forgotten. I can see Mother in my head, wearing a pink gown, holding onto Father's arm as he takes her to an opening night at the opera. She adored music—a passion Father shared as well. For a moment I can imagine myself alongside them, enjoying a glass of champagne before the performance, watching the stage together from velvet chairs as the curtains rise.

But these are not my parents. And I will never feel their love again, or share those luxuries.

I trail the couple as they whisper to each other all the way up the avenue to the main plaza. I freeze by the arched gates, standing under the winged horses and marble angels that guard the entrance. A cascading fountain carved with roses sits in the middle of the square, the water sparkling under the setting sun. But the beauty of the square dims next to the marvel just ahead. Lutèce's opera house towers over the plaza, with columns supporting golden arches and stained-glass windows. Every nook is carved to perfection, a structural wonder conjured from a storybook.

Here the crowd is all in formal attire: delicate lace necklines upon velvet collars, flowing gowns with trains of chiffon, silky suits, and sparkling jewelry. So much jewelry. Diamond necklaces, gleaming sapphire rings, sumptuous pearl earrings, and encrusted crowns, so colorful and bright.

The precious stones are mesmerizing. The things I could do if I could get my hands on just one of them.

I wonder which of these gems store magic under their vibrant glow. My sister and I used to play a guessing game when we were young—a rose gem for a ballerina, an aquamarine one for a teacher, perhaps. Whichever

Talents are among this crowd, there's no doubt that they are the finest in all of Lutèce—not mere craft skills, but gifts honed by the upper class long before any tradesmen could even dream of holding a magical gem.

I shift from one foot to the other, shrinking under the criticizing eyes that fall on my faded brown cotton dress with its frayed hem. The bitter taste of shame coats my tongue as I turn away from the gathering at the opera house's entrance. The couple has long since been lost in the crowd. There is nothing I wouldn't give to be among them: respected, welcomed, even adored—all the things I can never be without a Talent.

The sun sets behind me, bathing the white streets with orange hues as I plunge back into the city, away from the plaza. The buildings here are farther apart, beautiful cottages with wide gardens. I follow the line of round balconies until my eyes fall on a carriage a few houses down. A coachman stands on the sidewalk, securing the reins of two white horses.

"Where is that butler when you need him?" a call comes from the grand house to the left where an old lady leans against a heavy entrance door. "Leave the damn mare and hold the door for me, you fool."

The coachman pulls at the horses so suddenly they rear up on their back legs with all the force of untamed beasts. The carriage jerks forward as the startled young man grabs the reins only to fall to the ground. He hits the pavement, a cry of pain escaping him as he holds his elbow.

"Clumsy imbecile!" the lady shouts. "If I miss the show, it will come out of your salary."

I rush forward, leaning down to examine his injury. "Are you hurt?"

He shakes his head and takes my hand to stand before hurrying to grab the horses.

"Sorry, my lady. It's all my fault," the coachman mumbles.

"I'll help you with the door, my lady," I say, and the coachman shoots me a grateful look.

The woman scans me from head to toe as I pass through the gates and approach the house, her gaze lingering on each stray hair and stain on my dress. Her beak-like nose wrinkles in disapproval, but she nods, and I climb the four stairs to her doorway. From her straight back and the finery of her silver robes, I can tell she is used to being respected and served at all times—never one to hold a door for herself, or even comb her own hair.

"At least your manners cover for your poor appearance, girl," she says as I bow my head and hold the door, allowing her to stand with the poise fitting her status.

"Here." She takes out a bronze piece from a small clutch and drops it in my hand. "Hurry up now!" she shouts at the coachman, who rushes to open the carriage for her. "Just close the door, girl, it will lock on its own."

"Yes, my lady," I utter, letting go of the heavy door. But as the woman looks away, I shove my foot between it and the frame.

A moment later, the horses trot up the street, disappearing around the corner. My body is frozen, a tingling sensation spreading down my limbs. The street is empty, only birds chirping as they settle in the tree branches for the night. What am I even doing? The door presses against my foot, but I linger at the threshold. Inside this house, there are riches beyond anything I could imagine. A single teaspoon here would be worth more than the shop has earned in the last month; easily payment for the best doctor in the city. When you have so much, would you notice if anything were gone?

With a shaky hand I pull the door, swiftly slipping inside. A peal of nervous laughter bursts from my lips when I take in the foyer. A massive chandelier hangs above, like an array of stars dropping yellow light on red-carpeted stairs.

Heart racing, I sneak up the massive staircase. The metal railing is cold to the touch and my knuckles turn white as I grab it, holding onto it like a lifeline. Yet even through my fear, I can tell the riches here are undeniable—a soaring ceiling with a painted dome, golden-framed portraits. Even the air smells opulent, a mixture of vanilla and roses.

But I have no time to stand and stare. An estate always has servants, and if anyone sees me, I'm ruined. I hasten up the stairs to the second-floor corridor. From the corner of my eye, I register a tightly trimmed garden outside the windows at the end of the hall. Mouth dry, I rush to the closest door and press my ear to it. All silent. With a quick glance to each side, I twist the handle.

The room is just as big as I expected—a massive chamber covered with mahogany wood panels, lush red curtains, and containing a canopy bed. A giant vanity dresser stands by the far wall, a glistening mirror above it reflecting the array of colored glass perfume bottles and expensive tinctures. Their rich scents draw me in as my feet sink into the softly carpeted floors.

My hands shake as I reach for a heart-shaped bottle and sniff the orange blossom aroma. I glance over my shoulder before pressing the round nozzle, the spray landing on my wrist in a delicate coat. The experience is intoxicating: the cool oil against my skin, the refreshing smell of flowers. It draws a sigh from my lips, making me reach out for another bottle—just as steps echo behind the door.

Cold spreads down my limbs, and I freeze. The steps fade, but the panic in my chest lingers—a reminder that I don't have time to play around. Taking a deep breath, I open the drawers. I need to find something the lady wouldn't miss. Something small, insignificant, but expensive enough to cover the cost of caring for Anaella.

I pause at the third drawer, hand hovering over a golden box. It's round and heavy, engraved with the image of a songbird—a robin or a nightingale, perhaps. There is something enchanting about it, as if the bird might suddenly burst into song. Touching it alone feels like a crime. I lift the lid with trembling fingers and gasp. I'd been prepared for riches. This is something far beyond. The jewels are like rain beading a meadow, cascading onto one another as if fighting for a place at the top: gemstones and diamonds, sparkling from an endless sea of gold.

I close my eyes, twisting my ring. *My ring*. Once a promise for a bright future, now worth a silver franc that wouldn't even get the cheapest doctor out of his chair. This is the only way to get the money I need. Shaking my head, I dig into the box of jewelry, trying to reach the bottom where the long-forgotten pieces are sure to be found.

My hand closes around what feels like an encrusted necklace.

"Come on . . ." I mumble as I wriggle my fingers to pull it out. It is stuffed so deep that other jewels get caught in its chain, but eventually I release it from their grasp, mouthing a silent yelp of victory. The chain is solid gold, with leaves of silver attached along the neckline. It's simple yet elegant. But it is the stone that catches my eye—a tear-shaped ruby, sitting in a bed of silver flower petals. It's warm to the touch, so reflective it almost glows.

"That isn't yours," a deep voice says behind me.

I turn at once, but my vision goes black as a rough sack covers my head, muffling my scream.

CHAPTER TWO

My Little Nightingale

THE LEFT SIDE of my head throbs in pain. I open my eyes slowly, blinking through my blurry vision. The room around me is dark and stuffy, the scent of mold heavy in the air.

I try to move my arm, but it resists. I wince, squinting to see through the darkness. I've been tied to a chair, my hands forced together behind my back, my ankles wrapped with a coarse rope to the chair's legs. Panicked, I struggle against my bonds, the rope cutting my wrists.

Is my attacker here? I turn my head from side to side, but I'm alone. The last thing I recall is screaming and kicking while rough hands threw me over broad shoulders, and then a blunt blow to my head. These could not have been the actions of the police; they were too rogue. A personal guard, perhaps?

Should I scream? Try and call for help? Around me there's nothing but gray walls. No windows. No furniture. Only a short staircase leading up to a concrete platform with a bolted metal door. This has to be a basement of sorts—even if I try shouting, no one will hear me. No one except whoever put me here. My heart quickens, and my breath comes in short bursts.

What are they going to do to me? Torture me? Turn me over and throw me in jail? Kill me? What will happen to Anaella if I simply never return? Will she think I abandoned her? She'll die of heartache before the illness can take her.

I jump at the thud of heavy boots and fight in vain against the ropes. The rattle of keys chills my insides, followed by the shriek of the rusty metal door.

Two giant men loom in the entrance, their heads mere inches from brushing the ceiling. They step inside, forming a protective wall in front of a dark figure lingering on the stairs behind them.

"Boys," a young lady's voice says, "untie my guest, will you?"

One of the men marches toward me, a knife gleaming in his fist.

"Please don't hurt me!"

"No need to be afraid, my dear," the woman says as the man swiftly slashes the ropes around my ankles and wrists.

Something in her tone is sincere, yet the looming thugs make me cower into the chair. I massage my wrists as the man steps back, fingers tingling as blood returns to my hands. "Who . . . who are you? What do you want from me?"

The woman glides down the stairs, holding a candelabra with long, delicate fingers. The light falls directly onto her face, the flickering shadows accentuating her high cheekbones. Her slick black hair is tied into a tight bun, her dark eyes daggers. As she steps off the stairs, her lips press into a knowing smile. Yet the expression is far from one of simple kindness. There is a feeling of superiority to it, as though her grin guards countless secrets she could dangle over my head.

Against it I'm smaller somehow, weak, afraid. I shudder, my body more bound to the chair than when the ropes held me down.

"I'm Lady Sibille, but if our meeting goes as well as I expect it to, you could refer to me as Dahlia." She tilts her head almost playfully as she hands the burning candles to one of the men. The action is so confident, her control so natural, it's as if she were a great duchess—but instead of devoted countrymen, she commands an army of oversized thugs with knives. "And I think the better question is: what do *you* want from *me*?"

"I want nothing from you," I utter. "I just want to get home to my sister."

"Ah, but that is a lie, dear. I believe you showed a particular interest in this." She pulls the necklace I attempted to steal from within her robes. It dangles in the air between us, flashing in the dim light of the candles before she places it around her neck. The ruby fits seamlessly with the open neckline of her tight gown. Most ladies would deem her appearance inappropriate, the crimson silk hugging her curves so tightly it's as though the fabric has become a part of her skin, outlining her shape to perfection.

I wonder what it must feel like to wear such a gown, to allow yourself to be so sensual, so daring. It's almost admirable. An unfamiliar warmth spreads to my cheeks as I stare, the sensation unsettling . . . dangerous. Claws of fear dig into me and I shiver, turning my head away from her in a sudden panic.

"I'm sorry," I manage, but it's as though my mouth is filled with sand.

Thieves, thugs, bandits—the city's underground has always hidden them in its shadows. This woman, no matter how elegant she may appear, certainly belongs to them. People like her respond to power, bribes, or bargains, yet I have nothing to offer. My only choice is to beg.

"I'm not a thief," I say. "I swear. I only wanted something I could use to pay for a doctor for my sister. She's sick, you see, and . . ."

Dahlia lifts her hand and my voice falters, my courage all but disappearing.

"Yes, Anaella is terribly ill, isn't she?" Her voice is as soft as a cat's purr.

Dread spreads through my veins in waves. "How . . . how do you know her name?"

That calculated smile stretches again on her lips, and my skin crawls. What else could she know? Would she hurt Anaella for my stupidity? How could I have been such a fool? I deserve whatever is coming for me. If only I could spare my sister . . .

"I know all about you, Cleodora," Dahlia says. "I never go into business without doing my due diligence."

Her words make me pause, cutting through the rumble in my head. "Business?"

"Indeed."

This must be a trap. This woman cannot be trusted. Yet what choice do I have? The looming thugs seem somehow even bigger as they wait in the shadows.

"You can choose to refuse," she says as though she has read my mind, circling around me slowly. "Yet I doubt you will want to, once you hear my proposal."

"I . . . I have nothing to offer you. If you know everything about me, you must know I have no Talent."

"That is exactly why you'll do perfectly." Dahlia stops right in front of me, too close for comfort. "Your father left you with a shop you cannot maintain without his gift. Your mother gave her Talent to your sick sister, who can't even use it. No other friends or family to speak of—you are practically invisible. But instead of worrying about food on the table, you worry about medicine. So young to have such burdens. Only nineteen." The scent of jasmine envelops me as she leans closer, her lips nearly brushing my ear. "I know how you feel," she whispers, her breath warm. "Helpless. Worthless. I can help, if you'll help me in return."

Help her? There is nothing I can give a woman like her, nothing that won't mean delving into a world of shadows I want no part of. I should say no, beg for mercy, and pray for my sister's fate. Yet something within me stirs, making the words die before they reach my lips. How could she possibly have all this information?

I feel exposed, naked—my deepest regrets and shame laid barren. The urge to hide or wrap my arms around myself in protection is almost too strong to resist, yet I force myself to remain still. If she truly knows so much about me, could the rest of her words be true? Could she possibly help?

"What do you want me to do?" My voice shakes as I speak.

She draws back with a smile, and I'm not sure if it's that jasmine perfume of hers or simply her intoxicating presence that's making my head spin. "You see, the jewel you tried to steal from *Dame de Adley* wasn't hers to begin with."

"Lady Adley? The famous soprano?"

"Nasty woman, if you ask me. Wouldn't you agree, Henry?" Dahlia turns to one of her guards, who immediately nods on cue, like a marionette. "Anyway," Dahlia sighs, "this beautiful gem was a gift from my family that I have long planned to reclaim."

I furrow my brow as she takes off the necklace, her fingers circling the gem. "What does this have to do with me?"

"Haven't you guessed already?" Dahlia laughs, the sound too sweet. "This is Lady Adley's Singing Talent."

"*What?*" I search her face for the lie, for any hint that she's only toying with me, but I find none. "It can't be, it was just stuffed in the bottom of her jewelry box." I stare at the shining ruby in disbelief. "No one would treat a Talent with such . . ."

"Carelessness?" Dahlia suggests. "You'd be surprised how ungrateful some people are. Which is exactly why I'm looking for someone to assume this abandoned Talent. Someone like you."

"Me?" And even though my nerves are still tingling with fear, I nearly laugh. She can't possibly be serious. I'm a nobody—a Talentless girl with nothing to my name. I cannot be an opera singer. A lady. Why would she even want me to?

"Lady Adley has recently retired," Dahlia says. "She has become too old to be a prima donna. She has no children, and no one to take over her estate. I have been watching her for a while now, and I've decided it is time she took her leave. Tonight's performance is Lady Adley's last social event, after which she will depart Lutèce for her vacation house on the Riviera." Dahlia snaps her fingers, and one of the guards places a tiny vial in her palm, full of thick red liquid.

My mouth turns dry, my stomach churning. "Is that . . . ?"

"Lady Adley's blood." Dahlia flips the bottle, watching the fluid drip over the glass. "Darrin here fetched it from her after he carried you over. I have all the necessities to complete a transfer ceremony. Now all I need is for you to take her place."

My eyes shift between the gem and the vial. This is not a trick. Not a lie. She wants to give me a Talent—the one thing I thought I could never have. The one thing capable of mending the fragmented pieces of my life that have been in disarray ever since Father died. The hot waves of desire and chilling fear running through me are undeniable, crashing against each other as I fight the urge to grab hold of the ruby and never let go.

"You will be presented as Lady Adley's distant cousin, and her chosen heir," she continues. "You will become an opera star, and her estate will be yours. With the money, you could pay for your sister's care, even buy her a new house."

I shake my head, trying to make sense of it all. "But . . . I have no knowledge of singing."

"I don't deal with untrained Talents." Dahlia's eyes flash with anger before she blinks it away. "You will have all the skills to use it once we embed it with your blood."

My blood . . . bonded with a Talent. No longer ostracized. No longer living on the edges of society. It sounds too good to be true. "But why—?"

Dahlia cuts me off. "Oh, I can already see it." She steps behind me, brushing my hair with soft hands. Chills run through me as she places the ruby around my neck. "Under all the grime, you are a beautiful woman. The stage will love you."

I know I should resist, that no good can come of even toying with this idea—not when I can sense the dangerous shadows behind it. But her words ignite a spark buried inside me—that same desire I felt watching the Elite at the opera house, to be among them, respected and adored.

True, it's not the Talent I always dreamed of having, but somehow that only makes it more exciting—a fresh start, a way to save my sister and me, a life of luxury I've never even dared to imagine. The weight of the stone presses against my chest—it's so close. The desire burns through me as I've never allowed it to before.

I need it to be mine.

"There is a price, of course," Dahlia says.

"I'll give you anything!" I say before I can even think, my voice echoing in the basement.

The smile spreading on her lips is so breathtakingly beautiful it's unnerving. "I was hoping you'd say that. You see, Cleo, in my business, connections are everything. I need people I can trust. Can I trust you?"

I nod at once, even though somewhere in the corner of my mind warning bells scream at me. Who is Dahlia? I've never heard of the Sibille lineage, not even back when Father tailored most of high society's clothes. I am certain associating myself with her would be a mistake. But the pulse of energy coming from the necklace against my skin is too strong, and deep down I know that I would do anything to claim it. To save my sister. To change my fate.

"When my father gave that Talent on your neck to Lady Adley, she was nothing but a street rat," Dahlia says. "He gave her a life in exchange for her services. Now that she has retired, her duties will fall onto you."

"What do you need from me?"

"I need you to help me provide my clients with whatever they desire. I pride myself on never turning down a job. For the right price, of course." She lets out a long cackle.

My eyes dart to her two guards, standing still as statues. "Like . . . an illicit market?" I can't hide the hesitation in my tone.

The corners of her lips curl up. "You will be one of my workers. You will integrate yourself within the Elite, live their life, gain their trust, so that when I need you, you can use your connections for whatever I deem necessary."

"I'm not sure I know what you mean." I drop my eyes to the concrete floor. By my feet, dark red patches glisten in the candles' flickering light. My stomach quivers. What am I doing?

"My most lucrative currency these days is Talents. They are a rare commodity now that there are no new gems to be had."

A rare commodity is an understatement. The mines officially ran dry just before I was born, sparking riots in the streets. But no political uprising could change the reality: honing new Talents has become impossible, and each magical gem in existence has become ever more precious. But with all Talents claimed, how can they possibly serve as any sort of currency?

"Unfortunately," Dahlia continues softly, "not everything can be obtained through negotiation." Her long fingers lift my chin, compelling me to meet the depths of her black eyes.

Trapped within her gaze, I'm breathless. There is intimacy in this connection, a sense of vulnerability that frightens me. Only, somehow, I'm not weakened by it. I search her flawless face as she searches mine, and for just that moment I almost feel like her equal.

Dahlia doesn't blink, yet something shifts on her face—not uncertainty exactly, but perhaps curiosity? She narrows her eyes before speaking. "I need you to become my thief."

The connection is broken at once as I fumble, opening my mouth to protest but failing to produce any sound. I should have known this was coming. I did know. And instead of stopping it I allowed myself to momentarily indulge in this dangerous dream. But what she's asking of me is the stuff of nightmares.

I'm not a criminal.

Yes, I did try to steal that necklace, but it was supposed to be a one-time thing, a means to help my sister, nothing more. I only meant to take a jewel, something insignificant, forgotten, that no one would miss. Not a *Talent*. Stealing someone's gift is the most despicable crime there is. I know too well what it's like to have your fate, your future, snatched away from you.

After Father passed, taking his Talent with him, the world didn't delay in showing Anaella and me its cruel side. The customers were the first to disappear, and with them my dreams of following in the footsteps of my family's long line of tailors. Our friends didn't stick around much longer either, and my sister's health took a turn for the worse soon after. It was as if we were cursed, bound to live our lives in the shadows, just trying to survive each passing day.

Agreeing to this deal would mean that we'd never have to struggle again. I would never again worry about putting food on the table, or cry at night while contemplating all the ways I'm failing to provide for my sister—failing as the head of the family. I could finally build a life for us.

But at what price? I'd be selling my integrity, everything I believe in—gaining my dreams by stealing them from someone else, inflicting my own pain on the world.

"You are concerned," Dahlia whispers. "Afraid to ruin someone's life. Well, if you accept my offer, I promise you will take only from those who can *afford* it."

She's mere inches from me now, her breath warm on my skin. Everything about her speaks of softness—the smoothness of her face, the perfect rosy color of her cheeks, so unlike the darkness surrounding us.

She is like an angel or a fairy godmother, offering me a way out. Or is she perhaps like the devil, asking me to sell my soul for her gifts?

Can I become what she asks? A thief? Forever lying, scheming, cheating . . . stealing.

Her full lips part, and a sudden urge to close the distance and test if they are as soft as they seem catches me off guard. I swallow the lump rising in my throat with a wave of embarrassment. She is a seductress, a beast in disguise who knows how to lure her prey with their greatest desires.

"Oh, Cleo, you disappoint me." She sighs as I stay silent.

At once a hollow ache fills my chest. I'm still not sure turning her down is even a real option, if I value my life. But even if it were, I'm not sure I could. I'll never have another chance. Not to have a Talent, or to afford proper care for Anaella. Beast or not, how could I live with myself if I gave that up?

"I really hoped we could work together." Dahlia turns to leave, gesturing for her men to pick up the ropes.

"I'll do it." The words are out of my mouth before I can control them.

"Oh!" She clasps her hands. "Did you hear that, boys? I'm so glad!"

My heart is beating so fast I fear it might burst through my chest. What did I just do?

But Dahlia is already moving. No time to regret. One of her guards unclasps the necklace from my neck with rough hands, and I nearly jump when he crushes it in his fist. The ruby breaks free from the setting of silver leaves, which fall broken to the floor.

"Excellent, Darrin." Dahlia flashes a perfect smile. "Henry, dear, the blood." She beckons, her eyes still locked on me.

The second guard steps forward with a knife in hand. He grabs my arm, and though I know this is a vital part of the ceremony I tense at the gleam of the blade, instinctively trying to pull away. But his grasp is like steel. A moment later the knife slices deeply into my palm, much deeper than I thought it would be. A whimper escapes my lips and I pant, chest heaving as blood drips on my dress.

"The shinier the jewel, the bloodier the Talent." Dahlia's voice is like a lullaby. She brushes a lock of hair away from my forehead, and goosebumps rise on my arms. With steady hands, she takes the ruby and pours the vial of Lady Adley's blood on it. "Trust me," she says, before pressing the gem into my wounded palm.

I flinch as the cut flares with pain but keep my hand steady. Eyes closed, I take a deep breath as my blood mixes with the blood on the stone—the magic ready to be transferred from one to the other, erasing Lady Adley's connection with the gem and replacing it with my own.

I had always imagined what it would feel like to bond with a Talent. Father used to say it resembled fantastic ecstasy, like floating on a cloud.

Yet the warmth spreading inside of me is not soft. Instead, currents of static flow from the crown of my head down to my fingertips, as if my cloud is brimming with lightning. And when they quiet, I'm left breathless, but I'm no longer an empty vessel. The ruby pulses in my hand and my heart pulses with it. And all at once, I feel complete.

Dahlia kisses the top of my head, her lips the brush of a butterfly's wings. "You will make a fabulous diva, my little nightingale."

CHAPTER THREE

Golden Cage

THE FIRST RAYS of sunlight paint the horizon in shades of scarlet and tangerine, electric against the deep blue skies. I hasten down the quiet alley, the chirping of waking birds barely audible over my racing heart.

"Do not look for me—my men will make sure you get instructions soon," Dahlia said right before her guard put the sack over my head again, ensuring I wouldn't know my whereabouts. I suspect he made extra rounds with the carriage before finally letting me out a few blocks away from home.

What will I tell Anaella? I cannot possibly tell her the truth . . . she'll never understand. I'm not sure *I* understand. How will I explain where I've been? Did she suffer through the night without me?

I close my bandaged palm; the cut is still raw and painful, but no blood seeps through the white cloth. I never expected that binding myself with a Talent would require so much blood. But then again, I was never meant to have such a powerful Talent—an Elite Talent. This gem is for a true lady, for the aristocracy of Lutèce, who possess the oldest, most powerful Talents.

"Which jewelry would you like? A necklace? Earrings?" Dahlia's voice still rings in my mind.

"Can you attach it to my ring?"

The memory of Dahlia's full lips twisting into a smile surfaces as I close my eyes. "*So sentimental.*"

I shiver, pushing the image away, and stare at the ruby resting on my finger—the price of my soul. The pulse of energy from the gem creates goosebumps over my skin, unfamiliar yet exhilarating.

Morning dew sparkles on the weeds pushing their way through the cobblestones. Even the gray walls look refreshed, bathed in golden hues that mask their decay. For a moment, I'm a child again, watching the rising world through hopeful eyes. But the lightness in my step fades when I reach the wooden door to our shop.

The ruby shimmers in the light as my hand freezes on the doorknob. It seems too big for my thin fingers. I take the ring off, stuffing it into my pocket. The door creaks as I step inside.

"Cleo?" my sister calls.

The weakness of her voice sends a wave of guilt through me. I rush into the back room to apologize for abandoning her last night, but she's not alone.

I halt at the sight of the man sitting by her side, a woman in a white robe standing over his shoulder, holding a stethoscope. A doctor? Confusion furrows my brow—was Anaella's cough so bad a neighbor called for one?

"I thought you left me," Anaella says. She's joking, I know. Her eyes are half open, her skin flushed and covered with cold sweat, but still, she smiles at me.

"Miss Finley?" the man asks, blinking from behind a pair of thick glasses.

"Yes, and you are . . . ?"

"I'm Dr. Banks, and this is Nurse Dupont. We've been awaiting your arrival."

My jaw drops. I've heard of Dr. Banks before—a miracle worker with the Healing Talent to identify all illnesses at a mere glance and the skill to treat even the most apparently futile cases. His patients are either fabulously rich or so hopeless that they are willing to sell their inheritance, their family, or their soul. But I already sold mine. I have nothing of value to give him. No way to pay for his services.

"Your sister needs around-the-clock care," Dr. Banks says. "I prescribed a mixture of herbs, and Nurse Dupont will administer a weekly cupping therapy. The young mademoiselle also requires plenty of fluids, fresh foods, and sunlight."

I want to ask him for a diagnosis, but crippling dread tightens my throat. The blood Anaella has been coughing has already made me fear the worst. If I'm right, I do not want her to have to hear his answer.

He takes a bottle from his leather bag and places it in my hand. "I will be back in a few days to check on her, but if anything changes, Nurse Dupont knows how to reach me."

"Thank you," I blurt, and he tips his head slightly, revealing a shining sapphire on his earlobe, gleaming through his black curls. A second later, he's out the door.

"I will go prepare hot water," the nurse says, turning to the kitchenette.

Anaella lifts her brow. "I don't know how you managed it. When you didn't come home last night I started worrying."

"I'm so sorry I was out so long." I drop to my knees by her side. "I . . ."

"A secret boyfriend?" Anaella chuckles, her laughter turning into a cough. I hold her hand until she calms, careful to keep my other hand, the wounded one, by my side.

"Where is your ring?" my sister asks.

"My ring?"

Worry creases her brow, and my stomach twists. Even ridden with illness, my sister is so beautiful with her dark locks and hopeful eyes. How I hate keeping things from her. But as much as I want to share the burden, I cannot mention the deal I made, the price I was willing to pay—lying, cheating, stealing. No, I will not expose her to the dark underbelly of Lutèce. Not until she's strong enough.

"I sold it." The lie comes out of my lips too easily.

She pushes herself up on her elbows, the strain making her tremble. "Cleo, it's—"

"One of the only things left from Father. I know . . . But you are more important, Ann."

"If you would just listen to my ideas, we could sell my designs or—"

"I got a job."

It's not a complete lie. After all, I will be working in the opera house soon, and . . . serving Dahlia. Still, a bitter taste fills my mouth. "That's where I was last night. I sold my ring to this lady, and she offered me a job."

"Oh, Cleo, that's wonderful! What will you be doing?"

A fit of coughing overtakes Anaella and spares me from answering. The nurse hurries back into the room carrying a stack of clean towels and a large basin filled with steaming water, which she leaves by my sister's side to moisten the air.

"No more talking. You need to sleep," she says firmly to Anaella, pulling me up by the arm and grabbing the bottle of medicine from my hand.

I take a step back as Nurse Dupont applies a tincture to Anaella's chest. She moves with the efficiency that can only come from having a Talent. Her golden hair is tied into a tight bun; her white robe has many pockets containing bottles and syringes that clank together when she moves. Yet each gesture is as gentle as a spring breeze. I find comfort in the softness with which she tucks Anaella's covers.

I lean against the desk for support. My sister's designs are still scattered all over it, but Father's book is now sitting at the top. I hold it up. It's small, not much larger than my palm, filled with all the patterns and fabric choices Father used to bring Mother's old sketch designs to life. It's a guide—made especially for Anaella and me as a way to ignite the spark of fashion within us from a young age. Now it's a reminder of all I have lost. Yet my fingers tighten around it as the nurse turns to me, leading us to the front of the store.

"She will need all of my attention in the coming days," she says.

"I don't have money to pay you," I whisper. "I don't know who—"

"Lady Sibille took care of everything."

I freeze for a mere moment. Of course, this is Dahlia's doing. She promised to care for Anaella. To change our lives.

"I shall stay here in the extra bed with your sister until she's well again. And Dr. Banks will be visiting every few days."

"Extra bed?" The only free bed in the house is mine.

The nurse ignores me and draws out a letter from her robe. "This is for you."

I take the crisp envelope, fingers numb as I break the wax seal.

No time to rest, my little nightingale. Your sister is well taken care of, and we have work to do. Hurry up and go to your new estate. You know the way.

Love, D.

I turn the page over, but there is nothing else.

I'm supposed to leave already? It's all too soon. And what about Anaella? Dahlia can't expect me to leave her behind. My throat tightens as I look again over the words, wishing for an explanation to appear.

"Anaella is to stay here," the nurse says, as though reading my mind. "Lady Sibille gave clear instructions."

I bite my tongue, fighting against the anger that sets in my bones at the thought of leaving my sister. This wasn't a part of the deal. Or was it? I didn't ask many questions. Perhaps I have only myself to blame. But Dahlia should have been more upfront. At the same time, the nurse standing before me is proof of her power, of how she can change our lives. And as I glance at my sister breathing softly, more quietly than she has in weeks, after only one treatment, I'm filled with a sense of endless gratitude I cannot deny.

Nurse Dupont's blue eyes soften as she reads my face. "I'll take good care of her," she says. And I believe her.

I nod. The question that's been on my mind since I saw the doctor springs to my lips. "Did the doctor give a diagnosis?" I drop my voice, making sure Anaella can't hear us.

"Winter fever," she answers, just as low. "But she will heal. I never lose patients."

I close my eyes, my chest lighter by a thousand bricks. Winter fever is not a joke, but it is like music to my ears. Not consumption. She will heal.

The idea of leaving her to face it without me is physically painful, but that's what I get for putting my fate into the hands of criminals. Dahlia's reach still frightens me—how she knew about my family, my home, how quickly she managed to get a doctor and a nurse to make my sister their top priority. I have a feeling she could bring my ruin just as easily. Yet I know I have no choice. I'm doing this for Anaella.

"Don't disturb her." The nurse grabs my arm as I turn toward the back room. "She'll be out for hours after what I gave her, and she needs the rest."

My lips tremble. Now I don't even get to say goodbye.

I fight against the tears pulling at the corners of my eyes. "Tell her I'll be back as soon as I can, and . . . that I have to work."

"I will," the nurse says as I linger at the doorway.

I don't want to leave. I don't know when I'll next sleep in my own bed. The stuffy shop might be in ruins, but it's the only place I have to call home, the only place that connects me to my parents. And with Anaella left behind, I'll be leaving half of my heart with her.

I wipe a stray tear as I hold Father's book closer to my chest. I need to be stronger. "Thank you," I say, before stepping outside.

The walk to the other side of town passes in a blur as the city wakes from its slumber. Placing the ring back on my finger, I stare at its deep-red haze. I want to enjoy the sun on my face and the knowledge that Anaella is in good hands. Yet all I can think of is the price I agreed to pay to achieve that. Does Dahlia expect me to stay separated from my sister?

I should have found out more before accepting her deal, but somehow I doubt that would have changed the terms. I can still sense Dahlia's warmth around me, her perfume making me dizzy as she leaned in to whisper in my ear. There was such softness to her voice, yet at the same time it was full of so much power and command. I wish I had that type of strength and poise, but against her I stood no chance.

The polished streets sparkle in the morning light, but as I turn the corner my gaze focuses only on the estate looming right ahead. My new home.

Ivy climbs between the arching windows, while sculpted eagles perch on each side of the massive gates. They glare at me as I make my way between the rosebushes lining the path to the front door. Just yesterday Lady Adley stood upon these stairs, yelling at her coachman and judging my poor clothes. I look even worse now, with the stains of blood on my skirt and lack of sleep evident on my face. No one will ever believe I belong here.

I clutch Father's book more tightly; its presence is comforting in the face of the unknown future that awaits inside these walls. Taking a deep breath, I stuff the book into the pocket sewn into my skirt's side seam and take a hesitant step toward the stairs.

The door swings open before I can make it to the entrance. "Lady Adley, we've been expecting you!" A young maid curtsies before me.

"Adley? No, I—"

"We were all so worried when we heard about your accident." The maid steps aside as I climb the short steps to the entrance. "Those bandits should all face judgment for their sins."

"The bandits . . ."

"Oh, my lady, you are in shock. We are just so blessed that only your clothes and luggage were harmed."

The foyer spins around me as I walk inside, pressure building in my chest. Dahlia did not prepare me for her web of lies. Am I supposed to hold

Lady Adley's title as well as her Talent? Did she simply relinquish it? How can I possibly take her place? I'm not a Dame. No more than the maid.

"If you'll follow me, I have already drawn you a bath."

"A bath . . ."

"Yes, my lady." The maid bows her head, a posture of reverence and respect I don't deserve. She is young, perhaps sixteen, with an array of freckles covering her smooth skin and a white band holding up her fiery red locks.

On my own, I could have found myself in her shoes—without Anaella or Father's legacy to keep afloat, I likely would have been working a menial job for room and board, just like her. Is she Talentless? Perhaps she's a third child of irresponsible parents, forced to watch as her mother and father passed their gems to her older siblings, leaving her without a magical inheritance? Or maybe her abilities are best suited to caring for others, and living in a manor while doing it is not a bad deal.

I nod awkwardly, trying to seem dignified, as we climb the grand staircase.

When I snuck into this estate the day before, my frantic heart and shaking legs took over. I never imagined I'd see this place again. But now it is mine. The fine detailing covering the golden frames of the paintings, the light reflecting from the spotless marble, the symmetrical formation of round bushes and neat flower patches outside the window. All mine.

"What is your name?" I ask as we walk along a corridor overlooking the gardens.

"Pauline LaRue, my lady."

"Beautiful name," I say, before clearing my throat. "I'm Cleodora. But you can call me Cleo." She bats her eyes in surprise. Are ladies not supposed to befriend their maids?

Pauline just smiles politely. "You must be exhausted after your travels, Lady Adley."

I keep my mouth shut for fear of incriminating myself as Pauline leads me to a set of rooms on the second floor, connected through a series of open arched doors: a study laden with leather-bound books, a sitting area overlooking the garden, a massive bedchamber draped in pink, and a pearl-white washing room.

I force myself not to gape at the swan-like golden faucets, the marble tub, the rose petals floating over the steaming water.

"Hopefully the temperature is to your liking," Pauline says, reaching to untie the back of my dress.

"I can do it," I say.

"That's my job, my la—"

I grab her hand when she touches the dress, and she freezes. "I'll do it."

"Of course. I'll go prepare a dress for you." Pauline curtsies before shuffling out of the room.

Leaning against the sink, I feel the cold touch of the marble stabilizing my spinning head. Sending my maid away is certainly not the way to keep up appearances, nor is washing by myself, but the words flew out before I could think.

The steam rising from the bath clouds the air, and I stumble toward the window, cracking it open. Even the window frames are plated in gold. As I step away from it, a wave of nausea overtakes me. I do not belong here. Especially while my ill sister sleeps in the back room of a dusty shop.

I pull at my dress as the fabric sticks to my sweating skin and the book in my pocket bumps against my thigh. I can't let the maid see it. Not when all my luggage was supposedly stolen by "bandits." But where can I hide it? I'm not even sure why I brought it. It was an instinct. A need to have a piece of home with me.

Pauline knocks on the door far too soon. "May I come in?"

"One moment!" My eyes fall on a nearby set of drawers and I dash toward it, springing the bottom one open and stuffing the book under a large stack of fresh towels. I shove it shut before quickly fiddling with the back of my dress, letting it drop to the floor. My undergarments swiftly follow and a moment later, I step into the bath, careful to keep my bandaged palm dry.

The thick bubbles offer a safe cover, and the scent of roses is over-whelming. As if sinking into a cloud, I melt into the water's embrace. "Come in," I say.

Pauline peeks into the room. "I have prepared a dress for you, my lady. Is there anything else I can do for you?" Her smile is genuine and kind. If I weren't the lady of this house, I could imagine her being my friend.

I start shaking my head, but stop. As much as I may want privacy, I must be convincing in my new role. "Actually . . . I was wondering if I could ask you a few questions."

"Of course. I'm at your service." Pauline reaches inside one of the golden cupboards and takes out a soft sponge. "To help your skin glow, my lady." She takes a step toward me but stops, clearly unsure after I sent her away before.

I need to act my part better. I give her a tiny nod and she immediately sits on a stool by my side, scrubbing my arms.

"How long have you worked for Lady Adley?"

"Less than two years. Though I have the most seniority among the staff."

"Aren't you slightly young?"

"The lady had strict rules and expectations, and no patience for older, slower workers." She hesitates, a blush blooming on her cheeks. "We were all surprised by your arrival. Lady Adley has always been private when it comes to her family. But she must be very fond of you."

"Me? Oh yes. We were close. When I was younger." The lies scorch my mouth like burning pebbles. "I'm very grateful to her."

I fall silent, pretending to occupy myself with untangling a massive knot in my hair. The memory of Lady Adley's pout and her beak-like nose wrinkling in disapproval at our only short meeting fills my head. That old woman would never have approved of someone like me, let alone willingly given me the keys to her kingdom.

"How much did my *cousin* tell you about me?" I ask.

"Not much. It all happened so quickly." Pauline pulls at the hem of her long sleeve. "She returned home after the performance last night in an especially bad mood, shouting about leaving the city. Come morning, a letter full of her instructions was waiting for us in the lounge, and she was gone. I believe the prospect of watching someone young take her place on stage was just too much for her. She never could allow anyone else to shine." Her palm flies to cover her mouth. "Please forgive me, I did not mean any offense."

"Don't worry about it," I mumble. "So, how did you know it was me at the door?"

Pauline wipes her hands on her apron before taking out a worn photograph from her pocket, and I immediately stop fighting the tangled mess at the back of my head. It's faded at the edges, and ripped at the upper corner, but I recognize it at once. Father spent an entire week's earnings to have it taken just last year—he said it was a special gift for my birthday. I'm wearing a new dress Father had sewn for the occasion and smiling at the camera. My face is wide and open, unfearful. I haven't smiled that way since. How on earth did Dahlia get her hands on it?

"This was among the instructions," Pauline says, eyeing my bandaged palm. "She said she had sent you her gem a few weeks ago, and her lawyer came in at first light to confirm all the legal aspects of naming you the new owner of the estate and confirming the succession matters of the Talent and accompanying title."

Succession matters. Of course. The Elite bestow their titles along with their Talents upon their heirs. I should've known that.

"But then when the messenger boy came with the news about your travel party . . ." Thankfully, Pauline seems oblivious to my turmoil. "Never mind that, you are here now. Please, let me." She returns the photo to the safety of her pocket before her skilled fingers weave through my hair to untie the stubborn knots.

"Thank you," I manage once she's done.

"It's my job," she says, reaching for the bottom drawer holding the towels.

And Father's book.

My body stiffens.

The air locks in my lungs as Pauline hovers over the drawer, the seconds stretching. Then she turns to me with a smile, holding a large mint towel, and my breath returns.

"Here you go, my lady," she says.

I try my best not to glance toward the washing room when Pauline leads me back to the pink bedchamber. I sit silently by the white and gold vanity as she styles my hair into an elaborate updo, then applies blush to my cheeks and sprays me with perfume. By the time she's done and leaves to fetch a gown, I feel like a pampered sacrificial offering—a tribute of a soul in exchange for riches.

"I believe I found a dress that might fit you." Pauline draws my attention back as she returns, carrying a garment in her outstretched arms. "I have to apologize—it's from last season, but I'll make sure to arrange a meeting with the modiste first thing tomorrow."

She keeps talking, but I'm overtaken by the silver silk in her hands. It flows in layers, catching the light in a prism of colors with each tiny movement. Father would have called it a work of art—a reflection of a glossy lake under the bright moon.

"May I?" Pauline reaches for my bathrobe.

I nod, keeping silent as she helps me into a set of heavy undergarments before putting on the dress, tying the sash around my waist with a beaded bow. The fabric gathers high around my neck, caressing my skin with softness.

Stepping away from the vanity, I walk to the large mirror standing by the corner. I might be a fraud, but when I stare into my porcelain-like reflection, heat rises to my cheeks, adding natural blush, as my heart beats faster with excitement. I look like a lady.

Pauline's reflection smiles behind me in the mirror. "Absolutely beautiful."

"I . . ."

"Oh, you don't like it." Her face drops at my hesitation, and a moment later she's already moving. "I'll go search for another one! Don't you worry, I'm sure there—"

"It's perfect," I say, and she pauses by the door. "Just . . . finer than what I'm used to wearing while at home."

"Only the best for you, my lady."

A knock on the door makes us both jump. Pauline bows her head awkwardly to me before opening it to another young maid, who can't be more than twelve years old.

The girl curtsies deeply, almost falling over herself. "Sorry to interrupt, my lady." Her gaze sweeps over me quickly before dropping back to the floor. Her eyes are wide like a frightened deer's. "Madame is here."

"Already?" Pauline's face whitens. "I'm afraid we must hurry. I'm so sorry, my lady. Please forgive me. I was assured your lesson would be later this afternoon."

"Lesson?"

"Madame is waiting for you in the music room. I will show you the way at once."

I risk one last peek toward the washing room before following her. I will have to move Father's book later.

We cross the living quarters and return to the main corridor, walk back down the massive stairway, and make our way through a set of arched doors. Servants gawk at me as we pass. They drop their glances before I catch them staring, yet I can feel their eyes lingering on my back, trying to assess the new lady of the estate.

Pauline slows down by a closed door of a corner room, right at the edge of the house. "After you, my lady."

I nod, and she opens the door for me.

"You are late," a woman calls as soon as I step inside.

CHAPTER FOUR

Moon Serenade

THE WOMAN SITS by a white grand piano in the middle of the room. She wears an elegant black dress with a turndown lacy collar. Her dark auburn hair is gathered up into a fluffy bouffant, accentuating her strong jaw. She doesn't stand to greet me, or bow her head; instead, she scans me shamelessly with her beetle-like eyes.

"A bit skinny, but at least your posture isn't horrendous," she says. "Acquire plenty of salmon for her, and make sure it's fresh. She should eat vegetables and fruits. And I want her weight to be tracked weekly."

"I beg your pardon?"

"I was talking to your maid." She dismisses me with a wave of her hand. "Judging from the timbre of your speaking voice and that beautiful swan neck, you must be a dramatic coloratura. Am I correct?"

"A what?"

"A high soprano. A voice perfect for agile runs and gorgeous high notes, and yet suited for a more dramatic repertoire due to a full middle range."

I have never heard any of that terminology, and I have certainly never sung high notes or runs. What does running have to do with music anyway?

"What repertoire do you know?"

"I'm sorry . . . I don't."

She blinks before letting out a huff. "Oh, don't make me laugh. Old Lady Adley would never have bestowed her Talent on a girl with no musical training."

I press my lips tightly, crossing my arms. This is exactly what I feared. If I can't convince this woman that I'm Adley's heir, how can I hope to fool the entire city? Dahlia should have prepared me more, given me guidance. Instead, I've barely been a lady for a couple of hours and I'm already flailing. My legs start shaking under my long skirts.

Madame stands up as the silence lingers. "You can't be serious."

"I'm sure the lady will pick everything up quickly, Madame," Pauline interjects, immediately dropping her gaze to the floor. She's so quiet I'd almost forgotten she was in the room.

"Well . . ." The woman puts on a stretched smile. "We have more work ahead of us than I thought. Luckily, your maid is right. Your Talent is powerful, and under my guidance you should be able to access it fully within the week. We need to make sure you are prepared for your audition."

My throat tightens. Air has stopped reaching my lungs. "My audition?"

"For the opera house, of course. And if you have hopes of taking over your cousin's role as the leading soprano you'd better be impressive. They are waiting for the scheduling confirmation." Stepping away from the piano, she takes a crystal decanter from an engraved cabinet to her left and sniffs it before pouring herself a glass of the deep amber liquid. "My name is Lady Hélène Corbin, but you can simply call me Madame. I will be your maîtresse de chant—we will work together on your musicality, diction, style, and performance."

"Pleasure to meet you," I manage as she takes a sip, then lets out a loud sigh.

"I don't work with an audience." She shoots a glare at Pauline, who jumps at once, giving me a tiny, encouraging smile before shuffling out of the room.

Madame empties the rest of her drink in one gulp. "Stand over here." She points to the middle of the room, right next to the piano.

I follow her instructions, fighting my still trembling legs, as she sits at the piano, her hands hovering over the ivory keys.

"What do you know about your Talent?" she asks.

Nothing. The answer sits on the edge of my tongue, but I cannot utter it. I'm supposed to be Lady Adley's cousin, a member of her family. I'm supposed to know everything about my Talent.

I stare at the ruby on my finger, gleaming in the sunlight streaming through the window. Dahlia told me Adley used to be nothing but a street rat, yet with her gift she became a lady, a member of high society. Her Talent, like all the Talents of the aristocracy, does not involve menial labor—those all came later, when tradesmen were finally allowed to acquire gems. No, her Singing Talent is one of art, of beauty. Which means this ruby has to be one of the oldest Talents in all of Lutèce.

"It has been in my family for many generations," I lie. "I'm incredibly honored to keep up its legacy."

"I didn't ask for the obvious answer." Madame rolls her eyes. "I meant of *singing*. What do you know about singing?"

"Not much, I'm afraid," I admit.

"Your Talent was honed for the first time over three hundred years ago by the legendary soprano Marguerite Duval—her natural singing was so rare that the Crown gifted her with the ruby. She imbued it with her gift, tying it to her with her blood so it would forever be preserved, even after her lifetime. With each generation that followed, that gift only became more profound, the gem absorbing, growing, learning, adapting. All that knowledge runs in your blood now."

I had never heard of that soprano, but I nod along as though the history is all too familiar to me.

"Singing does not only involve your voice," Madame continues. "Your entire body must support the sound and make sure it carries over the orchestra. Your Talent has been trained to control and release every muscle, to give the exact amount of pressure and air needed to produce the perfect sound. But you must not interrupt it. Take this." Madame gestures toward a book resting on the piano. "Page thirty-nine."

"Interrupt it?" I ask as I flip open the heavy score, resting it on a music stand engraved with images of chirping birds.

"The magic runs through your blood like a river, with no beginning or end. When you let it flow, you can feel its pulse with every pump of your heart. But if you let your mind get in the way, you put a dam in that stream. You need to learn to give up control." She eyes me sharply before repeating, "Page thirty-nine."

I stare at the top of the page, reading the title: *Sérénade au Clair de Lune* by Annette Devon. Below it, neat symmetrical lines filled with musical notations narrate what must be a dream-like melody. But to my eyes, they are nothing more than black markings on a white page.

"I can't read this," I mumble.

"Unfortunate indeed. Luckily, your Talent holds the skill."

I twist the ring around my finger, but the ruby's energy is quiet. "What should I do?"

Madame smiles, and for once the expression is not unkind. "Look at the notes, but don't attempt to analyze them. Start at the top left corner and follow the line slowly, letting the shapes occupy your mind."

With a deep breath, I focus on the black dots and swirling lines. The first bar is short: only a few notes, marked together under a bow. I close my eyes, imagining the round shape of the first note—an elliptical mark floating in the middle of the five lines. At once my gem is humming, or, more accurately, *I'm* humming. The wave of energy from the ring resonates through my body, and I know that the pitch is perfect, even before Madame plays the note on the keyboard.

"You see, it's already inside you," she says. "Now open your eyes, look at the notes, and let them guide you."

She glides her hand over the keyboard and a note ripples through the room, like a raindrop on a clear lake. It is pure and bright, filled with possibilities. I'm still basking in its beauty when another one follows—sharper, demanding. Madame's hands travel over the keys, weaving notes together into an enchanting melody. I breathe in the music and my body sways with the rhythm, wanting to merge with it.

And before I can comprehend it, I'm singing.

The depth of my voice is captivating, round and soft, yet with a brilliant brightness. But more than the sound, the physical sensation is exhilarating—my blood is warm, the ring on my finger pulsing with each lovely note. The music is my heartbeat, my purpose. And for the first time in my life, I'm not lost.

Perhaps I can do this after all. Perhaps . . . this is my true calling.

I'm floating as my eyes follow the notes, my mind translating them instantly, combining them with the words without any effort.

> *Tonight, the hawk halts its hunt, while the snake slumbers*
> *on lilies' down.*
> *Tonight, the moon shimmers and mercy drops to earth in pale*
> *celestial light.*
> *Cradle his hand, dear moon, place it tenderly in my own.*
> *Hold us until dawn's soft light, and let him wake with me*
> *in his heart.*

My voice soars high, filling the air with a soft timbre. I'm the moonbeam dancing across the water, my song the whispers of lovers.

As I turn the page, the tempo picks up in a whirlwind of bewitching harmonies. The notes get closer together, crowding the page. There are too many. The music is moving too quickly. Panic clutches my throat, the fear of shattering the dream-like melody penetrating my mind. My voice falters—I no longer float under ebony skies. The pitch drops, and the notes on the page are again nothing more than random marks.

The trance is ruined.

Madame's eyes flash as she bangs her hands on the keyboard. The cluster of notes makes me jump.

"What happened?" Her voice is sharp.

"I'm sorry . . . We were going so fast, and the page . . . It all looked like a messy cloud of notes."

Madame shakes her head. "The fast notes are called coloratura, and they are nothing to fear, your Talent is trained for them. In fact, Lady Adley was famous for her coloratura, and so too will you be. If you trust your Talent."

Trust my Talent . . . I have a Talent now. A trained skill I can count on. I have nothing to fear. "Yes, Madame," I say. "It won't happen again."

"I hope not!"

I press my lips together. "Madame? If I may ask? That song felt so familiar, yet I'm certain I never heard it before. How—"

"It was one of Lady Adley's best arias. Your Talent has experienced it many times before. The stone remembers. This music is in your blood now." Madame cocks her head to the side. "It's good to see that beautiful ruby again. A Talent like this should be celebrated."

"All Talents should be," I say.

She raises her brow, staring at my ring for a moment. "Wasn't it a necklace?"

"The ring was a gift from my father."

"Oh?"

"He died before he could pass his Talent to me. I believe that's why my cousin bestowed her gift on me." I polish the lie with the truth.

"Well, Lady Adley had a wonderful ear, and she wasn't wrong in her faith in you. With her gift, your voice will be like a slice of heaven." Madame's eyes drift back to her own music score. "Start from the beginning, and don't let anything hold you back this time."

By the time Madame leaves, the skies are already darkening.

My stomach growls, but I'm too tired to even think about eating. The high of singing began to wane somewhere into the fourth hour. When I was allowed to rest my voice, Madame searched for the perfect audition piece. She contemplated different arias, while I absorbed the music, training myself to let my Talent take over, to hear the notes in my head without uttering a sound.

"I presume you had a good first day. Madame is rarely so elated when she leaves," Pauline says as we walk down the corridor.

"Yes, thank you. I'm just exhausted. I never knew singing was so physically taxing."

"We have prepared your dinner: fresh salmon, as Madame instructed. But perhaps you'd prefer taking it in your room?"

"That would be lovely."

"Can you find your way back from here?"

"It's just down and to the left?"

"Yes, my lady. I'll bring it to you immediately." She bows her head, then hurries down the steps to the first floor.

Candles flicker along the walls as I make my way to my room. The house is quiet, the garden outside the window draped in starlight. If only Anaella could see me now. Walking these great halls, draped in finery, a Talent adorning my hand. I can hardly believe it myself; it's a sculpted dream I hope never to awaken from.

But a dull ache settles in my chest as I sneak into the large washing room. The absence of my sister by my side carves a hole in the perfect image of my new home. My hand trembles as I reach for the bottom drawer and dig under the fresh towels.

The touch of worn leather calms my nerves. I pull Father's book out of its hiding place and head back to my bedchambers. It was silly of me to take it. Unlike Anaella, I haven't dared to browse these pages since Father died. Every design Mother drew, every note Father left, they are all physical proof of what I've lost.

Yet now the urge to look through them and read every word is overwhelming. What would Father say if he could see me now? Would he be proud of me? Or disappointed by my choices? I trace the cracks in the leather binding with the tip of my finger.

I've been failing as head of the family. Anaella's health is proof of that.

I imagine her flushed, fever-stricken face, a rough blanket wrapped around her frail body as she lies on a hard mattress. A lone tear trickles down my cheek as I sink into the canopy-covered bed, the impossible softness of the mattress mocking me.

I want to visit my sister this evening, but there's no way I can leave the house, not without raising suspicion. I'll have to settle for tomorrow. Nurse Dupont will be taking good care of her. At least that thought eases my guilt.

With tired arms, I take the pins from my hair. Soft curls fall on my shoulders, leaving my scalp aching. The moonlight shines through the window, draping shadows across the lush carpet. For a second, one of them moves sharply. I freeze.

One blink and the shadow is gone. But whatever cast it must still be outside.

Legs trembling, I push myself out of the bed, holding Father's book close to my chest as I inch toward the window. Could anyone climb this high to reach my balcony? The window is slightly open, allowing in a fresh breeze, but the small balcony is empty. Nothing but white marble and geraniums under starry skies.

I force myself to swallow as I quickly stuff the book into one of the drawers of a nearby oak desk. I haven't been acting carefully enough. Allowing myself to mope and cry over a life that's already been lost isn't going to help.

But my body still tingles with unease. With another glance toward the garden, I lean closer to the cold glass window when the door swings open behind me and I startle with a cry.

"I'm so sorry! I didn't mean to scare you, my lady." Pauline rushes to rest the silver tray with a domed plate on a side table. "Forgive me. I should have knocked."

"Don't worry about it," I say, forcing my breathing to slow.

For a second, I'm thankful for the mysterious shadow. Without it, Pauline would have probably found me with Father's book in my lap. Lying my way out of that is not a task I'm ready to take on.

"You are too kind, my lady." Pauline lowers her head, busying herself with setting the cutlery. "I hope the meal is to your liking."

"I'm sure it will be." After a week of eating stale bread and preserved meat, any fresh food would be divine, not to mention one that comes on a silver plate. "I noticed there are no locks on my windows."

"Yes, the former Lady Adley instructed against them."

"I see . . ." I bite my lip. The lack of security does not match the image of the great Adley I had built in my head. Why would a famous diva leave herself exposed? "Would it be possible to have locks installed?"

She nods. "Certainly. I'll make sure Mr. Vernier, the butler, takes care of it in the morning."

"Thank you," I say. Whatever the reason might be, this house now belongs to me, and I need to start accepting my new role. My new life.

I am the new diva.

"Your food is getting cold," Pauline says.

I force a smile, taking one last look through the window. Down in the garden, by the far line of trees, I swear a dark shadow moves.

CHAPTER FIVE

The House of Garnier

"GOOD MORNING!"

Light assaults my closed eyelids and I burrow deeper into the soft feather cushions. Wrapping myself in velvet, I nestle back into the realm of sleep, returning to my dream. I'm the lady of an estate, wearing fine jewelry, possessing a Singing Talent so grand the power emanating from its gem is almost tangible.

"My lady, it's time to wake up."

I snap my eyes open.

Pauline stands by the edge of the bed, a silver tray laden with breakfast in her hands. "I hope you slept well," she says as I sit up.

"Incredibly. I mean," I catch myself, "yes, very well indeed."

My stomach growls at the sweet smell of the golden apple turnovers and the buttery warmth of the freshly baked croissants resting on a china plate decorated with roses, sitting temptingly beside a steaming cup of hot chocolate.

"I thought you might prefer your breakfast in bed today, my lady, before your appointment with the modiste. You will also have time to enjoy the fashion houses and lunch at a café, since Madame will be coming only later in the afternoon for your lesson."

"Thank you." I smile at Pauline.

"Just ring the bell when you are finished. I'll be outside." She curtsies before leaving the room.

I lean back into the pillows, covering my mouth to stifle a laugh. My fingers dig into the blanket, the softness of the linen against my skin proof that I'm not dreaming.

But it's the hot chocolate sitting before me that fully grounds me in reality. I take a deep breath as I swirl it, watching the chocolate flow slowly, thick as cream. My mouth waters even before I take the first sip. I cannot remember the last time I had sweets, let alone drank cocoa. These were luxuries my sister and I couldn't afford.

Bringing the porcelain cup to my lips feels sinful, but I cannot resist. Dark and bittersweet richness coats my tongue before flowing down my throat. And when I dip the flaky croissant in the chocolate, I know this is the taste of heaven. I never want to eat stale bread or drink souring milk again. By the time my plate and cup are empty, I have a cream mustache—definitely not ladylike, but who's here to see?

My nightgown brushes the carpeted floor as I hop out of bed and open the door out to my balcony. A morning breeze caresses my face and I close my eyes, savoring the fresh scent of morning dew upon flowers. There are no traces of the shadows of last night. The world is still.

If only Anaella could be here with me.

And just like that, a chill takes hold of me. My eyes jump to the desk drawer holding Father's book. But I have no time for reminiscing. No time to doubt my choices. To keep this life and help my sister, I need to play my part—to be the lady of the house. A day of errands could help with that. Heading inside, I ring the tiny bell on my nightstand.

⋘⟡⋙

It takes Pauline an hour to style my hair and help me into a gown. Today's garment is a little too big for my frame, especially in the bust. Even the foundation corset is loose. I can probably fit two fingers between it and my skin, but I don't mention it. It's a layered, deep blue silk gown, with white lace ribbons along the neckline and at the sleeves' edges. Fitting with the current fashion, Pauline pairs it with a wide hat adorned with gray feathers that somehow even matches the purse she hands me—a reticule of gold taffeta with steel-cut beads and tassels.

I try to keep steady in my leather heels as Pauline leads me outside to a waiting carriage.

A coachman rushes to my side. "I'll help you with the door, my lady."

I'm nodding at him politely when recognition freezes my insides. This is the same young man I helped right before I snuck into the estate. The one Lady Adley shouted at for scaring the horses. But he couldn't possibly recognize me, not when I barely recognize myself in these clothes. Could he?

"My lady?" He offers me a hand to help me into the carriage.

The tall feathers sticking out of my hat force me to bend down as I climb inside. But when he closes the door, our eyes meet at the window, and for just a second I think a crease of confusion appears in his brow. A moment later, he's at the front of the carriage and the horses trot ahead.

My heartbeat accelerates. I could be imagining it. After all, our meeting was so short he might not even remember me. But if he does . . . he could expose me—not the cousin of the great Adley, but a common thief who stole an identity. I tug at the collar of my dress as I imagine the carefully cultivated lie unraveling. For once, I'm happy the corset is too large; if it fit, I most definitely would have fainted from lack of air by now.

"Are you feeling well, my lady?" Pauline asks.

"Yes. If only the roads were smoother, riding would be far more pleasant, don't you agree?" I say with the most aristocratic voice I can muster.

"Indeed, my lady."

The river sparkles outside the window as we cross the main bridge. Soon we are forced to slow down by the commotion and carriages clogging the streets.

"It's just up ahead," Pauline says as we come at last to a stop.

The coachman opens the door for us and my stomach twists, but his head is dropped in a bow. No hint of anything unusual.

I just need to play my part. Keep my head high. Pushing my chest out, I step onto the street, trying to exude the confidence of the rich lady I turned into overnight. But my spirit falters at the sign above the shop's entrance: House of Garnier.

"I made sure to pick the finest modiste in all of Lutèce, my lady," Pauline says. "Josephine Garnier herself is expecting you."

The image of Father sitting by the sewing machine fills my mind, his voice echoing in my head. "A perfect dress is a reflection of both the tailor's soul and the muse it's created for. That is what turns a garment into art."

"But Papa, look at the newspaper! How can we compete?" I said, fanning the crumpled page with the article about the House of Garnier's new factory in front of his face.

Father just laughed. "These stores might produce dresses faster. But, mon coeur, people like Josephine Garnier have the skills but not the heart of a true artist. Having a Talent is not enough. It's how you use it that counts."

He was wrong.

And here I am, about to be fitted by the woman whose ascension was the force behind his bitter end.

A bell rings over my head as I step into the shop, and I'm hit by the scent of vanilla perfume. The entire left side is dedicated to mannequins in beautiful dresses, while the right side displays gentlemen's suits. Between them stands a statue of a winged angel, surrounded by low benches covered with red velvet. Straight ahead, a wide set of stairs leads to a raised floor, where, I can only assume, are the separate fitting areas. My mouth drops in awe at the sheer size of the place.

"May I help you?" A woman rushes to my side.

"Lady Adley is here for her fitting," Pauline says.

"Of course." The woman curtsies. "Miss Garnier is just upstairs. If you please, follow me."

The second floor is broken into smaller rooms, each one decorated with opulent furnishings. Through the few open doors, staff members wait, readying themselves for a day of fitting customers and altering clothes.

The woman leads us along the corridor to the farthest edge of the store. I never imagined a fashion house could be this lush. Next to it, Father's shop is like a stuffy basement. What would he say if he could see me now, about to be fitted by his competitor?

The door ahead is closed, yet as we get near whispering voices drift through the air. I cannot tell any words apart, but it's clear the conversation is heated. I strain to hear better, just as a loud smack reverberates from inside the room.

"Wait here, please." The assistant hurries ahead and knocks on the door.

At once everything falls silent, and a moment later the door swings open.

"What?" a woman snaps.

"Lady Adley is here to see you, Mistress."

Another stretch of silence, and then the assistant moves to the side, revealing Josephine Garnier herself.

"Oh, Lady Adley!" She curtsies dramatically as the assistant waves us forward. "What an absolute pleasure."

Plump lips land on the back of my hand as Miss Garnier takes it. She's a tall woman, who definitely doesn't need the high heels she's wearing. Her hot-pink dress has a deep neckline of flowing fabric matched with an underlayer of lace that travels all the way up to a high collar. The sleeves are sheer, and there's a beautiful, trimmed finish on the skirt. But her garment is just the background for the true star—a square-shaped pink druzy gem, hanging from a gold necklace. The perfect display for the Talent of a high-end modiste.

"We were so stricken when we heard about your traveling misfor-tunes," she says as we enter the room. I turn my head from side to side, looking for whoever she was arguing with a moment ago. But the room is empty. "Rest assured, we will make certain your new wardrobe is tailored to perfection," she continues.

"That's very kind of you," I say, though I'm not focused on her words. I can't see any exit other than the door we just stepped through. Could she have been talking to herself?

"Always at your service, my lady." She curtsies deeply again. "I have a few dresses in mind for you already, and my designer has prepared new sketches for you to look at."

I follow the gesture of her hand to a book perched upon a nearby desk. Unlike Father's pocket copy, this fashion manual is massive, featuring detailed designs and patterns. A delicate sketch of a green gown stares at me from the open page, but what captures my attention are the numbers—measurements made not for a single lady but for a variety of sizes. This is a ready-to-wear gown to be sold for all who desire it. Prêt-à-porter. Something Father never had the chance to try and compete against.

"Oh, this one is not for you, my lady." Josephine closes the book quickly. "For you, we need dresses that are one of a kind. But first we have to get you out of that corset—that size is all wrong for you."

I only manage to nod before two more assistants walk into the room. A moment later, I'm standing on a raised platform as they undo all of Pauline's work from the morning.

If Josephine was truly arguing with the walls just a moment ago, her work doesn't show it. She takes my measurements efficiently, faster than I ever did for a client. Her gem pulses lightly with each movement, and my stomach tenses with a tinge of jealousy. I mentally check each measurement she writes down from the list Father taught me. Height, bust, waist, shoulder angle—she misses nothing, all the way down to the size of each individual wrist. She might be eccentric, but I cannot deny the grace of her Talent.

"Let's try this first," she says, helping me into a burgundy dress laced with black flowers. "With this bodice, you will have the thinnest waist you've ever seen."

She starts pulling at the strings to tighten it when the door bursts open. The two assistants yelp, and Pauline leaps forward to block me from sight.

"How long does one have to wait in this place until a competent person appears?" a young man says, his voice low yet filled with the undertones of a brimming storm. "Is competence too much to ask?"

"Monsieur le Vicomte!" Josephine hurries forward, and I panic as my dress almost falls. "If you will please follow me outside, my lord, I'll make sure my finest assistant takes care of you."

"With all due respect, *Mademoiselle*, your assistants have already done enough damage. Is this the House of Garnier or the House of Amateurs?" The man sneers and crosses his arms.

For a noble, his manners are certainly poor. And no matter how much I want to dislike Miss Garnier, she doesn't deserve to be questioned in such a manner by this arrogant man.

"There's no need to be rude," I say, and the room falls quiet.

The man shifts his gaze to me, his brow raised as though surprised anyone has dared to challenge his words. For a second I'm struck by his eyes' bright shade of green, like a cat's.

"Lady Adley, I'm so incredibly sorry." Josephine tries to make the man follow her out the door. "If you excuse me, I'll be right back with you."

But the man doesn't move. "Adley?" he muses. "I didn't know the old crone had relatives."

Even with Pauline and the assistants standing before me and my hands holding up the top of the bodice, my undergarments are clearly visible. Embarrassment bubbles within me, the need to hide overwhelming. "Well . . . I . . ." I bite my tongue to stop my stuttering. He needs to believe I am his equal. Relaxing my shoulders, I elongate my neck, placing one hand on my hip. "I demand you leave at once."

A lopsided grin stretches on his lips. No person this arrogant should be this handsome. His complexion is graced with warm hues of amber, and his hair is a rich brown, falling on his forehead in waves. There is something deliberately disheveled about his look, as though he didn't even care to straighten his vest, or button his cuffs. Yet somehow it only makes him more attractive, almost wild. Heat rises in my cheeks, spreading down to my neck, and a strange yet not unpleasant shiver passes through me.

"Make sure they don't mess up your seams," he says, his tone the perfect mixture of amusement and disdain. "The fabric on my jacket sleeves is puckering."

"It just needs more tension. That type of wool is probably too heavy," I blurt before I can think.

He raises his eyebrow at me once again.

"Yes, well. It is indeed an easy fix," Josephine says. "If you please, my lord. I'll be right back, Lady Adley."

The man finally tears his eyes from me, turning without another word and striding out of the room. I let out a pent-up breath.

"Are you alright?" Pauline asks me, hurrying to lace up the bodice of my gown so I don't need to hold it up any longer. "Such insolence."

"Indeed . . ." I say, my vision still lingering on the closed door the man disappeared behind. His rudeness left a sour taste in my mouth, yet my pulse quickens at the thought of his emerald eyes. I focus on slowing down my breathing.

Pauline finishes tying the dress. "I didn't know you could sew, my lady."

"Oh." I blush again. "It's just a hobby."

<hr />

Two hours, at least twenty dresses, and countless apologies and bows later, I'm finally out of Miss Garnier's shop. The sun is high in the sky and the ladies all around are strolling with open parasols, protecting their sun-deprived skin.

Even though my wardrobe will be sewn and sent to me in just a few days, Miss Garnier insisted I leave her shop already wearing a new gown from her collection. The lively orange satin is tailored to perfection, cinching me at the waist, and yet I feel like a decorated tangerine with the extra layers of tulle covering my skirt.

"For you, my lady." The coachman offers me a parasol as soon as I leave the shop and step onto the street.

I take it with what I hope is a graceful nod. We are at the upper end of the avenue, where endless displays stretch out—another fashion boutique, another jewelry store, another art gallery. Yet my mind is on the narrow alleys behind them. Getting home from here wouldn't take long.

"I'd like to walk for a while," I say.

"Are you certain, my lady? I can take you wherever you like."

I want to decline his offer politely but stop myself. If he suspects me, I cannot show any softness. "I believe I made myself clear. I shall be back within the hour." Not waiting for a reply, I turn down the street, with Pauline accompanying me at a deferential pace or two behind.

I need to see Anaella, and I refuse to let another day pass.

My mind skips between different apologies I can give for leaving without saying goodbye. I need to come up with an explanation for my new clothes, though, and why my new employer would have spent so much on me already.

I adopt a lazy, strolling pace, feigning interest in the changing displays. Gentlemen tip their hats at me as I pass; ladies offer smiles. Never before did any of them bother to acknowledge me, yet, with nothing more than a new, expensive dress, I've finally received my invitation into their secret club. The thought adds a few inches to my height as I hold my head higher.

The alley on my left calls to me; the familiar route home is inviting. I almost turn down it when I realize I can't go anywhere as long as Pauline is at my heels, trailing me like a watchdog. I need to get rid of her.

That's when the smell of fresh cake drifts through the air. Just ahead, the door to the bakery closes after a customer leaves. I halt for a moment. That same bakery used to be near Father's shop. It was one of the first businesses to relocate when the Elite abandoned our street after Father's death. I sigh, taking another deep breath. This sweet scent is the answer to my problem.

"Pauline, will you be so kind as to run to the pâtisserie to get me some cake?"

"My lady?"

"All these measurements made me hungry."

"Of course."

"I'd also like some pastry," I add, wishing to buy more time. "I don't mind which one, but I want it fresh, so just wait until they bring out a new batch."

"But what about you, my lady? I cannot leave you for so long."

"I'll be right here." I gesture to the nearby jewelry shop.

Pauline doesn't move. "I shall accompany you. Your first outing in the city should reflect your position. I could not possibly allow people to think you have no maid. But worry not, my lady. Mr. Basset will run to the pâtisserie."

"Basset?" My mouth dries as I follow her gaze. The coachman is just slightly farther up and across the street. He must be keeping his eyes on us, making sure I never truly have to walk. My heart sinks. I could never sneak away from them both.

"I'll ask him. I'll be just a moment." Pauline curtsies and then crosses the street carefully between the carriages.

Desperation clutches at my throat. I must see Anaella. We have never been separated like this. It's bad enough I can't tell her the truth, but I need to let her know at least that I'm safe. All the new dresses and luxuries mean nothing to me if my sister isn't well. Why didn't Dahlia allow her to come with me? My eyes dart to the alley, and for a second I debate making a run for it.

That's when I notice a young boy leaning against the brick wall. His clothes are nothing but dirty rags, his face is smeared with ash. Our eyes meet, and I expect him to drop his head in shame, but instead he blinks through thick lashes as if studying me.

Across the street, Pauline talks to the coachman. I don't have much time.

"Boy," I call. He inches closer, dirty blond curls sticking out from under his hat. "I need you to deliver a message. Can you do that?"

He nods silently, eyeing the purse Pauline handed me this morning.

I stuff my hand into it at once, feeling for any coin. My fingers close around a heavy velvet bag and I pull it out, emptying it into the boy's outstretched hands. The gold is enough to last him a month. "There's an old dress shop I need you to find. The name Finley will be above the door. Ask for Anaella. Tell her—" I drop my voice to a whisper as Pauline crosses the street back toward me. "Tell her, Cleo sends her love. Tell her I'm fine and that I'm doing all of this for us. And that I promise I'll take care of her."

A second later, the boy disappears into the dark alley and Pauline is by my side.

"Was that boy disturbing you, my lady?"

"Oh . . ."

Pauline shakes her head in disapproval. "Little criminals waiting to pickpocket hard-working people. It's all because of these foolhardy parents. Having more than two children should be outlawed, if you ask me."

The conviction in her voice is too strong, personal. I have wondered if Pauline's own circumstances are cruel—if, like me, she knows the pain of never getting to hold an inherited gift, denied by tragic, untimely death or reckless parenthood. Now it seems I have my answer.

"These young ones shouldn't be on the streets like this." The bitterness in Pauline's voice pinches my heart.

"Yes. They really shouldn't," I say before biting my lip and turning into the jewelry store, leaving the alley behind.

CHAPTER SIX

Sing, Little Bird, Sing

MADAME WAVES HER cigarette holder, rings of smoke circling above her head. "Hurry up! We'll be late!"

"I'm not feeling too well." My stomach gives an uneasy twist and the sour taste of bile reaches my mouth.

Pauline wraps a light shawl around my bare shoulders. "You'll be brilliant, my lady. I'm certain."

I press my lips into a smile, but inside, all my muscles are tight. Madame is already climbing into the carriage, but I'm still standing, frozen, in the doorway. At the end of the ride awaits the opera house, where a crowd of patrons, managers, and music experts are waiting to vote on whether my singing is impressive enough to hire me . . . to make me their lead soprano. The thought alone makes me want to run back inside the house and lock the door.

Madame sticks her head out of the carriage. "I refuse to be late! My reputation is on the line just as much as yours. You will not make a fool out of me."

I jolt at her words, nearly falling down the steps. Basset, the coachman, hurries away from the horses to offer me his arm. But before he reaches me his foot hits a paving stone. He stumbles, his arms flailing for balance.

"Are you alright?" I ask, leaning toward him.

He straightens up. "Thank you, my lady." His eyes meet mine for only a moment, and I draw back.

I lift my chin high. "Don't waste my time again."

He bows, yet the usual timidness I have come to expect from servants is missing. Could he have fallen on purpose? Was he trying to recreate our first meeting?

"Young lady," Madame calls, "if you don't get into the carriage this instant . . ."

I climb inside at once, avoiding the end of her threat.

"Toi toi toi!" Pauline calls right before the horses pull us away.

My confusion must be evident because Madame rolls her eyes. "It brings misfortune to wish 'good luck' before a performance. We say 'toi toi toi' or 'merde' to warn off the evil spirits waiting for your failure."

I cannot tell if she's joking about the evil spirits, but I simply nod and intertwine my fingers, resting my hands in my lap to stop myself from clenching them into fists or biting my nails. I will need a lot more than luck if the coachman exposes me. Will I go to jail if he does? What will happen to Anaella?

"Perhaps instead of sitting there like you've seen a ghost, you should recite your words again." Madame pouts.

"Sorry, Madame. It's just nerves."

"Ha! Nerves . . . I coddled you too much this week."

To call Madame's lessons "coddling" is like calling a horror story a lullaby, yet I keep the thought to myself.

"You are right, though. You are not ready." She takes a puff of her cigarette, and I fight the urge to cough from the smoke. "Your Talent, however, is. If you let it lead, you have nothing to fear."

"And what if I lose focus?" I ask, the coachman's wary eyes filling my mind.

"Do you have anything better to focus on?" She raises an eyebrow.

"The music is in your blood, and your ruby longs for the stage. It's time you let it shine."

The carriage comes to a halt, and I peer out the small window. I expected us to reach the main plaza, but instead we are on a narrow street bordered by brick walls.

"The artists' entrance is in the back," Madame says, answering my unspoken question.

I dodge eye contact with the coachman as we step outside. The wall to my left is bare, yet, though the street is grim, silk curtains gleam under chandelier lights through the opera house's open windows—a promise of the glamour contained within the walls.

"Come along!" Madame ushers me in the right direction.

A concierge is waiting for us by the entrance. "Madame, always a pleasure." He bows and opens the door for us.

Madame passes him by without a second glance.

I step forward to follow her when a shadow moves at the corner of my eye. I spin around to face the alley, but only the coachman stares back at me.

"Something the matter, my lady?"

I shake my head. The stress is clearly affecting my mind. I step into the tiny foyer before Madame has a chance to shout at me again. She is already near the top of a tall staircase. I gather the fabric of my skirts and rush after her.

The walls on both sides of the stairwell are covered in photos: colorful posters presenting the newest productions, autographed portraits of famous singers, framed glowing newspaper reviews, each speaking of the legacy of the opera house.

"Beautiful, aren't they?" Madame says as she catches me staring. "Your face will join them soon enough. If all goes well today, it won't be long before every person in Lutèce knows your name."

Her words are like an elixir. For just a second, the image of my portrait displayed on these walls enters my mind, the cheering of adoring fans, and the crying of my name. I drop my gaze to the floor with a wave of shame. I'm not here for my own benefit. Fame is not what I should care about. I'm here for Anaella. A pang of guilt stabs at me. I don't even know if the message I sent found her, or if the boy just ran off with the money.

"The stage is right ahead," Madame says.

My legs are numb. Air fails to fill my lungs; I'm light-headed. I have to grab the wall for support to keep myself straight. We are now in a narrow, dark passageway, and Madame stops at a heavy, red curtain.

"Wait here," she says.

"Where are you going?" I'm not sure why I even want her by my side. After hours spent in her company, I can certainly say Madame does not possess a calming energy. Yet beneath her roughness, she wants me to succeed. Without her, I have no one to root for me.

"I need to see that they are ready for you. I will meet you on stage. You don't think I'd let just any pianist accompany you, do you?"

"Oh . . ."

"Don't waste your voice now," she says before striding past the red curtain, leaving me alone in the corridor.

I let out a long, steady breath, wrapping the shawl tighter around myself. This is it. The ruby suddenly feels heavier on my finger. I stare into the gem, visualizing the currents of energy bubbling inside it, fueling my blood. Such a small jewel, yet it holds my entire future.

Absently, I twist one of my curls around a finger. Pauline spent an extra hour last night wrapping strands of hair in soft rags, and another hour this morning shaping the lush locks. Everything has to be perfect— from the milky tone of my skin and the pink blush on my cheeks to the scent of my velvet rose perfume. As if my looks will determine my success.

With each stretched second the unease in my stomach grows. What is taking them so long? I tap my leg under my long skirts. What were the words of the aria again? My mind draws a blank and the panic clutching my throat is enough to make me choke. *Tonight, the hawk halts its hunt.* The first line rings in my head and I let out a pent-up breath.

A dainty hand pulls the curtain. "They're ready for you. Toi toi toi, my lady," the young maid says as she takes the shawl off my shoulders, revealing my gown.

Madame insisted the garment I wear complement my ruby ring. And so Pauline laced me into an emerald bodice, with off-the-shoulder sheer sleeves and a silk layered skirt that cascades in voluminous waves. In my head, I can hear Father telling me how to reconstruct the pattern. Yet I have no time to think about the dress.

Goosebumps rise on my skin as I step forward into complete darkness. The heels I'm wearing are higher than usual, designed to accentuate the length of my gown, but with my trembling, I'm afraid I might stumble and fall before I reach the stage.

Then, light penetrates through, and I'm right at the stage's wings. At the center sits a grand piano and Madame is perched on its bench. She gives me a curt nod and I straighten my back. But as I walk out onto the stage, all thoughts of posture fly away. My vision is taken by a blur of gold and crimson. Rows upon rows of velvet chairs stretch before me, surrounded by massive columns along the walls that reach all the way up to a huge painted dome—a spectacle of blue hazes laced with delicate clouds, surrounding heavenly messengers. From its center an intricate crystal chandelier towers above us, its height making my head spin. Upon the stage, I'm but a tiny speck of dust, unworthy of the grandeur laid before me.

"Ahem," someone coughs, and I force myself to keep walking to the middle of the stage. "Lady Adley, what a pleasure to have you here."

"The pleasure is mine," I reply, repeating the words Madame taught me.

The man sits in the third row, close enough for me to make out the details of his slicked-back black hair and burgundy suit. He must be Maestro Lamar Mette, the musical director. Madame explained to me that he's the one who oversees all musical aspects of the opera house, and the single most important person I have to impress. Behind him, more people fill the seats, though I cannot tell them apart. They dot the empty rows, their eyes locked on me, ready to judge my abilities.

My Talent.

Maestro Mette leans back into his seat, fingers intertwined and resting on his chest. A flicker of light reflects off a giant gemstone sitting on his middle finger—his Talent on display. "We were deeply saddened by your cousin's retirement," he says. "Her voice was a gift from heaven. She shall be sorely missed."

A snort echoes from somewhere above and I startle, my gaze drawn to the opera box to my right. My jaw drops when I recognize the unmistakable emerald eyes staring at me. The arrogant man who barged into my fitting at the fashion house lifts a glass of champagne to me in a silent salute.

What is he even doing here? Is he a patron? A member of the board? One of the other musicians? The memory of the ease with which he looked at my undergarments bubbles within me, and for a second it's as though all the layers of silk caressing me have been stripped away, leaving me naked before him again. A renewed wave of embarrassment takes hold of me, yet it is clear the man doesn't share the sentiment. He doesn't seem any more humbled today, his chiseled face utterly glinting with amusement. I almost wish I could order him out of the hall the way I did back in the shop.

"What would you like to start with?" Maestro Mette asks, a tinge of agitation in his tone.

"'Sérénade au Clair de Lune,'" I say, but my voice shakes.

"Can you please speak up?" calls the man from the box, with a smug grin. A flash of anger tightens my chest. Is he trying to humiliate me?

I brush my hands along the length of my skirt, lifting my chin up in defiance. I cannot let him rattle me. "I'll be singing the Moon Serenade, by Annette Devon." My words come out strongly, filling the hall.

"Please," the maestro says.

I turn my head to look at Madame. Her lips are pursed, but she gives me the slightest nod. I close my eyes and she starts playing, allowing the divine harmonies to envelop us.

The ruby pulses with the rhythm and I give in to its beat. Magic flows through my blood as the music takes hold of my body. And when I start to sing, the world fades. All my fears, my anxiety, anger, guilt, all wash away through the song. The music releases all the emotions locked inside, as if showing them both the door and the key.

I don't need to think of the words or the notes; my Talent remembers them better than I ever could. It is a sense of freedom I have never known possible—as if I could jump off a cliff and land safely. But right now, I never want to land. I want to keep flying.

The music winds down, and the last note is drawn from my lips. I'm breathless, as if my body resents the separation from the music. The hall is silent, the type of stillness meant to savor the moment.

"Thank you," Maestro Mette says, his words shattering the magic.

I wait for him to say more. For others to speak, clap, or call me off the stage. But they are all already moving out of their seats toward the exits, chattering among themselves.

Madame is suddenly by my side. "Walk," she mutters under her breath.

I follow her off the stage, and my nausea is back. Did I just fail? What will Dahlia do once she discovers I couldn't keep up my end of the bargain? Will she take the Talent away? Will she take away the medical care for Anaella?

The thoughts wrap themselves around me like a noose tightening around my neck. I don't even notice Madame has stopped walking until I run straight into her.

"Careful, girl," she says, spinning to face me.

I blink in surprise at the smile on her face. Surely she must be furious I wasn't offered a part?

"Well, that ought to show those pompous snobs." Her words brim with excitement, an unexpected departure from usual austerity.

"But . . . they didn't even say anything."

"Common practice!" She waves me off. "With that audition, I'm certain there's a bouquet already on its way to your home."

"Indeed," a voice calls from behind us. "After all, it was prepared even before you opened your mouth for the first note."

Leaning in an open doorway, the man from the fashion shop stares at me again. He's wearing a buttoned-down white shirt with a stiff neckline, but his dark tie is loose, and his coat is slung over his shoulder. So improper, it's infuriating. I've spent so many hours getting ready for today, making sure I fit in. And yet he dares to have that judgmental look on his face, as though I'm the one needing to gain his respect.

"Vicomte Lenoir." Madame bows ever so slightly.

"Hélène," the vicomte says, not bothering to move.

No one refers to Madame by her proper title of Lady Corbin, by her own choice. Yet, ignoring both her wishes and her title by using her first name requires an entirely new level of rudeness. A strain tugs at her smile, but she doesn't reply; no one dared to call him out in the shop, either. Whoever this vicomte is, he must be important enough that everyone agrees to play by his rules.

"Congratulations." He turns back to me, his loose tie dangling as he shifts.

I follow the hand-stitched pattern of subtle white polka dots among the deep blue silk of his tie and am hit with the urge to reach out and straighten it . . . or perhaps rip it off? It's almost too much to resist. Heat rises to my cheeks, though I'm not certain if I'm abashed by my own thoughts or by my failure to keep my annoyance in check. I'm certain his bedraggled charms have brought many young ladies to swoon over him, but he won't have that kind of luck with me. I shake my head as he continues.

"I'm certain you'll receive your contract as soon as they finish collecting all the reviews from your audition and cast their votes."

"Shouldn't you be handing in yours?" I try to mask my emotions with a polite smile.

He smirks in return. "Didn't write one." Pushing away from the wall, he whispers, "It wouldn't change the results anyway." With that he goes back into the room he appeared from and shuts the door behind him.

The ride back to the house passes in a blur, with Madame muttering about youngsters and their lack of respect. She isn't old herself, maybe reaching into her forties, but the vicomte can't be much older than I am. I have already learned that Madame is not a woman who keeps her opinions to herself, nor is she a woman who will appreciate any comment on my part, even if it's only to agree with her. So I keep my mouth shut and nod.

Her mood improves only when we reach the estate to find Pauline waiting for us with a massive bouquet of pink and white carnations. Just as Madame predicted.

It did arrive rather fast . . .

The vicomte's dismissive smile surges in my head, and my excitement wavers for just a second. The audition was a formality.

But so what? After all, the opera house was familiar with my Talent. But it is *my voice* they have never heard before. The singing was all mine.

And so is my success.

"Well done, my lady," Pauline says once I'm finally back in my chambers and out of my corset. "I had no doubt you would succeed."

"Oh, Pauline, it was wonderful. I've never felt anything like it . . . Standing on that stage . . ." I can't keep the smile off my face. "It was like a dream."

Pauline lets out a laugh as she carries over a porcelain basin. Her fingers brush over my hands as she carefully removes my ring for the washing. For a split second, her round eyes linger on the ruby, her hold on it tightening. There is something eager in the way she looks at it—a mixture of hunger and awe. It passes quickly, though, vanishing as soon as she puts the ring down. But it's a look I could spot anywhere, because until not so long ago, it shadowed my face. It's the same way I used to stare at Talents after Father passed—a stare full of longing. Only now, the Talent provoking it is all mine.

Guilt gnaws at the back of my mind, but the euphoria of today is too intoxicating.

Pauline smiles as she turns to undo my hair. "It's a dream you get to live every day now."

Every day.

My smile grows.

Pauline finally leaves me in my nightgown, closing the door on yet another day. But I'm not ready for it to end. I cannot even comprehend how stressed I felt just a few hours ago. Now, all that's left is pure elation.

I sit by the vanity, staring at the vase holding my new bouquet. *I made it.* I close my eyes, and the memory of the song plays in my mind—the softness of the melody, the floating quality of my voice as it soared through the hall. I take a deep breath, the scent of sweet blossoms enveloping me.

For just a moment, everything is perfect.

Then a hand lands on my mouth and a voice whispers in my ear, "Don't scream."

CHAPTER SEVEN

A Midnight Stroll

I SNAP MY eyes open, a cry building in the back of my throat. The intruder stands behind me, poised with a palm pressed against my lips, ready to muffle any sound. Will he attack if I try calling for help?

But something is off. The hand is rough, yet too small. Too weak. I twist around easily and his arm drops at once.

He's just a kid. Couldn't be older than eleven. He stares at me with unblinking eyes, and I'm hit with a sense of familiarity. I've seen these eyes before. The torn clothes. The blond curls. This is the boy I saw on the main avenue. The one I sent to deliver a message to Anaella. But what is he doing here? Is Anaella . . . ? I can't even finish that thought.

"Lady Sibille sent me," he says, and the tension in my chest drops. Dahlia sent him. Not the nurse.

"Love your house." The boy takes a step back. There is an ease to the way he moves, a sense of freedom or carelessness. He heads for the tray of sweets resting on a round table in my sitting area, tilting his head from side to side before picking up one of the chocolate pralines. "But this room is way too pink." He pops the bonbon in his mouth.

I can't actually argue. The rosy shades of my chambers would never have been my first choice. But this boy clearly didn't sneak into the house to offer commentary about the interior design.

My eyes follow him as he circles the room, his unwashed hands leaving black stains where he touches. I instinctively wipe my chin with the back of my sleeve.

I wait for him to say more, but he keeps quiet. Did he find my sister? Is she okay? How did he get into the house? What does Dahlia have to do with him?

His appearance is like a wake-up call, or a slap to the face. I've been so self-absorbed, caught up in the glamour of it all. The house, the dresses, the audition, the promise of fame. All while my ill sister is in the dark, not knowing my whereabouts, left alone with only a nurse for company. It's been over a week since I told her I accepted a job in the city—over a week since I've seen her. The shame and guilt rise up my throat like acid.

I don't regret my decision. But the festering frustration is slowly overshadowing the gratitude toward Dahlia. I should never have accepted this separation from my sister.

I break the long silence. "Did . . . did you find Anaella? The girl I asked you to deliver a message to?"

"Oh yes, I knew where she was from before." He jumps up to sit on the bed, and I can already imagine the look on Pauline's face in the morning. "I've been keeping tabs on you for a while now."

I blink. "What?"

"I'm one of Lady Sibille's Eyes."

His words make no sense, but with the boy's unwavering gaze everything falls into place. I have been wondering how Dahlia gathers all her information. How she knew so much about me. How she got her hands on my photo to complete the web of lies tying me into my new life. It all seems so obvious now. Children, especially poor ones, are invisible. No one would ever pay attention to a kid in the street. They are the perfect observers. Spies, hidden in plain sight. How many kids run around the city at her command?

"Your sister is doing better," he says, and I perk up. "Her fever broke."

I sigh as relief washes over me. "When . . . when did you see her last?"

He shrugs. "Maybe two days ago. I've mostly been following you."

The shadow in the garden. Our meeting on the avenue. The prickling sensation of being watched at the opera house.

"It was you? Have you been stalking me all this time?"

"Not just me. You have personal security." He hops off the bed. "Speaking of security, those locks you added on the windows are silly. What with you being guarded and all."

"Guarded?" The word comes out with a huff.

"Lady Sibille provides the best care for her partners," he recites. "If I do my job well with you, she'll promote me!" The eagerness in his tone is undeniable.

I look out at the moonlit garden. The trees sway gently in the wind, casting long arms of shadow on the grass. Is one of Dahlia's henchmen looming behind them now? Making sure I am safe? Making sure I am doing my part?

"Well, we better go! You don't want to be late." He takes another sweet.

"Late?"

"Lady Sibille is waiting for you."

I immediately wrap my hands over my chest, suddenly overly aware that I'm wearing only a nightgown. The negligee is nothing but a thin layer of ivory chiffon with frills. Certainly not something I can leave the house in. I'm already too naked in front of Dahlia, too fragile, I don't need to have her eyes following my exposed figure as well. Especially if I want to muster enough courage to demand reuniting with my sister. I have to change. But the boy is already moving.

"Take a cape. It can get cold." He heads into my dressing area. A moment later he tosses a darkened-gold silk cape in my direction, its fur collar fluttering in the air. I catch a glimpse of the embroidered autumn leaves before the mink hits my face, making me splutter as tufts clump in my mouth.

This will have to do.

"How do we go out?" I wrap the cape over my shoulders and slip into a pair of shoes. "I can't just walk out the door in the middle of the night. The servants will ask questions."

His face lights up with a mischievous smile. "The way I came in."

He skids over to one of the giant tapestries that line the walls. The woven image shows a blooming meadow with graceful deer roaming among the flowers and songbirds flying above—a picture of perfect harmony. The boy, however, clearly doesn't care about the beauty of it.

With one swift move, he swipes the fabric away. I gasp. A small, round door is hidden behind it.

"Come on," he says, pushing it open.

I have to bend to not hit my head as I follow him into the low passage. The door closes behind us with a soft click, and darkness overtakes us. The boy shuffles, and a second later a small flame lights the way ahead. He's holding a silver lighter, his eyes twinkling in the glowing fire.

I have heard of secret passages in manors and castles, helping the servants travel from one place to another discreetly and efficiently, but I imagined they only existed in far larger estates outside the city. The passage takes a sharp turn, leading down a dangerously steep staircase. I reach out and use the wall to steady myself as I put one foot after the other. The boy skips ahead, unaware of any risk.

Another door waits at the bottom. The boy grunts as he pulls it open with both hands, the heavy wood and metal creaking. A gust of cool air hits my face, and I wrap the cape tighter around myself.

We are in the back garden now, round bushes bathed in dim silver moonlight. The boy walks briskly, his small feet making no sound against the soft pebble path. We stick to the edges of the garden, close to the massive hedge blocking it from prying eyes. I sneak a glance back at the dark windows of the house—not a single candle flickering at this hour.

"Over here," he whispers, right before disappearing through thick branches.

I take a deep breath. No point in delaying. Bending down, I follow him through the bushes. Right behind the dense foliage, the branches give way to a wider opening. I push through them as they grab my cape and scratch my skin. A moment later, I'm standing on a narrow street, a lone lamp at its corner attempting to cast away the darkness. Instead, it creates a myriad of ghostly patches that seem to dance to its, somewhat unnerving, buzzing pulse.

"Keep to the shadows," the boy says, already walking.

I follow his instructions, trailing just one step behind him. "Where are we going?"

The kid doesn't answer.

The streets are still, the houses sound asleep. I glance at each estate in anticipation, hoping it might be the one, but the kid pays them no mind. He hums to himself in low tones as he leads me deeper into the maze of the city. Here, rows of buildings tower above us. We are close to the river.

Just as this realization hits, we emerge onto a wide street. Ahead stands the arching bridge leading to L'Île de Lutèce—the true center of the city and the bigger of the two natural islands dotting the wide river.

It's the one place I wish I could avoid.

A tremble enters my gait as we step onto the bridge. Just ahead—somewhere along the darkened shore—Father's body was found. They said the river carried him for hours before he hit the rocks.

I can still hear Anaella's sobs piercing through me as the police handed me the report. The dreaded words are as clear in my mind now as if I were reading them for the first time:

Cause of death: Drowning.

Clear traces of alcohol detected. No signs of struggle. A possible accident or act of self-harm.

An accident. It had to be. Father would never have left us by choice.

But he also never drank. Not even the occasional sip of wine at dinner. Could he have been that desperate?

He never let Anaella and me see how dreadful our situation had become, never allowed the weight of it to reach us. He always looked strong, hopeful. Even after we lost Mother. But there are cracks even the brightest smile can't hide—an empty cash register, graying waters, a grieving heart. Father was drowning long before the river took him, stealing his life and dragging his gem into the depths, forever lost beneath the waves.

I gaze at the black surface of the river, imagining the spark of Father's Talent shining through. But the magic died the moment he drew his last breath. Talents cannot survive without a beating heart—they must be transferred while their last owner is still alive. Even if Father's gem were found, it would be nothing more than a useless rock.

My hand closes over my ring, the ruby warm to the touch. There is no point in dreaming of a lost Talent when I have one right in my palm.

Shrugging, I stare straight ahead—to where Dahlia is waiting, with the promise of my future. We are halfway across the deserted bridge when I glance over my shoulder. A man in black lingers in the shadows, pausing as I do. When I resume walking he does too, maintaining the same distance.

A chill runs through me. "Someone's following us," I whisper.

"It's just Edmund." The kid waves me on impatiently. "He's your guard for the night. Now hurry up."

Was he behind us this entire time? How did I not notice him sooner? The idea that someone is constantly watching me makes the tiny hairs on my arms stand up. But I have no time to ponder any of it.

We are now across the bridge, walking by the island's edge along the river. Soon we reach a wide garden stretching right below the massive cathedral that dominates L'Île de Lutèce. Large spires reach into the ebony skies, while intricate Gothic arches give way to stained-glass windows. In the dark, the stone gargoyles nestled between the flying buttresses and pinnacles seem alive, as if they could leap right off the walls and attack.

"Wait here." The boy points to one of the benches facing the river. "Lady Sibille will arrive soon."

My stomach tightens. The image of Dahlia's perfect figure wrapped in her sensual crimson dress resurfaces. But there is also the memory of the ropes cutting my wrists as I fought against them, the gleam of the knife held by her henchman. I sit down, the night suddenly colder, my cape doing little against the goosebumps rising on my skin.

At the edge of the garden, my personal guard is standing watch. Is becoming a watchdog the boy's future as well? He's so young, yet there's almost no innocence left in his eyes. Does his family know where he is? Does he even *have* a family? He shifts from one foot to the other, unable to stand still. Then his head turns.

"Good luck," he says, before rushing away.

"Wait! I don't even know your name."

"His name is Lirone," a voice says in my ear.

I turn sharply. Dahlia is sitting right next to me, as though she has been there from the start. Her jasmine perfume fills the air, enveloping me and lulling my mind. When did she get here?

"How lovely to see you again, my Cleo." One side of her mouth tugs up into half a smile.

Her raven hair is pulled again into a tight bun, revealing her perfect snowy neck. But every other inch of her is covered, cozily wrapped in a monochromatic coat. Black chenille adorns her collar and runs all the way down the front flaps to encircle the trim at the hem. I have to fight the urge to touch it and feel its texture. The crimped fabric is adorned with a pattern of black lilies, mixing silk and velvet seamlessly. It seems familiar, yet I cannot place it. It's a perfect example of masterful detailing, with richness and depth that denote true opulence.

"Do you like it?" Dahlia asks, and I realize I've been staring.

I drop my gaze, my hair falling to the sides of my face like a curtain. She has only just arrived, and I'm already dumbstruck by her presence. How am I supposed to negotiate anything with her like this?

Dahlia doesn't wait for me to respond. "I thought we should meet in person to celebrate my nightingale's first triumph."

"You know about the audition?" I cringe as the question leaves my lips. Of course she knows about it.

She stares straight ahead at the gushing river as though I haven't even spoken. In the silver shine of the moon her features seem softer, rounder, exuding an almost ethereal glow. Her lips are slightly parted, and her chest rises and falls in a slow, rhythmic motion that's undeniably sensual—desirable.

"You have done well," she says. "Luxury suits you. I assume you find everything to your liking?"

"Oh, it's wonderful," I blurt, the sudden need to please her overwhelming. I bite into my lip. I'm not usually like this. So why do my limbs feel weak? I shake my head to clear it, searching for the little courage and conviction that still reside under my skin. "Except . . ."

Dahlia raises her brow.

This is my chance. My opportunity to speak up right after a success. I've done well and she has acknowledged it. If there were ever a time to make demands, this would be it. And yet I can't bring myself to speak. What if she sees me as ungrateful? Or worse, what if I upset her? What if instead of helping Anaella I put her at risk?

"I always loved this little island," Dahlia says as my silence stretches. "My father used to take me to the great cathedral every week when I was a child. But he never wanted me to be a part of the deals he conducted under its shadow at night." Her voice is soft, yet each word captivates me fully, as though I'm being let in on a secret so intimate it can be mentioned only under the protection of the darkness. "I wasn't the one meant to take over my father's role."

A fluttering feeling rises in my chest as the meaning of her words sinks in. There is only one reason she wouldn't be in line to inherit. Is it a trick? A way to draw the question out of me? Could she have known what I was going to ask of her? I press my lips together, not wanting to lose in whatever game she's playing, but my curiosity is too strong.

"You had a sibling, didn't you?"

Her large doe eyes narrow as she examines me. It's possible I've crossed a line, fallen into whatever trap her story presents. But then she stands up, the moon peeking through the trees and casting dappled shadow on her face. "Walk with me," she says.

I follow as she trails closer to the riverbank, her gaze reserved only for the racing water.

"I loved my brother." Her voice is so gentle now that I have to strain to hear her over the current. "But he was always the destined one. The chosen heir. No one ever saw his fall coming. Life has a twisted way to mess with fate, though, doesn't it?" She pushes a stray hair behind her ear, and a lone, angelic tear gathers at the corner of her eye.

Her vulnerability presents such a striking contrast to the impression of unshakable dominance that has lingered in my head from our last meeting that I'm lost. I want to be mad at her, to blame her for not telling me the details of our bargain beforehand, for forcing me to deal with the guilt of leaving my sister behind. I'm not ready to let my anger go, yet it seeps out of me without my permission, stolen away with each word she utters. I want to tell myself it's all an act, but somehow I'm certain she isn't lying. There is a timbre to her voice, a breathy quality and fragility that strikes me as undoubtedly honest.

"What happened to him?" I whisper.

"He died."

"I'm so sorry. You must miss him."

"More than anything."

Maybe it's the way her voice brims with love and regret, or maybe it's the familiarity of the weight she's carrying. Whatever it is, I can't help but feel drawn to her and want to know more. "Would you tell me a bit about him?"

She turns to face me, her irises glinting like a moonbeam dancing across a black lake. At this moment she's a being of divinity, a rare beauty not from this world. Yet at the same time there is humanity in her pain, a sense of longing that mirrors my own. I'm suddenly struck by how young she is beneath the layers of composure—scarcely in her mid-twenties, yet clearly forced to act in a manner beyond her age for too long.

The urge to comfort her nestles within me as I take a step toward her. She freezes, her body hardening, as though my movement has awoken her from a trance.

She catches herself, a flash of anger crossing her face.

I drop my gaze to the ground. "I'm sorry . . . I . . ."

The gushing river fills the silence between us as Dahlia's fingers find my chin. She lifts it up gently, all traces of tension within her evaporated.

"It's a tough world, my Cleo," she whispers. "But the past cannot help us. To succeed we must defy the rules, reinvent them. And make sacrifices. No one wanted me to take my brother's place, to inherit. No one thought a *girl* should have anything to do with an empire."

There is bitterness in her words, mixed with a sense of conviction so complete that it echoes in every cell of my body. I cannot imagine anyone not seeing her as mighty enough to command whichever role she pleases, but her strength comes from a place of struggle. She proved herself while inheriting what was not meant for her. And even though she doesn't say the word, I know what she truly means—a Talent. With such power, what possible magic could lie within her?

"Why are you telling me this?" My voice trembles.

Dahlia's hand hovers uncertainly between us before she takes a deep breath and clasps my own. "I know you miss your sister," she says. "I need you to know that I understand what you feel before telling you that it must stay this way for a while."

My heart drops. She knew what I wanted to ask all along. "But I need her."

"Anaella cannot be at your side until your position is stable. I promise you she is in trusted hands, but her health is still too precarious. Do
you think it'll go unnoticed if the city's newest *Dame* suddenly has to
care for an ill sister? Never mind one whose condition worsened from
clear lack of proper Talented attention. Even her traveling 'from the
countryside' in such a state will raise too many questions. We must not
have that. I also cannot allow you to visit her at your father's shop. You
must not be seen in those parts of the city, not even at night."

My free hand curls into a fist by my side, and Dahlia cups my cheek in
her other palm. Her skin is soft, her fingers warm, her touch electrifying.

"However," she continues, "you can write to her. Letters I can allow."

Letters. At least that way I can tell Anaella I'm alright. I can let her
know I didn't just abandon her. That I'm thinking of her. And I hate
that the thought even comes to my mind, but letters will also allow me
to hide parts of the truth more easily. If I saw my sister now, I'd probably end up spilling all the secrets Dahlia wants me to keep.

"I know you wish I had been upfront with you before, but in my
business it is prudent to withhold a certain amount of information as a
precaution. But worry not, my Cleo. I promise you and your sister will
be reunited soon, and there are two things I never do: lie, or break my
word. I need you to trust that."

The sour taste of her earlier manipulation still lingers in my mouth,
twisting my stomach into knots, but Dahlia's unwavering gaze is honest.

I do believe her.

She will keep her word—Anaella and I will be together, and our
lives will be better for this unwanted separation. I glance down at my
fidgeting hands, the rough edges of my fingernails digging into my
palms. The best thing I can do for both of us is to keep going, make sure
it will all be worth it.

I nod my acceptance, and Dahlia sighs before continuing. "Good.
For now, you have to stay focused. Can you do that for me?"

"Y-yes."

She smiles, and the pain washes from her face as though my words alone are enough to mend her heart. With a single breath she pulls away from me, and my chest tightens, longing for the unexpected closeness we just shared.

"Well, my lovely, I didn't call you here just to chat. It is time we talked about your first assignment."

The shift in her tone is even more jarring than the sudden distance between us. Her pristine mask is back in its place—regal, confident, powerful, no cracks of pain or frailty to be found. I was so wrapped up in the moment I nearly forgot the role she expects me to perform. My mouth turns dry, my heart accelerating.

"My assignment?"

"You are my thief, after all." Dahlia chuckles.

"I don't want to hurt anyone." The words leave my mouth before I can think.

Her perfect brow rises, her dark eyes unblinking. "You truly mean that, don't you?" There is something unnerving in the way she studies me. Perhaps there's even a glint of confusion in her glare. But then she blinks, her smile returning. "Fear not. I have a feeling you will like this mission."

I doubt I can like anything that forces me to steal. Under the looming presence of the cathedral, just speaking about it feels like a sin already committed. Not that my feelings matter. Whatever the mission might be, I will perform it. For Anaella's health. For our new future. To become victorious and change my fate, as Dahlia has done for herself. I agreed to become a thief, and I will keep up my end of the bargain, just as Dahlia honors hers.

"You have met Vicomte Lenoir twice already, haven't you?" Dahlia tilts her head.

The vicomte's smug face immediately fills my mind, the image of his green eyes staring at me roiling my insides with a wave of anger. "Yes, I have."

"The vicomte has recently inherited a Mathematical Talent from his retired father."

"You mean . . ."

"You are to get close enough to him to steal it."

"But . . . he's—"

"A patron of the opera," Dahlia says.

"And from a noble family."

"Which only makes his Talent more lucrative."

Her voice is so casual, so certain, yet what she asks is far from it. Even among the Elite there is a hierarchy: the older the Talent, the stronger it is. And the nobles have been honing their gems for too many years to count, back to when the first enchanted mines were discovered, and the Crown shared their magical gems with only their closest court.

The vicomte's Talent must be one of the oldest in all of Francia, perhaps on the entire continent—a true legacy. I never thought I'd actually see one, let alone try to steal it.

"There's no need to be afraid." Dahlia's eyes soften.

"What if I get—"

"Caught?" Dahlia cuts me off again. "I've been planning this operation for a very long time. The *nobility* have become complacent. And in any case, I will not let any harm come your way."

I force myself to swallow. This was always a part of the deal. "Why . . . why *him*?"

"I've already told you, my dear Cleo, I supply whatever my clients desire. Besides, it has been too long since any truly powerful Talents have *disappeared*, don't you agree?"

I bite my lip as I watch the corners of hers twitch. She's referring to the great panic that took hold of the city about three years ago, when seven of the most prominent members of Lutèce's society woke up with their Talents gone—no magic pulsating in their veins. The thieves had stolen not only their gems, but worse, their blood, allowing the illicit transfer of their gifts. It was all anyone could talk about for nearly a year. The newspapers were filled with speculation, but the police never managed to trace the culprits. Though now, I have the sense that the main one is looking right at me.

"I . . ." My voice falters. "I don't think the vicomte likes me very much."

Dahlia trails her hand over my arm, tracing the leaf pattern of my cape. "You are a charming young lady, and I'm certain you can find a way to make him change his mind. You shall get close enough to him to steal a sample of his blood. The gem will come later."

I'm not sure what "later" means, but that secretive, knowing smile of hers makes it clear that the full extent of her plan will not be shared with me. Not yet, at least. All I can do is follow along.

After all, this is what I signed up for—the cost of changing my fate. And if anything, the choice of the vicomte only proves that Dahlia is a woman of her word. She promised I won't hurt anyone, that I will steal only from those who can afford it. None of those aristocrats who lost their Talents a few years ago were driven to poverty. None of them suffered the pain I know so well—they haven't lost their identity and future. Just like them, the vicomte will lose his social standing, at most—his pride. But as a noble, his life of comfort and richness is promised, with or without his Talent. In fact, chances are he doesn't even use his gift; most of the Elites only wear theirs for show. Taking it from him might well be a service.

Not to mention his entitlement, his rudeness.

Dahlia is right—of all the targets she could have given me, at least the vicomte is one I won't lose sleep over. And if the choice is between him keeping a Talent he probably doesn't even appreciate and my future, there is really no decision to be made. The only downside of this mission is the need to spend time with him.

Dahlia turns back toward the cathedral. "Expect Lirone in the evenings."

Lirone? It takes me a second to understand she's talking about the boy.

"You are to update him daily on any and all matters—nothing is too small or insignificant when it comes to creating connections with the upper class. And he can pass your letters and your sister's responses between you two." She pauses under a large chestnut tree, laden with late white blooms. "Can I trust you with that?"

I nod, and her smile makes my breath catch.

"In fifteen days, there will be a gala at the opera house to begin the summer social season, and if my sources are right, you are to open the concert. It's a chance for the opera to introduce their new star. The vicomte will be there. For now, focus on getting close to him. I shall eagerly await the news that he's completely taken with you."

"I won't disappoint you," I whisper.

Dahlia steps closer to me, so close her warm breath brushes against my skin. An unfamiliar heat grows inside me, responding to her presence, her sensuality. But more than that, I feel a yearning for the intimacy of the woman I saw behind the perfect mask. My body tingles, suddenly craving things I only ever dared imagine in the shelter of night. My head starts spinning.

And when she speaks, I'm left with no air.

"I know."

CHAPTER EIGHT

Stage Lights

"YOU HAVE A PLAN, right?" Lirone leans against the wall, munching on yet another praline bonbon. "I'll need to report something to Lady Sibille after you return from the gala tonight."

I suck in a breath and tug at the corseted-bodice Pauline laced me into before she left to check the carriage. Miss Garnier might be a famous modiste, but with the way the boning of this dress digs into my ribs, even with the addition of a padded liner, it's hard to understand why. The sleeves are also too puffy for my taste, matching the fullness of the skirts, which are held up by both horsehair and metal hoops.

Father's words fill my mind as I shuffle around, trying to find a position in which the dress doesn't hurt. "No matter how beautiful a garment may be, if it's uncomfortable, no woman will ever shine in it."

My eyes dart toward the drawer hiding Father's book. I'm certain if I dared to look through it, I'd find a note in perfect cursive telling me to use whalebone instead of that rigid steel boning to fix this bodice. So far, I've managed to muster the strength to open it only once, but just a glance at his neat handwriting was enough to bring tears to my eyes. The separation from home has been getting harder with each passing day.

"Will you stop standing in front of the mirror already?" Lirone rolls his eyes at me in his reflection.

"I have to perform in a few hours, in front of the entire social elite of Lutèce." I shake my head as I turn to him. "Not to mention that I must get close to Vicomte Lenoir, who I'm pretty sure wants nothing to do with me. And I can barely breathe in this dress."

"So you *don't* have a plan to win the vicomte over?"

I let out a huff and sit by the vanity. I don't have a plan, but I can't bring myself to admit it; not when every word I tell him travels straight from my lips to Dahlia's ears.

"Of course I do," I say.

"Well, what is it?" He crosses his arms over his chest in what I'm certain is supposed to be a serious pose, but he's so young it almost makes me laugh. Looking away from him, I grab a cotton pad from the dresser, already sprinkled with rose powder, and fluff it over my cheeks.

Just as Dahlia promised, Lirone's been visiting my room every day since our meeting. But so far, aside from receiving my invitation for the gala, I've had nothing to report. My rehearsals at the opera house have been short and concise, but, most importantly, private. Madame told me that Maestro Mette has decided to keep me as a surprise, which means my rehearsals with the orchestra were for his ears alone. I haven't met any of the other singers, and not even Madame was allowed inside. And so, all my hopes of making social connections—or perhaps seeing the vicomte again in the opera house corridors before the gala—have come to nothing.

Tonight, though, our meeting is guaranteed.

Not that I have any idea what to do when I see him . . . How does one get the attention of a man? Though I doubt his ego has been bruised, I've not been acting exactly like the shy, groveling ladies he is used to. Will he still care to speak to me?

"Fine, don't tell me," Lirone says when I don't reply. "But know that Lady Sibille does *not* like receiving bad news."

"I'll have good news by tomorrow." The conviction in my voice is surprising, even to me. "Speaking of news . . ."

Lirone rolls his eyes again and shakes his head, making his messy curls bounce. "I already told you, I gave your letter to that nurse. Your sister hasn't written back yet."

"But—"

"I'm not hiding any letter!" He flips the pockets of his patched-up jacket inside out, revealing a series of holes the size of his fingers.

I purse my lips, the crimson wax of my lipstick making them stick together. I wrote to Anaella nearly two weeks ago, but she still hasn't replied. Could it be that the nurse didn't pass on the letter? Or perhaps my sister is simply too mad at me? Or too ill to respond? The possible reasons circle over me like vultures.

I twist around in my seat, my knuckles turning white as I grip the intricately carved wood on the back of my chair and stare at Lirone. "Will you please go there again and—" A knock on the door makes me jump to my feet.

"My lady, the carriage is waiting," Pauline calls.

I turn to look at Lirone, but he's already gone. The only evidence left of his presence is the brief ripple of the tapestry hiding the secret passage. I have to give it to the boy: he's fast.

I take a second to brush down my black and white gown before opening the door.

"Everything well, my lady? I'm certain tonight will be a success." Pauline curtsies.

"Thank you." I step past her into the corridor and yank the door closed behind me, as if the room itself might reveal my secrets. "I wish you could come with me," I say as I stride toward the staircase, making Pauline rush to keep up with me. "It would be nice to have a friendly face there."

Pauline tugs a stray ginger hair behind her ear. "Perhaps one day, my lady. For now, you'll have Madame at the gala with you."

I chuckle. "Not exactly my definition of 'friendly.'"

Pauline smiles but stays silent. She accompanies me to my carriage and stays until the coachman helps me inside. Basset hasn't done anything to indicate suspicion since the day of my audition, despite driving me back and forth for rehearsals every day. Clearly, I was being paranoid.

He bows deeply before closing the carriage door after me. I watch the blur of streetlights through the small windows as the horses pull us forward, each light buzzing yellow, glowing like a firefly, showing us the way.

The concierge at the artists' entrance recognizes me at once, and soon I'm climbing my way toward the dressing rooms. I have become rather fond over the last two weeks of one of the smaller rooms by the end of the corridor. A secluded spot away from prying eyes. But a maid stops me before I can enter.

"Lady Adley, your dressing room is ready for you."

I look at her, and then at the closed door. "This isn't my room?"

"No, my lady. Please follow me."

She leads me up another set of stairs to a pair of arched doors. "If you need me, just ring the bell," she says before letting me inside.

My mouth drops. This is nothing like the narrow room I had until now. I'm not even sure "room" is the right word to describe it. It's massive, full of giant mirrors that reflect the golden candles, and adorned with too many flower-filled vases to count. The scent of white roses is almost overwhelming.

All of this is just for me?

My heels sink into the soft ivory carpet as I take a hesitant step, tracing my fingers over the gold cresting rail of an armchair. I'm gaping at the beauty when I notice a flash of red among the white flowers—a single scarlet rose demanding my attention. As I approach it, I notice a black silk string tied to its stem.

Heat travels to my cheeks. I don't need to ask who sent it.

A wish for good luck. A reminder of my mission. But there is also something sensual about it, like Dahlia herself. Each velvety petal speaks of softness, inviting me to delve into its endless layers and sink into the promise of a passionate embrace. Just thinking of Dahlia's lush lips, or the long lashes adorning her dark eyes, stirs something inside me—a sense of unfamiliar desire.

I'm not a fool; I know that Dahlia isn't an innocent maiden. I know I should detach myself emotionally, confine our relationship strictly to business. She is dangerous. A criminal. Yet there is more to her than just a mere outlaw, more behind all that perilous strength. The glimpse she granted me of the woman behind it all is etched within me—the pain, the difficulties she suffered after her brother's death, the raw emotions I accidentally touched with my questions. They are all the source of her immense resilience, the kind of resilience I can only dream of. Her struggles echo my own, as though I can see myself in her. Perhaps she feels the same?

Something about her hidden vulnerability mixed with the clear risk is almost thrilling. I have always lived my life by the rules. I've done everything I was expected to, just as my parents taught me. And where did it get me? Dahlia's way, however . . .

I stare at the golden dressing room, taking a deep breath of the flower-scented air. The Elite get to bask in this kind of beauty every day. Like Vicomte Lenoir—my target. My brief encounters with him have been enough to show me that he's taking all of it for granted—born with a silver spoon in his mouth and a legacy Talent just waiting for him. No matter how handsome he may be—messy curls, undone ties, glinting eyes I cannot forget—men like him drive me mad.

Taking his Talent from him to guarantee my own place in this world seems like a fair exchange.

I'm reaching for the red rose when the door opens behind me. I jump, pricking my finger on one of the sharp thorns.

"So *you're* the one who stole my dressing room," a woman calls from behind me.

I suck the drop of blood from the tip of my finger as I turn. Standing at the doorway, a lady in a shimmering gown scowls at me. Her dress is made of black lace trimmings over gold velvet bands, creating a mix of textures that only accentuates the glitter of the paillettes covering every inch of it. In comparison to this dress, with its long train and lacy sleeves, my own gown feels too simple.

"I'm sorry?" I open and close my mouth, not sure how to respond. "And you are?"

"Lady Véronique Battu." She flashes a smile with perfect dimples. "As consœurs, you may call me Véronique. Us sopranos have to stick together, no? I'm sure your cousin has told you about me."

I nod politely, even though her name is unfamiliar to me, and her collegial spirit feels somewhat too sweet to swallow. "Yes, of course. I'm Cleodora—Adley." I stop myself from using my own family name at the last second. I have never introduced myself as Adley before, and the sound of it tastes wrong in my mouth.

"Oh, I know." Véronique steps into my room, a dark lace fan clutched in her hand. With its tip, she lifts one of the closed flower buds before bending to smell it. "I've heard so much about you in the last couple of weeks. I only wonder how I didn't know your name sooner."

"Well, my cousin is a very private person."

It's not exactly a lie. Pauline did tell me that the former Lady Adley never shared much of her personal life. Yet Pauline is just a maid. If Véronique was close to Lady Adley, could she see through the facade Dahlia created for me?

Her blue eyes linger on my face longer than is comfortable, but she gives no indication that my words have stumped her.

"Well, this room was promised to me." She twists a perfect blond ringlet around her finger. "You had better find another one to wait in."

I only manage to huff in surprise before a man walks into the room, a wide grin spread on his face. "Véronique, you aren't picking on the new girl, are you?"

He's bulky and short, a feature made more prominent by the way his navy tailcoat hangs past his knees. Gold cufflinks adorn his sleeves, matching the buckles on his leather shoes.

Véronique opens her fan dramatically at his interruption, revealing an array of beautifully stitched butterflies.

"My fans call me Chevalier Muratore." He kisses the back of my hand, his lips grazing my ruby ring. "But to my friends I'm known as José. A delight to finally meet you."

His name I know at once: the famous tenor whose voice is said to be so divine it could make angels weep. I have always imagined him taller, and older. But both the singers standing in my dressing room are young; José is somewhere in his late twenties, and Véronique looks not much older than me.

"Please don't let Véronique's soprano drama upset you," he says with a wink.

"Soprano drama?" Véronique repeats after him, fanning herself with sharp wrist movements. "You know as well as I do that this dressing room was promised to me once Adley retired."

"You did one show in her place, Véronique. That's hardly a promise. Now there's a new Adley in the house." José takes a step toward her. "Besides, we have a concert to give! We should let the new girl concentrate." He offers his arm to Véronique, but she just snaps her fan shut and heads out the door without a backward glance.

"And the battle commences." José laughs and turns to me. "Enjoy tonight, ma chérie. I can't wait to hear the new diva! Toi toi toi."

I sink into the armchair as soon as he leaves the room. My head is spinning, and at this point I'm not sure if it's from the dress preventing air from entering my lungs or from Véronique's clear disdain. Suddenly the sweet scent of flowers makes me sick.

I didn't even have the chance to make an impression on the other singers. They clearly made up their mind about me the moment they heard the name Adley. The more time passes, the more I realize the gravity of taking on her Talent—the Elite gems signal more than just powerful abilities; they're a marker of social standing. High society is like an intricate game. Only my dice were rolled before I even saw the board, and now all I can do is try to catch up and understand where I landed and who the other players are.

"Breathe," I say aloud to myself.

One thing at a time. I might have started on the wrong foot with Véronique, even though I never wanted her dressing room . . . but José seems nice. And I'll have enough time to befriend them both.

Besides, tonight there's only one person whose opinion about me I need to change. I glance once again at Dahlia's red rose. I will not let her down. The vicomte is my primary goal, and I can't let anything distract me from that.

A maid rushes through the door. "My lady, the concert is about to begin. You are needed by the stage."

I nod politely and stand to follow. Even though I've been backstage almost every day these past two weeks, I have never seen it bustling with this much activity. Maids dash from one room to the next, while stagehands dressed all in black mutter among themselves. Musical scales drift from under closed doors as singers sneak in one last warm-up before the performance.

"There you are!" Madame appears from one of the rooms.

In all the time we've spent together, I've only seen her wear dark colors—black, brown, shades of gray. But tonight her dress is royal blue silk with wisps of silver chiffon. Her hair is held up by an elaborate flower comb inlaid with a sparkling sapphire. Could this be her Talent? I have never seen her display any jewels before.

"Where have you been?" She grabs my arm and pulls me toward the spiraling stairs leading down to the stage.

"My new dressing room." I glance over my shoulder. "One of the maids took me there. It's upstairs."

"They gave you Old Lady Adley's room already?" Madame blinks in surprise. "That will stir some drama, I'm sure."

"You mean Véronique? You know her?"

Madame laughs. "I know the ins and outs of not only this theater but the entire music scene of Lutèce, my dear."

I want to ask more, but she's already talking again.

"We don't have time for any of that tonight. You are the first singer on the stage this evening! It's a big honor. The gala is the opening event to the entire summer social season, and you are the symbol of it."

"I know," I say. She's given me the same speech every day since the invitation letter arrived.

"Sing just the way you did in the rehearsals. Don't let the crowd distract you."

"I won't."

"Five minutes!" a stagehand calls.

Madame leads me to the stage wings. The orchestra is already seated on the stage: rows upon rows of string instruments, followed by harps, wind instruments, and percussion. The musicians are all wearing black attire and sitting at attention. Massive curtains block the hall itself from view, chattering voices drifting from behind it.

"Madame, shouldn't you already be in your seat?" Maestro Mette joins us, holding his conducting baton with gloved hands. "Lady Adley, you look absolutely divine," he says.

"Thank you, Maestro." I bow my head.

"Well." Madame clears her throat. "I shall be in the audience." She turns to leave, but stops. "Cleodora, don't forget to enjoy."

Another call comes—"One minute!"—and when I turn back Madame is gone.

A rush of adrenaline pumps through my veins.

"It's a full house," the Maestro says. "Let's make sure they all fall in love with you."

My throat clenches. Suddenly the voices behind the curtains ring louder. There must be thousands of them. I try to take a deep breath and my corset tightens around me painfully. This is not the time to panic.

"Raising curtains!"

The ruby on my finger vibrates, but my mouth feels dry. From the corner of my eye, I see a stagehand leaning close to the ground as he pulls on a massive rope. The heavy red curtains ascend. A roar of applause hits me like a wave of sound, and my vision is blurred by the bright stage lights.

Maestro Mette steps onto the stage and the orchestra musicians rise to their feet. His hand rests on his chest in a gesture of humble gratitude, and as he bows, the light reflects off his ring, his Conducting Talent ready to shine. Other singers have gathered in the wings to watch, and somewhere in my mind I register Véronique and José standing on the other side of the stage. Stepping onto his raised podium, Maestro Mette turns his head to me.

My heart skips a beat. That's my cue.

CHAPTER NINE

Champagne and Biscuits

DEAFENING APPLAUSE FILLS the hall as the curtains fall. The cheers are a magnetic pull, demanding that we step back on stage for multiple curtain calls. I'm wrapped in a daze when Maestro Mette gives the signal and the entire row of singers bows once more.

Rose petals land on the stage, and the trance between me and the audience quickly meshes with reality as a colorful bouquet is delivered to my hands. My heart hammers in my chest, the rush of the performance stretching a wide grin on my face.

"Brava!" The shouts ring out as we step once more off the stage.

"Last time! Just for Lady Adley!" Maestro Mette orders.

I'm too entranced to pay any mind to the muttering of the other singers as I once again step in front of the crowd, this time by myself. The cameras erupt in blinding flares and curling smoke as Maestro Mette gestures to me. I take a step forward alone, bending at the knees so deeply I almost lose my balance.

The orchestra musicians are also on their feet now, their standing ovation adding to the thunderous applause of the crowd. I turn to the Maestro and gesture to him, but instead of bowing himself, he takes my hand and kisses the ring on my finger; the glow of the ruby bathes his face in a red hue.

The crowd cheers. "Bella! Viva la diva!"

Both hands on my heart, I lower myself into one last sweeping curtsy, savoring the moment as the curtains envelop the stage one last time.

"A star is born," Maestro Mette proclaims.

Around us the orchestra is already moving, breaking into chatter. But I'm still floating—the admiration of the crowd, an opium I can't get enough of.

"Fantastic, ma chérie!" José is by my side. "I always knew Adley had a special Talent, but it shines even brighter with your voice."

The other singers are scattered around the stage, congratulating each other on the successful evening. I try to catch their names and faces, but my mind is hazy, my heartbeat still synced with the beat of the music and the pulse of my ruby ring.

"Come, ma chérie, let's go have some wine and meet your new fans." José offers me his arm and I take it with a smile, my cheeks already sore.

We follow the steady stream of musicians away from the stage. Soon we descend a massive marble stairway: the famous Grand Escalier of the opera house. My jaw drops. The foyer is bustling with people drinking wine and champagne, while servants carrying silver trays present them with a variety of hors d'oeuvres.

Having only used the artists' entrance so far, I have never seen this side of the opera house. Its grandeur is striking. I slide my hand down the elegant banister, the spider-veined marble chilling to the touch. There is marble everywhere, stretching across the entire space and dappled in gold. My eyes skip from the grand columns to the bronze and crystal sculptures that rise above the mingling crowd. Murals in shimmering colors are reflected in giant mirrors, making me feel as though I'm a part of the art, not just walking alongside it.

"Lady Adley!"

As soon as I'm spotted, I'm surrounded by people. *Fans.* They call for José as well, but most of them fixate on me—wishing to tell me how wonderfully I sang, how grateful they are for my voice, how they can't wait to hear me again. They are the Elite of Lutèce, the highest, most Talented members of society. I'm not just accepted among them, I'm *cherished* by them. Recognized. Adored.

My dream, truly realized. All thanks to the ruby.

"What a splendid opening for the summer." A woman in a deep-purple gown takes both my hands in hers.

"Yes, she's a marvel, isn't she?" Maestro Mette is beside me. "I didn't know you were back in the city, Lauretta."

"I wouldn't have missed this! Besides, what better way is there to spend a Thursday evening?" The woman lets go of me and exchanges a set of kisses on each cheek with the Maestro. She tilts her head as she pulls back. "Isn't this the same tailcoat you wore to our réveillon two years ago?"

Maestro Mette's smile tenses a bit. "I don't recall."

"Yes, it is! We were together at Baron Thomas's and you had the foie gras." As she speaks, I notice her amethyst earring glowing. "We should plan another dinner soon. You both must come."

"We would love to." He puts his hand on my shoulder and I nod along.

"Oh, are those gougères I see?" The woman turns to look at the passing servant, her eyes widening at the sight of the cheesy pastry. "Will you excuse me?" She bows her head before heading after the tray.

"Lady Lauretta Toussaint—one of our richest patrons," Maestro Mette whispers to me. "I'd recommend avoiding her dinners unless you're interested in a detailed recounting of every social event from the last five seasons. I do not envy her husband with that Memory Talent of hers."

I let out a polite chuckle at his joke, but inside I'm trying to wrap my head around the concept of a Memory Talent. I knew these types of Talents existed—any honed skill can become one, be it memory, public speaking, or even negotiation. But these Talents are very rare and uncommon among the working class. After all, you can't use your memory to put food on the table. But here, I guess, anything is possible.

Maestro Mette grabs two tall glasses of champagne and hands one to me. "To our best season yet. Santé!"

I take a timid sip and vivacious bubbles burst across my palate, nearly making me giggle with surprise. The champagne tastes fresh and slightly sweet, matching its delicate scent of lime blossom.

The buzz around me has finally dwindled, and my heart starts slowing down. So many people approach me, their faces all mix in my head. Yet there is clearly one face missing. Vicomte Lenoir hasn't come to congratulate me. Not that I care for his praises. But, in fact, I haven't seen him at all this evening.

As much as I want to revel in my success, my work for the night is not done. Worry gnaws at my stomach. Could he have left already?

I scan the grand foyer before turning to Maestro Mette. "It was a pleasure to see all the patrons tonight. I've only officially met Lady Toussaint and Vicomte Lenoir so far." I take another sip of champagne, trying to sound casual. "Is he here tonight?"

"Oh, yes. I've seen him about," the Maestro says. "But you should meet our more cordial patrons. Allow me to introduce you."

Before I can protest, he heads toward the stairs, obliging me to follow him to one of the higher floors. We walk down a corridor with a set of small balconies that overlook the foyer. Standing and chatting by the nearest balcony is a group of ladies. Madame is among them, and so is none other than the modiste Josephine Garnier herself.

The adrenaline of the evening has managed to subdue the pain from her dress, but at the sight of Josephine's round face the boning of the bodice digs deeper into my skin. No doubt I'll have bruises when I get home tonight. How has she even attained such a high position in society to be invited here tonight?

"Lady Adley!" Josephine bows her head as we approach. "What a pleasure to see you again."

Madame gulps her red wine, emptying the glass. "See her, or your dress?" She sneers, her cheeks flushed from alcohol.

"Well, it is a masterpiece of mine!" Josephine boasts, as if unaware of Madame's tone.

"I thought I recognized your style, Miss Garnier," says a short woman with chubby cheeks in a pink frilly gown. She turns to me. "You looked so beautiful on that stage!"

"Lady Adley, allow me to introduce you to Lady Hardy and Lady Paradis." Maestro Mette gestures to the short woman and to a second lady leaning against the rail of the balcony. "They are two of our most esteemed patrons, and they are both professors at the Grand Collège."

"An honor to meet you," I say, noticing the glinting gems on their rings. They must be Teaching Talents, either for their subjects or for the art of tutoring itself.

"You are a true revelation, Lady Adley," Lady Hardy continues. "I suggest you start carrying a pen with you. Soon enough you won't be able to walk down the street without being stopped for autographs. A true idol in the making!" She flashes a wide grin before turning to Maestro Mette. "Lamar, you'd better have something special in store for the upcoming season now that Lady Adley is here."

"I have indeed," he says.

"Oh, you have to give me a clue!"

I know I should listen to the conversation; they are talking about my future, after all. The promises of fame and adoration are almost too sweet to dream of. What is his plan for me? Will he turn me into the lead soprano? A prima donna? Yet the discussion doesn't hold my focus for long. My eyes dart to the shifting crowds on the floor below—the vicomte has to be among them.

"Good luck!" Madame grabs yet another glass of wine. "The Maestro is a fortress. He won't even tell *me* his plan."

Lady Paradis chimes in from her place by the railing. "Lady Adley's voice will go fantastically with José's, don't you agree? Oh, speak of the devil. José, dear!" she calls, waving her hand in the air.

I turn just in time to see both José and Véronique approaching.

"Ladies." José raises his glass. "What brings you all here this fine evening?"

The women all giggle.

"We were just talking about the upcoming season. And how Maestro Mette won't give up his little secrets."

"Well, we do know one thing." Véronique steps forward, her voluminous skirts pushing me aside. "José and I will be this season's leading duo."

"All still remains to be decided," Maestro Mette says, and Véronique's face twitches, presenting a sharp contrast to the wide smile stretching on Madame's lips.

Lady Hardy is speaking again—something about a matinee concert—but my attention is stolen by brown curls and the glint of an unmistakable pair of green eyes on the floor below.

"If you'll excuse me," I say, not bothering to wait for a response before heading back to the Grand Escalier.

I push through the crowd, nodding and smiling as they call my name or raise a glass to me. Vicomte Lenoir seemed awfully close to the entrance, and I cannot allow him to slip away.

Broken pieces of messy plans spiral through my head in a hazy cloud: Is he wearing his gem? Maybe he'll be drunk, and I can persuade him to tell me more about his Talent? Or perhaps I should *get* him drunk . . . Do I really have to seduce him? Maybe I could simply break a glass and make sure he cuts his hand so I can steal a sample of his blood—that might be easier than making him desire me.

I shake my head at the ridiculousness of my own thoughts.

The foyer is bustling with too many people. I circle around and rise to my tiptoes to look over the crowd, but the vicomte is nowhere to be seen. Dahlia will not forgive me for this.

"Looking for someone?" The vicomte's low voice is right behind me.

I spin on my heel, my voice stolen by his closeness.

One corner of his lips is up in a lopsided smile, and his startling eyes look straight into mine.

"I . . . Monsieur le Vicomte, a pleasure to see you tonight." I curtsy deeply, but Vicomte Lenoir just continues to stare at me, his gaze intense and unyielding.

I take a deep breath, and the fresh scent of bay rum invites me in; the warm blend of rich and spicy notes clings to his clothes. This is the first time I've seen him properly attired, and I hate to admit how dashing he looks. He's wearing a crisp black jacket and trousers, leather shoes, and white gloves. But it's his waistcoat that catches my eye—an intricate paisley pattern is embroidered on the shiny silver satin. It is tightly fitted, showing off his masculine build.

I search for any hint of a gleaming gem, but nothing reflects the light aside from his golden cufflinks. I swallow. I knew this wasn't going to be easy.

I clear my throat as I catch myself staring. "Did you enjoy the concert?" I ask, trying to collect myself.

"Not especially."

His words hit me and send my stomach churning. I should brush off his comment, not let it affect me. I shouldn't even care what he thinks. Yet my mind spirals. Could he really have not liked my singing? Everyone else loved it—adored me, in fact.

The vicomte turns away without another word, and the pang of disappointment turns to bubbling anger. He thinks he can just walk away like that? And even though I know I'm meant to charm him, I can't stop myself as I follow.

"For a patron of the arts, you sure don't seem passionate about them."

He stops next to a servant with a tray of biscuits. Collecting a few in his palm, he bites into one, the crumbs sticking to his gloves. "Want one?" He stretches his hand to me.

I only glare at him, and he shrugs. "That's all you have to say?" I ask.

"Oh, my apologies. I should have known you'd expect me to lie by your feet and praise you for a performance you had nothing to do with."

I huff in disbelief. Perhaps stabbing him is the right plan to go with. How can Dahlia expect me to get close to someone like him? "Had nothing to do with?" I have to keep myself from shouting. "I sang on that stage."

He stuffs another biscuit into his mouth, not bothering to swallow before speaking. "You mean your Talent did. With that gem on their finger, anyone could have done it."

"That—that's not true!"

"If you say so." The vicomte eats the last biscuit and brushes his hands together, the crumbs falling onto the floor.

The bubbling in my chest comes to a boil; the heat of anger rises up my neck. I take a step closer to him, speaking under my breath. "If that's really how you feel, why are you a patron at all? Why are you even here tonight?"

"The truth?" He leans so close I can feel his warm breath against my ear. I shiver, my heart accelerating, rage muted by that spicy scent of his that envelops me with surprising sweetness. "I just like the free champagne."

I almost snort.

"Well, well, well . . . you two seem awfully close." My stomach drops at the sound of Véronique's voice. Is she following me around?

Vicomte Lenoir draws back with a smug grin, as though he's actually enjoyed the argument. I can barely stop myself from rolling my eyes, but with Véronique as an audience I muster my self-control.

I shouldn't have let myself get carried away. What was I even expecting from a man like him? But even for an arrogant, self-centered, pompous nobleman he lacks too much refinement. It's as though each word that came out of his mouth was designed to get my blood boiling. Perhaps he's simply bored, tired of being the perfect specimen of his Elite birth.

"How wonderful to see you tonight, my lord." Véronique bats her long eyelashes. Her fan is open and covering a part of her face, as though she's blushing. "It has been too long, hasn't it?"

"Long indeed," he says, but his tone is cold.

She reaches for his arm, thumb trailing over his muscles. "You should really come to dinner! Father will be thrilled to see you. How about this Sunday?" She shoots me a quick glance with narrow eyes before returning straight to the vicomte. "It will be lovely, I promise. Just a small family gathering."

Her act is so complete, polished to perfection by years of training and glamorous social seasons. In contrast, my rudeness screams out like a garish, clashing color on an otherwise refined, classic palette. Yet somehow the vicomte doesn't seem charmed by her elegant social dance.

He pulls his arm away from her, and I can't deny the wave of satisfaction passing through me at the tension I see grabbing at the corners of Véronique's lips.

"Unfortunately," the vicomte says, "I already have plans. There is a new art exhibition opening I promised to attend."

"Well, perhaps—"

"Some other time." He gives her a curt nod before walking away.

How strange. Did he wish to get away from Véronique even more than from me? My eyes follow him through the crowd until the back of his jacket disappears through the entrance doors.

"You're welcome." Véronique turns to me.

I let out a chuckle. "I'm sorry?"

"No need to apologize. It's not your fault." She shakes her head. "You are not from the city, after all, and I've known Vicomte Lenoir since we were children."

"I—"

"No need to thank me. It was my pleasure to stop you from embarrassing yourself further."

The sweetness of her tone is sickening.

"A man like the vicomte requires finesse." Véronique shifts her hips from side to side, her skirts sweeping the marble floor. "Our families have been pushing for our engagement for some time now. It will certainly happen by the end of the summer."

I raise an eyebrow. With the coldness the vicomte expressed toward her, it's hard to imagine him getting down on one knee. True, their arrogance and air of self-importance clearly make them compatible, and socially they are the perfect match. But no one should have to marry just for status or prestige. Not even a man like the vicomte.

Besides, I can't have Véronique claim him for herself—not before I steal his Talent. Not that she needs to know any of that.

She's looking at me expectantly, awaiting my response to her big reveal. I plaster on a smile. "Congratulations, you are perfect for each other."

Véronique blinks, clearly surprised by my positive reaction. The sweet taste of the small victory makes me hold my head higher.

"Well—um—" She stammers for a second. "Yes, we are."

"If you'll excuse me."

She doesn't follow me as I turn away.

Dahlia won't be pleased about the exchange I had with the vicomte. I might not be a "promised fiancée" he's running away from, but somehow I doubt he is any keener to spend time with me. If anything, my impertinence probably only made him resent me more. But thanks to Véronique's interruption, I know the vicomte is attending an art exhibition on Sunday.

Now all I have to do is make sure I'm there too.

CHAPTER TEN

Headlines

A TRIUMPH FOR Le Nouvel Opéra de Lutèce!

Last night's opera gala is one to be remembered, not only as a fantastic start to the summer, but as the beginning of a new chapter for the grand opera.

This morning, the name on everyone's lips is Cleodora Adley—the young successor to the great soprano Dame de Adley herself.

But who is this new prima donna, whom many are already calling "Lutèce's Nightingale"?

Coming from a country estate to the big city, the young Dame conquered the stage as soon as the first note flew from her lips. Not a single eye in the audience could have missed the glow of the ruby on her finger. Five levels of seats were flooded with her sweet soprano notes as her petite figure, clad in black and white, swayed with the emotions of her song. The most precious of silences followed her performance, as if the air itself wished to hold on to the spell. It lasted for only mere seconds, though, before the hall was rocked by the force of applause, echoing all the way from the first row to the top-most gallery.

At that moment, a star was born.

Read more in an exclusive interview with Maestro Lamar Mette, the musical director of Le Nouvel Opéra de Lutèce, on page 5.

"A positive review, I'm certain, my lady?" the head butler asks as he sneaks a glance at my copy of *Le Petit Journal* while filling my cup with hot cocoa.

I nod, utterly speechless.

"That's wonderful, my lady. You ought to celebrate."

Just like the rest of the estate's staff, he is far too young for his position, barely into his twenties, with only a hint of a mustache gracing his upper lip.

Another servant enters the dining room, carrying a silver tray with fresh pastries. Without waiting, the butler places them on the already heavily laden table.

"Thank you, Godfrey." I muster a smile before glancing once more at the page.

Breakfast delicacies surround me, yet I'm queasy. Last night's memories are like a dream, something that couldn't possibly belong in my life. But it is my photograph that stares back at me from the front page, just between an ad for ladies' riding hats and an announcement about traveling cheques. I'm on the stage in mid curtsy, holding my bouquet. I trace my finger over the black lines. If I didn't know this was me, I wouldn't have recognized myself, and not only because of the grainy texture of the photo.

Lutèce's Nightingale, I read the name again, and the memory of Dahlia's kiss brushing my forehead fills my mind. "My little nightingale" she called me. It's so specific, I wonder if she had a hand in suggesting the public nickname. A smile tugs at my lips at the thought.

I put the paper down. "Is Madame scheduled to arrive later today?"

"No, my lady. Madame usually spends the day after any event at home," the head butler clears his throat, ". . . recovering."

The image of Madame's wine-flushed cheeks resurfaces.

"I see."

I stare at the pool of gold sunlight falling on the mahogany table. The dining room is on the ground floor, and its massive arched windows and airy drapes welcome the garden greenery into the room. I'm looking over the rose hedges when a familiar face peeks out of them.

I stand up so quickly that I push the table, spilling the cup of hot cocoa over my full plate. Instinctively, I grab a clean cloth and dab at the spill, but all I manage to do is burn my fingers. "Merde!" The curse slips from my lips before I can suppress it.

"My lady!" The head butler rushes to me. "Are you hurt? Please allow me."

I step away from the table, flashing another glance at the window. The face is already gone, but I know what I saw.

The head butler shouts orders to the servants, the tiny topaz gem on his cufflink gleaming—the Organizational Talent that earned him his position springing into action.

"I'm so sorry, my lady." He turns to me while the other servants are already running to the kitchen to replace my ruined breakfast. "If your ladyship would like to go and change her dress, we will arrange for your breakfast to be brought to your room. I will have Pauline sent up to you at once."

Looking down, I notice the brown stains marking the pink lace of my gown. "Oh . . . that won't be necessary. I'm not that hungry anyway. And please allow Pauline to finish her breakfast. I will change on my own."

Without waiting for his response, I hasten out of the room and up the staircase to my chambers. I've just managed to close the door behind me when Lirone jumps off my bed, cutting short a low melody he was humming.

"What took you so long? And what happened to your dress?"

"You showed up mid breakfast." I keep my voice low. "I thought we were supposed to meet tonight."

"You were asleep when I arrived yesterday." There's something accusing in his tone. "This can't wait."

"You mean . . . you were in my room while I was sleeping?"

Lirone shrugs.

"What about my privacy?"

He ignores me. "Lady Sibille enjoyed your performance last night."

"She was there?" I'm not really sure why I'm surprised by this point, but the knowledge that she saw my triumph in person is undeniably exhilarating. If nothing else, it strengthens my position despite not making enough progress with the vicomte.

"She hopes you like your new nickname." Lirone keeps talking, as if I didn't say anything.

Lutèce's Nightingale. It really is her doing.

"But how did you do with the vicomte?"

"Well . . . things didn't go quite so—"

"Damn it, Cleo. I told you, you needed a plan."

I flinch. "Hey, watch your tongue."

"Merde!" he spits back at me, his tiny face full of defiance. "What, were you too busy getting drunk?"

"No!" I cross my arms. Who is he to talk to me this way? He's just a kid.

"Was talking about your big upcoming role more interesting?"

I open my mouth and close it, stumped for a second. "Upcoming role?"

"Don't play dumb, it's right here." From within his patched-up jacket, he draws a copy of today's paper. "That conductor talked all about it in the interview."

I swallow my surprise over the fact he even knows how to read and snap the paper from his hand, spreading it on the bed. Just as Lirone said, there it is.

Maestro Lamar Mette announces a newly commissioned opera to open the upcoming season, starring tenor Chevalier José Muratore and soprano Dame Cleodora de Adley.

"He chose me?"

"You really didn't know?" Lirone asks.

I shake my head.

"Well, now you do. But this won't help you when Lady Sibille realizes you aren't doing your job with the vicomte."

I tear my eyes from the paper. "But I *am* doing my job. I know where the vicomte will be this Sunday."

"Where?" He puts his fists on his hips. Somehow that makes him look even skinnier than he already is. When was the last time he had a meal?

"Some gallery, for a new art exhibition." I fold the paper confidently. "I need you to find out which one."

"Me?" He scoffs. "Why do I have to work double because you can't do your part properly? You're on your own."

Before I can say another word, he turns his back to me and disappears behind the tapestry and through the secret door.

But I can't let him leave. I race after him.

"Lirone!" I whisper as the door closes behind me, leaving me enveloped in shadows.

A soft click precedes the tiny flame of Lirone's lighter.

"What?" he asks.

"There are so many galleries in the city, I don't even know where to start."

"Not my problem." He turns away, the tiny flickering light moving farther down the passage with him, leaving me in darkness.

I follow him, running my hands along the scratchy walls to avoid falling. "Please, I can't exactly ask anyone else. I don't want anyone to know I'm interested in the vicomte."

"I don't work for you."

It's my turn to roll my eyes at him, but I'm not sure he can even see it in this light. "You want to be promoted by Dahlia, right? Isn't making sure we *both* look good a part of it?"

He halts at once, and I know I've won. "Fine," he huffs, walking back and closing the distance between us. "But you better get this man interested this time. You got a plan?"

I'm about to lie again and claim I do when I meet his eyes. "No."

"So we better come up with one."

"We?"

A sudden noise makes me freeze. Something between squeaking and hissing. Could there be someone else in the passage? The thought makes my heart quicken. I'm about to ask Lirone about it when something furry scurries over my foot.

My scream echoes from the narrow walls around me as I jump, almost tumbling backward.

"Shhh!" Lirone grabs my arm. "What the hell are you doing?"

"R-rat."

"And here I thought you were just pretending to be a spoiled lady." His voice is teasing, the fire gleaming mischievously in his eyes.

"Oh, shut up."

"I almost forgot. I have something for you." He draws out a wrinkled envelope from one of his pockets.

Even in the faint light, I recognize the handwriting at once. *Anaella.* The seal is already broken, but I have no time to question it. My fingers tremble as I take out the thin page, each stroke of ink carrying a piece of my sister within it. I hold it to my face, taking in the aroma that lingers from her touch—a faint scent of mint and cinnamon.

Lirone steps closer, allowing the light to illuminate the words, and yet it takes me several moments to be able to comprehend them and not just stare.

> *My dear Cleo,*
> *I hope this letter finds you well.*
>
> *I was so happy to receive a message from you. It has been too long since I saw you, and I didn't even get to say goodbye. I know you're doing all of this for me, and I'm grateful, but I miss you.*
>
> *Nurse Dupont treats me well, she is kind and skilled. And the doctor has already been here twice since you saw him. He says I'm getting better.*

Maybe I could come visit you soon? Nurse Dupont told me you work for a fine lady here in the city. I can't wait to hear all about it!

P.S. Is Father's book with you? I can't find it anywhere.
Love,
Your Ann

A lone tear leaves a warm trail on my cheek before landing on the page and smearing a part of the ink. Everything inside me is spiraling, the emotions crashing into each other like cruel waves.

My sister is going to be okay. She is getting better. My relief is like a breath of fresh air. Yet the pain of the separation cuts through me.

This is the sacrifice I made. My burden to bear.

The weight of lying to her sits on my chest like a ton of bricks. But at least I'm not left in the dark . . . Anaella is all alone in this, confused and abandoned.

Perhaps taking Father's book with me was selfish. I knew Anaella was attached to it; she used to sleep with it under her pillow for the longest time. But I didn't think about any of that when I took it. I just wanted a piece of home with me—a slice of memory of my parents and Anaella.

"Here." Lirone hands me a dirty, oddly damp handkerchief.

I dab at my running nose, wiping the tears with the back of my hand. "Thank you," I say.

"You miss her, don't you?"

"More than words can say. She's the only family I have left."

Lirone turns quiet. I've never seen him so still, so unlike his usual hyperactive self.

"What about you?" I ask. "Do you have a family?"

"Lady Sibille is my family."

"I meant a mother or father? Siblings?"

He hardens for just a moment before taking a step farther into the dark tunnel. "I'll be back tonight with the information about the art exhibition, so we can start planning."

"But—"

"Don't fall asleep before I come." He dashes away, disappearing around a corner and taking the only light source with him.

Snatching my skirts, I scurry toward the hidden door. I don't know if anyone heard my cry, but I've been in here too long already. The letter is heavy in my hand—a treasure I must hide and protect. A piece of home. Of my true identity.

Soon my free outstretched hand lands over the rough surface of the tiny door. I just manage to grab the metal doorknob and pull when another sound sends chills down my spine. But this time it's not a rat, and the sound doesn't come from the dark passage behind me. It comes from inside my room.

The tapestry hides me from view as I hold on to the open door, heart pounding in my ears. The butler must have sent Pauline, or one of the other maids, after all. Should I head back and try to find a different way out? The idea of retreating into the rat-infested darkness where I could tumble to my death makes me shudder.

No. I'll stay here and wait until whoever it may be leaves.

But a thumping of boots startles me. I lean closer. These are the steps of a man, not a maid. The sound of shuffling, like someone is rifling through my things, is clearly audible from behind the tapestry.

Could it be a thief? None of these riches feel like mine anyway, so there really is nothing in this room I'm attached to. Except . . . Father's book.

The thought of someone finding it or stealing it turns my blood icy. I can no longer stand still. Inching closer, I pinch at the fabric, trying to sneak a peek at the intruder.

A sliver of light illuminates the darkness of the passage as I stare at my sunbathed chambers. My view is narrow, and for a moment I don't see anything aside from my vanity and the pink carpet. Then a tall figure enters the frame. His back is toward me, allowing me to take in only his brown jacket and casquette hat. Even before he turns, cold spreads through my body all the way to my toes. And when he finally does, it takes all my self-control not to cry out loud once more.

I let the tapestry drop and hide me just before the coachman's eyes can meet mine.

CHAPTER ELEVEN

Paint Me a Picture

LIRONE WAVES HIS hand in front of my face. "Cleo, are you listening?"

"Keep your voice down," I whisper, hoping the rattling of the carriage will drown out my words.

"What crawled under your skin?" He narrows his eyes. "I snuck in here for you, you know."

"Well, I didn't ask you to do that."

"Yes, you did. When you asked for my help." His voice is rising, and that's the last thing I need with the coachman sitting up front.

I clutch my purse tighter, feeling for Father's book, now hiding inside. It's been two days since the coachman snooped in my room. Two days of utter panic. I have no idea if he saw the book or not. But I no longer feel safe leaving it behind. Luckily, Father made it small so that Anaella and I could carry it around as children—a "pocket version" he called it—so fitting it in my purse was easy enough.

My first instinct was to run to Dahlia and tell her everything— admit that the coachman might suspect me, that he saw me right before I broke into the estate and tried to steal the ruby. And yet I promised Dahlia I wouldn't let her down. Told her I was ready for the job. What would she think of me now if I burdened her with my fears while still having nothing to show for all her efforts?

The mere thought of looking into her angelic face and admitting my faults twists my insides into knots. I cannot deny I fear her anger. But more than that, I cannot bear to imagine the disappointment in her eyes—those beautiful dark eyes that stare into my soul and fill my stomach with fluttering butterflies.

And there's always the possibility that I'm wrong. Surely, if the coachman knew anything, he'd have mentioned something by now. There might be a simple explanation to it all, one that has nothing to do with him attempting to reveal my identity.

And so, moving Father's book as a precaution and keeping my mouth shut seemed like the only logical choice. I need to be certain before making any move.

Next to me, Lirone pulls at the carriage curtain, sneaking a glance outside, the afternoon sun coloring his face momentarily.

"Cut it out!" I grab his hand.

His glare is as sharp as a knife.

"Look, I'm sorry." I let him go. "I just need today to go well."

"Why do you think I'm here?" Lirone leans back in his seat, his fingers tapping on his thigh absentmindedly, as though he were playing the piano. "To the vicomte, you are just a girl from the country. You need to show him that you are at his level."

"I know," I say pointedly. "I'll be the picture of decorum."

"Don't joke. I'm trying to help you."

He's right, of course. Lirone went above and beyond to get information about the vicomte. We've spent last night going over everything in detail. From how the vicomte's family used to work for the Crown generations ago, to their estate matters, and right down to their current daily occupations.

I can't deny my initial surprise when I learned that the vicomte's great Mathematical Talent is being used for something as mundane as being an accountant for the opera house and managing his family fortune. Generations ago those skills were considered a form of art—a tool for military glory.

I wonder if that is the reason the vicomte seems to disdain the opera so much. Does he find his work degrading of his Talent? His family must have orchestrated some of Francia's most glorious wartime victories—nothing less would do if you held the crème de la crème of the Elite Talents.

I can't even imagine how much blood would be needed to transfer such an enormous amount of power. Did the vicomte have to slice both his hands to fuel it? The small scar on my palm is nothing compared to it. Would I need to acquire such an amount of blood from him as well? Just the thought makes me queasy.

Lirone risks another peek out the window. "We're almost there."

On cue, the carriage slows down.

My heart starts beating faster.

"I'll be back tonight for a full report," Lirone says. "And Cleo, don't be rude."

"Look who's talking," I mutter, but a second later he's already jumping onto the busy street side, not waiting for the carriage to stop.

"My lady." The coachman bows his head as he opens the other door, missing Lirone by a split second.

I clutch my purse so tightly my knuckles turn white: did he hear me speaking to Lirone? I search his face for any proof that he suspects me. But there is nothing—not a single twitch in his eye or strain in his mouth.

Putting on a smile, I relax my hold on my purse and take his gloved hand without a word. There's no time for me to focus on the coachman. I need to concentrate on the vicomte—on putting all the information Lirone found to good use. I hate admitting that Lirone is right, yet I know that my rudeness cannot continue. Our plan is simple: be proper, stroke his ego, and get him interested. If I want to succeed, no matter how much the vicomte irritates me today, I need to be a perfect lady. To hold my tongue.

The street we're on is narrow, lined with tall buildings on both sides that flow almost imperceptibly together, creating the feeling of a stone valley. There's no sign pointing to the exhibition, or anything at all that indicates where I have to go. Could Lirone have got the wrong address?

"—nothing like Bussière's detailing! How can you even compare?" A voice draws my attention to two women entering a nearby building.

"I've always appreciated your opinion, Esme, but your lack of understanding of art astonishes me," the other lady answers as they push open a grand red door and disappear behind it.

I trail them to the entrance, not sure if I'm meant to knock. But the door isn't even fully closed, and voices drift from the other side. Taking a deep breath, I push the door open.

The foyer is elegant, with a railed staircase leading to the apartments above, where the source of the lively chatter seems to echo from. I follow it all the way to the second floor. Already in the hallway, gentlemen and ladies sip champagne from tall glasses, utterly unconcerned with the early hour of the afternoon.

I step through the open door of the apartment, smoothing down my dress, the rich lilac velvet soft to my touch. It's one of the fanciest of my new gowns, highlighted with extensive, contrasting gold embroidery. This is my first outing since my debut at the gala merely three days ago, and Pauline insisted I must look my best. But as I glance around, I notice almost all the ladies are in light day dresses of linen, cotton, and silk. It wasn't my intention to stick out.

I push through the crowded corridor and into a large sitting area. This is clearly someone's home, yet every inch of the walls is covered with portraits and vibrant landscapes.

A footman passes by, carrying a tray of champagne. I grab a glass, doing my best to fit in. None of the faces around me look familiar, even though many of them keep glancing my way. I scan the room for the vicomte but he's nowhere to be found. Instead, a blur of orange catches my eye.

Across the room, rich shades of tangerine and crimson cover a small canvas, a million strokes of a rough brush creating a vivid sunset over a bay.

"Look here, mon coeur!" Father's voice brims in my head as though from a lost dream. "Look at the colors. Up close, they are nothing but blurry smudges. But take a step back and they become a work of art!"

"The water looks alive, Papa!"

"How does it feel?"

I wrinkled my brow. "Feel?"

"Every piece of art, from a painting to a song to the dresses we make, is meant to evoke an emotion—to tell a story." Father smiled at the painting. "What does this one say?"

I stared at the painting in silence, watching the beautiful lilies seeming to sway as if wanting to leap off the canvas. "It's . . . happy. Free."

The painting before me now feels the opposite. On the surface, it's peaceful. Serene. But something about it speaks of urgency—of pain. As though the ocean itself is set ablaze.

"Do you like it?"

A tall woman stands beside me wearing an elegant jacquard cream dress, contrasting her dark skin. Her tight curls are collected into a high, rounded bun that curves away from her head. A brooch gleams right below her shoulder, embedded with a polished moonstone.

She stares at me expectantly, her warm brown eyes fixed on my face.

I clear my throat. "It's beautiful, but . . . sad."

"Oh?" She raises a thin eyebrow. "And why is that?"

"I—I'm not sure." I stare at the burning waves a moment longer. "Please forgive me. I don't know much about art."

"One doesn't need knowledge to feel," she says. "Do you come to exhibitions often?"

I chuckle. "My father took us once to Le Centre du Rêve, for my mother's birthday—" I stop myself. Noble families don't celebrate by going to art shows.

But the woman doesn't seem to mind. "Your father has excellent taste. It's one of my favorite galleries."

"I've only recently moved to the city." I try to recover from my blabbering. Suddenly the book in my purse seems heavier. "I've inherited my cousin's estate."

The woman's face lights up. "Oh, I know. You are—"

"Cleodora, what are you doing here?" Madame's voice startles me.

"Chère, you didn't tell me your protégée would be here today." The tall woman smiles at Madame.

"I wasn't aware the lady had an interest in art," Madame says, and though her words are polite, there's a strange bite to them.

"It's a pleasure to welcome you to our home, Lady Adley." The woman turns back to me. "I'm Lady Brooks, but you can call me Renée."

Our home? Is she the lady of the house?

"Renée," Madame interrupts before I can reply, "it's time for the opening speech. Though it seems many of our guests are preoccupied with staring at Lady Adley. We had better start before they realize it's really her and begin asking for autographs."

My face turns hot. People truly are staring, but not because my dress stands out . . . I didn't realize the effect of the gala would be so quick. These people actually recognize me. Or at least this new version of me as an opera diva—as a star.

Renée chuckles. "I'll probably ask for your autograph myself after the speech. But we had truly better start. Will you excuse me?" She turns away from us both.

"Speech? Is she—?"

"The artist you came to see," Madame says. "Or did you wander here by accident?"

The clink of metal on glass hushes the room. Standing by one of the largest paintings—a dazzling portrayal of a mother and her child— Renée smiles warmly at the guests filing in from the corridor.

"Dear friends, welcome! I cannot begin to tell you how thankful I am that you all decided to join me on this special day. I've been working on this collection for the last few years, and though I've had a few small exhibitions in that time, they were all stepping stones, leading to this day. *Un Enfant de L'Océan et du Feu* is a tale and a product of love. A love I wish to share with you today." Renée holds up her champagne glass. "Please, enjoy yourselves. Santé!"

"Santé!" the crowd cheers back, with applause, before returning to drinking the bubbly alcohol.

I follow suit, sipping from my glass before turning back to Madame. But she's already gone, talking with a group of old ladies sitting on a massive blue couch by the window.

"I didn't know you were an art lover."

The voice makes the back of my neck tingle. *Vicomte Lenoir.* I spin around to find him right by my side. How does he keep sneaking up on me? Is this a game?

He's back to his unkempt look today, nothing like the upstanding gentleman persona from the gala—there's a loose button on his mint vest, which is matched yet again with a crooked tie. To make matters worse, his silky hair is messy, as though he didn't even bother to comb it after waking up. For a man with a legacy Talent, he's certainly not acting the way I would expect. Or perhaps his status has made him simply too arrogant to care.

I swallow the rude comments already filling my mind and bow my head. "What a pleasant surprise to see you, my lord."

"Is it?" He cocks an eyebrow. The expression is challenging, daring, and for just a second there's a soft fluttering in my chest. It's almost as though he's expecting me to retaliate. But I won't resort to banter today—I will prove to him I'm a lady.

A sweet smile stretches on my lips as I answer. "Certainly, my lord."

His jaw clenches, but he doesn't reply. I need to keep the conversation going.

"So, what are you doing here?" I regret the question as soon as it leaves my mouth. He's here to look at the exhibition, same as everyone else. Great start to creating the impression of an educated lady.

"Didn't we establish this last time? I'm here for the free drinks."

Again with the snide remarks. I barely hold myself back from telling him he can get champagne at a tavern where the drunks might be more tolerant of his shoddy conversation.

Instead, I sweeten my tone. "Do correct me if I'm wrong, my lord, but I believe you have enough fine drinks back at your manor. In fact, your family's wine cellar has won much praise."

There, that's better. Give him a chance to gloat about his riches.

But the vicomte doesn't even smile. He empties his glass and grabs another from a footman before answering. "I prefer my drinks cheap." I'm taken aback by the sharpness in his voice. For all his jeering, his tone has always stayed at a level of light amusement. The sudden harshness of it makes me startle.

"And what about the art?" I manage.

"What about it?"

"As a patron of the arts, you must go to plenty of exquisite galleries. Do you acquire many paintings from such events?"

He stares at me for a moment, his eyes scanning me from top to bottom, lingering on my gown. Perhaps Pauline was right in choosing an expensive one after all—if not enchanted by my conversational skills, the vicomte might at least find me attractive. My heart beats faster and I hurry to take another sip of champagne.

"If you are looking to acquire art that will match the price of that dress, you are at the wrong exhibition." His words are a slap to my face, but I don't even manage to think of a retort before he nods his head and says, "I believe your fans are getting impatient." He shoots a glance at a group of muttering women clearly waiting for our conversation to be over to surround me. "Now, please excuse me." He turns his back to me, and one of the ladies is already taking a step forward.

I can't let him leave. Not like that. It's too soon.

But my mind draws a blank. All excuses and topics of conversation evaporate into a foggy mess in my head. The lady is closing in on me, and the purse in my hand weighs me down with a dreaded sense of failure.

"Do you think the water is burning?" I end up calling when he's already halfway across the room. The lady halts mid step, and another woman quickly draws her back into the awaiting group.

He stops in his tracks, turning around to face me. "I'm sorry?"

"The . . . the water. In this painting." I turn awkwardly to point at the landscape of the bay behind me. "Do you think it's burning?"

I'm not sure why he even bothers to entertain my foolishness. This is quickly turning into a disaster. How am I supposed to show him I deserve my place in society if I can't even maintain a ladylike discussion?

The vicomte traces his steps back all the way to my side, then cocks his head as he stares at the colorful canvas. "So you *are* interested in the art?" he finally says. "I assumed you were here just because Hélène invited you."

Hélène. Once again, he demonstrates complete disregard for Madame's social status. Does he really think of himself as so far better than the rest? But I can't show any sign of unease, not when my ability to maintain his attention is so fleeting.

"Why would you think that?" I ask.

"This is her house, after all. Hers and Renée's."

"And what a wonderful surprise seeing you here, my lord." Renée approaches us, and the vicomte offers her a rare genuine smile, no hint of a snicker in sight. "I didn't think you'd come, after you didn't respond to my invitation."

"I wouldn't have missed it." The vicomte kisses her outstretched hand, and all I can do is stare. He is so polite, it's unsettling.

By Renée's side, Madame ogles the vicomte without blinking.

"A marvelous exhibition, as usual," he continues. "You both must be proud."

"I take no credit for Renée's work," Madame says.

But Renée laughs. "You are too modest, chère. You are my muse, after all."

Madame says nothing in response, yet the blush on her cheeks turns a shade deeper. There's an ease to the way Renée looks at her—a mixture of respect and adoration combined with tenderness and intimacy. It's the face of someone in love.

Their shared home is more than a mere arrangement. It's one of those unspoken romances whispered about in secret—a love accepted and welcomed as long as it's out of the spotlight.

The memory of Dahlia's delicate hand brushing against my cheek colors my mind, the depth of her dark irises promising a taste of a forbidden delight. Have our shared looks contained even a fraction of the passion Renée is showing?

"Well." Madame clears her throat, and I pull myself out of my reverie. "We'd better continue our rounds. Lady Adley, I shall see you at the opera house tomorrow."

"Tomorrow?"

"The Maestro has scheduled the first meeting regarding the new production."

"Oh yes, *L'Enchanteresse.*" The vicomte mulls the name in his mouth as if it were a sweet nougat confection. "I've heard of it so many times over this weekend, I'm already tired of it."

Madame opens her mouth to answer, but Renée beats her to it. "Oh, Nuriel, if I didn't know any better, I'd take every word coming out of your mouth far more seriously."

Nuriel. I repeat the name in my head in wonder.

The vicomte smiles again, revealing one annoyingly charming dimple on his left cheek.

How did they come to be on a first-name basis?

"I hope you stay a bit longer," Renée continues.

"I shall," he answers, as Renée takes Madame by the arm and turns to the next group of visitors.

We stay silent for a moment, my gaze wandering back to the painting. I feel the vicomte's eyes fixed on me and fight the urge to turn back and face him—I cannot let him know that those green irises of his have the power to get under my skin. My breath comes short, catching in my corset, and everything in me is itching to fidget with the hems of my sleeves for a distraction.

"To answer your question . . ." he finally says.

His voice is low and warm—a trap I cannot avoid. I turn to him.

"Yes, I *do* believe the water is burning."

He walks away, and a moment later I'm surrounded by chattering ladies and their overly excited smiles.

CHAPTER TWELVE

Scribbles on a Page

A SALTY SCENT of sweat hits me as I walk into the rehearsal room. Located in the rear part of the opera house, it's a vast round space adorned with decorative columns around the walls. Six large windows look out over the city below—packed streets threading together like veins, feeding Lutèce's pumping heart.

"Ma chérie!" José plants kisses on both my cheeks. "I was starting to fear you weren't coming."

"Am I late?" I scan the room, taking in the circle of chairs in the middle, most still empty.

"Not at all, I just took you for an early bird." He laughs, the sound booming in my ears. "Come sit by me."

I smile as we sit down, nodding my greetings to the rest of the people in the room. I recognize some of their faces from the gala, though I do not remember their names—a short-haired mezzo-soprano in a frilly blue gown, a broad-shouldered baritone with a thick mustache, another young man I recall being an assistant to Maestro Mette. But the musical director himself is still not here, nor is Madame.

Véronique is the next to enter the room, floating in with a cloud of silver chiffon and white feathers. "What a god-awful smell. Someone, open the windows!" She wrinkles her dainty nose as her clear blue eyes fall on me. I feel almost compelled to follow her order before a maid darts from behind her.

Taking a seat opposite me, Véronique pulls out a round bottle of perfume from her beaded purse and sprays the air around her, acting as I imagine a proper diva would. I have to fight to stifle a laugh. Am I supposed to act this ridiculous? She smiles as the sickly-sweet scent of roses laces the stuffy room. Thank heavens the maid opened the window.

Soon the circle of chairs is full, and Maestro Mette walks into the room, followed closely by Madame, who takes her seat at the grand piano in the back. She doesn't even bother to nod or smile when her eyes meet mine.

Could I have offended her by going to her house uninvited yesterday? Is she the type of person who wants to keep her personal life away from her job? Maybe she's upset that I stole some of the attention. Or perhaps . . . did she not want me to meet Renée?

Whatever it is, I have no time to ponder as Maestro Mette claps his hands, demanding our attention.

"Bonjour, everyone!" He smiles at us, though as his gaze moves around the room his eyes remain markedly severe. "I trust by now you all know why I gathered you here. I'm aware this is earlier than usual to start working toward the upcoming season, but I've decided this to be appropriate, since we'll be working on a newly commissioned opera."

Maestro Mette waves his hand and two men scurry inside, carrying piles of books. They go around the circle, handing a copy to each of us. The book is heavy, the red cloth binding velvety and adorned with golden letters: *L'Enchanteresse by Léo Chabrier.* "Each of your copies is already marked to indicate your assigned role. If you look at the first page, you can find the full list, as well as a brief synopsis of the story, courtesy of our wonderful librettist, Ernest Barbier. Now—"

"Is this a joke?" Véronique cuts in.

"Lady Battu?" Maestro Mette raises an eyebrow.

"I believe there must have been a mistake. This copy cannot possibly be mine."

"Is your name not on it?"

"It is, but—"

"Then I can assure you, no mistake was made. I prepared the copies myself."

Véronique's powdered face turns a shade whiter, then scarlet. Her nostrils flare as she glares at Maestro Mette, as if she's ready to pounce and scratch his face with her well-manicured nails.

I risk a glance at the list of roles, finding my name next to the first one, "Nova—The Enchantress," followed by José Muratore as "Alain—The Lover." I skim the rest of the names until I reach Véronique's, almost at the bottom: "Valerie—Jealous Sister of Nova."

"As I was saying," Maestro Mette continues, "we have less than two months to rehearse, and the premiere is set for September 3."

"What about the summer social events?" the mezzo-soprano asks. According to the list, her name is Marie Arnould, and she will sing the role of Nova's mother.

"Not to worry, Lady Arnould, all events have been taken into account," Maestro Mette says. "Now, please open your scores. I'd like to start with a musical reading."

Véronique stands and clears her throat. "I'm afraid that won't be possible."

"Lady Battu—"

"Given how low it is on the list, the role I've been assigned cannot have more than a line. I will not play second fiddle again just because there is a shiny new toy around."

The room erupts into chatter, but I can't understand a word over the ringing in my ears. José is now also on his feet, and Maestro Mette is striding to the middle of the circle with his arms raised. My pulse quickens; my mind is foggy from the heavy scent of Véronique's perfume. Head spinning, I'm about to stand when Madame's eyes meet mine. She shakes her head—a warning. It's enough to keep me glued to my seat.

I watch as Madame stands, full of elegance and command. Her black dress sweeps along the wooden parquet behind her as she steps out of the room. No one seems to notice.

"This is not the place to discuss this!" Maestro Mette's voice rises.

"Would you rather I gave an interview to the paper instead?" Véronique lets out a high-pitched laugh, each note sharp and clean. "No . . . that's more *your* style."

The vein in the Maestro's forehead is now bulging. He's about to retort when a knock on the door makes the entire cast turn.

Madame is standing at the entrance, followed by a group of what I can only assume are patrons, draped in finery and jewels no person should be allowed to flaunt on such an unremarkable morning. Bitterness fills my mouth. I clench my fists in my lap, and the ruby ring digs into my skin, a reminder: I am one of them—pearls adorning my neck and ears, a Talent sitting on my finger.

"We hope we're not interrupting," a short man with a squeaky voice says. "We couldn't possibly resist Madame's invitation to watch the musical reading."

Véronique opens her mouth when Vicomte Lenoir peeks into the room.

I straighten my back at the sight of him. But it's Véronique's transformation that's truly shocking. One look at him and her entire posture shifts—the sneer replaced by a delicate smile, the fire in her eyes muted by fluttering eyelashes. From a tigress ready to attack, she has turned into a kitten.

"Anything for our dearest patrons," she purrs.

Maestro Mette lets out a huff, and pats his vest before smoothing down his slicked-back hair. "Please, sit down," he says to the patrons.

"My lord, you can have my chair," Véronique says.

But the vicomte lingers at the doorway. "I'm afraid I cannot stay. I only came down to see what the commotion was about. Though I'm certain Albert would appreciate sitting."

The short man nods, already crossing the room to claim Véronique's chair.

I have to bite my lip not to smile at Véronique's scowl. The battle still clearly rages within her, but for now she has lost. Changing her mind in front of the patrons will not do her any favors.

The vicomte tips his hat goodbye, and a stray brown curl falls across his forehead. I trace it down to his emerald irises, and our eyes meet. Something between us shifted back at the gallery, a current of unspoken energy that left me unsteady. I can't quite put my finger on it. Every word coming from his mouth still makes me see red, yet his strange games have ignited a sense of curiosity within me. And for some reason, I feel he shares the sentiment. I can't call this a success yet—I'm still no closer to figuring out how to steal his Talent—but it's a start.

Neither of us shies away as we stare at each other, but as I nod my head in acknowledgment the vicomte's face shifts in response—a subtle twitch at the corner of his lip that leaves me wondering what he's really thinking. And then he's gone. And I'm left with no air.

I shake my head to clear it when I notice Véronique is glaring at me.

"Please open your scores," Maestro Mette says once all the patrons settle down.

"Ignore her," José whispers to me. "Just have fun rubbing your beautiful Talent in her face."

I chuckle, and force myself to focus on the first page. By now, the musical symbols aren't completely unfamiliar to me: the five lines, the curving key signature, the bows above the notes. All I have to do is let the gem take control—let its magic flow through my blood, and my voice will do the rest.

The Maestro gestures with his baton and Madame starts to play. Yet no sense of familiarity washes over me, no matching pulse from my gem. There is a flow of magic, a steady stream that lets me follow the notes on the page, but nothing more. I try to slow my breathing, to soften my gaze. I even rub the ring with my thumb. But the melody, as beautiful as it may be, feels strange.

José starts to sing, his tenor voice powerful and warm, commanding yet effortless. He is no longer the cheerful man meddling in the soprano drama, he is a lover. A knight from a far-off land, saving innocents on the battlefield. Goosebumps cover my skin. It makes no sense that such an immense sound could come from one man.

He gestures with his arm, letting his emotions lead him, and a bracelet appears from under his long sleeve—a delicate band of silver, embedded with an amber gem. With each beautiful note drawn from his lips, the gem gives off a faint glow—a pulse of magic fueling his blood.

But his lines are passing quickly, and Nova's lines are drawing near, and the music still feels unfamiliar, and my gem is not thrumming, and Véronique is staring at me, and *everyone* is staring at me. And all of a sudden the notes on the page look like meaningless scribbles.

I take a deep breath, focusing on the magic in my blood—my Talent knows what to do. Generations of knowledge accumulated within my ruby. The gem remembers . . .

But the gem cannot remember what has never been experienced.

And this opera has never been sung.

It is Véronique's smirk that fills my head when I draw out the first note, and I know I have failed.

⬦

It takes all I have not to sprint out of the room as soon as Maestro Mette ends the rehearsal. Instead, I plaster on a smile, doing my best to avoid Madame's glare as I head for the door, down the stairs, and onto the street.

I just embarrassed myself, not only in front of the musical director and other singers, but in front of the patrons.

Someone bumps into my shoulder and a second later Véronique is in my face. There's no more anger in her eyes, just a glint of triumph. She flicks a perfect golden curl away from her forehead as she leans in and whispers, "And for a second, I thought I had to worry about you."

I don't get the chance to answer before her carriage pulls up.

She throws me a dazzling grin and climbs inside. Then she sticks her head through the small window. "Mark my words—this role is mine. You'll be out within the week."

"We'll see about that," I say, but her carriage is already pulling away, swallowing my voice in the sound of turning wheels and stomping hooves.

Even though my words were confident, that's the last thing I feel inside. The magic in my ring was enough to help me stumble through, but everyone could see I was struggling. And the more stressed I became, the worse it got. Notes slipping away. Pitch faltering. The markings on the page shifting in and out of focus. Lines sounding clear in my head, only to be replaced by deafening silence. Thank heavens the vicomte didn't stay to watch.

My future depends on establishing myself among the Elite, and this role will define that. I cannot let Véronique take it. If she does . . . Will I be fired? Will Dahlia fire me too? And what will happen to my sister?

The thought of Anaella pinches my chest. I haven't answered her letter. I'm not sure if it's because I hate lying to her, or if it's because of the guilt I feel for leaving her behind while I play dress-up, no matter how justified it may be. If she were here instead of me, I'm sure she'd handle it all with grace and ease. She has always been the one who knows what to say, what to do, how to act—a lady in every sense of the word, except the title. Yet, somehow, I'm the one who is trying to fake my way through it, forced to keep her away from a life that should be hers. She'd be better at it all—all except the part of being a thief. My sister is too good, too pure, for that.

Unlike me.

My carriage finally rolls up, and the coachman hops off. "My lady, I apologize for the delay."

I wipe a stray tear from my eye. "Not to worry. I wasn't waiting long."

"Are you alright, my lady?" The coachman offers me his arm.

The genuine concern in his voice catches me off guard, and I glance up at him. I see him several times a day, on the way in and out of the carriage, but fear has kept me from truly looking at him until now. He's even younger than I thought, only in his early twenties, his tall hat sitting on tightly trimmed blond hair. His skin is pale, his cheekbones high, giving him a skeletal look that fits only too well with his dark eyes. But I can't see any malice in him. Only pure interest and worry.

"Thank you for your concern, Basset," I say, my voice betraying the unease that grips me. "Unfortunately, I have not had the best day."

"I'm sorry to hear that, my lady. Is there anything I can do?"

"I don't believe there is." I hug my purse, the hard binding of Father's book pressing against my chest. "I simply need a bit more time to adjust."

"I remember the first time I came to the city. I grew up on a farm, so it wasn't easy to become accustomed to all the people and the noise. It must be quite a change from your family's country estate."

I force a smile, but my muscles tense. "Yes, different indeed."

"You must miss your family. I know I miss mine. My *sister* most of all."

My blood turns cold. "I'm sorry?"

"My sister . . . She was pretty sick when I left. But I knew the money in the city would help the family more."

He's staring right at me, his eyes not shying away from mine the way a servant's eyes should. The weight of it is suffocating, accusing. My breath catches, my throat is tightening, as the meaning of his words seeps in.

That story could not be his. It isn't his.

It's *mine*.

Suddenly the book weighs like a ton of bricks, pressing hard against my chest as though trying to protect me from him.

"I'm sorry, my lady." He bows his head, finally breaking his gaze. "I overstepped my bounds."

I'm too frozen to speak, to act. Fear crashes into me in waves as I stare at him, but I force my face to remain blank. I cannot show any weakness before him, cannot betray my position.

"Take me home," I order, but the words falter.

He follows my command nonetheless.

The streets roll peacefully outside the carriage window, but inside everything twists and turns, threatening to overflow.

Why hasn't he told anyone yet? Everything around me spirals as I try to make sense of it all. Could I make him keep quiet by paying him? Is that why he hasn't said anything before now? Is he trying to extort me? Or perhaps . . . could he be working for Dahlia? The glint of hope burns within me; I'm praying for an easy way out. But then why would he tell me a fake story instead of admitting it? Still, I have to know.

I don't wait for him to help me out of the carriage once we arrive. I stumble out on my own and rush into the house without looking back. Pauline greets me, but I push her away with the claim of a headache.

As soon as I've closed the door to my room, I head for the window. Throwing my hands up in the air, I start waving my arms like a lunatic. I know they're out there, Dahlia's henchmen—my personal guards. And I need to see Dahlia. Now.

Just as I expected, within moments Lirone emerges in my room, sliding from behind the tapestry.

"What happened?"

"Tell me he works for Dahlia, please."

Lirone's brow creases. "What? Who?"

His blank face gives me the answer. My heart sinks. My secret is no longer safe. It's resting in the hands of a man whose intentions I do not know.

The truth I tried to bury comes to my lips. "He knows."

"What? Who knows what? The vicomte? What the hell did you do?"

I shake my head. "No. Not the vicomte."

"Cleo, what—?"

"The coachman. Basset. He knows I'm a fraud. He knows about my sister."

"That's impossible. How would he even—?"

"He met me before, on the day I broke in here . . . I suspected he recognized me, but I wasn't sure. And then he was sniffing about in my room."

"In your room? But there's nothing here . . ." His eyes dart to the purse still hanging from my wrist. Lunging at me, he snatches it from my hand and spills its contents on the bed.

"Don't touch it!"

But Lirone ignores me, picking up Father's book in his tiny, dirty hands. "I should've tossed this away the moment I saw you had it."

"Don't! It's my Fa—"

"Your Father's, I know." His voice is lower, nothing like a child's. "You think I didn't know you had it? I've been following you since the day you arrived here! You just looked so damn miserable, I figured it couldn't be that bad for you to keep it. After all, no one here knows a bloody thing about you, right?" A bitter laugh escapes his lips. "But the coachman does know you. And he found it, didn't he? That's why you started carrying this with you?" He shakes the book at me.

"I wasn't sure before . . . but now I am. I thought there must be another explanation. And I didn't want to—"

Lirone curses before hurling Father's book on the bed.

I flinch, fighting the urge to run and grab it. "We need to tell Dahlia."

"No!"

"What do you mean, no? He knows about me."

"We cannot tell Lady Sibille. We need to deal with this ourselves."

"But—"

"If you tell her, we're both in trouble." He closes the distance between us and grabs my hand. His fingers are frozen, making me jump as they wrap around mine. "I was supposed to make sure your transition was smooth—without obstacles or risks. No loose ends. But I missed the fact that a member of the staff has seen you before, and I let you keep that incriminating book. And *you* . . . you kept it from her for far too long."

I walk to the bed and pick up Father's book with shaking hands. It's open on a random page featuring strokes of pink and writing in cursive letters. I remember the day Mother and Anaella sketched this design. Father and I spent hours figuring out the sewing patterns. He could have done it in minutes without me, but he wanted me to do it myself, guiding me along the way. It was the first dress my sister and I were fully involved in making—her design, my tailoring. I trace the scribbled notes on the page, my eyes landing on one in the bottom corner.

"Jan. 12, 1881. Dress is ready! I couldn't be prouder of my little girls."

Tears sting my eyes, but I fight against them. Bringing the book with me was a mistake. A desperate need to hold on to a life that's gone. If only I'd fully embraced my new identity, none of this would be happening. My secret would be safe. Anaella would be safe.

My sentimentality brought this on me. And yet I still can't let it go. I shut the book forcefully and press it to my chest. "What are we supposed to do?"

Lirone is silent, his forehead so creased with concentration that I can almost see the wheels turning in his head. "Fire him."

"What good would that do?"

"You need to hurt the coachman's reputation. To make sure whatever he says about you will be taken as the blabbering of a fired servant."

"I don't—"

"Do you want to get out of this or not?"

"Of course I do."

"Then you have to! And it needs to be done in public. Somewhere with a big crowd so that everyone can see his incompetence."

"Incompetence?"

Lirone nods. "I'll take care of that part."

"Don't you think I should try and talk to him? He hasn't said anything so far. Perhaps I can pay him or something?"

"And let him hold this over you? To be able to run and talk

whenever he wants? No. We need to make sure that even if he tries to talk, it can't hurt you."

"But . . . this will ruin his life."

"And he can ruin yours!" Lirone pushes. "If he exposes you, you will go to jail. Your sister will not be cared for anymore—she could die. And you will lose everything. Is that what you want?"

I fall quiet. Of course he's right, I cannot risk this. Still, I hate his idea, and all the many ways it could go wrong. But what choice do I have? The fear in Lirone's eyes is startling. Just the thought of telling Dahlia has terrified him, and though I have only seen her kind side so far, I am fully aware of her darkness. After all, she kidnapped me the first time we met.

"How did you even find out he knows?"

"I had a bad rehearsal . . . I was feeling down and he pretended to try to cheer me up. I almost believed him until he told me a story about his 'sister.' There's no other way he'd know Anaella even existed if it wasn't for the book."

"Bad rehearsal?"

"I couldn't read the notes." I wave my hand to dismiss it. "We have more important issues—"

"You couldn't read the notes?" Lirone covers his face with his hands.

"Well, it's not like I had any musical education, you know."

He snaps his head up and glares at me. "You will now."

"Lirone, I really don't think this is the time."

"You will do everything I say. You will keep *that thing* close to you at all times." He eyes the book, making me involuntarily clutch it tighter. "You will fire the coachman, publicly. And I will be teaching you music every night."

"Wait, you know how to read music?"

He ignores my question. "Say you'll fire him, Cleo. Say you'll fire him, and I'll teach you."

I stare at his stubborn face, so young, yet full of the burdens only grown-ups should carry. But I doubt Lirone ever had the chance to be a child or have a real family. At least I knew the warmth of a loving home once.

With Father's book still embraced in my arms like a relic of a past life, I shake my head and sigh. "Fine. I'll do as you say."

CHAPTER THIRTEEN

Rearing Horses

"ARE YOU FEELING alright, my lady?"

Pauline stares at my reflection in the mirror. Worry creases her brow, and with the way I look, I can't claim it unjust. My face is pale, even without powder, my lips are dry, and my eyes are surrounded by faint, dark circles. I look like Anaella the last time I saw her. Weak. Sick. Beauty washed away by sleepless nights, anxiety, and guilt.

"I'm fine," I say, a fleeting grimace betraying a twinge of pain as Pauline's hairbrush tugs my head back. "Just didn't sleep well."

"Do you wish for a laudanum tea?"

"No, thank you," I say, though a stubborn cramp stabs at my abdomen. Mother used to swear by that tincture. I was so young, yet I still remember how, on similar mornings, she would quietly sip her tea before drifting into a tranquil, pain-free nap. It's been a few months since I even needed to think about such methods. Taking an opium tincture would surely stop the pain, but it's a luxury I cannot afford today. The concert demands my utmost clarity and focus, and after my latest failures, I cannot mess up again.

Pauline picks up a hairpin.

"Can we leave my hair down?" I ask before she can insert it. "I do have a headache."

"Of course, my lady." Pauline puts down the pin, draping my hair over my shoulders instead. "Don't you worry, I'm sure the matinee concert will go smoothly. The garden party was always one of your cousin's favorite summer events."

For the past week, all everyone has talked about in between rehearsals is the garden party, a lavish event hosted by the Marquis de Canrobert at his private chateau on the outskirts of the city. Maestro Mette informed me that I would be singing at the event only two days ago, and he did not seem pleased about it. After only one week of rushed lessons with Lirone each night, I'm still very far from being a musical expert, and the Maestro will not forget my messing up so quickly. But the Marquis's wife asked for me personally after hearing me at the gala. With the entire social elite attending, this could be my chance to regain Maestro Mette's respect.

And the perfect opportunity to fire the coachman in public.

I've been avoiding any conversation with him over the last few days, and he hasn't approached me, either. But now that he has revealed his knowledge to me, I'm certain he won't stay silent for long. The paranoia has made me cling to Father's book even more, and I have been carrying my purse with me at all times. For all I know, he's already making plans to steal it and sell the truth about me to the highest bidder. I need to act quickly.

Layer after layer of makeup covers any cracks in the perfect mask of a lady I am cultivating, and when Pauline is done, I once again stare into a stranger's face in the mirror. She helps me into a light pastel dress with delicate gold trimmings, as pretty and sweet as a fine macaron.

Something in the design is familiar—the way the delicate ruffles weave together, how the chiffon gathers at the neckline. I can almost feel Father's arm over my shoulder, as if it were just a moment ago when we'd huddled together by the fire, studying famous designs. It is clear Miss Garnier has also done her homework.

Pauline pulls at my corset and I wince in pain. "Not so tight today."

"Sorry, my lady," she says, loosening the grip and moving on to tying the strings of the bodice into perfect bows. But she doesn't let her hands fall. Instead, she bites into her bottom lip as if fighting the urge to speak.

"Pauline? Is everything okay?" I turn away from the mirror to look at her directly.

"Oh, yes," she blurts, and pushes away her long, fiery braid over her shoulder. "I just . . . wondered if you might want me to join you today. The former Lady Adley sometimes liked me to accompany her for events outside the city."

Eagerness plasters her face, shining in her round brown eyes. I'm certain it's the same hunger I used to display whenever I watched the ladies shopping on the grand avenues or strolling in parks. It's the hunger of a person wishing to belong in a world that can never be theirs.

I still don't know Pauline's full story, but from the little I've gathered it seems my first guess was right. She was born to a family of carpenters with multiple children, and a large part of her salary is going every month to support her younger siblings—yet more youngsters who will never know comfort. How different her life could have been . . . Instead, Pauline has to fend for herself out in the world.

All I want is to tell her to join me, to have her at the party, even just as a companion—to allow her a taste of the ambrosia I've tricked my way into sampling.

But her presence could undermine the task ahead of me. She knows the coachman too well, and I cannot have anyone around who might speak on his behalf.

"Thank you." I try to keep my voice level. "But I think I'll be fine on my own today."

Pauline darts her gaze to the floor. "Of course, my lady. I'll go check if the carriage is ready for you."

A pang of guilt passes through me as she curtsies and hurries out of the room. But I cannot let that distract me. Not today.

Lirone didn't tell me the details of his plan, insisting the less I know, the more believably I'll react. I tug on my dress, fighting the impulse to rip it off and go back to bed, but my wishes don't matter. Failure is not an option.

Taking a deep breath, I turn back to the mirror. "I can do this," I say to my own reflection.

My stomach twists as the carriage rolls over the bumpy road, each jagged stone and shuffle sending a wave of pain through my abdomen. The crowded streets of the city have given way to wide-open country, with rolling hills, and large trees swaying in the summer breeze.

I squint as the sun shines through the foliage. The fresh air is sweet, intoxicating, carrying within it the essence of the flowers dotting the greenery. I can't remember the last time I left the city. Perhaps when Anaella and I were still children. I remember a checkered blanket spread out on the grass, a basket full of fruits, cheese, and bread, and ringing laughter as Father taught us how to roll down the hill. Mother shook her head as we ran back up, our dresses covered in fresh grass and twigs in our hair.

The urge to jump out of the carriage and run up the hill takes hold of me, the wish to return to that lost world burning within.

The road turns, and we pass through an arched gateway. Soon, a cacophony of hoofbeats and rolling carriages fills the air as we circle an immense fountain. The commotion is such a contrast to the quiet road that I find myself retreating farther back into my seat.

But before I can even take a breath, the carriage jerks and I jolt forward. My purse flies from my grasp, the string attaching it to my wrist threatening to snap. I scream, and the horses rear up, while shouts from outside echo my alarm. The carriage is shaking, and to my utter terror it starts tilting, threatening to fall on its side. I grasp my seat, bracing myself for impact, when the doors fly open. Arms grab me and pull. Suddenly, there are people all around.

The horses are surrounded by men holding their reins and attempting to calm them. Someone asks after my well-being, but I'm focused on the large crowd that has gathered right ahead, circling someone on the road.

I push through, blood pumping in my ears as I ignore the voices calling my name.

Stretched out on the dirt is a child wearing a simple stable boy's uniform. He writhes in pain, holding his elbow close to his chest in clear agony. My pulse quickens, cold spreading through my veins. Did the carriage hit him? Has anyone called for help? Then his eyelids fly open, and his familiar, unblinking eyes stare right at me, a malicious smile flickering on his lips.

Lirone.

I go numb.

The coachman pushes through the crowd. "My lady! I'm so sorry, my lady! I don't know how . . . He came out of nowhere."

I gawk at him, but no words come out of my mouth.

"What's this?" someone calls. I turn to see a man holding out a flask that he clearly just unearthed from beneath the coachman's carriage seat. Opening the cap, he takes a whiff and wrinkles his nose. "He's a drunkard."

Mutters rise from all around, and Lirone lets out another well-timed cry of pain.

"No . . . That's not mine. I've never seen that in my life." The coachman's eyes widen.

"You're drunk," I spit, hating myself as the words leave my lips.

He takes a step toward me, hands outstretched as if ready to strangle me or grab my skirts and beg for mercy. Two men snatch him by his arms before I can find out which.

"His jacket reeks of alcohol," one of them says.

"No one can trust a word that comes out of your mouth." I lift my chin, throwing him a look I hope is full of disdain. "I never want to see your face again."

"My lady!" He drops to the ground while the men still hold him, his eyes full of tears.

"Leave at once! And know that I will make sure you never find work in the city again." My voice trembles, but it doesn't matter. All everyone can see is a lady shaken to her core, firing a drunk servant. "Be grateful I don't call the police."

I grip my purse tighter; the incriminating evidence that caused all of this is tucked safely inside. If only he hadn't found Father's book. Then none of this would be happening. Fear is written in every line of the coachman's face, and a slight tremble weakens his knees. I wish there were another way, but it's too late. I've gone too far.

"Take him." The words come out as a broken whisper.

"No, my lady, you have to believe me! It was an accident!"

But the men are already dragging him away, and his cries are muffled by the rising voices of the crowd.

I have just condemned a man's life.

My head spins. This is all wrong. This was a horrible plan. Even if he *was* going to extort me. No man deserves that. But I can't undo any of it.

I grab my stomach helplessly, my breath comes in short bursts as Lirone is carried away as well. I can only hope the carriage drops him off at the nearest theater after the doctor finds nothing wrong with him—he missed his calling as an actor.

"Lady Adley!" A woman taps my shoulder.

I spin and wobble on my heels. A lady wearing a flowery dress with an excess of frills is by my side. A bonnet sits on her light sandy curls; it's adorned with bows and roses, making it seem like she's carrying a garden atop her head.

"Are you alright, dear?" She bats her eyes at me. "You must be completely shaken. Please follow me inside. We'll get you some water and you can sit down for a bit."

I manage to nod, though the world is spinning around me. She takes me by the arm, waving her other hand for a servant to follow us. Even with my dazed head, I still register the grandeur of the house. By comparison my estate is shabby. My throat makes a choking sound, something of a mortified chuckle. Back home, Anaella is still sleeping in a stuffy room at the back of a dusty shop, drinking gray water.

Am I a horrible sister? Am I a horrible person?

"Sit down, dear," the lady says, and I sink into a velvety sofa.

A maid hands me a glass of water and I take a timid sip, but all it does is make my stomach lurch.

I fired the coachman and ruined his life to keep my secret.

I did it to save my sister. To make sure she can join me in this lavish world. I did it to keep her safe.

I had to do it.

But even as I cling to these words, all I can see in my head is the coachman's face as they dragged him away.

And though I'm sitting, the room whirls around me, the world disintegrating into blackness.

Then Madame's face is inches from mine.

"Oh, thank heavens." Relief is written in her eyes.

I'm still on the couch, but somehow I'm now lying down. "What happened?"

"You fainted."

I push myself up, heat rushing back to my cheeks. "I'm sorry . . ."

"No need to apologize, dear!" The short lady is still here, smiling at me warmly. "After what you've been through, I'm surprised you even made it into the house. I would have fainted on the spot. One simply cannot trust servants these days."

A lump rises in my throat, but I push it down. I cannot think about the coachman now or I won't be able to go on.

"The boy will be alright," Madame says. "Looks like nothing was broken. Now, let's get you home."

"Home?"

"Well, I assumed—"

"I wish to stay. I have a concert to give."

Madame presses her lips together. But my mind is made up. I did not come all this way just to fire the coachman. I need to gain back Maestro Mette's respect, or all of this will be in vain. I need to find Vicomte Lenoir and get closer to him. I need to prove to Dahlia that I'm worthy, and that I've established my position among the Elite well enough for her to allow my reunion with Anaella. I need to make all this madness worth it.

I stand and nearly lose my balance again. "I feel fine. I just need some fresh air."

"Well, we have plenty of that in the garden," the short lady says. "I haven't even introduced myself. I'm Madame la Marquise de Canrobert. It's a pleasure to meet you at last, Lady Adley."

The Marquis's wife, the marchioness, the woman who insisted on my presence. I drop into a deep curtsy, though the need to lean against the couch to stand back up smears my attempted elegance. "The pleasure is all mine, your ladyship."

"The ensemble has already set up in the garden and the concert can start whenever you're ready," Madame says. "I have already told Véronique that she will open the event instead of you. I had better go find her."

"Don't worry about it. I don't mind singing after her." The last thing I need now is extra drama with Véronique.

Madame raises an eyebrow but nods. "Shall we go outside, then?"

I plaster on a smile, ignoring the painful cramps in my stomach as I follow her and the marchioness out the door.

CHAPTER FOURTEEN

Birds in the Garden

THE GARDENS OF the chateau are like nothing I've ever seen—circling the marble fountains are rows and rows of flower beds in vibrant hues of rouge, violet, navy, and specks of gold, all standing out against cushions of emerald green foliage. The air is redolent with their fragrance and filled with the chirping of birds.

Among the blossoms, gentlemen stroll accompanied by ladies in elegant dresses, their gowns as fresh as the garden itself. Servants in black-and-white uniforms blend among them, carrying trays of canapés and crystal glasses rippling with fizzing drinks. It's the perfect image of luxury.

I only take a few steps before I'm recognized.

Josephine Garnier blocks my path, grabbing my hand sympathetically. "Lady Adley, I'm so happy to see you. I was certain you'd have gone home after that terrible accident."

"I wouldn't have missed this for the world." I pull my hand gently out of her grip. Of all the people at this party, the modiste is the last I want to see.

She's wearing a pink dress again, only this time the shade is soft, befitting the outdoor event. Her dazzling gem necklace rests peacefully on her décolletage and sparkles in the light as she moves.

"I was shocked to hear what happened with your servant." She puts a hand on her chest as if mortified by the mere mention of the disaster. "You did the right thing firing him on the spot. A man like that has no place among civilized people."

I swallow hard, hoping my face doesn't betray my shame. At least Lirone's plan worked—the accident is front and center as a conversation topic.

"After such an event, most people would look a mess," she continues. "But you are as lovely as a rose. And your dress! I couldn't have created a better one myself!"

Of course she'd find a way to pat herself on the back, seeing that my closet holds nothing but rows of her designs. I let out a polite laugh at her joke.

For a second she just stares at me with her brow raised comically high. Then her wild laughter overpowers mine, forcing me to take a step back in discomfort.

"Cleodora." Madame is suddenly by my side. "The concert is about to begin."

"If you'll excuse me." I bow my head to Josephine, but she just nods, still laughing.

"Keep your guard up with that one," Madame says under her breath as we walk away.

"I'm sorry?"

"Miss Garnier might seem unhinged at times, but don't let it fool you. Her wits are as sharp as a guillotine."

"Why are you telling me this?"

She stops abruptly and takes a drink from the tray of a passing servant. "I'm your mentor. It's my job to look out for you."

"You've barely looked at me since the art exhibition. You didn't even offer to help with studying for the role, though everyone can see I'm in over my head."

Madame's face hardens, her lips pressing into a thin line. "You don't need my help. You're not in over your head—you're too much *inside* your head. True, it's not an opera your gem has honed, like everything you've sung until now, but your Talent should be enough to help you sight-read to a tolerable degree." Her words are reassuring, but the sneer on her face betrays her true intentions. "And you are welcome at any exhibition you like."

"Is this about Renée? Did you not want me to meet your partner? I don't know if I offended you somehow, but I don't care that you are both wom—"

"Take my advice or don't," she says, cutting me off. "That's all there is to it." She strides past me, effectively ending the conversation.

No matter what she says, it's clear she's mad at me. Madame might claim her lack of help is innocent, but I know when I'm being punished. I just wish I knew for what.

A group of gentlemen walks by, tilting their hats to greet me. I force a smile. There are too many curious eyes around for me to break down. Too many people I have to impress if I hope to ever establish myself among them—to appease Dahlia.

Pushing down the hurt and nerves, I follow Madame past a rose arch and around a massive green hedge to a separate part of the garden. A wall of palm trees surrounds it, while bronze and marble statues dot the scene—ancient, draped figures, angelic babies playing harps, and majestic warriors in full armor. They are beautiful, ethereal, and cold— perfect figures meant to entertain all who look at them for eternity. For a moment I can relate to them, as though I too am just a flawless vessel designed to allow my Talent to amuse and charm those around me.

Elegant round tables covered in white cloths sit atop the freshly cut grass, their chairs all facing a massive white canopy. The ensemble is already on the stage under it, tuning their instruments in a cascade of discordant sounds that slowly merge into a single note. The crowd settles in around me, enjoying champagne, and cakes covered in colorful icing.

I notice Maestro Mette sitting in the audience at the front, with José and a few of the other singers. I should join them, but I'm frozen.

Véronique steps forward on the stage, not waiting for an introduction. She looks beautiful. A light blue silk gown drapes from her frame, its entire bodice dotted with pearls that spiral all the way down her skirts in an undulating pattern. With each movement, they capture the light like dazzling rainbow drops. But it's the tiara adorning her blond ringlets that grabs my attention—silver bands interlaced with palmette motifs and topped with a diamond ribbon, while at its center sparkles a heart-shaped aquamarine stone. It's breathtaking.

I have never seen Véronique's gem before. A few years back, in the wake of the great panic when those seven Elite Talents disappeared, many of the aristocracy abandoned the habit of wearing them. After all, physical closeness isn't needed for the magic—the blood we feed the stones binds them to us like an imprint within our veins. Yet being far away from your gem isn't easy. It's like a part of you is missing, calling you to reunite.

I remember how Father's high-class customers stopped wearing their gems for fittings, how they all swore to bring them out only on special occasions—a small reprieve from the ache of separation and a way to flaunt their Talents as riches. They hoped storing their gems in safes would protect them from potential thieves. Somehow, they thought it easier than keeping their blood out of criminals' hands, making the transfer ceremony impossible. As time passed, though, more and more of them started wearing them to the shop again, extra safety measures forgotten and abandoned. Certainly, at this event they have all fallen into a false sense of safety—unaware that right among them stands a thief.

The crowd quiets without Véronique uttering a word; her presence is a magnet no one can ignore. She stands with her chin tucked down, her eyes closed, and I'm drawn to take a step closer to her. She lifts her head, and the first violinist gives the mark. The ensemble of instruments follows his lead, no conductor required for such a small group of musicians.

The strings tremble with each graceful stroke, joining together in a rich harmony. Their sound is clear in the open air, a burst of joyful celebration as vivid as the nature surrounding us. Véronique smiles, pure exhilaration sending tendrils of thrill through the audience. Then she opens her mouth, and the sound is as light and graceful as any of the birds in the garden.

Her tiara shines—it almost gives her a halo—as her voice glides and soars. She is a diva in the full sense of the word—a goddess, a singer with a Talent so bright it deserves to be celebrated.

Goosebumps cover my arms at her brilliant trills, like a songbird in flight. How could I possibly compare? Yet, when her song dies and her eyes meet mine, there is a glint of fear in them. No. Not fear. Disdain. Jealousy.

Because all her threats and gloating don't change the fact that I'm still the lead singer, the one who was requested personally by the marchioness. With Lady Adley's Talent I'm not just her equal—I'm her rival.

Suddenly, my ring feels like a massive weight on my finger.

The crowd claps and the marchioness steps forward. "Magnifique!" She raises her glass. "Thank you, Lady Battu, for such a marvelous opening."

Everyone cheers again as Véronique curtsies before walking off the stage.

"And now," the marchioness continues, "I'm very pleased to welcome a special guest to the stage. Please give a warm round of applause to 'Lutèce's Nightingale'—Dame Cleodora de Adley."

The crowd's polite cheers turn into an enthusiastic wave and my legs carry me forward as if I have no will of my own. A maid takes my purse for safekeeping, while whispers about carriages and accidents accompany me on my way to the stage. Not a single person has missed the newest piece of gossip I'm starring in.

My stomach churns again, pain stabbing my back as a wave of nausea passes through me. Perhaps I should have taken that opium tea this morning after all . . . My body truly has the worst timing.

Just breathe. This is an aria my Talent knows, one the former Lady Adley sang countless times and one I've practiced myself more than once. This should be easy.

Maestro Mette's gaze beckons at me from the first row. This is my chance to show him why he chose me for the lead role. I can do this. I give a slight nod and the ensemble starts to play.

I let the music flow through me, the familiar hum of my ruby reacting at once. The sea of faces fades and blurs, leaving only the swaying trees, their branches dancing as if to the beat of the music.

A flash of green grabs my attention—a pair of striking catlike eyes. The world snaps back into existence.

Vicomte Lenoir winks at me, and a hot flash shoots through my body. But the music doesn't wait for me to collect myself. Letting the Talent take control, my lips part, allowing the notes out.

I sing, the melody and words all coming out perfectly—but something is off.

The usual power of my voice is weakened, and with each note, a raspy, unpleasant sensation grabs my throat as though my vocal cords are covered in gravel. I take a breath, but the air doesn't fully go in; instead it hits my stomach with another stab of piercing pain. The magic still sings in my blood, making my voice ring out, but my body heaves under the pressure to support it.

The warmth of a cello line takes the lead, and my melody winds down to a delicate pianissimo—a shimmering silver line stretching among the clouds of harmony. I sense my muscles tensing before it happens. My stomach twists in agony, and the line breaks. The strings pick up again, and I follow them in a whirlwind of sound, and when the song comes to an end, I'm all but breathless—head spinning, stomach readying to empty itself right there on stage.

Clapping enters my mind as if from far off, and I curtsy, strictly from habit, before stepping away. The marchioness is speaking again, but I cannot understand her words. My head is throbbing. I snatch my purse from the maid as I stumble away from the crowd, past the green hedge and the flower beds, until I'm far enough away that the next singer is just a distant background noise.

Collapsing onto a bench, I try to force air to fill my lungs.

"What was that?" Madame's voice makes me jump. I didn't even realize she had followed me.

"I don't . . ."

"This is your time of the month, isn't it?"

My heart rate accelerates, my nausea threatening to overtake me. Discussing my female calendar with Madame is not something I thought I'd ever be doing.

"I—"

"Foolish girl," Madame snaps. "I blame myself. I should have had your maid report your schedule along with your weight."

She's upset with me, this time openly, but I don't deserve it. Not for this, at least. "I don't understand . . ."

"You're lucky your Talent holds an exquisite singing technique, or this would have been a total disaster. Didn't you sense your vocal cords are swollen?"

My eyes widen. "Is that what it was? Why my pianissimo broke?"

"That, and the lack of support and breath control. You cannot possibly expect your muscles to act normally."

I open my mouth to answer when another cramp passes through me and my hands fly to my belly. Madame's glare softens.

"Are you regular?" she asks, her voice now gentle.

"Not usually," I admit, avoiding her gaze.

"Well, you've been gaining weight, so we can only hope it'll stabilize. I expect to be informed, so I can make certain you will not perform like this again."

I nod as another throb skewers me. I should definitely have taken the opium tincture this morning.

"The Maestro won't be happy, but I'll take care of it," she continues. "But, Cleodora, if you wish to keep your role, you cannot afford to mess up again. Now let's go back to the party."

"Can I have a few minutes?"

"Don't take too long," she says, turning away from me and heading back toward the crowd.

As soon as she's gone, tears spring to my eyes. This day has been nothing but a massive failure. I ruined a man's life. Condemned him to a fate worse than what I've been running from. Humiliated myself in front of the marchioness. Broke while singing for all to see. Lost Maestro Mette's favor. Managed to make Véronique shine even more. And worst of all, I did all of that in front of Vicomte Lenoir.

It'll be a miracle if I can make him see me as anything but a joke after this.

The tears are now streaming down my cheeks, smearing the makeup Pauline worked so hard on and revealing the broken mess I am inside. I reach into my purse. My hands are shaking as I take out Father's book and press it to my chest.

I knew letting go of my past was a part of the deal. I knew I could never again be the Cleodora Finley whose future was promised inside these pages. But it's as though every step I take strips away a part of me. If I keep going, will anything remain? And what is the point of maintaining this facade if I keep messing up at every turn, my own shortcomings pushing my reunion with Anaella further and further away?

I haven't seen my sister in over a month. I haven't even answered her letter. I disappeared—allowed this role I'm playing to take over. Yet even while failing at it, I'm still here in this lavish world, while she's left behind in darkness.

I cannot keep going this way. Whatever heinous acts I have to commit, whatever parts of myself I have to bury, I need a guarantee that this will all be worth it.

I cover my face with my hands, wishing the world to vanish— hoping that when I open my eyes, I'll be back at Father's shop, with Anaella by my side.

Instead, a cough startles me. I flinch, hurrying to stuff the book back into the purse.

"Having a cloudy day in your everlasting sunny kingdom?" Vicomte Lenoir is leaning on the side of a bronze horse statue. If he thinks anything is odd about me crying over a book, it doesn't show in his tilted smirk.

I don't know what he's doing away from the crowd, and I'm aware I should be grateful he's even still talking to me. But I have no energy left to deal with his smugness. Today won't be the day I win him over.

"I have no kingdom. And no sun." I rise to my feet. "Now, if you'll excuse me."

I try to push past him, but he grabs my arm. An electric shock passes through me at his touch. My head turns back toward him. He's so close that his breath is hot on my neck. A shiver runs down my spine. His hand still grips me, warmth radiating off him in gentle waves. I should pull away, but his touch has left me rooted to the spot.

The smirk is gone, replaced by an uncertain line on his forehead. "You . . ." He suddenly lets me go, shaking his head as if to clear it. "Are you alright?"

It's a stupid question, seeing as tears still smear my face, but the sudden worry catches me off guard.

"You were there. You heard it."

"It's just a concert."

"To you. To me, it's my entire future." I don't know why I'm being so honest with him. All I know is that my emotions are in turmoil, and I can barely hold myself together, let alone bring myself to speak politically. "What are you even doing here?"

"At the party?" He raises an eyebrow; his cockiness has returned.

"No." I will not let him turn this into another sparring match. "Here. With me."

He shrugs, sticking his hands in his pockets. "It was getting boring there. I was actually heading for my carriage."

"You're leaving?"

"Wasn't that what you were doing? Or was your plan to sit here and wallow over your diary?"

"That's not my—" I bite my tongue. No wonder he didn't think it odd; he simply sees me as a hysterical woman.

A flash of anger rises in my chest when I notice the smile at the corner of his lips. He's teasing me. Is this his way of offering comfort? I can't decide if his behavior is infuriating or charming. Maybe it's a bit of both. I examine his sculpted face; his expression is guarded, giving nothing away. What game is he playing?

"Well, I would go home," I say, trying to regain control of the conversation. "But if you haven't heard, I lost my coachman. I have no way to leave."

"I can take you."

I blink, waiting for him to laugh. But he's not joking.

"What about the marchioness?" I mumble, suddenly aware of how secluded we are. "We didn't even say goodbye."

"With what you've gone through today, people have enough to gossip about. Believe me, no one will care."

The concert is still going on in the distance, Véronique and José's voices echoing in a passionate duet. Just the thought of going back makes me squeamish. There is nothing I can salvage there, but here I have a chance I never thought I'd get—an opportunity I've been begging for.

The vicomte just stares at me, waiting for my reply.

"Thank you for your kindness, *Monsieur le Vicomte*." I add his title and lower my head, trying to regain a measure of decorum. "I'd be delighted."

He bows his head in return, gesturing for me to lead the way.

As we reach the waiting carriages, he speaks again. "Your Talent is impressive, but you are still human."

"Pardon?"

He opens the carriage door, allowing me to climb in first before following and settling himself on the velvet seat opposite me.

"You aren't perfect," he says, as his coachman closes the door behind us.

I don't know if it's meant as an insult, but at this moment I don't really care.

CHAPTER FIFTEEN

Candlelit Dinner

THE HEAVY DOOR shuts behind me, and I wince at the loud thud. When Dahlia's henchmen placed the sack over my head on the way here, I should have known our meeting would be in a strange place— at least this time we're not in a basement.

After the day I had, I should be exhausted. I *am* exhausted. But at the same time my nerves are prickling, keeping me alert. The large room is elaborately decorated with furniture in mahogany and walnut, reflecting in ornate mirrors that are elegantly poised on the walls. All around, chairs are propped upside down on distinctive brocade-silk cloaked tables. Yet in the corner of the room, on a tiny stage, a performance is taking place. The tender sound of the violinist's music caresses me as I stare at the contortionist bending her legs over her shoulders in an inhuman pose. Why are they here in the middle of the night?

"Do sit down," Dahlia calls over the music. She sits at a round table in the center of the room. The tall candles flicker as I move closer to her, taking in the porcelain dinnerware and silver cutlery laid before me.

After Pauline left my room this evening, it took Lirone less than a minute to appear, bowing and expecting me to praise his "once in a lifetime performance" earlier that day. Seeing that he was showing absolutely no sign of having been trampled by horses, I couldn't argue that he deserved applause. Even if I regretted ever having given him the chance to earn it in the first place. But he wasn't there just to check in on me. Dahlia was calling, and as Lirone said, "Lady Sibille doesn't like to be kept waiting." The sack over my head came as soon as I entered a darkened carriage at the end of my street.

"I hope you don't mind—I took the liberty of ordering already." That perfect smile stretches on Dahlia's scarlet-colored lips as I sit down across from her, tucking my dress under me.

The restaurant is clearly the type frequented only by the wealthy, promising fine dining and company. A fancy dinner and a performance . . . Is this a date? My heart flutters.

"Wine?" Dahlia asks, already pouring me a glass.

In the candlelight, the liquid looks purple, rich, and velvety. "Thank you."

Her doe eyes stare at me as I take a sip, the fruity flavor of plum coating my tongue.

"Exquisite, no?" she says. "Much like your *performance* at the garden party today—and I certainly don't mean your singing."

I choke at her words, a fit of coughing overtaking me as the wine slides down the wrong pipe and into my airway. I'm not sure what I was expecting. After all, I would have been a fool to think she didn't already know all the details about today. There was only one part of the day unaccounted for.

The time I spent in Vicomte Lenoir's carriage.

She tilts her head in amusement, one long finger resting on her chin.

"I—" I clear my throat, finally able to stop coughing. "After the . . ." I fall silent as a door flaps open behind me.

A man carrying a tray enters the room, and from his perfectly white outfit and tall hat, it's clear he's not just a servant.

"Ladies." He bows his head.

To my surprise, Dahlia stands as he approaches, revealing a smooth cream gown with a deep-cut neckline and delicate purple lace that spirals across her skirt. On the back of her chair hangs the same coat she wore when I last saw her on our midnight stroll—black lilies shimmering in the candlelight.

"My dear," Dahlia says just as the violinist plays a soft trill, "I'd like you to meet someone very special to me."

I hurry to my feet. "Pleasure to meet you, monsieur."

"Adolphe Dugléré, the proud owner and chef of Café Anglais," he says, and my jaw drops for just a second before I recompose myself. Even *I* have heard of Café Anglais. In truth, I doubt there is anyone who hasn't. Is this where we are? The waiting list for a table here is as long as any novel ever written. How did Dahlia get the chef to be here in the middle of the night for her?

"And you must be the lovely Lady Adley—your reputation precedes you," he continues, droning each syllable. "An honor to make your acquaintance."

He looks like a caricature of what I might expect the most famous chef in Lutèce to be—plump, with a short, almost nonexistent neck and flushed cheeks. Pinned onto his white jacket is a silver brooch indented with an onyx gemstone, its aura so powerful it bewitches me to stare.

Adolphe sets two plates on the table before ceremoniously removing the silver cloche on each one. "Soupe à l'oignon, with brandy, caramelized onions, and herbs, topped with a freshly baked cheese brioche."

"Thank you, Adolphe." Dahlia sits down, running her hand over Adolphe's arm, and my stomach hardens. There is such adoration in the way he looks at her that all of a sudden I want to shove him away, tear him from her grasp. The chef turns away with a bow, and I suppress the urge, though my breath remains shallow.

Dahlia puckers her lips, blowing air over a spoonful of soup before taking a sip. She accompanies it with a soft, low moan, and I force down a lump in my throat as she licks her lips. "Won't you eat? It's best served warm." She blinks at me demurely and I automatically reach for my own spoon as if under a spell.

Her eyes follow me as I take a bite, immediately burning the roof of my mouth. She smiles as I gulp at the wine to cover it.

"So, a little bird told me you had quite an eventful day. Firing your coachman, fainting, ruining your aria." Dahlia counts each one on her fingers as if listing off my crimes. "Should I be concerned?"

"He was a drunkard." The lie springs to my lips. Lirone warned me to stick to the official story—even with Dahlia—and though it feels like putting a nail into the coachman's coffin, coming clean now will do nothing to undo the damage. I brought this on myself the moment I chose to keep my suspicions from Dahlia to begin with. I have only myself to blame.

"Yes, I heard he hit a child," she says. "Tragic, really." Dahlia's gaze is unnerving, unmoving.

My knuckles turn white as I grab the spoon, bringing more scalding soup to my mouth to avoid her eyes. She leans in, and my hand freezes in the air mid bite.

"But I'm more interested in what happened after . . . I hear you went on a joyride with our *friend*. How is Vicomte Lenoir these days?"

I force myself to swallow. Of course this is the reason she brought me here.

"The vicomte was kind enough to offer me a ride home, since I lost mine."

"I don't have any interest in facts I already know." Her glare speaks of danger. "Tell me what happened in that carriage."

I take another long sip of wine, stalling, as I watch the contortionist twist herself into a knot. The alcohol releases the tension in my body, taking away some of the pain still lingering in my abdomen. I close my eyes for a second, the vicomte's well-sculpted features filling my mind.

⤚⟡⟡⟡⤙

"Do you often rescue damsels in distress?" I teased as the carriage lurched forward.

Vicomte Lenoir gifted me with one of his smirks. "Only the interesting ones."

"You find me interesting?"

"Only if you consider yourself a damsel in distress."

My pulse quickened, unbidden.

The vicomte leaned back, one arm gracefully draped along the backrest of his velvety bench seat. "Did you always know you wanted to take your cousin's Talent?"

I shook my head. "I never imagined she'd give it to me . . . But it's my future now."

"And you enjoy it?"

"Of course I do." The words all but flew out of my mouth. Almost too quickly.

He raised an eyebrow but didn't argue.

"What about you? Do you enjoy your Talent?" I directed the question back to him, clutching my hands together in my lap. "I've never seen you wear it."

The line of his mouth hardened at that, but he passed a hand through his hair, ruffling his rich brown locks as if to shake my question away. "I prefer things that are flawed."

My brow knitted together, but it was clear he wasn't about to elaborate. "Like me? You claimed I'm not perfect."

A spark danced in his bright eyes. "Yes. Exactly like you."

<hr />

The words ring again in my mind softly, a strange flutter stirring my heart. The vicomte is so infuriatingly arrogant, and yet, there's something captivating about him. I can't deny a part of me enjoyed his teasing and biting wit today. He's like a puzzle I can't quite solve, drawing me in with each new piece that falls into place.

Yet I can't say any of that to Dahlia. The vicomte is my target, and thinking about him as anything else is a dangerous game I can never hope to win.

"Well?" she whispers.

"It was nothing of importance." My lip trembles a bit as I speak. "Though I do think he's starting to like me. I tried to ask him about his Talent, but he changed the subject. All I managed to get from him is that he likes things that aren't perfect."

"Well, you've clearly been less than perfect the last few days."

I'm about to defend myself when Adolphe returns, carrying the main course of our meal. "I hope all is to your satisfaction."

"You know it is, dear," Dahlia says.

The chef straightens his back, his chest filling up with pride. "I have prepared for you my signature dish. Confit de canard—duck legs in shallots, garlic, and thyme, accompanied by red cabbage slow-braised with apples and red wine."

Steam rises from the plates, and the delicious smell of spices makes my mouth water even through my recurring nausea. This time Adolphe doesn't leave; he's waiting expectantly for us to taste his masterpiece.

I follow Dahlia's example, taking a forkful and biting into the rich meat. It falls off the bone at once, a perfect, sinful combination of crisped skin and silky meat. Tears form in my eyes; the taste is too good to be true— clearly created with a Talent so grand it makes others pale in comparison.

Yet all I can feel as my mouth longs for the next bite is guilt. I must not forget myself in pleasures. None of this is about me. I put down the fork, suddenly struggling to swallow.

But Dahlia and Adolphe are staring at me, and I cannot let them down. I force a smile. "It's the most wonderful thing I have ever tasted," I say.

Adolphe bows to me modestly before turning away again.

Dahlia takes another bite, looking at the performers on the stage with a soft gaze. "Enchanting, are they not? They are some of my brightest stars." She smiles as the contortionist goes into a deep split, locking eyes with her for a moment longer than I'd like. "I actually imported Adolphe's

Talent all the way from Londinium. Have you ever been?" She doesn't let me answer before continuing. "I never regretted gifting any of them their Talents, and they have never disappointed me in return."

The violin's enchanting melody fills the room as I let her words sink in. They are like me. The chef. The contortionist. The violinist. They are her thieves. This romantic dinner is about more than just information. It's about showing me the future that awaits me if I hold up my end of the bargain.

Did she take all of them on moonlit strolls? Did her lips brush against their skin as well?

"Such precious things," Dahlia says. For a second, I'm sure she's talking about the performers, but then I notice her eyes are following the gems glinting from their rings—a beautiful amethyst and a rare black opal. "It's a shame how limited the supply is, isn't it? Who would have thought those enchanted mines would ever empty . . . Perhaps one day we can go see them together, if you'd like. Maybe we'll find some forgotten gems."

Her smile is sweet, inviting, her words full of promise. But promises can be dangerous; they can lead to heartbreak. And I know Dahlia can rip my heart out if she desires. Does she truly care for me? I shouldn't even play with that thought, yet I can't help but weave that dream in my head. And the way she looks at me makes it practically impossible to resist. I long to see the full world Dahlia has to offer.

"I'd go anywhere with you." The words leave my mouth despite myself.

Her eyes sparkle. "One day." She grows silent, her gaze falling down to the ruby on my finger. "I often wish things had been different. Don't you?"

A genuine question dances on her perfect features. Does she refer to the story she told me about her brother? About her Talent? She sighs, gently biting her bottom lip. Could she be nervous? Does she wish to share more with me?

"I . . ." The last thing I want now is to push her or pry, no matter how curious I am. I hesitate, my breath shaky. Reaching out, my fingers land on the back of her hand. Her skin is soft, warm, an invitation to intimacy.

She looks up at me at the touch, her head tilted, her brow knitted, as though the concept of being comforted is completely unknown to her. The rest of the room fades as a magnetic energy moves between us—masks falling off, emotions dancing close to the surface. I'm lost within her, mesmerized by the soft spark glinting in her eyes.

She drops her voice to a whisper, her words reserved for my ears alone. "If I had my way, every child would have a Talent of their own." The passion in her words speaks of truth, revealing that vulnerable side of her that only draws me in more.

This is the Dahlia I daydream of. The Dahlia who mirrors my own struggles. And in that moment, I'm certain that this Dahlia is mine alone. I feel my body aching for her. Longing. Falling.

The violin picks up and Dahlia dispels the fragility with a chuckle, pulling her hand away to grab her glass. "Though I suppose that would hurt my business. The rarer something is, the higher the demand. Speaking of which . . ." Dahlia pauses, taking another sip of wine. "Did you know that on his first mission Adolphe collected his blood sample within one week?"

And just like that, her tone is back to business. And though I know I should follow suit, I can't help but wish for her tenderness, her warmth.

"What about you, Cleo?" she asks. "You sat with Vicomte Lenoir alone in his carriage, yet barely any progress has been made. I have not even asked you to worry about his gem yet. When can I expect your blood sample?"

"I don't . . ."

"My sweet Cleo. So innocent. So pure. I truly admire that about you." She swishes the wine in her glass, the deep purple liquid threatening to spill as it swirls but never surpasses the edges. "Lirone has kept me up to date about your little plot: being proper, stroking the man's ego. But you are *not* a proper lady. You are nothing like the women the vicomte knows." She takes a long sip of wine, a single drop dripping at the edge of her lips. My stomach tightens as she licks it away, and I mimic her gesture with a sudden hunger that has nothing to do with the food. "Use it," she says.

"I don't know how," I mumble.

She lets out a delighted giggle. "You are innocent, my love, but not naive."

I focus on the plate before me. She means I should seduce him by any means necessary. Just the thought makes my heart race and my palms sweat. It's what I signed up for when I agreed to her deal, but each step I take toward completing my end of the bargain feels like a step toward the edge of a cliff.

I can sense her eyes on me, compelling me to look up. There's that softness in her gaze, in the way her lips are parted ever so slightly, in the single lock of raven hair falling on her forehead. I cannot say no to her. For her, I would jump right off the cliff into the abyss.

"I will make it happen. But . . ."

Her brow rises at the conditional word.

"I need to see my sister." My resolve, after today, makes my words come out stronger.

She's quiet for a moment, not answering as she cleans the last bite off her plate. Then she rings a tiny bell and Adolphe rushes back from the kitchen.

"I think we're ready for dessert, dearest."

Pressure builds in my chest when she doesn't respond. Yes, I would do anything she asks of me. I would lie, cheat, steal. But if today has taught me anything, it is that without Anaella, none of it is worth anything. I need a guarantee that she will be taken care of, no matter what. I need Dahlia to understand that. I need her to let my sister be a part of my life so I can dedicate myself to it wholeheartedly. Having Anaella by my side is the only way I'll truly be able to put the past behind me and build a new future without regrets.

Adolphe clears the table—my plate is nearly as full as when it arrived, but luckily he shows no sign of feeling insulted—before placing a single bowl of crème brûlée before us.

Taking a silver teaspoon, Dahlia breaks the round sugar disc with a firm tap. "We've talked about this," she finally says, once the chef has left again. "It's not safe yet."

"When, then?" I ask as she digs into the custard. "I need her to come live with me. Keeping her this way, while I . . . It's just wrong. Wouldn't you feel the same in my place?"

She stills, my unspoken words lingering between us: *What if it were your brother?*

For a moment I wonder if her anger might reemerge, if I have pushed too far, but the glint in her eyes is one of sadness, not fury.

"I can assure you," she says, "that Anaella wants for nothing. She is well fed, dressed, and taken care of. As long as you are mine, she will never suffer."

A pleasant shiver runs down my spine. I want to be hers. But even though her claims are comforting, it's not enough. Not anymore.

"When?" I ask again.

She keeps silent a moment longer before speaking. "Once you deliver Vicomte Lenoir's blood and gem to me, I promise to bring your sister to live with you. You shall never be apart again."

Never apart again. The words I longed to hear. Yet I still want more. "And when can I see her?"

Dahlia lifts the teaspoon to her mouth, closing her lips around the sweet delight. Then she rises to her feet, and my pulse quickens. Her gown shows every curve of her body as she circles around the table and bends to face me.

The warmth of her breath is sensual—the sweetness of the crème brûlée's vanilla scent, mixing with her signature jasmine perfume and enveloping me with her presence. Her long eyelashes flutter against my skin as her fingers trace my jawline. I cannot think anymore. The violin, a background noise. The contortionist, nothing but a blurred, meaningless shape. The room is gone. The world is gone. The only clear thing is her. She is everything.

Her lips are an inch from mine when she whispers, "Soon."

And that's all I can take.

Leaning forward, I close the distance between us, tasting the sugar that still lingers on her perfect lips.

CHAPTER SIXTEEN

Keeping Time

"CLEO, FOCUS!" LIRONE snaps at me. "Your tempo is all off again."

I groan, holding back from throwing the music notebook at the wall. Almost a month of studies and I barely have anything to show for it. Yes, I did manage to learn the new role for the opera, mostly . . . leaning heavily on the private lessons Madame finally felt inclined to give me. But Lirone still insisted I should learn to read music on my own.

He has a point. Father always told me that one could never take full advantage of a Talent without knowledge. That was the entire reason he created his book for Anaella and me, to teach us the importance of our skills. "We are not machines, mon coeur," he once said as he put yet another comment in the margins. "Anything worth having takes work. Never forget."

I glance at my purse sitting on a nearby armchair. Even though the danger of the coachman no longer looms over my head, I have left the book there, always in reach and out of sight. I guess I've grown too used to its weight, though it no longer evokes sentimentality within me. Instead, it's a reminder that the pressure on my chest will lift only once my sister is by my side. And that I have to do everything to make sure there are no cracks in this new life I'm building for us.

Letting out a long breath, I compose myself. "Where did I go wrong?"

Lirone rolls his eyes. "You are the one with the *Talent*. You really can't tell?"

"Are you going to mock, or help?"

He snatches the notebook out of my hands and squints to read it in the faint candlelight. "Right here." He hands it back to me and points to a bar where the rhythm changes from 3/4 to 6/8. "You kept counting like you're in three, when 6/8 is counted in two. Start from the top."

I nod, grabbing the tuning fork by the stem and hitting it lightly against one of the elaborate bedpost columns before pressing it close to my ear. The note reverberates softly. Now I just need to find the note two steps up. My gem pulses, itching to give me the answer, for me to surrender to the magic, but I push it away and focus. I need to do this on my own. I bite into my lip as I hum an upward scale to the right pitch.

Lirone nods approvingly. With no metronome handy, he taps gently on the dresser, giving me a beat. I bob my head with each tap, my voice soft as I mark the new solfège line. Lirone insisted on writing new exercises for me himself, claiming my Talent would already be familiar with all the known solfège teaching books.

My eyes run ahead, scanning each coming musical interval and translating it in my head.

Do, re, fa, re, la, break, trill on sol, fa, mi, jump an octave, sol, break.
Si bémol.

Bémol!

My throat clenches, and I wince as the note rings false—far too sharp.

Lirone slaps his forehead, singing the correct note back at me with annoying accuracy.

This time I can't stop myself from throwing the notebook. It hits the wall with a thud before landing on the carpet with its pages crumpled.

"What was that for?" Lirone all but stomps over to pick it up.

"It's useless. I'm too tired anyway, and I have a staging rehearsal in the morning."

"You're just lazy."

"Easy for you to say! You have perfect pitch."

"You think I can read all of this," he waves the notebook over his head, "just because of my hearing?"

I bite my tongue. I asked Lirone once how he knows music so well, but all I got from him was "passion" and "good ears."

"Hearing the notes is not enough to know how to read notation, not to mention rhythm."

"I don't—"

"No, you don't know." His face hardens with anger. "I had no fancy mentors, but I wanted to learn so much that I spent nights in the saloon, begging the pianist to let me stay by his side. I taught myself, from listening and watching. And you . . ." He pushes the notebook into my lap again. "You get everything handed to you, and still you complain."

The image of Lirone standing in a stuffy saloon, surrounded by drunkards, makes my stomach tense. He's just a child. A child showing clear promise and resourcefulness. But just because he doesn't have a Talent, his life can never be fulfilled. If there were new gems, his own musical gift could have been enough to hone a new Talent. But instead, he's forced to live in the streets—lie, cheat. How long has he been alone in this world?

I press the notebook to my chest, shame burning in my cheeks. "I'm sorry."

Lirone huffs. "Just try harder."

"I *am* trying," I say, but even in my own ears the words sound whiny. What would Father have said if he heard me? "I will do better."

He eyes me with pressed lips before relenting and flopping on the bed next to me. "Maybe it's enough for today."

I nod.

"Lady Sibille is still waiting, you know," he says, after a few moments of silence.

I straighten, my heart beating faster at the mention of Dahlia's name.

"It's been nearly three weeks since you saw her," he points out.

I'm painfully aware of how much time has passed since our dinner. She is expecting progress—progress I'm desperate to achieve with the new promise of having Anaella by my side after this mission. Yet since my carriage ride with the vicomte, my advances have been depressingly futile—foiled by constant rehearsals, silly dinner parties, and people bustling around us, blocking any private moment.

My longing to see Dahlia again, to bring her good news, has been growing inside me with each passing day. With each night filled with dreams of her lush lips kissing mine. Of the sweetness that coated my tongue. And of the way her touch turned from melting softness to passionate hunger as she pressed her body against mine. I thought with time the sensation would fade, yet somehow I still feel as if it happened mere seconds ago.

Could she feel the same? It's hard to imagine Dahlia losing concentration while daydreaming of our kiss. Yet I wish it were true.

I wish I could talk to my sister about it all, about the candlelit dinner and the way butterflies fluttered in my stomach at Dahlia's gaze.

I wish I could tell her about the kiss.

I remember my clammy hands and racing heart after Gabriel Martin, the baker's boy, and I stole a moment behind his parents' boulangerie. Anaella waited up for me, ready to hear every single detail ten times over. My sister always had a way of painting the world in pink—sitting on the bed, weaving romantic dreams. I need that now.

Every kiss, every touch . . . we always shared our experiences.

But not this time.

"I have another letter for you to take," I say.

"Another?" Lirone props himself up on his elbows. "She still hasn't answered the other twenty."

"I don't care." I stand, reaching for one of the drawers in my vanity. "Here."

Lirone stares at the sealed envelope, his reluctance evident. "I told you not to seal them. I'll have to break it to read anyway."

I circle my finger over the red wax. He did tell me that, but I simply don't care. Something in the act of sealing each letter makes it real—a stamp that proves I wrote down the words. I've been writing to Anaella each day since the garden party. As if that could somehow make up for how horrible I've been for neglecting her. There is so much I want to tell her, though I don't dare write about the kiss, or my feelings for Dahlia—not while I still have to keep Anaella in the dark.

But my sister hasn't been replying, and each time I ask Lirone about her, all he has to say is that he handed the letter to the nurse. I don't blame Anaella for holding a grudge. I deserve to be kept waiting.

"Just take it," I plead.

"Fine." He relents, stuffing the envelope into an inner pocket of his patched-up jacket. "I'll be back tomorrow night."

The horses slow down as the carriage rolls into the familiar alley, stopping right in front of the artists' entrance to the opera house.

"My lady," the new coachman says as he opens the door for me.

My head butler hired him the morning after I fired Basset. He's a young man, but there's nothing youthful about him—his face remains a somber mask, his shoulders never slacking. He has the air of a proper and upstanding man, someone to erase the memory of the "drunkard" no one dares to speak of anymore.

Lirone's public scene remained on everyone's lips for days, but in a city like Lutèce, even the juiciest gossip is soon replaced. In this case, it was overtaken by a scandalous affair between a patron and a ballerina. Now all that lingers is my own guilt.

Soon I'm handing my hat to a maid before walking onto the main stage. The other cast members are already here, stretching and humming to wake their voices from a long night's sleep.

Maestro Mette is waiting at his conductor's pedestal, while Madame is at the piano, running her fingers smoothly over the keyboard in enchanting scales and arpeggios.

"Settle down, everyone!" Maestro Mette calls. "Patrice and I discussed it, and this morning we would like to skip the overture but start again from act 1, to see how the opening scene works."

Véronique lets out a displeased huff but luckily says nothing. Since we started working with *Le Visionnaire*, the gentilhomme Patrice Agard, on staging, she's been holding her tongue more often. Despite his honorary titles, the stage director's proclivity for yelling until his face turns red and the vein on his forehead bulges has been enough to keep most of the cast silent.

The rehearsals have also brought another side of Maestro Mette to the surface—a colder side, calculated and precise. It's written on his brow and in the hard line of his clenched jaw, in the way he holds his baton as though it's a sword. It's a side, I learned quickly, I do not want to cross.

The two of them together make for a fearful sight.

"Please take your positions," Mr. Agard says.

Following the stage director's order, José winks at me as we face each other from opposite ends of the stage, and a smile tugs at my lips. At least I have one ally through this.

Madame starts playing and merely four musical bars later José stumbles forward. He wanders across the stage singing in full voice, bringing the story of the battlefield to life with each note.

The rest of the cast has split up, either watching from the wings or sitting in the front rows of the hall as an audience.

José's tenor voice soars as he drops to the ground, and that's my cue.

I gather up my skirts and glide forward, my steps light and ghostly, as instructed. A chair marks the hill I'm supposed to mount, and I nearly lose my balance as I climb on top of it, pretending to watch the scorched earth below.

My ruby is already pulsing, recognizing the music at last. I let the Talent take hold, embracing the lack of control and trusting the gem, as Madame instructed me to. The melody springs from my lips, each note a shimmering drop of magic. My body is no longer my own, and I am no longer myself. I'm Nova, The Enchantress. And like her, my blood is fueled with power.

I sing out a long and mournful trill when the stage director bangs his fist on a desk and my voice all but disappears.

"No. No. No!" He stumps toward me, and my entire body stiffens. "Lady Adley, how many times do I have to tell you, you look at José *after* your cadenza."

I was looking at José? I didn't notice . . .

"I'm sorry," I say, but he's already turned away from me.

"Chevalier Muratore," he shouts at José. "I need more agony from you. You are looking for survivors on a battleground. There is nothing but death around you. I need to see it in your eyes. The horror!" He doesn't allow José to answer before yelling again. "From the top!"

We spend the next hour just on the first scene, and by the time José and I are allowed a short break, I'm already tired. But mostly frustrated. My Talent is for singing, not acting.

"Don't look so worried." José nudges my shoulder lightly as we step backstage. "Making mistakes is what rehearsals are for."

"You coddle her." Véronique's voice echoes from behind us.

She's leaning on the door frame leading into the dressing areas, her blond hair undone and cascading off her shoulders. Her dress is simple, practical for rehearsals—a light fabric covered in a floral print, with only the slightest lace embellishments around the cuffs and collar. Even I could have sewn this dress within a few hours, and I wouldn't have needed any of Father's notes or a practice muslin to construct it.

"She lacks skills," she continues, her eyes running up and down my length. "Maestro Mette will come to his senses soon enough."

"Véronique, I have no patience for your insistent blubbering today." José sighs. "Stop obsessing about Cleodora and do your job."

Véronique narrows her eyes. "I'm not obsessing."

"If you say so. Come, ma chérie, we only have a few minutes for our break." He interlaces his arm with mine, pulling me along the corridor—my knight in shining armor.

But Véronique isn't giving up.

"You might have managed to learn the music, finally, but you're not fooling anyone," she calls after us.

I pause, closing my eyes for a second to keep calm. "Go rest," I tell José. "No reason we should both miss out on our break."

He shoots Véronique a fake smile before entering one of the dressing rooms up ahead.

Alone, I turn to face Véronique. "Well? Have at it."

She blinks at me, clearly taken aback. I take pleasure in her hesitation. Then she steps toward me.

"You think you have it all figured out, don't you? Waltzing in here with your Talent." Her voice drips with venom. "Well, you're wrong. I have been preparing for *my Talent* since I was born. I studied music, acting, dancing, even languages. The only reason the Maestro indulges you is your *cousin's* name." She's so close now that her perfume assaults me—sharp, like a bee sting. "But he already has doubts. After that catastrophe at the garden party, it was bound to happen. You have no idea how to deal with your Talent. You are a wild card—a fleeting excitement. But when the dust settles, I'll be the one left standing. Do you understand?"

I bite my tongue, acid and anger seething within me. I don't care how justified her resentment toward me is, and I don't care about her expertise. Her attack is personal, belittling all my efforts, as if they were nothing but a joke—as if *I* am nothing but a joke. My nails dig into my skin as I clench my fists, doing all I can to keep from slapping her.

That's when a door slams farther down the corridor. I jump and turn my head to see Vicomte Lenoir walking in the other direction, away from us. Without thinking, I spin around swiftly, feeling my hair hitting Véronique's face.

"My lord!" I call after him.

He stops in his tracks and looks back at us. There's a stack of papers in his hands with sketches of buildings, delicate lines accompanied by countless calculations. He shoves these quickly under his arm.

"Lady Adley, shouldn't you be in rehearsal?" he asks.

Not exactly the greeting I was expecting, but I push it aside. Heat still courses through me, the need to spring into action. To pull Véronique's hair out, or at least shove my newfound understanding with the vicomte in her face.

"I'm on break," I say. "What about you? You seem in a hurry."

He tucks the stack of papers closer to him. "Budget issues," he says, though I'm not sure I believe him. He's holding sketches, not balance sheets. His hair is disheveled even more than usual, his golden vest wrinkled as if he's slept in it, and there's a crease of worry on his forehead.

"I'm certain it's nothing you can't handle, my lord," Véronique offers, her voice now soft and sweet. "My father has been asking about you—you still owe him a hunting trip."

I can't help but roll my eyes, catching myself too late. The vicomte lifts his brow and blinks, a hint of a smile forming on his face. But he focuses back on Véronique. "Please tell him I shall write to him soon to set a date."

"But—"

He cuts her off. "Lady Adley, have you ever gone hunting?"

"No, my lord. I've always considered it a rather masculine pursuit," I say, savoring the shock plastered on Véronique's face.

"A shame. I would have invited you to join."

Warmth creeps to my cheeks at the thought of spending more time with him. Dahlia did tell me to seduce him . . . This is all just a part of the game. "Perhaps I could be persuaded."

There's a spark in his eyes as he laughs, the sound low and warm, so unlike his smug persona. "I'll take that as a challenge."

Véronique opens her mouth just as a bell rings from the stage, calling us back to rehearsal.

"I won't keep you any longer," he says. "Enjoy your rehearsal, ladies."

He turns away from us, and my eyes follow him until he disappears around a corner.

"I don't know what you think you're doing." Véronique bites into each word, all sweetness evaporated. "But you're playing with fire."

I should probably worry about her more, but I don't care. This is the most progress I've made with the vicomte in weeks. A real step toward stealing his Talent, pleasing Dahlia, and getting my sister back. I should almost thank Véronique for goading me.

The smile is still stretched on my lips when I return to the stage, but Maestro Mette's cold glare and the director's tomato-red face are enough to wipe it right off.

CHAPTER SEVENTEEN

The Merry Women

"HERE YOU GO." José flashes a smile at the giggling girl as he hands her his autograph. "We look forward to seeing you in the crowd on opening night!"

It's become so customary for people to gather in the street and wait for us each evening that getting back home only after dark seems normal.

I sign my name—or *Lady Adley's* name, to be more accurate—on a piece of paper and hand it to the last girl still waiting. Her eyes light up as she stuffs it deep into her pocket, sneaking a glance at my ruby.

"Can I touch it?" she asks.

She looks so entranced that I'm tempted to say yes, but then the concierge shouts out for everyone to make way for the arriving carriages. I shake my head as I watch the young girl getting swept up with the rest of the fans, reluctantly forced to leave. I can't deny that I'm enjoying my new status as an opera diva. The recognition, the adoration—it's everything I could ever dream of.

But something about it also feels hollow. Perhaps it's the fact that it isn't *my name* I'm signing. Or the fact that, even with the Talent, I still struggle in rehearsals, and the shouts of the directors are a constant reminder of that.

"I'm so hungry I could eat a whale," José says, buttoning his closely fitted jacket up to his neck. "All these signatures seem to take longer each night."

"Lucky you have dinner plans, then," the mezzo, Lady Arnould, teases.

He winks at her, and a blush blooms on her cheeks.

"What about you, ma chérie? Already tired of your adoring fans?" he asks me as his carriage pulls in.

"No. I'm just tired," I say as he helps Lady Arnould into the carriage.

"Well, rest then." He climbs in after her, before sticking his head out the window. "Tomorrow will be a long day. Bonne nuit!" He sends me a kiss through the air as the horses pull them away.

I lean against the wall, waiting for my own coachman to arrive. My head is pounding, weakness creeping down my limbs. As much as I enjoy being a diva, I have to admit I didn't expect the job to be this hard. A full day of being shouted at has clearly taken its toll. And even though I can't say I regret standing up to Véronique today, it certainly didn't make her more pleasant to work with.

In truth, I can't remember her ever sinking so low with her blows. From correcting my musical lines while I'm singing to practically putting her leg in front of my feet for me to stumble over, she took every single opportunity she had to belittle me and show Maestro Mette that he made the wrong choice.

The problem is . . . the more time passes, the more I fear she might succeed.

No amount of fans can help me if I can't maintain my position in the opera house.

I'm rubbing my eyes with the backs of my hands when my own carriage pulls up, but before I can climb inside, Madame steps out of the building.

"Cleodora, wait," she calls.

What now? Does she want to yell at me as well? Did I not get enough for one day?

"I'm glad I caught you," she says. "I want you to come earlier tomorrow for another session with me. You're still making mistakes in the duet."

"Fine," I mutter.

"This is serious, Cleo."

I gather a handful of fabric from my skirt in my fist, doing my best to keep my posture calm and my temper in check. "I know that."

"Maestro Mette needs to know he can count on you."

"I said, I know." The words come out sharper than I intended, and Madame takes a step back.

"Now you listen to me, young lady," she snaps, pointing her finger at me. "You should be grateful for all my help! I spent so many hours training you because of your lack of preparation. You think I have nothing better to do with my time? You young people think the entire world revolves around you!"

Her accusations pierce through me, each one like a nail digging into an open wound. I try to keep my head high. To take it all with pride. But after today, I have no strength left. Tears form at the corners of my eyes. Tears of frustration. Of anger. Of defeat.

I hold such a powerful Talent, yet I still feel worthless. I'm a diva, but only on the outside, like a beautiful wallpaper that hides deep cracks within the walls. Not like Véronique—she was raised to be a singer. To be a star.

Perhaps I don't deserve a Talent at all.

"Here." Madame offers me a handkerchief from her purse.

"Thank you." I take it from her, dabbing away the tears.

"This isn't your time of the month. Why are you so upset?"

I let out a hollow laugh. "It's just . . . a lot harder than I expected."

It's Madame's turn to laugh. "Nothing worth having comes easily," she says, echoing Father's words from so long ago. I almost smile. "Well, I know just what you need." A wide grin unexpectedly lights up her face. "Going out. Enjoying the night."

"But we have rehearsals in the morning, and you said—"

"Forget what I said." She waves her hand as if to banish my words. "What you need is to get rid of some stress. You!" She signals to my coachman, and he steps toward her with a deep bow. "Follow my carriage. Lady Adley has a social engagement this evening."

"Yes, my lady," he says, holding the door for me to climb in.

"I'll see you there," Madame says.

Before I get the chance to argue she's already heading for her own waiting carriage.

The horses charge forward, and I lean back into my seat. I'm really not in the mood for going out. I'm not even dressed for a social engagement. I huff at the ridiculousness of the thought. This dress, though simple, is something I could only have dreamed of owning not so long ago. I rub my hand over the smooth fabric. The quality of it alone would make Anaella squeal with joy.

Outside, the dark streets twist and turn as the horses trot, their hooves clacking against the rough pavement. I don't recognize the way, so I can't even begin to guess where Madame is taking me. I just hope there won't be too many people.

We come to a stop, and I glance outside nervously; Madame is already waiting on the sidewalk when my coachman opens the door.

"Well, hurry up," she says, turning toward a familiar red door.

This is Madame's apartment complex.

Last time I was here, ladies and gentlemen waited with champagne on their lips, their hum of conversation beckoning me toward the art exhibition. This time, the foyer is empty and there is no polite chatter. But the night isn't quiet, either. Music echoes from above us, growing louder with each step as we climb up the grand staircase.

I have to do a double take as we walk into the entrance hall. There are no more paintings covering the walls, no servants dashing around— even the smell is different: a heavy mixture of smoke, alcohol, and something that reminds me of hot cocoa. The only thing that is still the same is the crowd. But these are not the usual courteous social elites I expected.

The space is bustling with *women*, arguing, drinking, and laughing far louder than any proper lady is allowed. I watch their freedom with wide eyes. Some of them are even dancing right in the middle of the room, swaying to the sound coming from a golden phonograph.

"Who are they?" I have to raise my voice to be heard over the music.

"Les Rieuses." Madame's voice is low and warm, almost soft, her cheeks flushed as if she's already been drinking. "We don't host the association too often in our salon, but Renée wanted to celebrate."

I still have no idea what she's talking about. Is this a women's association? A private club? Does Madame always turn her house into a salon at night?

At the very center of the swaying ladies, a pair of women dance closely together. I watch as their bodies weave into one another with the beat of the music. They both laugh as one takes a big gulp of wine straight from a bottle before leaning in, their lips crashing into each other with hunger.

I avert my gaze, heat rushing to my cheeks.

Madame watches me, her eyes bearing into me as if searching to read my mind. That's when Renée rushes over to us, throwing her arms around Madame. Her tightly coiled curls encircle her head tonight, adorning it like a crown; she's wearing a light silver dress with a plunging neckline that creates a dramatic effect against her smooth dark skin. She's practically radiant.

"Chère! What took you so long?" she says as she draws back with a giggle. "Oh, you brought a guest."

"Lady Brooks." I bow my head, but she just laughs.

"It's Renée," she says. "I'm so happy you could join us! I keep telling Hélène to invite you over."

Madame purses her lips, but there is an ease to her I've never seen before. "Well, Cleodora, would you like a drink?"

I nod, still flustered as I follow them into the crowd. Before, I believed that Madame wanted to keep her private life hidden from me, that she was upset I'd even met Renée. But now she's brought me right into what I can only describe as an incredibly intimate, lustrous party. Not the type of event any of these women will admit they attended in the morning. What changed?

Renée hands me a glass of red wine. "Hear you go, dear! Santé!"

I take a sip while both Madame and Renée down their entire glasses.

"Better drink more if you want to have an excuse to skip our extra rehearsal in the morning," Madame says. "I brought you here to let off steam, not watch from the sidelines."

I put the glass back to my lips and Madame tips it up, making some of the wine spill over and stain my dress.

"Oops," she says, but there's no guilt on her face.

"Oh dear!" Renée laughs. "I guess you'll have to borrow one of my dresses."

I choke down the forced gulp. "It's fine, really—"

"Nonsense! The night is still young. I wouldn't want you to spend it in a ruined dress." She interlaces her arm with mine and starts pulling me away. Madame flips an entire bottle upside down, filling her glass all the way up.

Renée hands me another drink as she leads me to a large chamber with carved wood paneling and light mint drapery. She sits me down on a velvet armchair before disappearing through another door that I assume is a closet.

I take small sips of wine as I wait for her return.

The room is meticulously ordered, as if every single item was chosen specifically to complement the space—from the book with the golden cover by the nightstand, to the delicate painting of a forest right above the bed, to the collection of porcelain miniatures sitting in a glass cabinet. Observing it feels like sneaking a peek into Madame's mind. Or heart.

Renée returns with a black and white gown in her outstretched arms. "I hope this will fit you—I haven't been able to squeeze into it in years. I only keep it for sentimental value, really." She keeps talking, but I cannot focus on anything she says, my full attention stolen by the familiar lines of the dress.

The striking contrast between the black velvet and ivory satin creates an illusion of delicate, filigreed ironwork. I can visualize the way it was constructed, as though the design patterns lay right before my eyes—the unique weaving of the textile, custom made *à la disposition*, making sure the pattern of the fabric is intrinsic to the design of the dress.

Could it be? Could this be one of Father's gowns?

The urge to pull out his book from my purse and flip through the pages, to verify that my mind isn't tricking me, is almost too much to resist. But how could I possibly explain that to Renée?

"This dress. Where did you get it from?" I ask instead. I don't even realize I've risen to my feet until the fabric runs between my fingers.

"It was a gift," Renée says. "It was one of Josephine Garnier's first dresses at the launch of her independent fashion house."

Miss Garnier's. Not Father's.

I can see it now. The differences between the memory and the gown before me. The way the waist is cinched, the frills around the wrists, and the way the hem is stitched. Father would never have left that much space between stitches; his would have been tighter, fanning out only toward a curve.

Looking at it closely, the dress is still beautiful, but it isn't the masterpiece I remember in my head. The book could confirm it for certain, but now that I think of it, perhaps the pattern itself is different. This is just a black and white gown, not a piece of home.

"Are you feeling well, dear?" Renée rests the back of her palm on my forehead. "You turned pale."

I force a smile. "I'm fine."

"Well then, put it on!" She takes the wine from my hand.

I slip out of my own garment, and she whirls around to face the wall to give me privacy.

"I'm really glad you came tonight," she says. "Last time you were here, we didn't get the chance to talk. I know you mean a lot to Hélène."

I do? Madame certainly had me fooled on that account.

"I'm happy to be here . . . though I have to admit I didn't expect . . ."

Renée laughs, the sound like little bells chiming in the wind. "Oh dear, Hélène didn't tell you, did she?"

I step into the dress, holding the corseted-bodice up. "Umm, could you . . . ?"

She turns to me, immediately taking over the lacing of the back. "The ladies outside are Les Rieuses, The Merry Women. We are an association that creates opportunity for ladies like Hélène and me to . . . *express* ourselves freely."

"You and Madame live together, right?"

"Yes. Hélène is my partner. And while some will look at our 'arrangement' as one simply offering financial and social benefits—two spinsters sharing their income and companionship—Hélène is my life." She tightens the lacing and moves to rearrange my hair. "There are many Talented ladies out there who would prefer to keep their choices a secret on a daily basis, as you can imagine. We have to be selective with invitations . . . though I'm sure none of them would be against having a célébrité like you here tonight." She lets out a chuckle. "Hélène is a private person. But I told her that if you are important to her, she should let you in. I had a feeling you would understand."

"You love her," I say.

"That I do."

The taste of sugar is suddenly in my mouth, the memory of Dahlia's body against mine as her teeth gently bit my lips. Heat courses through me all the way from the pit of my stomach, making me shiver.

Renée spins me around to face a mirror. The dress fits perfectly, as though it were tailor-made for me. It embraces the natural curves of my body, accentuating them with the fashionable reverse S-curve silhouette. With its long train following behind me, I look almost regal. Renée lets my hair loose, and the curls fall down my back.

"Divine," she says. "And with that natural blush, you need no powder. Perhaps just a few extra sips of wine."

My cheeks turn a deeper red at her words, and she laughs.

"So, what about you? Anyone special in your life?" she asks.

Dahlia's dark eyes fill my mind, like two pools so deep I could drown in them. But at least that death would be sweet.

"You and Nuriel seemed rather close last time you were here . . ."

Nuriel. She means Vicomte Lenoir.

I blink away the image of Dahlia, the memory of Nuriel's glinting, catlike eyes and teasing smirk taking its place.

I forgot how close he and Renée seemed to be, despite Madame's clear distaste for their friendship.

She stares expectantly at my reflection in the mirror, and curiosity overtakes me. This could be an opportunity to learn more about the vicomte, about a side of him I suspect not many get to see.

"The vicomte and I are on friendly terms," I say, picking my words carefully. "He's a . . . charming gentleman."

"Oh my, I never thought I'd hear these two words together. Attractive, yes. Smug, certainly. But charming?" Renée laughs again.

I chuckle in return. I cannot really argue, not when, up until recently, I saw the vicomte as nothing but an arrogant man. Yet our last meetings hinted there is more to him, and Renée clearly knows it as well.

"Are you close to him?" I ask. "I'm sorry if I overstep, but I couldn't help but notice you are on a first-name basis."

"Nuriel and I have a long history." Her face is soft, as though she's recalling a long-lost memory. "He was my very first client—walked right into my first exhibition and bought a painting on the spot. He's been one of my greatest supporters ever since. Of course, Hélène hates to think anyone competes with her for that spot."

Her first client. How many years ago was that? The vicomte is a young man, while Renée has seen many more years. Did she inherit her Talent at such a late age? I suppose there are families that pass along their Talents only on their deathbeds. I can imagine only too easily what a full life of waiting must be like.

"Come on, then! Let's get back to the party." Renée squeezes my shoulders and hands me back the wineglass before heading out the door.

Back in the sitting room, the ladies all seem to have downed many more drinks in the time we were away—empty bottles litter the sideboards. I can now recognize some of their faces: a few patrons, ladies I've met in passing and can't name, a woman with a dazzling emerald necklace who I'm pretty sure is the founder of an athletic club I've read about in the paper. In one of the corners of the room, a group sits at a gambling table, hiding their wide grins behind cards while their gems glint with each new deal. Trying to guess all the Talents displayed here would be a thrilling game I'm sure I'd lose.

Renée breezes to Madame's side, planting a kiss on her flushed cheeks. With the dress she lent me, I fully fit in among the other women and their sparkling jewels. Yet I'm still like a weed among the flowers. They all came here to let themselves be free. To shake off the masks they wear every day of their lives. But I cannot shake mine. Not even for a second.

I down my glass of wine in one big gulp, weaving among the swaying bodies of the dancing ladies. The air around me is heavy; the bodies press in from all sides. I let their movement take me, my head somehow light and drowsy at the same time. With each minute, the music rings louder in my ears, and my heart beats faster. The sensation is intoxicating, dangerous. The women entangle together—arms wrapping around each other, hands finding their way under silk. My body tingles in a rush of longing.

Closing my eyes, Dahlia's perfect figure fills my mind, gliding through the sea of dancers, her gaze only for me. Her rousing jasmine perfume envelops me when she grabs my waist, her delicate fingers tracing my skin with a touch so gentle, yet commanding. I melt into her, not caring for the watchful eyes.

Then my eyelids snap open, and the illusion is shattered. I heave at the sudden ache in my chest. I need to sit down. Is it the wine? I've never drunk more than a few sips before. I'm heading toward the couch on the other side of the room, fighting the sudden wobble in my feet, when a voice grabs my attention.

"Why isn't Miss Garnier here?" a woman asks.

She's standing with three other ladies by one of the windows overlooking a circular terrace. I shake my head to focus as I step closer to them, trying to hear over the music.

"Oh, Josephine wouldn't dare show her face here," another lady, wearing all black, answers. "She knows better than to come to Madame's house."

"Oh?"

"Madame will have her head," the lady continues. "Rumor has it Renée and Josephine have some *history*."

My senses are tingling, yet their words cut through the haze in my head. Could this be the reason Madame warned me to keep my distance from Josephine? A lover's spat? Could this be the reason the gown I'm wearing has been hidden away, for its "sentimental value," all these years?

I try to inch closer but instead I crash into one of the dancing ladies.

"I'm so sorry!"

Her laugh is boisterous, as though she's had a few too many drinks, but her eyes still focus on me. "You're Lady Adley!" she says. "Can I have your autograph?"

I glance desperately at the group of women. I have no time for this. "I . . . don't have a pen," I say, my mind failing to come up with a better excuse.

"I've been longing to meet you since the gala!" The lady rushes on, pausing only to hiccup. "Your voice is just so beautiful, and you're even prettier in person! I wish I had such flowing hair—"

"I think I saw a pen in the kitchen," I say, cutting off her drunken rambling. "Should we go get it?"

Her face lights up and she turns to head for the kitchen, already talking again, but I don't follow after her. Who knew being famous could be so uncomfortable?

I need water. I need to focus. But all I see are more wineglasses.

"Santé!" someone calls, and the ladies cheer back.

I take a deep breath, struggling to keep my balance as I try to make my way back to the gossiping ladies. They're all giggling gleefully now. Nothing like romantic entanglements and complications to keep one entertained.

"—expanding her business." I catch only the end of the sentence. Are they still talking about Josephine? Did I miss it? "I was at her shop just last week and I heard her talking about it. She's opening another factory and has plans for overseas shipments. Can you imagine—the great *Mademoiselle Josephine Garnier* going international?"

"International?" one of the other women chimes in, cigar smoke coming out of her mouth.

All of a sudden, I'm nauseous. They *are* talking about Miss Garnier. About her business and her apparent upcoming expansion. Another factory. Like the one that stole all the business from Father.

"I will fix it, mon coeur!" Father's voice thuds in the back of my head. "I have a meeting with a new supplier. You will see, it'll all be alright. Just keep working on the beading on the bodice. We'll add a note on that later, together." He kissed my head before grabbing his coat and rushing out.

But he never fixed it, and we never got to add that final note to his book. How fitting that the last words Father ever said to me were a promise unfulfilled.

I don't even know if he ever made it to the supplier. Maybe the deal fell through . . . or maybe there never was a supplier to begin with. Maybe he just wanted an excuse to hide his drinking. They found his body the next day. He wouldn't have been driven to such desperate acts if it hadn't been for Josephine Garnier's exclusive deals with the suppliers. How many more Talented tailors is she trying to put out of business now? How many lives will be ruined when she's done?

Even while wearing yet another of her stunning gowns, I can't help but think Josephine doesn't deserve her success. At least, not at the expense of true artists like Father was.

I want to find out more—to go and ask the woman for details. But before I can do anything, the music falters.

"Someone crank the handle!" a woman calls.

A moment later a lively and invigorating cancan comes out of the phonograph. The high-spirited rhythm echoes all around, bringing the ladies to their feet.

I can't do anything as I'm swayed with their carefree dance, all thoughts and questions swallowed by the music.

CHAPTER EIGHTEEN

The Prettiest Flower

BY THE TIME I make it back to the estate, dawn is already painting the sky. I don't even ring for Pauline to help me undress. Instead, I flop onto the bed in exhaustion.

My eyelids droop, too heavy to stay open. Wine runs through my veins, its intoxicating effect now a soft lullaby.

I'm drifting into the realm of dreams when a tiny hand taps my back.

"Not now, Lirone," I mumble.

"Wake up, Cleo," he persists.

I groan as I force my eyes open, meeting his unblinking gaze. "What? Why are you here at this hour?"

"That's exactly my question for you." He shakes me by the shoulders, and I push myself up on my elbows.

"I went out," I say as a massive yawn overtakes me, distorting the words.

"I know that. My question is, why would you go out when you know we're meeting for a lesson, *and* you have a rehearsal in the morning?"

"Who are you, my mother?"

He glares at me. "This isn't a joke."

"I'm not laughing."

"This isn't about you," he shoots back at me, and even though he's whispering, there's anger in his voice. "It's about protecting Lady Sibille's investment."

"I'm not an investment."

"Business partner, whatever. It doesn't matter." Lirone shakes his head. "So where were you? Henry managed to follow you to that pianist's house, but he couldn't go in."

I sit up, trying to prevent myself from leaning into the soft pillows. "I was at Madame's. There was a party, and she invited me."

"A party . . . you skipped our lesson for *a party*?" He's so enraged he's shaking. "Mon Dieu! What am I supposed to tell Lady Sibille?"

Now fury starts bubbling in my chest, too. "That I need to keep up appearances. Ladies go to parties!"

"You're hopeless."

"Lirone, please." I cover another yawn with my hand. "I have to sleep. Can't we discuss this when I wake up?"

"We can." He presses his lips together tightly. "But I thought you'd like to know you have letters."

All my senses perk up at once and I hurry to my feet.

In the dawning light, Lirone pulls an envelope from his pocket.

Anaella.

I snatch the letter from him, tearing the envelope with haste before taking in my sister's familiar handwriting.

> *My Cleo,*
> *I'm sorry it took me so long to answer you. I tried to sit and write before, but each time the words refused to come.*
> *You just left . . . disappeared.*
> *And all of a sudden, this flood of letters.*
> *But you've given me no address, or a way to write to you on my own, or visit you.*

I don't know what it is you are doing to support me . . . But
Cleo, it's not worth it if it keeps you from home.
I miss you.

Your Ann

A lump blocks my throat, tears welling in my eyes. I expected her to be angry with me, to be hurt, but seeing the words on the wrinkled page sends a shock of sharp pain to my heart.

Could she be right? Could all of this not be worth it?

The image of our stuffy back room fills my head—the narrow beds, the creaking floors, the cloudy water, and the dusty shelves displaying only cheap fabrics after moths had eaten their way through Father's collection just last fall—a shadow of the home we used to have. At least now there is food in the house, and medical care. But would Anaella hate me if she knew the price? If she knew why I cannot see her? Shame and guilt grab me, threatening to squeeze the air out of my lungs.

"Cleo?" Lirone's voice pulls me back.

I lift my eyes from the page and notice he's holding a second envelope. This one is heavier, the paper expensive, with an elaborate, but broken, wax seal and delicate lettering forming my name.

"I said *letters*."

I wipe away a stray tear from my cheek. Who else could possibly be writing to me?

"Seems like you're not doing *everything* wrong after all." Lirone places the other envelope in my hand, a hint of a smirk on his lips. "It's from Vicomte Lenoir. He wants to take you out in two days."

Pauline follows close behind me as I step out of the carriage, glancing at the letter clenched in my hand one more time.

Dear Lady Adley,

I have an important meeting at the Jardin Botanique this Thursday.
I hope you might accompany me afterwards for a walk.

If you're agreeable, I shall expect you by the entrance to the
round greenhouse at 17:00.

Nuriel

The vicomte's handwriting is delicate, artistic in its curves. I circle his signature with the tip of my finger.

Nuriel.

He signed his first name. That must mean this is a courtship meeting. It has to be—he would have used his title if it were a simple social call.

I ignore the butterflies in my stomach as waves of nerves and excitement pass through me. It's all just a game. I need him to fall for me only so I can steal his Talent. But if that's the case, why is my heart racing at the thought of his closeness?

Shivering, I fold the letter and tuck it carefully into my purse beside Anaella's. The two sit next to one another innocently, just two sheets of paper. Yet one holds the chance for a future, and the other is a reminder of the reason I cannot let this chance pass me by.

Having my sister's reply has sparked a fire inside me—an urge to prove her wrong, to uphold my end of the bargain and grant us both the life of our dreams. A life where I can make sure Anaella never shivers at night or goes to bed with an empty stomach. Where I can make sure she is healthy, happy, maybe even fulfilled.

I close my purse and turn back to Pauline, my chaperone. Yes, I did go into the vicomte's carriage alone once, but this is a public outing—being seen alone together this way would be like poking a hornet's nest.

"How do I look?" I ask, smoothing out my dress.

The gown is made of light blue silk, with a sheer gold organza lining the off-the-shoulder collar and sleeves. But its real beauty lies in the skirt—rhinestone butterflies flutter upward from the hem, growing gradually smaller as if disappearing into the distance.

"As radiant as any flower in this garden, my lady."

Pauline smiles as we walk past the main gates. She seems happy to be outside and out of her maid's uniform. I wonder when, if ever, she last had a vacation. Being stuck on the estate, taking care of me—it's surely not the life she dreamed of. Her obvious pleasure today brings me joy.

I've never been to Lutèce's botanical gardens before, though I know they draw visitors from afar. I can definitely see why. Large trees line both sides of the main lane, throwing scattered shadows on the stone paths and keeping the air cool. The scent of freshly cut grass lingers in the air, mixing with the sweet aroma of the tidy flower beds. I take a deep breath, my ears ringing with the sounds of bees flying among the blooming buds as we follow the signs toward the greenhouse.

We stop by a majestic, perfectly round glass building. Wide stairs lead up to its entrance, and its polished walls sparkle in the sunlight, tinted by shades of blue, green, and turquoise from its metallic structure.

My pulse quickens. This is it.

But the vicomte is not by the entrance, and I cannot see him approaching from any of the paths.

"Don't worry, my lady," Pauline says. "I'm sure he'll be here."

I nod, my body rigid with tension. Am I early? Did he change his mind? Or worse . . . what if the letter is a fake? A cruel joke meant to embarrass me. I can imagine Véronique behind such a ruse. I glance around as though she might appear from behind a nearby tree, ready to laugh in my face.

Before my mind can spiral further, muffled voices drift from inside the greenhouse. I strain to hear. Their timbre is low, masculine, but the cadence is heated. It sounds like an argument.

In a split-second decision, I pull the glass door open and enter the building. A wave of humid heat and the potent aroma of saturated earth wash over me. Giant exotic trees reach all the way up to the tall ceiling, while wild bushes and vines spread below. Flowers the size of my palm bloom in silky whites and tangerine hues, their scent citrusy. It's as though I've stepped through a portal to a different world, a jungle.

The voices are stronger now, echoing under the tall ceiling as I move toward them, making my way between the massive plants.

"I'm telling you, this is exactly what you're looking for," a man says. A thrill of anticipation and relief grabs me when I recognize the vicomte's voice.

He is here.

"Yes, the plans look great on paper," another man says. "But I already told you, I need to meet the man myself."

"And *I* already told you, he is unable to travel. I'm here to represent him, and my word should be more than enough." Vicomte Lenoir's voice is sharp and commanding. It reminds me of the first time we met, when he barged in during my fitting at Miss Garnier's fashion house, brimming with anger. But something about it strikes me differently now, a sense of passion within the storm, alluring, like watching lightning in the night.

"My lord, I didn't mean—"

"You deal with me, or you find someone else. But I promise you, you won't find anyone better."

They are just around a corner now. I lean past the bushes blocking my view and take in the scene. A delicate round table is set among the greenery, with an endless array of sketches covering every bare inch. Immediately I'm taken back home, to Anaella's designs spilling everywhere in our room. But these aren't fashion designs I'm looking at. These are buildings.

Vicomte Lenoir leans over the desk with his jacket draped over his shoulder. His tie is off and his white shirt is unbuttoned at the collar, revealing a glimpse of his toned chest. He brushes a hand through his hair, causing the strands to fall in damp tendrils, like ivy after a summer rain. It gives him a careless look, wild, like a man who has just emerged from a night of unbridled passion. A flush of heat spreads within me and my hands turn clammy, though it could simply be the fault of the humid greenhouse.

Next to him, an older gentleman with glasses inspects the sketches, his face a hard mask.

I take another step forward, and a fallen twig crunches under my heel. The two men turn to me immediately.

"Lady Adley." The vicomte straightens.

"Sorry to interrupt, my lord," I say, my voice somehow richer, as though the humidity adds another velvety layer to it. "I was waiting outside and didn't see you."

"Were you?" He checks the time on his gold pocket watch. "The day did run away from me. I apologize."

"I didn't know you had another engagement, my lord," the other man says. "We can pick this up another time."

The vicomte rolls up one of the large sketches and holds it out. "Take this, to consider in the meantime."

"Oh. No . . . no need, my lord. I will see it the next time we meet." He bobs his head, taking a few steps back. "My lady," he mutters to me before walking away.

The vicomte's grip on the sketch is so tight I fear the paper will tear. I've never seen him so anxious, so constrained, lines of frustration creasing his brow. This is definitely not the mood I imagined for our meeting. I shift from one foot to the other, not sure if I should speak. Does he regret inviting me?

"My lady." Pauline's voice reaches me as she emerges from behind a large bush. "I thought I'd lost you. I didn't even realize you'd stepped inside—" She freezes when she notices the vicomte and falls silent at once.

"You've brought a chaperone?" The vicomte raises an eyebrow, but finally loosens his grip on the paper.

I release a pent-up breath. "This is my lady's maid, Pauline LaRue."

He nods in acknowledgment before turning to the table and beginning to stack the papers. I exchange a quick glance with Pauline, her smile soothing my nerves. She tilts her chin subtly forward, silently encouraging me to make the first move. I never thought of her as bold, but her reassurance fills me with confidence. I take a step closer to the vicomte while Pauline draws back, giving us a little privacy.

Standing next to him, I examine the sketches. The architecture is exquisite: stunning glass structures between Neo-Baroque pavilions, massive columns supporting iron frames, winding staircases, and large glass domes. These buildings would be the jewels of any city.

"They are breathtaking," I say, running my hands over the lines of a beautiful stone structure that could easily function as a gallery.

The vicomte stops stacking the pages and turns to look at the sketch I'm holding. "It's one of my favorites."

"Who made them?"

"A friend. I came to show his designs to the manager. They're looking for an architect to build a new greenhouse." He pauses, his hand hovering over a large, rolled sketch, as if unsure whether to proceed. Then he relents, slowly spreading the sketch on the table, his movements tentative and careful. So unlike his usual sure self. "This is the one he planned."

I take a step closer to him—that same bay rum cologne of his blending seamlessly with the natural scents of the greenhouse, spicy and earthy notes mingling to create a complex aroma that is both refreshing and invigorating. But I cannot allow it to cloud my mind. Not when the vicomte is finally opening up to me. I force myself to take shallow breaths, trying to focus.

The building in the sketch looks massive, constructed from separate components that weave together into a shape resembling a star. Elaborate spiral staircases are sketched at the pointed edge of each of the five main halls. I follow the straight lines, trying to imagine the space in my head— climbing the stairs, walking along the hanging bridge, gazing down at the plants from above. Like a miniature glass city.

"Each area will feature different types of plants from separate regions," he explains.

"That's genius," I say. "But . . . the manager didn't like it?"

"He liked the designs." There's anger again in his tone, that fiery energy that marks true conviction. "What he didn't like is the fact that my friend isn't here. He wants confirmation of the power of the gem involved. As if anyone without a magnificent Talent could have designed these."

How very elitist. Though I'm not surprised. This is how high society functions, after all: a Talent means status, and there is nothing more important than that. Taking on an unknown architect would be like expecting Véronique to suddenly buy her dresses from a modiste without a renowned Talent to precede her—absolutely ridiculous.

The vicomte snatches up the sketches again and places them in a wide satchel before hanging it over his shoulder, his jacket now carried in his hand. "But enough about business. You didn't dress up for that."

There is that teasing voice again, that twinkle in his electrifying eyes that catches my breath. But it isn't arrogance I see on his face. It's confidence, and the urge to challenge me. It's as though every interaction he conducts is a part of an elaborate game, a test to see who will figure out the rules.

But I'm also playing a game—one in which he's not in charge.

"I'm not exactly sure myself what I dressed up for, my lord." I twirl a loose curl around my finger.

"Considering you've brought a chaperone, I believe you had a pretty good idea."

As much as I try to hide it, a smile tugs at my lips. He *is* courting me. And maybe . . . he likes what he sees. Somewhere in the back of my mind, I remind myself that this is all part of the plan. That he is a rich, entitled man I'm about to rob blind. That I should care nothing about him. Especially not whether he might happen to fancy me. But when his gleaming eyes meet mine, my knees turn weak, and a strange flutter brims in my chest. His voice, his scent, his teasing smirk—they all make me forget why I'm here. Or maybe it's the danger of it all, the thrill of the unknown, the need to figure out the puzzle he presents.

I break my gaze, staying in control as I walk farther into the greenhouse. "Won't your fiancée mind?" I ask as he follows me, matching my tone to his light banter.

"Fiancée?"

"Lady Véronique Battu? Aren't you two practically engaged?"

The vicomte snorts. "Hardly."

"Oh?" I try to keep my face clear, but I can't help the sense of elation spreading through me.

He lifts a giant leaf with the back of his hand, allowing me to pass under it first—a perfect gentleman. "Our families have history. I won't deny that my parents would appreciate the match. But expectations and reality are two very different things."

"Like for your friend the architect? You expected today to go differently."

He is quiet as he wipes a drop of sweat from his forehead.

"You seem to care about him dearly," I continue. "I believe I saw you carrying his sketches a few days ago at the opera house."

"I care for all things touched by passion," he says, staring right ahead.

I follow his gaze to an indoor stream leading to a round pond with swaying lilies. A painter sits by the water, gently stroking a canvas with his brush. On his finger rests an onyx ring, pulsing lightly as he works.

"Nothing is more passionate than a Talent," I say.

But the vicomte shakes his head. "It isn't magic that made this man fall in love with art. Look at his face."

My brow creases, but I do as he says, studying the man. There is a serenity to him. His eyes are tender, filled with adoration, a gentle smile playing upon his lips, growing with each stroke of color. He appears as a man consumed by love, lost in the beauty of his creation.

"Since I know you carry a diary, I can imagine you are an ardent woman." The vicomte's voice is low, inviting. "What are you passionate about, Cleodora?"

Just like that, he uses my first name. So casually, as if we are the oldest of friends. A part of me startles at his rudeness, my instinct to bite back at him kicking in, and yet the sensation of closeness is not unpleasant—as though a barrier between us just broke.

He is staring at me, waiting, testing. This question matters to him.

"I . . . love fashion." The words come out as a surprise even to myself.

"Ah, is that what you write about? That must be why you discerned the issue with my sleeves back at Josephine's shop." He turns to smell a round flower, its blue buds resembling the shade of my dress. "Do you have much knowledge of sewing?"

I open and close my mouth like a broken doll. Why did I have to speak? How could I be so foolish as to let his stupid charms bring my guard down? Telling him the truth is out of the question. No one can know about Father. About his book. About my memories from our dress shop. About the endless rows of fabrics that used to call to me as if longing to become art.

I turn away and step onto the curved bridge to the other side of the stream, the water bubbling softly below. "I dabble, my lord."

"Nuriel," he says, grabbing my arm. An electrifying shock passes through me, a tingling sensation somewhere between pleasure and pain. I need to break away from his hold, to detach myself from him, but I'm frozen. "Call me Nuriel."

"Nuriel . . ." I repeat after him as if entranced. "I . . . I do love singing."

"I'm sure you do."

"This ruby has been a blessing for me, that's why I always wear it." I'm not sure if I'm trying to convince him or myself. "Don't you feel the same about yours?"

"In my family, we wear our Talents only on special occasions: a new hospital wing initiation, a premier night." He waves his hand to dismiss it. "It's best this way."

"How so?"

"It's a heavy burden, is it not?" he answers with a sigh. "Carrying generations of expectations within your blood." He grows silent for a moment before taking another step closer to me.

I can feel the heat radiating from his body, the salty scent of sweat and the sweetness of his cologne. Now that I've finally got him to talk about his Talent, I need to push further, to learn more. But my heart quickens like a bird flapping its wings in a cage. I ache for his closeness, his touch, to press his body close to mine. Panic prickles up the back of my neck, overwhelming and sudden. This is supposed to be a game. I'm supposed to be in control. I'm not supposed to feel this way.

Not with *him*.

"Cleo . . ." He leans in, and I stumble backward.

But my heel doesn't meet the ground. I let out a yelp as my arms flail, trying to regain my balance. My hand reaches for the rail but swipes only air. I tip toward the flowing stream when the vicomte grabs me. His strong, sure arms yank me forward, pulling me to safety. But just as I find my footing, he loses his.

Everything slows as my hand wraps around his wrist, ready to pull him back to solid ground. Then the stones down below catch my eye, their sharp edges like the claws of a hungry beast. And for an instant I'm transfixed, the image of the water turning crimson playing with my mind.

I can almost hear Dahlia's soft whisper in my ear, "*Let go.*"

Why am I even hesitating? Why do I want to keep him safe?

But his weight is too heavy, and my hands are drenched in sweat. I feel my grip slipping. And before I can do anything else, he falls right over the unusually low railing, tumbling down into the water with a crash.

A woman screams, and I turn to see Pauline staring in wide-eyed horror. I had forgotten she was here, following and watching from afar.

Cold spreads inside me as the vicomte reemerges, blood staining his white shirt.

What have I done?

"Pauline! Call for help!" I shout, and then she's running.

I grab onto Nuriel's arm, trying to pull him out of the water. He pants and curses—a stream of profanity not appropriate for any lady's ears. But I cannot blame him.

A large rip on his arm reveals a nasty bleeding cut.

From the corner of my eye, I see the painter leaving. So much for basic decency.

"Merde," Nuriel spits, finally lying back on solid ground. Even his jacket is a casualty, now a heap of soaking reddish wool. His hair is dripping wet, his white shirt all but see-through and sticking tightly to his body, revealing firm muscles I didn't know existed.

I force myself to stop gaping as I crouch by his side. "Are you alright?" The stupid, yet expected question leaves my lips.

"What do you think?" He winces as I reach for his wound.

The cut is deep, gushing blood that trickles down his arm as if tracing his veins from the outside. My stomach twists but I ignore it, grabbing my purse in search of a clean cloth.

"We need to clean it," I say.

Bandages would be better, but all I have is a white handkerchief. I bring the fabric to his wound, my fingers hovering uncertainly for a moment before pressing down to stop the bleeding.

He sits up with a groan, pushing his wet hair out of his eyes. "Thank you," he says.

"Don't thank me. It's my fault." More than he knows.

"Could've happened to anyone." He rubs his head, wincing.

I reach out with my other arm, still not letting go of the cloth, and his hand intercepts mine when it grazes his forehead. A tremor runs over my skin. I freeze, breath catching in my throat as his thumb circles my palm. His face is so close I can trace every flawless line, from the curve of his jaw to the arch of his eyebrows. He's like a sculpture of a god, a work of art. He's too handsome to be real.

His striking green eyes stare right into mine. From this distance, I can see they are speckled with flecks of golden honey. It gives them a warmth I've never noticed before, as if daring me to observe the man behind the smug, perfect mask.

"Cleodora." He draws out my name, his voice husky.

He reaches for my cheek, cool drops of water tracing a path from where his fingers meet my skin down to my neck. My heart races at how close we are, how intimate this moment has become. A part of me tries to rebel, to resist, but his touch is a magnet, drawing me in despite my better judgment. My lips part ever so slightly, my breathing becoming shallow.

I feel myself leaning in just when the sound of hastening footsteps startles me.

"My lady!" Pauline is by my side, two young men following her.

They rush to the vicomte, pulling him up from under his arms. "Lean on me, my lord," one of them says. "We'll get you to the doctor."

"Well, Lady Adley, I'm afraid we'll have to cut our meeting short." The vicomte adopts a formal tone. "Until next time."

"My lord." My legs tremble as I shuffle to my feet and curtsy.

Then the men carry him away, and I'm left alone with Pauline, and a handkerchief utterly soaked with *blood*.

CHAPTER NINETEEN

Bathing in the Moonlight

I HAVE HIS BLOOD.

The wheels of the carriage turn under me as I clench the purse resting in my lap. The drenched bloody handkerchief is stuffed safely within it, weighing like a pile of rocks.

I should be happy.

After all, this was the goal—acquiring the vicomte's blood is the first step to stealing his Talent.

Dahlia will be pleased. I can only imagine how she'll reward me . . . And success means I'll get to see my sister. To have her live with me, far away from the arms of poverty.

So why do I feel like throwing up?

I'm not supposed to care about Nuriel. He's supposed to be my "perfect target"—the one I won't lose sleep over. Yet I cannot deny the exhilaration that passed through me at our touch, or the way my heart flutters every time I meet his speckled emerald eyes. There is something challenging about him, and yet . . . safe.

In our relationship, *I'm* the dangerous one.

"It wasn't your fault, my lady." Pauline touches my shoulder, pulling me out of my thoughts. "I'm certain Vicomte Lenoir will ask you out again. I think he likes you."

I can't even fake a smile this time. "I would rather he didn't."

"My lady? You seemed to be getting along so well. Did he say anything to upset you?"

"No . . ."

"You must be exhausted, my lady. Too much excitement for one day."

I nod, my head pounding.

The carriage finally stops at my estate, and soon I pass through the gates and up the wide stairs to the entrance. The door is already open, but I pay it no mind. The head butler must have heard us arriving, though he's not waiting in the foyer. Strange.

I take my hat off and hand it to Pauline, but when she reaches for my purse I clutch it tightly. I have far too many reasons to not let it out of my sight.

"Leave it," I order, my voice sharper than intended.

She drops to a curtsy, her fiery-red braids falling on her shoulders. "Sorry, my lady."

The bitter taste of guilt fills my mouth. None of this is her fault.

I turn to apologize for snapping at her when a loud crash echoes from the next room.

Startled, we both sprint to the main sitting area and burst through the double doors. Shards of glass cover the needlework carpet, while the main table lies on its side, toppled over, with one of its legs missing.

"Mon Dieu . . ." Pauline mutters. "What happened here?"

I take a step inside just as a dark shadow emerges from the corner of the room, holding the missing table leg. "I was waaaiting for you," he slurs.

A chill runs down my spine.

"Basset?"

The coachman I fired stumbles forward, and the stench of cheap whiskey assaults me. This time he truly is drunk. A messy beard covers his face, his hair unevenly cut. There are tears in his coat and on his pants. Unemployment has not been kind to him. He sways as if struggling to keep his balance before throwing the wooden leg aside, grabbing a vase from a shelf and smashing it on the floor.

Pauline screams, covering her ears.

He takes another wobbling step. But I cannot bring myself to run. I am utterly frozen in horror.

"I . . . kn-know your secret." He hiccups before bursting into a frightening laugh.

My blood runs cold. My secret? But he already knew my secret. That's why I had to get rid of him. "Basset, please." I raise my arms in surrender.

"Don't move!" he yells. "You—you did this to me, to keep your seeecret hidden."

"I don't know what you're talking about—"

"SHUT UP!" He grabs one of the large chairs and flings it across the room. It crashes against the wall, breaking apart from the sheer force of impact.

Pauline shrieks again and grabs my arm to drag me out of the room. When I don't move, she dashes out herself, yelling for help.

The coachman doesn't pay her any mind. "You-you ruined my life. I was a good man. An honest m-man. All I wanted was to provide for my family. For m-my sister." He is choking on his tears. "But I know your secret now. Just like I was promised—" He hiccups again. "And now I will ruuuin you."

His words make no sense. His sister? His family? He knows my secret *now*? But it can't be . . . He was on to me from the beginning. He saw me from before. He was searching my room.

"Basset . . ." I draw out his name slowly, too scared to make any sudden movement. "What were you doing in my room the day after the gala?"

He halts for a second, his eyes squeezing as if to clear the fog of alcohol. "Your . . . your room? P-Pauline had a headache. She . . . sent me to find a torn blouse. To mend it."

I let out a short burst of air. It can't be. But with so much alcohol in his body, I doubt he's even capable of lying. Which can mean only one thing . . .

He is innocent.

I ruined his life, tore it to shreds and cast him aside, made him into a laughingstock—a condemned man. All for nothing. I made him into a monster. And now he will take me down.

I deserve it.

"And m-my poor s-sister . . . they need a doctor to come to the farm." He sobs, and my heart writhes in pain. His family are farmers, hard workers who probably never had enough luck to hone a magical Talent. Everything he shared with me was true; he only came to the city to help them. And I took everything from him.

He is not the monster. I am.

"I . . . I can help you. I will help your family."

But the coachman shakes his head. "Sh-she was right about you."

She? Does he mean Pauline?

He advances again, now only inches from me, his boots smashing the glass under his feet. "*Cleodora Finley*." He spits my true name in my face, and a stab of shock pierces my heart.

That's when two officers burst through the open doors. "Stop right there!" one of them yells as they yank the coachman away.

He curses and kicks in the air, his words a nonsensical mess as he fights against the restraining men, hitting one of them in the gut. "She will get you!" he manages to scream before the second officer hits his head and he goes limp.

"My lady!" Pauline shakes me. "I can't believe it . . . Mr. Basset was always such a gentleman. Are you alright? Did he hurt you?"

I shake my head, unable to speak.

I did this.

This is my fault.

One of the officers puts shackles on the coachman's hands, while the other turns to me. "My lady, you're safe now."

I force my eyes from the coachman's unconscious body and look at the officer. A shout nearly escapes me when I recognize his face. This isn't an officer staring at me. It's Henry, one of Dahlia's henchmen, wearing an official police uniform.

"You are very lucky we were patrolling the area," he says. "We heard your maid shouting and ran right over."

He means they were right outside watching me, but all I can do is nod, keeping up the facade. "Thank you, officer."

"I'll need you to come to the police station to make a statement," he says, staring at me without blinking.

Translation: Dahlia is waiting for me.

"No!" Pauline snaps, an unusual harshness in her tone. "I mean, surely this can wait until morning." Her face is a cold mask, eyes wide and unblinking as she stares at the coachman.

"It's alright, Pauline. It's over, nothing to be afraid of." I try to soothe her. "I should go with them. Better to get this over with."

"I'll come with you, my lady," she says, finally tearing her gaze from the horrific scene.

"No need. I will accompany the lady myself to the station and back," Henry says. "Edmund, take this man to the carriage."

The other henchman flings Basset over his shoulders as if he were nothing more than a broken mannequin. I cringe. The poor man doesn't deserve this.

"My lady, please follow me," Henry says.

We step into the cool evening air, where a black carriage already waits. Edmund shoves the coachman in the back before offering me his hand to follow. I hesitate for just a second before taking it. He climbs in after me and shuts the door. Then we are moving.

The coachman's head flops from side to side with the rocking of the carriage. I swallow as Edmund shoves his unconscious body into a corner so his head won't hit his shoulder.

"Be gentle with him," I utter.

Edmund doesn't even glance my way.

"Where are we going?"

Again, no reply.

My teeth chatter and I clench my jaw in an attempt to control the tremors.

Edmund makes sure to keep the shutters closed the entire ride, not saying a single word. At least this time they didn't cover my head. After what feels like an eternity, we come to a stop.

My heart hammers as the door opens. "Out," Henry orders, waiting for me to join him outside.

"What about Basset?" I ask.

"None of your concern anymore."

My eyes jump between the coachman and Edmund's cold stare—the bulging muscles in his arms, the tension in his jaw. A sickening sensation overtakes me. I don't want to leave this innocent man with him. Even if he wishes me harm.

"Lady Sibille doesn't like waiting." Henry repeats the words I've heard from Lirone before.

I have no choice. I guess I never had a choice. Not after I pledged myself to Dahlia. My thoughts are in turmoil, one following the other in an incoherent jumble. I tighten my grip on my purse, still clutched close to my chest. The bloody handkerchief inside it is yet another proof of how low I have sunk.

Yet it's too late to turn back.

"I'm so sorry," I whisper, though I know the coachman can't hear me.

Taking a shaky breath, I step out of the carriage. We are standing in a dark street with no lampposts in sight. The building before us is short, with two sculptures of lions' heads mounted above its wide doors. There are some letters painted between them, but in the darkness I cannot make them out.

Henry grabs my arm, pulling me inside as the sound of trotting horses echoes behind me—the coachman is being taken toward his fate.

But I cannot allow myself to think about that. I wince at the strength of Henry's grip, but he doesn't let go.

Candles light the wide entrance area, revealing a vivid mosaic floor and a colorful array of silk, cushioned alcoves right within the walls. A fountain sits at the center, its water covered with rose petals. Henry drags me toward a side corridor, forcing me through an open doorway.

The aroma of purifying oils envelops me as soon as we walk inside—a fresh mixture of rosemary, lemongrass, lavender, and what I'm pretty sure is myrtle. I blink in surprise at the imposing columns standing all around a large rectangular pool, each one linked to the next by a perfect archway. Above, the ceiling is lined with carved stars inlaid with gold. Hot steam rises from the water, as blue as a summer sky.

And right there, within the fog, is Dahlia, her body submerged in the water, which reaches just below her clavicle. Her raven hair is free of its usual tight bun, cascading in tousled waves around her, while her cheeks are flushed from the heat. The gentle sound of rippling water surrounds her, adding to the peaceful aura that emanates from her serene form.

"Leave us," she orders, and Henry obeys. "Cleodora . . ." She spreads her arms over the cold marble edge of the pool. "What an unfortunate sight."

Her words stab me like a knife to the gut. "Dahlia, I—"

"I thought I made myself very clear the first time we met," she says, circling the surface of the water with one finger. "I work only with people I trust. You broke my trust."

I want to explain to her what happened. To defend myself. To tell her none of this is my fault. But my voice is stuck in my throat. I cannot lie to her.

"What a mess you created," she continues. "If only you had come to me before, all of this could have been avoided."

"I wanted to, but Lirone and I—"

"Tsk, tsk, tsk." She hushes me. "I haven't given you permission to speak yet."

I watch in silence as she swims toward me. Even through the water, I can see she's naked, ripples caressing every soft curve of her bare body. Heat courses to my cheeks despite myself, luckily masked by the rising steam.

"So, let's see if I understand it all," she muses. "The man who broke into your estate is the same coachman you fired a few weeks ago. The one you told me was a drunkard. But in truth, you fired him because you believed he knew your secret. And now he does."

None of these are questions. She isn't looking for information; all she wants is to show me that she already has it. That I can't hide.

"You lied to me—abused my trust." She barely whispers it, yet somehow it's worse than if she'd shouted at me. "This wasn't supposed to go this way. I had hoped . . ." There is disappointment in her tone, a glint of pain in her eyes that makes me want to reach out to her. But before I can make a move, she shakes her head. "Now I'm in a difficult position, Cleo. I don't like to be in difficult positions." She dips her head backwards, letting her hair fall back into the hot water. It swirls around her like a black halo of shadowy tendrils. A moment later, she sighs. "You are special, my lovely one . . . I truly did want it to be different, but I believe we must part ways."

I gasp as though she has just ripped my heart out of my chest with her bare hands. No. She cannot leave me. I need her. I need my Talent. I need to help my sister.

"It pains me more than I expected it to. But I can no longer trust you. You have failed me," she says, her voice soft, tinged with sadness. "I will have to find someone else to get Vicomte Lenoir's Talent."

"But I have his blood!" The words spill out of my mouth.

She pauses, her brow lifting ever so slightly before a delicate smile dances on her lips. With a graceful move, she stands, walking toward me without shame or modesty as droplets glisten over her naked body. My eyes travel from her face to her collarbone, then down . . .

"You have his blood," she repeats after me.

I nod, hands shaking as I dig into my purse and pull out the hand-kerchief, the fabric still wet, leaving red marks on my fingers. Her eyes light up at the sight of the crimson cloth.

"Oh, my Cleo . . . how happy you've made me!" She claps her hands and Henry marches inside, not even blinking at her naked form stand-ing before him. "Henry, dear, store the blood sample properly so it doesn't dry. Our client will need it for the transfer ceremony."

Henry takes the handkerchief from me, his rough hands gentler than I thought possible. For just a second, a pang of guilt stabs me at the betrayal of the vicomte. Though my treachery already happened the moment I hesitated to pull him to safety—in truth, it began the very first moment I smiled at him. He trusted me, opened up to me. He is not who I thought he was; there is so much more hiding behind his arrogant mask. But I cannot allow myself to think like that. I push the thoughts out of my mind. This is all worth it.

"Oh, and Henry," Dahlia calls. "Please bring in the gift I saved for Cleodora."

He bows once before heading out the door.

"Gift?" I mumble. "Does . . . does that mean you forgive me?"

"Almost." Her wet hand caresses my cheek. "It means you've earned another chance. But you must never abuse my trust again. Do you understand?"

"Y-yes. I promise," I stutter. "I will deliver Nuri—Vicomte Lenoir's Talent to you."

Dahlia freezes for the slightest moment, her dark eyes searching mine. Can she see my reservations? The emotions I'm trying to hide? The new connection with Nuriel feels like a direct betrayal of her.

"Yes . . ." She draws out the word. "Focus on staying close to *the vicomte*. The time to steal his gem is almost here. I need you to be ready." She flashes a dazzling smile that makes my heart skip a beat. She takes my hand, her soft skin warm, inviting. "And Cleo, don't you worry about the coachman anymore." She squeezes my palm. "I promise he will no longer be a threat to you."

The meaning of her words is both comforting and frightening. But with her looking at me this way, I'm not sure I care.

Henry's heavy boots announce his return. "As you requested, Lady Sibille," he says.

Dahlia doesn't even look at him, stretching out her hand without breaking her gaze at me. "Thank you, Henry, dear. Now, leave us."

I barely notice as he walks out again, every bit of me focused on Dahlia and the coat now resting in her hands. It's the same coat she's worn every time we've met—on our midnight stroll, in the restaurant . . . Her fingers run over the monochromatic fabric, tracing the lines of black chenille along the collar. Once again, I'm struck by a sense of familiarity I cannot place.

"Do you recognize it?" Dahlia asks, wrapping it around her naked body, the fabric soaking up the remaining droplets.

"I saw you wear it."

She tilts her head before pushing a lock of wet hair from her face and tucking it behind her ear. "Is that all? Maybe you should look in that book you carry."

Father's book?

I stare again at the coat, now hiding her perfect body from my eyes. The seamless mix of silk and velvet, the play in the textures, the elegance of the cut, and those black lilies . . . I have seen those black lilies before.

I dig into my purse at once, pulling out the book and flipping through it with trembling hands. The countless notes, the designs, the patterns all mix on the page, hard to read through the haze of fog. But the drawing of the lilies is unmistakable. I freeze as I stare at the page, the memory flooding my mind.

A bolt of fabric on the top shelf.

The scent of dried lavender keeping the store refreshed.

Father standing up on a chair while a five- or six-year-old me holds it for balance.

"Aha!" he exclaimed. "Mon coeur, this is it! Our next masterpiece!"

"But Papa, won't the fabric be too heavy? The stitches might not hold."

"No, mon coeur." Father laughed and patted my head. "A good tailor must trust the designer." He leaned in to kiss Mother and toddler Anaella, who was propped up in her arms. "Our job is to make sure her vision comes to life, to help it manifest into the world. Finding the way to work with the material is a part of the art."

Dahlia's long finger wipes away the tears from my eyes. "You remember."

"It . . . it's my father's."

"One of his earlier creations," she says, taking the book from my hand and storing it back safely inside my purse. "I acquired it when you and I decided to work together. I want you to have it."

My gaze snaps up to her face, to her beautiful doe eyes and thick eyelashes. Innocent as they may seem, there's so much hidden behind them. Too many secrets to count—her past, her motivations . . . her magic. But at this moment I can see right through them, to the woman behind it all, to the Dahlia who is not a criminal working in the shadows. She is the Dahlia I ache for most . . . her pain, her tenderness, her excitement . . . her lust.

Without a word, she takes off the coat, revealing once again her smooth porcelain skin. "You should try it on."

I take it from her, savoring the soft fabric in my hands.

"Your dress is in the way." Dahlia smiles before spinning me on the spot. "May I?" she whispers in my ear, and I nod.

My heart picks up as her hands run along my back, untying the bodice. Goosebumps rise on my arms at the touch of her fingers against my skin. When she's finished, my dress falls to the ground. But she's not done. My undergarments soon follow, silk brushing my thighs as they drop to the floor.

A shiver passes through me as Dahlia's eyes move up and down my length. Compared to her, I'm no more than ordinary. I lower my head, a wave of insecurity passing through me. Yet when Dahlia's hand lifts my chin, her gaze searching mine, I'm struck by the pure admiration written on her face—as though I am the most beautiful woman in the world. She bites her bottom lip as she takes the coat from my hands and drapes it over my bare body. It wraps around me like a cloud—soft and caressing.

"It suits you," Dahlia purrs.

My heart has climbed out of my rib cage all the way up my throat. "I—I'm sure it looks better on you."

Then she's pressing her lips to mine, her arms wrapping around me as the coat falls to the marble floor, forgotten as our bodies entwine in a frenzy of desire. Her touch is electric; every nerve in my body is burning against her skin. She is a drug, intoxicating me with every light stroke, every gentle pull on my hair, every brush of her lips, every soft bite.

I lean into her, my hands searching the curves of her body with ravenous hunger I doubt I could ever quench. Her kisses flow down my neck, her warm breath making me shiver as her nails dig into my back, the hint of pain turning into a symphony of pleasure that sends me spiraling.

She is danger incarnate, her impure ways a vortex of thrill and peril that has already damaged me beyond repair. Two monsters forged by struggle, claimed by unruly passion.

Her long fingers graze my inner thigh, trailing upwards. A broken sigh escapes me, and I shudder as electrifying currents light me from within, begging her to move her hand higher.

Instead, she bites my bottom lip, so softly it's merely a taunting brush. Her breathing is heavy as she pulls away, and my chest heaves, aching for her. The rising steam circles around us in a frenzy that echoes the turmoil within me. Pushing my hair away from my face, she smiles, her dark eyes meeting mine. She doesn't say anything, but a question dances in her gaze, a slight tremble of hesitation in her bottom lip. She won't go further without my consent.

Dahlia is every bit the seductress I feared her to be from the first time we met—the beast stalking its prey, her softness the perfect trap leading to an endless abyss. But just another second of her love is worth delving into the darkest void.

I want her more than I've ever wanted anything. The craving in my body lingers on the verge of pain. "Please . . . " My voice is but a broken rasp.

Her nails dig into my thigh, bringing a surge of divine pain that draws a moan from my lips. She grants me one of her dazzling smiles. Then her hand moves higher, circling, teasing.

"Say it," she whispers in my ear.

"What?" I pant.

Dahlia nibbles my earlobe gently, sending another wave of goose-bumps through me before repeating, "Say it."

And when the words leave my lips, I know there is no going back. "I need you."

She obliges.

I gasp as her fingers slip the missing inches upwards. Pressed together, we move in a steady rhythm, like waves in a sea of desire. I feel a sense of wonder at how perfectly we fit. As if we were made just for this, to fall into one another.

My body starts to tremble, my knees weakening as Dahlia pushes my back against the wall, the cool stone against my skin reviving my senses. I cling closer to her, utterly entrapped in a slow, sensual dance.

My moans echo around us, the watery depths turning them into a chorus of passion. Ripples of energy pass through me, growing, shift-ing, multiplying. The tension in my body is almost unbearable. My back is arching, my toes curling, my heart soaring. And just when I think I might burst, a wave of pleasure takes me with the most euphoric release.

Dahlia's lips find mine. Her hand moves to the small of my back, its confident touch pulling me irresistibly closer. "How beautiful you are," she whispers in between kisses, her voice a soft melody. "My lovely Cleo . . . promise you are mine."

I'm not even sure why she's asking. How could I possibly be anything but hers?

"Only yours," I say.

With another low moan, I give myself to her as she draws me into the steaming pool.

CHAPTER TWENTY

Ruffling Feathers

THE DRIPPING CANDLES cast a glow over my painted face as I stare into the mirror of my private dressing room, awaiting the afternoon's rehearsal. My finger hovers over the circle of blush on my cheek, tracing my jawline and down to my collarbone, following the same route Dahlia's kisses marked last night.

My body tingles at the memory of her—her smell, her touch, the taste of her lips against mine. She is not pure, but neither am I—our twisted spirits wrapped together in sweet darkness. There is no going back now. Her siren call has lured me in too deep, and I can't find a bone in my body that still wishes to fight.

I used to imagine what it would be like to surrender entirely to passion, to follow lust. What I wasn't prepared for was the vulnerability— the level of intimacy. Simply sharing a kiss with Dahlia was enough to entrance me. Giving myself to her fully did far more than that. It entwined more than just our bodies—it linked my heart to hers. It shifted my fate and etched something new into my soul.

I'm not really sure what this sensation is, but even my own reflection seems different today: stronger, confident, mature. As though with Dahlia's touch I turned into a woman.

My chest puffs out a bit at the realization, the blush on my cheeks deepening.

Not only has Dahlia granted me a life of power—she has made me worthy of it. She has set me aflame. There is nothing I wouldn't do to keep that fire burning. Stealing the vicomte's Talent is a small price to pay for that.

I smile into the mirror, at the perfect lady Dahlia has created—rich, respected, adored. Someone with a Talent that can leave a mark on the world. On my finger, the ruby sparkles as if the magic inside it is becoming impatient, waiting for the coming rehearsal—a full run-through with the orchestra, going over the entire opera from start to finish.

Standing up, I accidentally shove my purse and its contents spill onto the floor. My stomach clenches at the sight of Father's book, its pages crumpling. I quickly reach for it, then freeze.

Anaella's letter is peeking from under it, staring at me in defiance, as if each word is ready to put me on trial.

The wrinkled page feels heavier than it should as I pick it up and read over the last words in my sister's note.

> But Cleo, it's not worth it if it keeps you from home.
> I miss you.

> Your Ann

"I miss you too," I say to my empty dressing room.

She's wrong, though. After last night, I have no doubt about that. Dahlia will keep her promise. She cares for me, and I will not let her down. And once I succeed, my sister and I will reunite.

Soon Anaella will have her share of luxuries. We will throw grand parties together, and her laughter will ring all the way through our estate halls and out to our blossoming garden. I can already imagine us sitting on a bench, sharing all our secrets as we did when we were children. Once Anaella is by my side, I will no longer have to hide anything from her . . . though the thought of telling her of last night makes my cheeks burn.

Maybe one day she could even meet Dahlia. I never imagined introducing my young innocent sister to a shadowy mob-woman, but Dahlia is so much more than that. I know all my sister cares about is my happiness. Once she sees all the good Dahlia has done for me, *for us*, she will support me.

This will be the beginning of a different life for Anaella and me—a life I'm already a part of and have no intention of letting go. Anaella will understand, once I can explain it to her.

It *is* worth it.

I stuff my sister's letter inside Father's book, placing it gently back in my purse—the weight of it a reminder that every note I sing is bringing me one step closer to our reunion.

"It will be worth it," I repeat, just before the doors of my dressing room shoot open and bang into the wall. The sheer force rattles the dresser, knocking over a vase full of flowers; the porcelain cracks as it hits the floor, water spilling and soaking the carpet.

"Comment osez-vous!" Véronique strides into the room, stepping right over the scattered roses. "Mother was right about you Adleys. You have no shame, do you?"

Her mother? What is she even talking about?

"Don't act like an innocent maiden." Véronique advances on me, shoving a newspaper in my face. "We both know you did this just to antagonize me. You don't even like him."

I gape at the headline staring at me from the gossip column.

Vicomte Lenoir and Dame de Adley—a budding romance?

Under it is a short description of our meeting in the botanical gardens, confirmed by an anonymous eyewitness. A pang of guilt resurfaces, but I have no time to pay it any mind.

No wonder Véronique's blood is boiling.

"Well? Do you deny it?" She crosses her arms. "You went out with a man you know is soon to be engaged!"

I huff and follow her example, crossing my own arms over my chest in defiance. "I know no such thing. If that were true, it would have been *your* name in the paper, not mine. But you haven't had a single outing with the vicomte all summer. Have you?"

Véronique's eyes are burning, as if trying to set me ablaze. "Watch yourself, *Cleodora*. Keep pushing me and I'll make you regret it." Her voice is a threatening growl.

I let out a laugh, half to irritate her, half to ease the tension building in my chest. "And how exactly will you do that?"

"I have my ways." She takes another step, nearly pressing up against me with her chest puffed out like a bird's. With the feathers stuck in her hair, she looks like one, too.

"What on earth is going on here?" José calls from the doorway.

Véronique spins on the spot and glares at him. "None of your business, José."

His eyes dart between the two of us before landing on the broken vase and scattered flowers. "Perhaps it isn't, but you two had better pull yourselves together and get to the stage. Mr. Agard is fuming."

I bite my tongue; dealing with our angry stage director is the last thing I need at the moment. At least the mention of his name makes Véronique retreat. She lifts her chin and throws me one last glare through slitted eyes before striding out of the room, her heels crushing the roses under them.

José lifts an eyebrow.

I sigh and hand him the paper. He'd pry it out of me soon enough anyway.

"Oh, you are good, ma chérie!" Laughter rumbles in his chest as he scans the page. "C'est incroyable! But you should know she won't forget this."

"This isn't about her." I snatch the paper back.

José's smile grows. "Oh my . . . You *like* him. I didn't know you fancied arrogant, entitled men. If I'd known, I'd have offered my brother."

I roll my eyes, but my heart races. I did enjoy the vicomte's company, more than I should have. Yet the memory of Dahlia's soft skin against mine is overwhelming in comparison—the curves of her figure, the warmth of the water, the aroma of the oils surrounding us. José truly has no idea who I fancy.

He only laughs. "Come on, we need to get to the stage." He gestures for me to lead the way.

I ring the bell for a maid before stepping out, feeling a small prick of shame for asking someone else to clean up Véronique's mess. But I have no time to deal with a broken vase, not with Mr. Agard's shouts already echoing backstage.

"This is not what I asked for!" His yelling pierces my ears as I approach the wings. "How many times do I have to explain myself? Are you an imbecile?"

"Patrice, relax. We can get this all sorted," Maestro Mette answers.

"Sorted? This woman is making a mockery of me."

Reaching the stage, I freeze. Maestro Mette and our stage director are standing behind the curtains, but next to them is the modiste, Miss Josephine Garnier—the latest victim of Mr. Agard's temper.

"Sir, *you* are the one making a mockery of *me*," she throws back at him. "I don't have to stand here and listen to you insult my art."

"Aha!" Mr. Agard calls when he spots me. "Here is a fine example of your *art*!" A second later, he is pulling me to the center of the stage. "They call me *Le Visionnaire* because my productions are a manifestation of dreams! Yet *this* is the dress you think is going to star in my production?"

I look down at my costume. I was asked to wear it to check if I'm comfortable moving in it on stage, but now I think my comfort is the last thing that matters to anyone here. The gown is not my favorite, I have to admit, even though the tailoring is admirable. It reminds me a bit of lingerie, fashioned from rose-printed chiffon in shades of blues accented with turquoise, and adorned by white ruffles. It's definitely not the type of dress I had in mind for the character of Nova, The Enchantress—a woman in search of immortality in the midst of war.

"I said I wanted her to look like a blooming flower, not a . . . withering garden," he continues, his eyes scanning me up and down before turning back to Josephine. "You, woman, have no vision."

"How dare you?" She puts a trembling hand over her heart, clutching her shining gem. "Maestro Mette, when I agreed to create the costumes, I didn't agree to be belittled and humiliated! My Talent doesn't deserve this treatment. I'm leaving."

"Miss Garnier, please." The Maestro blocks her path. "Let's all take a deep breath."

"I don't need to breathe. I need respect."

The stage director opens his mouth to answer her, but Maestro Mette puts a hand on his shoulder. Stuck between them, I'm like a rabbit caught between three lions. I try to take a step away, but Maestro Mette glares at me to halt.

"How about this . . ." he says. "We'll prepare a detailed description capturing Patrice's vision and deliver it to you this evening, Miss Garnier." He is so careful with his words, it's like he's attempting to defuse an explosive weapon. "After the weekend, Lady Adley can go to your studio and try some other options that might fit better. Can we all agree?"

"I'll accept the terms," Josephine crosses her arms, "if they come along with an apology."

The vein on the director's forehead is bulging again, but I can see Maestro Mette's fingers dig deeper into his shoulder. "*Excusez-moi, Mademoiselle,*" he utters through clenched teeth. "Please accept my apology." The words could not sound less sincere, but Josephine's pleased grin suggests that this is enough to let the matter drop.

She huffs as she takes a look at my dress one last time before striding backstage, her footsteps sounding over the wooden floor as she retreats, muttering about unappreciated art.

The moment she's gone, Maestro Mette lets out a long sigh. I can relate. "Everyone, gather round!" he calls.

The rest of the cast assembles on the stage—singers and dancers ready for a full run-through of the opera. The tension in my stomach lifts; I'm relieved to no longer be standing alone under the scrutiny of the directors. Véronique's shoulder shoves into me as she takes her spot, timing her strike exactly when the directors are looking away.

I let out a tiny groan and rub my arm. Maybe I'll be lucky and Dahlia will choose her Talent as my next target. After all, basking in darkness must have some rewards—a way to hold up my end of the bargain and be rid of Véronique all at once. The thought almost makes me smile.

"We will work our way from the overture until the end without a break," the Maestro announces, and a wave of displeased murmurs follow. He hushes them all with one raised finger. "A few of our patrons will be watching today's run-through. Don't disappoint them." His eyes scan us, resting on each face a few seconds longer than comfortable. "We start in five."

The cast disperses as crew members rush to their stations, checking on props and ropes. I should be moving too, yet I'm rooted in place, looking out toward the hall, in the sudden grip of nerves. A group of patrons enters through the open doors to the gallery level, taking their seats. Three ladies and two gentlemen. But Nuriel isn't among them.

"He's not going to be here," José says in my ear. "Vicomte Lenoir never comes to rehearsals."

A sigh escapes me, though the tension in my chest remains unchanged. Should I be happy? Upset? I still have to play my part with the vicomte—seducing him is what Dahlia expects of me. Yet the disappointment that nestles inside me at his absence is too real for comfort. I'm not supposed to find the thought of seeing him thrilling. He cannot be allowed to have any place in my heart. Perhaps it's best he's not here now, since I clearly need to control myself better.

In the pit, the orchestra members are already tuning their instruments in an array of sounds, and Maestro Mette is taking his place at the raised podium. Pushing my emotions down, I find my place backstage just before he taps his baton for attention. Then the music begins.

The difference between the piano and the fully orchestrated accompaniment is immense. Madame's Piano Talent is incredible, but it cannot be compared to the intense beauty of combining the musicians together into a symphony of Talents. The instruments weave together into one living, breathing unit, filling the entire hall with their harmonies.

The dancers glide over the stage, telling a moving tale of pain—they are the spirits of lost soldiers on the battlefield. They move like wind transformed by music, bringing a wordless interpretation to the soft strings and the quickening beat. The hair of each ballerina is pulled back, gathered together and secured by a silver comb, embedded with a gem. I catch the light glow emanating from the various gemstones, each Talent shining brighter than the one before.

Then José starts singing, and the dancers plummet to the ground in graceful arcs—souls reenacting their deaths, never to rise again. The music swirls around me in a whirlwind, my own Talent responding with gushing magic coursing through my blood and notes leaving my lips.

The Lover and The Enchantress meeting at last—her quest for immortality leading her to him, as the magic in her blood calls her to take his life and have his years as her own. But her plans are derailed, a massive explosion wounding her mortally.

José's warm tenor voice soaring as The Lover in him tends to the wounds of The Enchantress.

The Mother, in a vision, warning against the cost of the immortality spell, with a deep mezzo-soprano voice and fearful notes.

The Sister, wishing the power to be hers, her jealousy ringing all too authentically in Véronique's voice.

And the feelings of The Enchantress for The Lover, *my feelings*, growing with each heart-wrenching note.

Each scene flows to the next in a blur—music, movement, and emotions combining into the most complicated form of art.

A flash of light enters the corner of my eye—up in the private booths a door has opened. Could the vicomte have decided to come after all, just in time to watch the last scene? The edges of my nerves tingle as I bring another melodic phrase to an end; my eyes wander up to meet him.

But it isn't Nuriel leaning into the red velvet seat.

My heart skips a beat at the sight of Dahlia's perfect porcelain features staring at me. I might be imagining it, but even from afar I can see the seductive hunger in her dark eyes, the smile tugging at her lips. Her hand rests on the shoulder of another lady—a young woman in a mint dress, with brown locks and rosy cheeks.

I know that girl.

This time, my heart stops altogether. I blink, certain my eyes are deceiving me. But the woman next to Dahlia is not a mirage.

She's my sister, Anaella.

CHAPTER TWENTY-ONE

A Songbird or a Crow?

MY MIND TELLS me it can't be true, that I must be wrong. Yet, deep inside, I know I'd never mistake anyone else for Anaella.

José's hands wrap around my waist as he moves and blocks my view, bushy eyebrows raised in expectation. The last notes of his phrase are drawn from his lips, and I'm meant to answer, but my head is blank, filled only with the image of my sister.

A flute trills, and Maestro Mette waves his baton, giving me the cue to enter. I open my mouth to sing, and for a second my voice falters. A flash of cold anger passes in the Maestro's eyes; a warning rings in José's tightening lips. The gem pulses again, yearning to take over, to become one with the music, and with the next breath I give in to the magic, my singing stabilizing.

José joins me, our voices melting together in a passionate duet—The Lover willingly offering his life to grant The Enchantress more years, the dagger resting on his chest.

My hand trembles as I let the blade fall—The Enchantress finally accepting mortality, not willing to kill a man she loves for her own gain.

And the final sacrifice.

A whirlwind of harmonies tangle, cascading in gushing waves as The

Lover takes his own life to heal The Enchantress's wounds, her name parting his lips in one last call . . . *Nova.*

The orchestra responds with a final crescendo, a cry for lost love and dreams. The sound reverberates through the hall, lingering for a moment longer before Maestro Mette drops his hands, and the magic is broken with a wave of movement and talking—cast members, crew, and instrumentalists releasing the tension built throughout the show all at once, like a corset snapping open.

Up in the gallery some patrons clap, already on their feet and heading toward the exit. But my eyes go straight to the private booths.

Empty. No sign of either Dahlia or Anaella.

"Bravissima, ma chérie!" José wraps a sweaty arm around my shoulder. "Though you scared me there for a moment."

"I . . . forgot the words," I mumble, scanning the hall, row by row, for any sign of my sister. There is none. Just empty velvet seats in red and gold.

Lady Arnould skips over next to us, planting a kiss on José's cheek. "You were fantastic!"

The costume and makeup for The Mother have added a few years to her round face, but José looks at her as though she's the most radiant of stars.

"Not as fantastic as you!" He untangles from me before grabbing her by the waist and spinning her around while she laughs.

"Settle down! Settle down!" Maestro Mette shouts over the noise.

Next to him, our stage director is standing with lips pressed tight, flipping through a notebook filled with corrections for us all.

I tap my leg restlessly under my skirt. I have no time for this. I need to find Dahlia. To see my sister.

"Well done, everyone!" Maestro Mette wipes his forehead with a white handkerchief. "A successful run-through indeed. Patrice has gathered all his notes for you, and we'll make sure you fulfill each of them well before the premiere in two weeks."

José leans in to whisper something in Lady Arnould's ear, and she giggles.

"In the meantime . . ." The Maestro clears his throat, throwing us a warning glance. "We think you all deserve some well-earned rest, so we'll leave the commentary for the beginning of next rehearsal."

"Woohoo!" one of the crew members cheers, causing laughter to ripple through the cast.

Maestro Mette nods in response. "Enjoy the rest of the evening."

Nerves on edge, I push toward the stage exit as soon as the words leave his mouth. If I hurry, I might still be able to somehow catch Dahlia and Anaella.

"Lady Adley, a moment, if you please," the conductor calls before I can make it out the door.

I halt, a sudden pressure building in my chest. The rest of the cast pass me by as I turn back with a pained smile. "Yes, Maestro." My tone comes out colder than intended.

I notice Véronique lingering near the curtain at the back of the stage, bent over, as if she's dropped something on the floor. My jaw clenches. If she had truly dropped something, she'd have asked a maid to search for it.

Maestro Mette stuffs his handkerchief into a pocket in his dark blue vest, which is adorned with straight lines of decorated silver buttons. Droplets of sweat cover his forehead, his breathing heavier than usual. Perhaps the singers aren't the only ones who need rest. The ring on his finger shimmers as if his Talent still longs for the music, no sympathy for the tiredness in his bones.

"Do you know why I asked you to stay?"

Of course I know. Anaella's appearance made me lose my concentration, actively interrupting the flow of magic. My singing suffered for it, and now I'm paying the price. But I cannot tell the conductor the truth.

"I'm sorry, Maestro. I lost my focus. It won't happen again."

Behind me, Véronique gives a soft chuckle. I almost turn to yell at her, but that would only give her what she wants—another reason for Maestro Mette to pick her over me.

He eyes my gem for a long moment in silence, and I have to keep myself from shuffling in agitation. "You were gifted an incredible Talent, Lady Adley," he finally says. "In your cousin's hands this ruby shone. It never faltered. I still hold out hope that you can make it shine just as brightly. Don't make me regret putting that faith in you."

"No, Maestro," I utter, but he's already walking away to the other side of the stage, where Mr. Agard is scribbling furiously in his notebook.

Mouth dry, I turn toward the exit, only to meet Véronique's gaze. She stares at me with a smirk on her face but says nothing, only snickering as I pass.

Darting into the corridor, my heart pulses so quickly I fear it might burst out of my chest. Thoughts swirl in my head in a messy tangle of strands, the fights and the performance twisting together— flashes of sneers, shouts, broken melodies, disappointed eyes, a mint dress, rosy cheeks.

I run through the halls, my head turning from side to side as though Anaella and Dahlia might be around any corner. But there's no sign of them—not in the foyer, not on the Grand Escalier, not in my dressing room. The opera house is too big for me to search, and, in truth, my sister could be anywhere by now, whisked away by Dahlia. The image of her long fingers clasping my sister's shoulder is etched into my brain. Those same delicate fingers that traced over my skin and explored every curve of my body just last night.

Why would Dahlia do this? Why did she involve my sister? How much did she tell her? Why didn't she tell *me*?

I clutch my purse and coat—Dahlia's gift—as I finally drag my feet toward the exit. The cool evening air hits my face as I step onto the street, a welcome reprieve from the heat of the day and the gas lights of the stage. The alley is abandoned—none of the usual fans, not even the concierge at the door. For a moment, the odd emptiness crushes me, and all I want to do is scream.

The frustration rages inside me like a clash of notes, screeching all at once in atonal chords. I pull at my hair as I pace, trying to avoid the urge to shout or beat my hands on the ground.

The neighing of approaching horses echoes, and I struggle to regain my composure. I cannot have my coachman see me this way. But the carriage pulling in isn't mine.

The unfamiliar coachman wears all black, matching the pair of dark horses before him. His face is tucked into a gray scarf and a hat hides his eyes. I take a shaky step back just as the side door is flung open.

"Join us," Dahlia calls from inside, her voice like dripping honey. And like a bee, I climb into the carriage. I should have known the empty alley wasn't a coincidence.

Then Anaella's arms are around me, her beautiful brown curls brushing my face as she nestles into my neck. "Oh, Cleo!" she cries. "I missed you so much!"

I squeeze her tight, afraid to let go in case she disappears. It has been over two months since I saw her lying in her bed, plagued with illness. But Anaella isn't the fragile sister I left behind. There is strength in her limbs, a shine to her hair, a healthy glow to her skin. The doctor and the nurse have performed wonders. Dahlia didn't lie to me when she said Anaella has been taken care of. Even her mint dress is new—a simple yet elegant bell-shaped gown, with minimal frills around the collar.

She draws back from me, round brown eyes sparkling with tears. "How . . . I don't understand," she says, her hand running over my face as she studies me—from my makeup, to the costume gown, to Father's coat.

Recognition dances in her eyes as she touches the soft velvet. "Is this . . . ?"

"Papa's," I choke, trying to hold back my tears. I'm surprised she remembers it . . . she was so young. But then again, I'm not the one who used to sleep with Father's book under my pillow. My hand slightly trembles as I brush a stray tear from Anaella's cheek. "It . . . it was a gift." For a split second, my gaze darts to Dahlia. She sits perfectly still on the bench across from us, her face an unreadable mask. Did she bring Anaella to me as a reward—a promise fulfilled? If only I'd had time to prepare.

"Ann . . ." My voice drifts. What do I tell her? How do I explain?

"Oh, Cleo," she says again, grabbing a handful of the fabric in her hand. "Look at you. You are *a lady*. When Lady Sibille showed up at the store and told me she was your employer, I never thought . . . How? You can sing? Why didn't you tell me?"

"So, she didn't tell you what I do?" I ask, gauging Dahlia's reaction. The warmth and passion from last night are hidden now. She remains a statue, examining the situation in silence.

Anaella shakes her head. "She only invited me to come see you."

"Ann, I swear, I didn't want to lie to you. I wanted to tell you everything, but the situation was . . . delicate. I had to stay away for a while."

Her forehead creases. "I don't understand."

Of course she doesn't. How could she?

As far as Anaella knows I sold my ring, relinquishing it along with Father's broken promises. But in reality, the ring found a way to fulfill its destiny. Only by means my sister could never have imagined.

My thumb instinctively moves to circle the ruby, the movement catching Anaella's eye. Her mouth drops.

"Whose Talent is this, Cleo?" A tremor enters her voice as her gaze shifts between Dahlia and me.

I turn to Dahlia, desperately seeking her guidance. How could she just bring Anaella here without any explanation or warning? How could she drop this on me?

She tilts her head, one eyebrow raised. Testing. Daring. She wanted it this way. She wants to see my reaction.

"Please," I mumble. And a smile blooms on her lips.

"I gifted Cleodora her Talent," Dahlia says. "It's an old family heirloom. In exchange, Cleo now works for me."

"Doing what?"

Anaella addresses the question to me, but Dahlia is the one to answer. "Acquiring new 'family heirlooms.'"

The color drains from Anaella's face, and in that moment, she almost resembles again the sick sister I abandoned. "Cleo, what is she talking about?"

"I—this Singing Talent used to be Lady Adley's. You know, the famous soprano." The explanation sounds insane as I speak it, but I need her to understand. "She used to work for Dahlia, and when she retired, I took her place. I'm a lady now, Ann. I have her estate, her money, her career, her name. And you will have it all too!" I clasp her hand in mine. "You can come live with me, as my sister, a young Adley. We can be happy!"

"Adley?" She tastes the name in her mouth. "That's not who we are . . . That's not Papa's name. I don't need a fancy estate. I just want you home."

"We'll have a new home. A better home."

"What about the shop? My designs?"

Dahlia answers before I can attempt to. "If that's your worry, dear, I will make sure to turn you into the most famous designer in Lutèce." She takes a cigar out of her purse and lights it with a steady hand. The sweet aroma of tobacco and spices fills the carriage. She puffs a perfect circle of smoke as she leans back in her seat. "You already have your Talent, Anaella. But *both* of you should have had one. By giving a Talent to Cleodora, we've done nothing but restore the natural order and bring about justice. And clearly you both deserve to enjoy the finer things life has to offer. Your sister knows I'm a woman of my word, and I give my word to you, Anaella. There will be a masquerade ball, the closing event of the summer social season." Her gaze meets mine briefly, but before I can wonder why, she turns back to Anaella. "We will introduce you to society then."

There is a spark of eagerness in my sister's eyes. That same hunger that awoke within me when Dahlia first offered me my future. Now we can finally share in it together. We can have it all. But then suspicion enters her gaze, her head tilting as she presses her lips together.

"But . . ." She turns back to me again. "What do you do? What does 'acquiring heirlooms' mean?" From the angle of her eyebrows, I can tell she already knows the answer.

I open and close my mouth, hoping Dahlia will chime in, but when I look at her, she remains silent. This one is on me.

"Well, I didn't . . . I mean, not yet . . . this will be the first. But . . ." I take a deep breath to stop my blabbering before the truth finally leaves my mouth. "I steal Talents."

Anaella snatches her hand from mine, as if my touch were an open flame. "No." She shakes her head rapidly. "It can't be. You're lying. You wouldn't."

"It's not as bad as it sounds."

"Not as *bad*? Cleo, how could you? After what happened to Papa?"

"Leave Papa out of this."

She lets out a burst of hysterical laughter. "Leave him out of this? You are in denial! After everything we've gone through . . ." Anaella's words sting like a whip, mirroring the harshness of her glare. "You know better than anyone what it's like to have your life slip through your fingers, yet you steal dreams without any sense of shame. Do you kill them, too?" She turns to Dahlia. "Is that what you have my sister doing?"

"No," I shout back at her in horror. "Of course not! How can you think that?"

Her chest is heaving. "What am I supposed to think, Cleo? You said that you sold Papa's ring. That you're working for a lady in the city. Clearly, it was all a lie. You agreed to some shady deal and left me . . . And what if you get caught? Did you even think about that? I'll be left all alone."

This isn't how this conversation was supposed to go. I'm clearly not explaining it right. "I'm not going to get caught . . . Dahlia—"

"This woman has twisted your brain." Anaella closes her eyes, her face contorting as if in pain, and she turns to Dahlia again. "Who are you, really?"

"I told you. My name is Lady Sibille." Dahlia takes another deep puff from her cigar. "I run the illicit market of Lutèce. Your sister is one of my . . . employees. And just as I promised her"—Dahlia stretches her hand, stroking my cheek with a single finger that makes my skin prickle—"you, Anaella, are now under my care."

The illicit market. The shadowy organization whispered about in fear—Dahlia runs *all of it*? The empire she inherited. I should have seen it. I should have figured it out. She is not a mere shadow woman, she is a true Reine des Ombres—a queen.

There was no faltering when she said it, no sense of shame or guilt. Is she not even the slightest bit worried about sharing that information so openly?

For all the connection we shared, she never did tell me much. Apart from her magical hold on me, do I really know Dahlia at all?

Anaella lifts her chin in defiance. "I don't need your care."

Dahlia laughs, a hollow sound that makes my skin crawl. "You definitely did when your fever was consuming you from within. My dear, I promise you, I can be your best friend if you'll let me."

Anaella starts shaking. "Cleo, we need to leave. Promise me you will never see this woman again. Come home with me."

"I can't." The words leave my mouth faster than I thought possible, and I can't help but notice Dahlia's lips tug into a smile. I force myself to swallow before continuing. "I need to do this," I say. "I'm doing this for you. For us!"

"Don't lie to me," Anaella says. "You're doing this for yourself! For the fame, the jewels. You know I would never have asked you to do such a thing. Do you think Papa would have agreed? You're wearing his coat, the perfect image of one of the ladies he created it for. But you're not a lady. Not a real one. You're a thief."

Her accusations pierce my heart like bullets, each one aiming to kill. I want to tell her she's wrong. To prove to her that this is the right thing for us both. To have the chance to share this new life with her and show her what our future could be like.

But before I can open my mouth, she gets up on her feet, crouching to keep her head from hitting the carriage's ceiling. "Stop the horses!" she cries, wobbling as she bangs her fist against the wall.

The coachman obliges, and a second later Anaella throws open the door.

"Where are you going?" I call after her.

"Away from you," she shouts at me through tears before running down the busy street.

I move to follow her but Dahlia grabs my arm. "Let her go."

"What?" I falter as I stare into her eyes—those beautiful, dark pools that make me go weak at the knees. I can feel her gaze penetrating through my defenses, luring me to obey her words, to please her. But Anaella's cry is fresh in my ears. I cannot let her go. With a burst of strength I didn't even know existed within me, I snatch my arm away from her grasp.

"No!"

I throw the word at Dahlia, far more aggressive than I have ever allowed myself to be in her presence.

Before she can stop me, I jump out of the carriage and start running.

CHAPTER TWENTY-TWO

The Underbelly

MY LEGS SHAKE as I dash forward, my heels striking the uneven pavement. The crowd on the streets is thick and loud; among it, Anaella's small figure is but a single blade of grass in a field. I scan the sea of ladies and gentlemen in their fine robes, the well-groomed horses, the imposing carriages that block my path. My breath becomes short, my eyes darting around in a desperate attempt to find my sister. A child giggles to my right and I turn just in time to catch a glimpse of a mint dress across the road.

"Ann!" I shout, sprinting forward.

"Watch out!" a coachman yells from atop his speeding carriage. The trotting horses rushing past miss me by a hairsbreadth.

I falter backward and nearly crash into a mother carrying her toddler. "I'm so sorry!" I blurt as the child begins to cry.

Heads are turning my way, whispers of recognition and perplexity. But I have no time to stop. I push away from the gathering crowd, throwing sideways glances as I cross the busy road, barely avoiding the approaching horses. But there's no sign of Anaella, just an open alley to my left.

"Ann?" I call out as I venture into it, leaving the bustling crowd behind.

I plunge deeper into the dark alley, letting my feet carry me forward in the hopes that around the next corner I'll find my sister waiting. Soon the lively sounds of the large avenue fade away to background noise, replaced by an eerie stillness. I don't know this side of town well, nor does Anaella. Would she be able to find her way home from here?

Anger sizzles within me. Why did Dahlia do this? When she promised I would see Anaella it was meant to be on my terms. I was supposed to tell her the truth myself. To have time to ease her into it. To find the right words when the time came. But that chance was stolen from me. I have only just found her . . . I never imagined our reunion could be so bleak. I never imagined her fury, her hurt . . . her fear. She looked at me as if I were a stranger.

Tears sting my eyes. It's the lies that did it all. If only I had told Anaella everything right away, she'd have supported me. I'm sure of it. We were always so close, sisters and best friends. But now my actions have created a rift between us, and I don't know how to fix it. I have lost both her and the chance to try in this maze of unfamiliar narrow streets.

The stench of sewage reaches me, and I cover my mouth and nose with a trembling hand. There's a man slumped on a broken staircase right ahead, an empty bottle in his hand. He shuffles as I approach; his bloodshot eyes stare me down, taking in my expensive dress and lingering on the purse clutched in my hand.

"Are you lost, ma belle?" He leers, letting out a hiccup. "Come! I'll help you find your way."

Staggering backward, I scan the empty street. The crumbling alleys stretch onward: shattered windows, cracked pavement, rotting waste, and squirming rats.

"Ann, where are you?" I mutter under my breath.

"Hey!" he shouts. But I'm already walking. Right ahead, the sounds of laughter and clinking glasses echo from an open door, and I head for it, eager for the safety of a crowd.

Darkness envelops me as soon as I'm inside, making me blink my eyes to adjust. I'm in a tiny foyer, lit by a single dripping candle. The laughter is coming from somewhere farther inside, while, from the floor above, the undeniable sounds of grunting and soft moaning reach my ears.

My stomach tenses. Perhaps the dreadful street is the better choice after all.

A door to my right bursts open and a giggling woman crashes through, pulling a man along by his collar. Her hair is wild, her feet bare, her body is covered by what can only be described as undergarments—frilly lace over naked skin. My cheeks run hot at the sight of the woman's breasts sticking out from her dark purple robe. But right over her ample bosom is a large tourmaline gem attached to a silver necklace. It glows as she passes by me, her gaze meeting mine with a striking smile. For a second, I'm drawn to follow her right alongside the man, waves of desire washing over me. She laughs as they stumble up the staircase, and the magical hold breaks.

I shake my head, stumbling back. I never thought a place like this would have Talents . . . did the madam who opened it years ago procure gems to hone seduction skills for her workers? What other Talents could be in here?

The aroma of tobacco and spirits wafts through the open door the man and woman left behind. I risk a glance, but all I can see is a dimly lit, narrow corridor. The clicking of a spinning roulette wheel draws me closer.

My heels make no sound as I walk along the carpeted floor of the corridor, my head turning from side to side at each open door I pass. In a stuffy room, gentlemen sitting at long tables deal with piles of money too large to suggest legal business, while a man with a shining yellow gem glinting atop one of his teeth pours them drinks. Another room is devoted to cards, a cloud of smoke floating above the men as they hunch over the round tables. In another room, a roulette wheel is constantly spinning as the crowd shouts, and more ladies in undergarments strut.

The people in here are either Talentless—the lowest members of society, driven by poverty—or those who use their Talents for pursuits

I have never dared imagine. This is the underbelly of the city, the darkest side of a glinting world filled with magical gifts.

Another door is flung open and a man steps out, admiring his exposed arm. His skin is raw and red, marked by black ink in the shape of a skull. For a moment his eyes linger on me, and I cower backwards, then another man bumps into him, knocking him to the floor with a grunt.

"I told you this was your last chance, Remy," the second man barks, long white scars marking his face, weaving together like a delicate, brutal lacework and disfiguring his features. "You pay rent or you're out!"

More men gather around, yelling, flocking from the various devilish rooms like a pack of hungry wolves smelling blood.

A scream escapes me. Luckily, no one can hear me over the commotion. The men shove me with their elbows, brute force and violence blinding them. My entire body shakes with fear; black spots dance across my vision as I pant for air. I should never have walked inside. Stumbling, I search for a way out of the mass of heaving bodies. A closed door stands to my right and, without thinking, I turn the handle and fall inside.

The room is dark, with large wooden planks blocking the windows. Broken glass litters the floor between splatters of alcohol and darker patches I don't want to identify. I lean against the closed door, trying to calm my quick breathing. Once the commotion quiets, I'll sneak out of here and never look back.

A cough makes my heart stop. I lift my gaze, and my eyes fall on two dark figures sitting in the shadowy corner.

"Are you lost, sweetheart?" a man calls with a low baritone voice.

My instincts scream at me to run, but fear makes my limbs numb.

The man stands, his tall frame threatening to reach the low ceiling. "What is a flower like you doing here among the weeds?" His narrow eyes leer as they run over my full length.

"What's your price?" the other man asks with a slick tone. "I'd be willing to pay extra to rip that dress off."

I try to open my mouth and speak, to say no, to shout, but nothing comes out.

The tall man is now mere inches from me, his dirty fingers running up and down my arm as I shudder. "Fabien, can't you see, this little woman is a proper *lady*?" He suddenly grabs my hand. "What a shiny gem you have there."

"Let me go," I finally say, but the man just laughs.

Alarm bells ring in my head. This is my punishment for leaving my sister. I only hope that she didn't wander into these parts of the city like I did, that she never set foot in this place, that she was smart enough to find her way home.

Will they be able to identify my body when they find me? Will police officers once again knock on our door, and notify my sister that she has lost the last remaining part of her family? Or will she have to read about the demise of Dame de Adley in the papers, forced to visit a tombstone that doesn't bear our family name?

The tall man starts pulling me toward the door, my body too weak to resist. He jerks me forward, and a scream finally escapes my lips. His hand flies to cover my mouth, but I kick and bite, using every bit of strength I have to rebel against him.

I cannot let this be the end. Not when I have already sacrificed so much. The weight of Anaella's absence crashes over me. I had just got her back, and I lost her. Now I'm about to lose my dignity and Talent at best . . . or my life at worst.

But I will not go down without a fight.

"Grab her! And get the gem!" the tall man shouts.

I let out another cry when the door bursts open and a gunshot pierces the air. The two men drop their hold on me at once. Another man appears, his fist crashing into the tall man's face with the crackling sound of breaking bones.

I crouch to the floor, shielding my face and shutting my eyes tight as another shot is fired and glass shatters, raining down on us from above. A cry of pain. The grunts of struggle. The sound of a slammed door. Then silence.

A moment later, a delicate hand rests on my shoulder.

"They are gone now." Dahlia's voice is in my ear. "You are safe, my love."

The sweetness of her jasmine perfume is like a breath of fresh air, cutting through the stench, enveloping me in a warm embrace. A sob escapes me as I bury my face in the crook of her neck. Her arms wrap around my frame, like the protective wings of an angel.

"Hush now, I'm here," she whispers. "No one can hurt you. I will *never* allow them to."

Her hand pats my back in soothing circles as she helps me to my feet. I sink into her touch, following her lead through a back door into the grim street. Her guard trails closely behind, and for once I'm grateful for his presence.

"What about Anaella?" I murmur.

"Your sister is safe," she says. "I have one of my men following her."

The pressure crashing down on me disappears with her words. Anaella was never in danger. Not while Dahlia watches over us. She promised to protect her, to protect me. I should never have doubted her.

I lean closer to her, and soon we emerge back onto the bustling street, the shiny storefronts and lively clatter a stark contrast to the underbelly of Lutèce I just witnessed. Without Dahlia, my sister and I might have suffered this fate—thrown out onto the cold street, left to the mercy of the city's darkness, forced to sell our bodies for shelter.

Dahlia helps me back into her carriage, sitting close to me and brushing my hair with long, gentle strokes. Her tenderness subdues me, the drop of tension in my body making me weak.

"Your sister will come around, trust me," she says.

I painfully detach from her, forcing myself to look her in the eye. "Why did you do that?"

She lets out a cackle. How can she possibly be pleased after what just happened?

"Why are you . . . ?" I press my hands to my temples, struggling to properly form the words. "Why?" I say again, unable to keep the helplessness out of my voice. "Why did you bring her to see me like this?"

"Isn't this what you wanted? To have your sister in your life?" Her words are innocent, yet her dark eyes are calculating. She's just made a winning move in a game I never even knew I was playing. Not with her.

"That's not the reason," I say.

She flashes me a dazzling smile. "Then you already know the answer."

And I do. This wasn't simply another gift for a job well done. And allowing me to wander off to the wrong side of the city wasn't a coincidence either. This was a warning. A reminder that my life is hers—that her reach is endless and that I'm at her mercy. That she can grant my dreams and light my life with passionate fire, but those same flames can burn me to ashes and take with them all I care for.

It's a lesson that's written in every angle of her perfect face, in her lush red lips, her raven hair, her skintight gown, and in the depths of her eyes.

I want to curse her, hate her, to leave this carriage and turn my back on her devious plans, just as Anaella told me to.

I want to kiss her, love her, to stay by her side forever and fulfill every one of her dark desires.

"You are safe with me." Dahlia leans closer, her thigh pressing against mine. "Anaella will calm down. And by the time of the masquerade ball, all of this will be forgotten, and you'll have your sister back in your life."

Her words are so certain, so sure, I find myself nodding along.

"Neither of you will know hardship ever again." She lifts my chin with a single long finger, the gesture commanding and yet intimate. "Not as long as you are under my protection. You just need to focus on finishing your task, and your new life will be promised. *Our life.* And since I'm in a giving mood, I will help."

"What . . . what do you mean?"

Dahlia plants a soft kiss on the top of my head. "You need to steal the vicomte's gem for me, and the moment I've been waiting for is approaching—the perfect opportunity."

CHAPTER TWENTY-THREE

Dress the Part

THE PERFECT OPPORTUNITY.

The final event of the summer social season.

The masquerade ball, the one Dahlia brought up in our carriage ride, will be held a mere five days from now. What she failed to mention is that it's being hosted by one of the top Elite families in Lutèce—the Lenoir family.

This is what Dahlia has been waiting for. There won't be a single nobleman who would dare to miss such an event. It's the perfect opportunity for the grandest of thefts—a crime so bold that the chaos that will follow will make the panic of a few years ago pale in comparison. I have no idea how many Talents she's planning on stealing. All I know is that I'm far from being her only employee, and that with her sight set on the most desirable Talents in society, the Elites have no idea what's coming for them.

My job is to find where in the lavish mansion Vicomte Lenoir keeps his gem. The bustling party will provide the ideal cover as I search for it—as I secure a future for Anaella and me.

"You're not a lady. Not a real one. You're a thief." My sister's harsh words, her tears, the horror in her eyes are like a bleeding gash across my heart. Anaella and I have never fought this way before. In fact, we've rarely ever fought at all. But I have no time to lick my wounds now. No time to question myself.

Dahlia's instructions are clear: Steal the vicomte's gem at the ball. Don't stray. Don't go looking for Anaella. *Or else* . . .

She never voiced the threat, but it is there. I feel it in my bones. She saved me from the evil of those predatory men. She watches over my sister. She can make certain we never end up on those horrific streets. But she equally could have left me for dead, if that had been her choice—abandoned to face a fate I cannot even fathom. Just the thought of it makes me shudder. She claims that she will never let anyone hurt me, and a part of me believes her, that same part that saw the vulnerability within her, that connected to her heart. But I'd be a fool to think this promise will save me if I defy her. Dahlia can spread her protective wings over me . . . or confront me as the angel of death, in the blink of an eye.

The fear and desire within me clash with every thought of her. But the yearning to please her, to gain her love, to find the woman behind the mask is etched too deep, smothering the instinct to flee.

All I can do is put my trust in her and follow her orders.

I flinch as the prick of a needle pulls my thoughts back to the room.

"Lady Adley, I'm so sorry!" Josephine Garnier fusses, readjusting the pin on my sleeve.

The newly reimagined Enchantress costume she has put me in is grand, full of embellishments—from the lavishly beaded flower-pattern front to the standing Medici collar and the sheer silk sleeves, with their six rows of puffs caught by velvet banding. The only element that shows restraint is the color scheme: a burgundy satin for the bodice, paired with velvet in such a dark red that it almost looks black. Ivory lace contrasts it along the sleeves, joined by obsidian beading that provides shiny counterpoints.

The design is inspired, and the garment is well made, fitting for how I'd imagine an evil queen would roam around her castle. I'm certain

Mr. Agard will hate it, though. There's something heavy about it, in the choice of fabrics and the way the skirt falls—it lacks the hunger for life that is the essence of the role of The Enchantress.

"Absolute perfection." Josephine admires her work in the mirror. "This will show that director of yours . . . insulting my art." She wrinkles her nose in disdain.

I bite my tongue. Arguing with her and siding with Mr. Agard will only turn her anger toward me. She'll simply have to face the music when I show up to the next run-through in this dress. I can already imagine the modiste and the director locking horns in a battle of insults.

"We should find you a new gown for the coming ball, my lady," Pauline says. Standing by a rack of dresses close to the window, she traces a long velvet sleeve as if revering the soft texture.

I stare at the beautiful garments hanging next to each other in pastel shades and glittering threads. The epitome of everything I wished for lies before me, just waiting for me to take my pick. It reminds me of the dresses Father used to display. Of how Anaella and I used to sneak into the shop at night, trying on the most beautiful gowns, the ones Father wouldn't let us touch during the day. I think he always knew what we were up to—we were never especially careful putting things back in place—but he never said a word, allowing us to have our nightly adventures and nurturing our love for fashion at the same time.

Will Anaella truly come to the masquerade ball, as Dahlia said? Will she take a role by my side as a young Adley? Will she be able to accept my choice?

The way she threw Father in my face still stings. I always thought his sudden death affected me more than it did my sister. Yes, we were both forced to fight for our survival once he was gone, but Anaella always took after Mother. She had Mother's Talent with her, and Mother's legacy to keep alive. I, on the other hand, was always glued to Father's side, had been groomed by him to inherit his gift. When the river took him, I lost both my father and the future he had prepared me for.

Anaella obviously thought that reminding me of what we had lost would stop me. But it is *because* of what happened to Father that I must do this. I cannot let desperation drown us, too.

"What do you think of this one?" Pauline holds out a forest-green dress with a jacquard woven damask pattern of morning glories. Her face shines as she looks at it, the shade of pine standing out against her skin and complementing her fiery hair.

"You should try it on," I say.

Josephine, startled, almost pricks my arm again in response. "My lady, I'm certain your maid meant to offer the dress for you. This is a gown for *a lady*."

Pauline nods quickly in agreement, putting the dress back on the rack as if her touch could somehow taint it. As if she's not worthy of holding it.

"I'm aware of her intention." I look straight at Miss Garnier. "And I stand by my words. I want her to try it on."

Pauline's gaze jumps to me, her entire face lit by a sudden glow of excitement.

The modiste bows her head. "Certainly, my lady." She snaps her fingers, and an assistant appears at the door. "Agatha, please take Miss . . ."

"LaRue. Pauline LaRue," Pauline blurts.

"Yes . . . Please take her to try on the Fresh Green gown."

The assistant stares at Pauline for a moment in shock. "Of course, Mistress," she says a second later. "Please, Miss LaRue, follow me."

I stand taller as they leave the room, warmth spreading in my chest. Pauline deserves to feel like a lady. I used to share her dreams of feeling beautiful and pampered—experiences neither of us should have been denied in the first place. I might not be able to change how society views those unfortunate enough to not have Talents, but I can have an effect on those around me. Just because Pauline wasn't born to the right family doesn't mean all her dreams have to be snatched away. I can help her fulfill them.

"You are very kind, my lady," Josephine says as she reaches to undo the back of my dress. "Not many would treat their servants to such luxuries."

"Pauline is a beautiful young lady, and my dear companion," I say. "I wish to reward her."

Josephine bursts into a fit of giggles, and I chuckle politely. But her laughter only grows as she speaks. "That girl is ever so lucky," she lets out. I glance at her face in the mirror, and even though she's laughing, her jaw is clenched. She almost looks angry, her fingers tugging at the laces of the bodice roughly.

My stomach tightens as I shift my uneasy gaze away from her, waiting for her laughter to die.

I draw in a sharp breath when the dress finally loosens. Somehow, all of her gowns always feel too tight. Definitely not ideal for singing.

"So, how about a dress for the ball?" She heads for her design manual, still giggling strangely. "What about this lovely red one?" She points to one of the sketches. "I already have it sewn. Though I originally made it for someone with a larger bust, there's enough time to alter that."

The fact that Josephine has so many ready-to-wear dresses is baffling to me. How is she able to spend so much time and energy making a gown without knowing who her client will be? Not to mention those off-the-rack dresses she sells on the first floor, delivered straight from her factories and awaiting anyone who comes into her shop. Father always tailored his gowns to the woman standing before him—the perfect work of art to allow the person to shine.

"Oh, I know!" She shuts her book. "I have the perfect gown in the other room."

I step out of the costume's crinoline as she rushes out the door, leaving me to wait for her return.

I walk slowly to her desk, allowing my hand to hover over the thick binding of the large manual. These pages contain the skill and hard work of generations of Garniers, yet, from the few glances I've caught,

I can tell that this manual is nothing more than a business product. A way to make the job quicker, to teach the patterns to the workers, to make them accessible for the factories.

Father's book wasn't created out of necessity. It was a creation of love, of passion. I let out a sigh. If only he were here, he'd have made me a dress truly worthy of the event. Perhaps we could also have worked together on the costume for The Enchantress, bringing the director's vision of her to life.

I turn to the window, overlooking the bustling street below. The cafés are brimming with customers, their bellies full of chocolate pastries and warm drinks. Father's shop isn't far from here, buried under darkening rooftops, stuffy alleys, and years of neglect. Anaella must be there, sitting among the pitiful remnants of cheap fabrics, and her endless designs. All alone . . .

I could go to her, leave right now while Pauline is being fitted, walk through the narrow paths until I reach the familiar faded sign above our door. I could run inside and hug her, tell her how much I miss her. How much I'm sorry for everything. We could have the reunion we both deserve. For just a second, the idea plays dangerously in my mind, my hands already picking up my purse. Then my gaze falls on a man sitting at one of the busy brasseries across the street.

He is sipping from a steaming mug, a casquette hat hiding his face. I narrow my eyes when he looks up, as if sensing my stare. I stumble away from the window, my heart jumping into my throat. I recognize those sunken cheeks and bulging muscles. This is one of Dahlia's henchmen—one of my guards, watching my every move, keeping me safe, making sure I follow orders.

Dahlia's instructions ring in my head. "Don't go looking for Anaella." *Or else . . .*

I let out a shaky breath. If only I knew my sister was okay, that she was starting to come around, or that she forgave me for lying to her. At least then I could go on without the dread pressing on my chest.

I wish Lirone could go to her and report back to me. But the kid hasn't come to see me in the last few days.

Actually, I haven't seen him since before my outing with Vicomte Lenoir.

Where is he, anyway?

Is Dahlia mad at him for helping me cover up my suspicions about the coachman? Could that be the reason he hasn't been around?

I sneak another glance at the busy street, as if I could somehow spot his tiny frame hidden behind a passing carriage or sneaking out of a nearby bakery, slick fingers grasping stolen goods.

"—they should increase patrolling in this area." One of Miss Garnier's assistants flings the door open and I jump, dropping my purse, its contents spilling on the floor. "I'm so sorry, my lady," she says.

But her apology is the least of my concerns, because Josephine has followed the assistant inside and has now bent to pick up the mess I made. I can do nothing but stare as her fingers close over Father's book, making my blood run cold. For a mere second, the sketch of a lime-colored gown peeks from under her grip before she shuts the book. Did she see it? Could she realize what she's holding? And more importantly, could she possibly recognize Father's distinctive style—his artistic fingerprint, within the pages?

"Here you go, my lady." Josephine offers me the book.

I take it with a trembling hand, noticing the strength of her grasp, almost as if she doesn't want to let the book go. But then she smiles brightly and turns to take a subdued aquamarine dress with vivid dark blue and gold accents from her assistant.

I must have imagined it. Surely if she had recognized Father's book, she'd have had questions. Or at least a polite comment.

"We were just discussing the latest news, Lady Adley," she says instead. "Have you read today's paper?"

"I'm afraid I haven't," I say, forcing my heart rate to slow.

"Oh, it's horrible, my lady," the assistant says. "They found another body in the river this morning. It was bruised beyond recognition. The police say it will take time to identify it."

My heart rate spikes yet again. No chance of finding rest.

"Can you imagine going on your morning walk and finding a body? The horror!" Josephine clutches her gem in fright, but her voice is light, giddy.

I shake my head at the sharp contrast. The way her actions clash with the mood she's displaying is unsettling.

"I'm betting it's another drunkard," she continues. "They get into fights, stumble into the water reeking of alcohol, and drown. I say good riddance."

Even though chances are she's right, her words are like drops of venom. Was that what everyone thought when Father's body was found? Was Josephine also laughing back then? I clutch the book tightly as I push it back into my purse. Suddenly the fact that Josephine's fingers have touched it makes me sick. I can almost see her, giddy to gossip about the dead man, without knowing she was the one who drove him to the edge, smothered his future, and all but pushed him into the turbulent water. I struggle to breathe, the air in the room thickening. Even though I'm in nothing but undergarments, I'm sweating.

The assistant giggles. "Maybe it was a passion crime."

"You can romanticize anything, can't you?" Josephine pouts. "What do you think, Lady Adley?"

"I . . ."

"My lady, are you alright?" the assistant asks, the sweetness of her smile matching her faded pink dress.

"I'm . . . not feeling so well."

"You look pale." Josephine's voice is no longer light. "Get her a chair!"

The assistant leads me to the plush armchair in the corner of the room, fluffing the cream and pink pillows behind my back. "Should I call for a doctor, my lady?"

I shake my head. "I'm fine, though I'd appreciate a glass of water."

The assistant is out the door before I can finish my sentence.

"We can set a different time for your fitting. The ball is not until the weekend," Josephine says as she sets down the gown and cracks a window open for fresh air. "If you come tomorrow, I'm sure I can—"

"No need." I push myself up against the weakness in my limbs. "I will be fitted today."

"But, Lady Adley—"

"Now."

She bows her head before reaching again for the gown she chose for me. As much as I wish to run away from her shop, the thought of coming back tomorrow is even worse. I need to keep up appearances, to be ready for the ball and for my mission. For that, I have to dress the part. But the less time I have to spend in the House of Garnier, the better.

Luckily, Josephine remains quiet as she works, making light altera-tions to the dress with incredibly precise movements, her gem shining with each one. She finishes quickly, much faster than I would have. I thank her while her assistant helps me back into my own dress.

"Your maid is across the corridor," she says. "She should be ready soon."

I do my best not to dash out of the room and put as much distance as possible between Josephine and me. This place is like my own per-sonal hell, a constant reminder of everything that was taken from my family. At least Anaella saw me on the opera stage and not here . . . walking through the halls of the fashion house that ruined us, with a false name that doesn't honor our father's legacy.

Pauline is easy enough to find. The door to her fitting room stands open, revealing her alone, admiring in the mirror the green silk that is wrapping around her petite figure. She notices my reflection before I step inside.

"My lady." She drops to a rushed curtsy.

"Pauline, this isn't a dress for subservient displays." I let out a laugh. "You look stunning."

A blush blooms on her freckled cheeks. "Thank you, my lady."

I step closer to her to examine the work. Toggle buttons and wrapped thread run along the front of the bodice, creating a false closure on the crisp, fan-pleated front. There's a double layer of fine piping finishing at the waistline, seamlessly connecting the bodice to the wide, bell-shaped skirt.

At the hem, I notice the row of silver pins the assistant has placed to mark the alterations. My brow knits together and I lean closer, circling around Pauline. The length of the skirt looks right, reaching just past the ankles, but the draping of the fabric feels off. I can already see it pulling up at the back from the tension—the weight of the silk satin not properly accounted for. Once refolded and stitched, it will be almost an inch higher than it is now, exposing the heel.

Bending down, I start reordering the pins, releasing the tense fabric with light strokes.

"My lady, what are you doing?" Pauline takes a step back.

"I'm fixing the hemline. It will be too short otherwise, and you won't be able to wear it."

"But . . . this isn't your job. I'm your maid . . . Besides, I can't even afford this gown, and I certainly don't have anywhere to wear it."

"You'll need a decorative cotton undergarment." I ignore her as I move another pin. "And we'll need to find a mask in the right shade to fit it, maybe something in silver."

"A mask?"

"For the masquerade ball, of course."

Her jaw drops, her gaze shifting back to the large standing mirror. Within its golden frame, she looks like a lady in a painting—a princess of the forest, or a dryad draped in green silk. She passes a hand over her tightly bundled hair.

"For the ball, we'll have to style it for you. Perhaps a high bouffant with a few ringlets falling at the front. Then we'll also need to do your makeup, and I'll lend you jewelry."

"My lady?"

"Maybe a pearl necklace to fit the low neckline, or a pair of emerald earrings to draw attention to your eyes. We'll also need shoes . . ."

"But—"

"Something with a modest heel, or I'll have to alter the hem again."

"But, my lady—"

"Don't worry, Ann, you'll be beautiful!"

I realize my mistake immediately, and let the hemline drop as I look at her in horror. Her brow is furrowed in confusion.

"Pauline." I make sure to use the right name this time, cold spreading within me. I miss my sister so much. I miss my home. I reach for my purse, for the reassuring weight of Father's book, and I realize it's missing. "I . . . I think I forgot my purse in the other room," I say. In my turmoil, I actually left my most prized possession behind.

"I can go get it for you, my lady."

"No." I raise my hands. "The assistant will be back soon. You should finish your fitting. I'll meet you downstairs." I push away from the room before she can object, ignoring the look of bewilderment plastered on her face.

My legs tremble as I close the door behind me. All I want is to leave this place and never set foot in the House of Garnier again. The shop clearly has a bad influence on me. Pauline is not Anaella. I'm not a modiste. I will never be like Father. I cannot match Josephine Garnier's Talent.

I feel as though the corridor is closing in on me, and my feet sink into the soft carpet as if it were quicksand. I hold on to the wall for support, closing my eyes. I need to get a grip. To maintain the perfect facade, and not let anyone see my seams tearing. No one can see me breaking apart this way.

With a deep breath, I straighten myself and look up just in time to catch a glimpse of Josephine's rose skirts disappearing behind the door to her private fitting room as she closes it.

I have to get my purse . . . I cannot leave it alone with Josephine.

Not after she saw Father's book. Not when there is a chance her curiosity might overcome her respect for my privacy.

My limbs shake, but I push on faster, gaining control and stabilizing myself with each step. And when I knock on the door, there is only the slightest tremor left in my wrist.

"Miss Garnier?" I call.

The door doesn't open.

I knock again. "I'm sorry to bother you, but I forgot my purse."

Silence.

The pressure in my chest builds. I need to get inside. Hesitantly, I reach for the handle and push. My gold taffeta purse lies innocently on the armchair by the corner, calling to me. But otherwise the room is empty. There is no sign of Josephine.

I pick up the purse, sighing in relief at the weight of the book still inside it. Did I imagine her walking into the room before? I spin around, almost expecting the modiste to jump out at me from behind the heavy curtains. I even check behind the standing mirror, as if she could be hiding, like a child playing hide-and-seek. But there is no one.

"My lady?" Pauline's voice reaches me from the corridor. She must have gone downstairs after her fitting to look for me and come back up when I wasn't there.

I look around one more time, scanning the flowery wallpaper, the open sewing kit on the desk next to the design manual, the large wooden wardrobe, and the rack of dresses—everything in perfect order.

"My lady?" Pauline taps my shoulder, approaching from behind. "Is everything well?"

No. Everything is not well.

"Oh, yes." I force my voice to remain calm. "I'm just tired."

"You should sleep early tonight," she says. "They've been working you too hard in rehearsals lately."

I nod and smile, but my eyes keep searching for crevices along the smooth walls.

Gently, Pauline rests a hand on my shoulder before leading me toward the exit. I follow her, though my muscles are tense, my body screaming at me to search for the truth I already know.

I did not imagine Josephine walking into this room, just as I didn't imagine her arguing with someone the first time I was here.

The House of Garnier has a secret passage.

CHAPTER TWENTY-FOUR

Hide Your Face

"STOP FIDGETING. You look stunning!"

Pauline smooths down her skirts one more time, giving me a timid smile that screams of nerves. Her mask is sleek and elegant, covering the upper half of her face with strands of silver, her bright eyes glistening behind it.

"I'm sorry, my lady," she says. "I'm just . . . maybe I should wait for you in the carriage."

"Nonsense." I pull her by the hand as we walk up the wide staircase to the Lenoir manor's entrance. "And I told you to call me Cleodora for tonight," I add in a whisper.

A guard nods to greet us at the door; a footman awaits to collect our belongings—the number of decorated coats hanging in the room behind him yet another testament that the summer social season is at its very final breath. My fingers linger on my purse a moment longer than necessary before I hand it over. I don't like separating from it, but then again, the only real danger here is from Dahlia's associates.

I watch as another guard examines a guest's mask, his actions no more than another piece of the evening's choreography. From his fellow household comrades who follow the carriages outside to the ones standing at the door, these guards' very presence here is no more than a dance of decorum, their concerns containing petty matters like guests complying with the masquerade attire, rather than identifying any actual threats. The irony isn't lost on me. *I* am the one they should worry about. A threat they will never see coming.

Pauline takes my arm, pulling me back from my thoughts. "What if someone realizes who I am?" Fear echoes in her voice, the same familiar fright that lingered in my bones long after I first assumed my role as a lady.

"No one will ever know." I push a stray red curl behind her ear and smile. "That's what the mask is for. Just enjoy the evening."

The trembling notes of strings drift through the air, echoing between the marble columns of the foyer and mixing with the laughter of the attendees climbing the golden staircase. There's an air of mystery to the people in the crowd, their masks hiding their features with ornate jewels and feathers. I can't help but stare at the way the masks enhance the dramatic aspect of each dazzling gown and dashing suit that sparkles under the flickering candlelight.

I try to read the faces, to guess who's hiding behind each mask, but on a night such as this, no one can tell the difference between a maid and a lady.

Under a mask, there is a sense of freedom.

Could Anaella be among the crowd, as Dahlia promised?

Pauline squeezes my hand as we reach the top of the stairs. Before us a long corridor stretches in both directions, leading to the private living quarters. But just ahead massive double doors stand open, revealing a railed balcony that overlooks a giant hall draped in yellow light.

Even though we just went up, a pair of elaborate staircases flank the balcony, gracefully descending on both sides. It's an entrance fitting a fairytale ballroom, allowing for an elevated lookout over the magnificence that awaits below. A set of sparkling chandeliers hangs from the soaring ceiling, its warm candles reflected in the large arched windows. Outside, a darkened garden bathes in silver moonlight, a stark contrast to the gold that rules the ballroom. Masked dancers glide like swans across the wooden floor, circling the hall to the enchanting sound of an orchestra playing the valse.

I've never seen a home this grand; the hall alone feels bigger than my entire estate. I've known all along that the Lenoirs are a true noble family, their immense legacy Talents shining from days of old. But I didn't understand the full meaning of that until this moment. Calling this place a manor is not enough to describe these riches. This is a palace.

"It's magical." Pauline's voice is full of awe. "Am I dreaming? Tell me I'm not dreaming."

I pinch her arm and she squeaks. "Definitely not a dream," I say.

Her smile beams, warming my heart.

As we cascade toward the dance floor, the train of my dress flows behind me, a river of delicate seafoam silk topped with overlays of dark blue and gold net lace. I gather the open skirt in my hands, letting it drop only when we reach the last step. It is a gown meant to make heads turn as it sways in dance, the excess fabric coming alive in movement. But all I can think about is accidentally stepping over the long train and falling for everyone to see.

Perhaps it would be better to avoid dancing tonight.

A servant wearing a simple black mask approaches us, carrying a tray of tall champagne flutes. I take one with a grateful nod and hand another to Pauline. With her eyes still darting across the hall, she takes a sip, and a short burst of giggles escapes her.

"It's bubbly," she says.

I laugh and take a sip as well when a young man in a deep-purple tailcoat approaches us. His mask is dark gold, mimicking the rich embroidery running along his attire.

He gives us a curt bow before turning to Pauline and offering his hand. "Would the lady honor me with a dance?"

Pauline shoots a wide-eyed glance at me.

"Go," I mouth without a sound.

Ever the maid, Pauline drops to a curtsy, but in her radiant gown it is a far cry from the obedient gesture of reverence. It is the epitome of decorum any lady would envy. With a dazzling smile, she takes the gentleman's hand as he leads her to the center of the dance floor. A second later, they join the wave of masked couples swaying gracefully. With her air of innocence and her fiery red ringlets, dotted with pearls, I'm sure Pauline will capture the eye of many men this evening.

If my sister comes tonight, I'm certain she'll understand why I cannot turn my back on all this. Just like Pauline, she'll get to taste this life and see what I can provide us. I can imagine her, healthy and strong, her beauty and inner flame radiating as they used to back when Father was alive. I can see her taking over the dance floor, turning every head in her direction as she puts every woman in the ballroom to shame.

I take another sip of champagne. As much as I want to follow my own advice and enjoy the ball, I don't have that luxury. Not if I want to secure that future for Anaella and me.

I walk around the outskirts of the hall, adopting a leisurely pace as I scan the crowd. I haven't seen Vicomte Lenoir since the disastrous ending of our outing at the botanical gardens over a week ago—since I stole his blood. I am here to fulfill my mission—to perform the ultimate betrayal—yet I still cannot erase the part of me that twists at the image of the soaked cloth dripping red . . . at the memory of his defined muscles, and the tingling sensation that pricked my skin when I leaned into the touch of his fingers tracing my cheek, entrapped in his penetrating gaze.

He grew up in this glamour, in this house, under its sparkling chandeliers. This is his world, his domain. And it is only because of Dahlia that I even have the chance to set foot in it.

Dahlia has set me ablaze, her essence and closeness so powerful that nothing can compare to them. But she is a creature of the night, her claws leaving marks of pleasure and fear on my heart. Here in the realm of gold and light, her shadows are weaker, giving way to all the emotions I tried to bury inside. To how Nuriel's smirk made my heart flutter with rage or excitement. To how his unkempt hair made me want to run my hands through it and pull him closer. And to how his arrogant banter made me feel his equal, like a partner in a sparring match.

Light and darkness. Safety and danger. Integrity and deceit.

But under it all is desire.

And the realization that, deep inside, I'm torn.

Torn between Dahlia and Nuriel—the red and white roses. Roses full of passion and hunger, or roses of grace and wonder.

But no matter which I pick, both have thorns, and I am bound to bleed.

I shudder, shoving the thoughts away as goosebumps rise on my skin. I cannot let my emotions rule me. Not tonight. Not when my entire future, my sister's future, depends on keeping myself in check. I will not let anything distract me. Tonight, I am not Cleodora—I am a thief. Before morning, the vicomte's Talent will be mine. All I need to do is find his gem . . .

But how?

There could be hundreds of rooms in the manor. Even if I manage to sneak away and search all night, there's no guarantee I'll ever find it, especially with guards and servants around. Not that they would suspect the famous Dame de Adley, even if they caught her wandering about. After all, that is the real beauty of Dahlia's plan—integrate among the Elites and win the vicomte over, so not a single eye will glance my way once things implode. Still, getting caught would cut my attempts short.

For all I know, the Talent could be locked in some box, hidden in a forgotten cupboard. And yet . . . it is hard to imagine that, with all these riches, the Lenoir family wouldn't want to put their biggest asset on display. No. The Talent won't be stuffed somewhere out of sight, the way Lady Adley kept my ruby. It will have a place of honor inside these walls—a special room, perhaps, or a study meant to showcase it.

I veer around an approaching gentleman in a dashing all-white suit, clearly on his way to ask me for a dance. A group of giggling women behind me is the perfect cover. I join in their tittering, taking in their perfectly coordinated flowery masks. I push on, putting more distance between me and the dancers, until high-pitched laughter catches my attention, each note exact, like a staccato line.

I do not need to see who's behind the mask to recognize the woman leaning on a balcony rail overlooking the garden. Véronique's gown is exquisite, a display of deep navy and emerald green woven with speckles of shiny beading over an asymmetrical skirt. It's a dress meant to draw attention, a perfect match to the peacock-feathered mask covering only the upper half of her face.

Her delicate fingers brush over a gentleman's arm suggestively before she covers her mouth to hide another wave of flirtatious giggles. There is only one man who makes Véronique act like a delicate maiden. But, with his back turned to me, I cannot tell if the vicomte has finally given way to her advances. I clench my teeth with a flash of unexpected jealousy. Nuriel deserves better than her.

The man leans to whisper something in her ear, and I draw closer. If he'll just turn around a little . . . I step sideways just as a servant passes, colliding straight into him. The silver tray in his hand tumbles to the floor with a crash of shattering glasses.

"My lady, I'm so sorry!" he blurts in horror. "It's all my fault."

A small crowd has gathered to watch the commotion, but all I care about is Véronique and the man by her side, both now looking right at me.

Brown. Not green.

The man's eyes are brown.

I can't help but smile.

"Are you alright, my lady?" The man leaves Véronique's side, turning to me with concern.

I nod as I step away from the broken shards of glass; servants are already laboring to clear the mess. "Thank you, I'm fine."

"A drink, perhaps, to calm the nerves?"

"Don't badger the poor girl, Hugo." Véronique wraps herself around his arm.

"How very kind of you, Véronique," I say.

Her blue eyes narrow behind her mask before she stretches a smile. "I should have known it would be you who makes a mess, Cleodora."

"Cleodora?" The man looks between us. "You mean, you are Lady Adley? Your performance at the gala was divine! I've wanted to meet 'Lutèce's Nightingale' ever since."

Véronique tightens her hold on his arm. "Hugo, I'm parched. Would you get me another drink?"

He blinks for a moment before bowing his head. "Certainly."

"And here I thought you and the vicomte were practically engaged?" I say as he leaves.

Véronique snorts. "Keep your filthy paws to yourself. Do you even know who that was? Hugo de Canrobert, son of the Marquis de Canrobert. He will inherit his father's Diplomatic Talent within the year. We met at the matinee concert, you know . . . where you choked." She smiles unpleasantly for a second as though pleased with her jab. "Not that I need to explain myself to you."

Of course Véronique would find herself a new man to pine over, one of an ever higher social standing. She is the epitome of the Elite, interested in status more than anything else.

"Don't worry, he's all yours." I exhale sharply through my nose and turn away from her.

"I'm surprised you even came tonight," she calls after me. "Or did you think that pathetic mask of yours would keep the scandal away?"

Scandal? What on earth is she talking about now? I turn back to her with my brow raised.

"But then again, it seems you simply have a way with servants." Véronique eyes the men still cleaning up the floor.

"What are you referring to?"

"You didn't know?" She lets out a delighted laugh, basking in my ignorance. "They identified the body that was found in the river earlier this week. A *Monsieur Basset*."

My heart skips a beat.

"The same drunkard who recently lost his job as a coachman after accidentally running over a poor child. Did you not get enough satisfaction from firing him? You had to kill him off, too?"

Her voice is joking, teasing, yet each word is a stab to my gut. Basset didn't stumble into the river drunk. He was murdered by Dahlia's men. Because of me. That isn't how I wanted things to end. I was going to try to repent for my mistake and help him, help his family. And yet I didn't speak up when I could, didn't fight for him. And now it's too late. The need to break down or scream builds inside me, but Véronique is still talking. I must hold myself together.

"Such a shame," she says, and somehow her voice sounds genuine. "I'm certain he was a man of great knowledge."

My eyes snap to hers. There's something else buried under the veil of mockery. She cares about his death. But why? What possible reason would make a famous soprano, a proper lady, care about a drunkard who drowned in a river?

"Refreshments for the ladies." Hugo returns, armed with tall glasses and a smile. A small group of people follows behind him like a flock of vibrant birds.

A strong arm wraps around my shoulder as José's familiar tenor voice booms in my ear. "You didn't think you could hide from me for long, ma chérie?" He laughs. "What are you doing tucked away in the corner?"

"I'm certain our divas were having a civilized conversation." Maestro Mette's voice comes from under a full face mask, adorned with stripes that match the lines running across his yellow vest.

"Forgive me for not keeping your identity to myself." Hugo kisses the back of Véronique's hand. "When I ran into your colleagues, I couldn't resist bringing you all together. I hope we aren't interrupting?"

I force a smile, as if stitching the pieces of myself together with the gesture. After spending most of my time in the opera house over the last few weeks, I'm almost certain I can identify the faces under the masks without any mistakes—our stage director's frown gives him away, while the low timbre of Lady Arnould's laughter betrays her, and Madame's stiff posture and watchful gaze are unmistakable.

"How thoughtful of you." Véronique flutters her eyelashes at the marquis's son. "Your company is always welcome. I was just offering Lady Adley my sympathies on the death of her former coachman."

"What a horrible way to go, is it not?" Hugo says. "My condolences."

"Why should Lady Adley require sympathy?" Madame joins the conversation without a greeting. "It's not as though she had anything to do with the man after firing him—justifiably, if I might add."

An argument ensues quickly, but my mind drifts away from it, the memory of the coachman's last conscious moments replaying in my head. His wobbly steps, the reek of alcohol on his breath, the slurring of his words. "She was right about you," he said. I thought at the time that he was referring to Pauline, who had sent him to my room on an errand for her, but now I'm not so sure. There was something else he shouted at me, right before Dahlia's man hit him over the head. "She will get you."

It made no sense. He was drunk and out of his mind. And I was too rattled to pay any attention to it. But those aren't random, unintentional words. It seems so obvious now. After all, I was completely wrong about him—he was an innocent man who never suspected me to begin with. And yet, when he came back, he knew something about me that he hadn't known before. He knew my real name. Firing him drove him to drink, but he had no reason to look into my past.

Not unless someone else used his hatred and vulnerability for their own gain. And as I look into Véronique's cold eyes, I'm certain that person is staring right at me.

"It was you who sent him, wasn't it?" I stare straight at Véronique.

The group falls silent, all turning to me.

"Cleodora?" José pats my shoulder.

"She's clearly had too much to drink." Véronique laughs, but her fake amusement does little to alleviate the tension in the group.

"Do you know what she's talking about?" José asks her.

"Absolutely no idea," she says, but the smile on her lips is as good as a confession.

The taste of bile reaches my mouth. I force myself to swallow and push it down. All of Véronique's threats finally make sense. She wanted to get rid of me from the moment I stepped onto the stage and snatched Adley's dressing room and the leading role from her grasp. And that desire only grew as I made advances with Vicomte Lenoir—advances she promised I'd regret.

But if the coachman had been able to tell her the truth about me, surely she'd have used it against me by now, while there was still time to steal the lead role for herself. That's why she cares about his death. She was using him to bring me down, but without him, her schemes stop dead in their tracks. Did he come to confront me before he made a report to her? For a second, relief washes over me, knowing Dahlia's men have silenced Basset for good. But the guilt is quick to gnaw at me, even more harshly than before, mixed with a wave of shame. He was an innocent man. He didn't deserve his fate.

Everyone is still staring at me. Speaking up tonight was a mistake, a stupid impulse. I cannot accuse Véronique of spying on me without admitting there is something worth looking into, or without implicating myself in the coachman's death.

"I . . ." I struggle to find the words. "I'm afraid Véronique is right. I've had too much to drink. You should have seen the mess I made when I stumbled into a servant just a few moments ago."

"It was rather spectacular, with all those glasses broken," the marquis's son says.

The rest of the group relaxes as José takes the champagne out of my hand with a chuckle.

I force myself to laugh along, even though my stomach is twisting, and every second in Véronique's presence churns it further. My eyes dart around the hall, searching for the nearest escape behind the sea of dancers. I spot Pauline's forest-green dress swaying among them with ease. If only I could be as carefree and not weighed down by deception, thievery, and death.

"In any case, it's a grim subject to discuss on such a night," Maestro Mette says, pulling back my attention. "Best forgotten."

"Indeed," a tall woman with a mane of tight curls chimes in, brushing her hand over Madame's shoulder as she takes a place in the circle. Her light blue lace mask fits her moonstone brooch, featuring her now familiar Painting Talent. "I much prefer talking about your upcoming premiere."

"Renée, how wonderful to see you." The Maestro nods in greeting. "We see you so rarely, I sometimes think Madame is hiding you from us."

"I believe your suspicions are accurate, Maestro Mette," says a man by my side.

I didn't even notice he had joined the group, but Vicomte Lenoir's catlike eyes are unmistakable. His now familiar spicy cologne stirs something inside me, drawing out the memory of his wet shirt sticking to his taut muscles. Yet there is nothing disheveled about his look today—from his fitted silver waistcoat to the stiffness of his standing collar and the shine on each button on his long tailcoat. He is the very image of a perfect host. His mask is black and simple, adorned only by a narrow silver outline.

Was he standing there when I blurted my accusation at Véronique? If so, there's no indication of it on his face, only the regular teasing smirk resting on his lips.

"You have a wonderful sense of humor, my lord," Madame says, the muscles around her mouth tight.

The vicomte laughs, and the warm sound washes over me. "I just wanted to ensure you are all enjoying your evening."

"Certainly, my lord," the Maestro answers, grabbing the shoulder of our sulking stage director, who forces a nod. Without his usual shouting, Mr. Agard is like a loose thread in a fine tapestry.

The pleasantries are too much to bear. I need to stop wasting time. I must sneak away and find the vicomte's Talent, or all of this will have been for nothing. Everything I sacrificed, all the horrible things I did—lying to my sister, manipulating the vicomte, ruining the coachman's life, bringing about his death . . . At least none of that will have been in vain if I succeed tonight.

"If you'll excuse me." I bow my head to leave, just as Vicomte Lenoir offers me his hand.

"Lady Adley." His bright eyes glisten under the flickering candles. "May I have this dance?"

CHAPTER TWENTY-FIVE

Toss It!

I STARE AT the vicomte's outstretched hand, momentarily frozen.

"What a wonderful idea, my lord." José winks at me before offering his hand to Lady Arnould. "Shall we?"

She takes it without a second thought, a smile lighting up her round face.

"Well?" the vicomte prompts.

Do I dare allow myself to be so close to him? But with everyone staring at me, a refusal would be unacceptable. Véronique digs her nails into Hugo's arm as I give the vicomte a small nod. At least dancing will give me an excuse to get away from her and her deadly schemes.

"It will be my pleasure," I say, putting my hand in his.

A tingle rushes up my arm at his touch. I've never been much of a dancer, and the long train of my dress isn't a helpful addition, but the valse is not too complicated. I just need to make it through one dance and excuse myself.

The vicomte leads me to the dance floor, maneuvering us between the couples before turning and bowing to me. I curtsy back, holding my skirts up. Keeping his eyes on mine, he takes my right hand in his left before placing his other hand over my shoulder blade. His hold is strong yet gentle, assuring, almost protective.

"You look lovely this evening," he says, as he steps forward with his left foot.

I follow his lead, stepping back in time before moving my leg to the side and crossing for the upcoming turn. "Thank you, my lord," I say, trying to keep the count.

"Are we back to formal titles, Cleodora?"

My pulse quickens, but I ignore the sensation. *Tonight, I am not Cleodora. I am a thief.* The words repeat on an endless loop in my mind.

"I judged it to be proper, considering that you are tonight's host," I answer.

"And have you ever known me to care for what's proper?" He steers toward the center of the dance floor and spins us around. I nearly stumble from the surprise, but his hold keeps me steady. His movements are full of ease, gracefully rising and falling with the steps. "Not much of a dancer, are you?" he teases.

"It's the dress."

"Doesn't seem to be in the way." He spins us again before pushing his leg back and allowing me to lean into a dip. "Perhaps you just have two left feet."

I suck in a breath as he pulls me up. For a second, his head faces mine, a twinkle of a smile on his lips. "I haven't stepped on your toes yet, have I?" I ask.

He chuckles. "I attribute that to my fantastic ability to lead."

I barely resist rolling my eyes. After not seeing him for a week, I had almost managed to forget how arrogant he can be. Only now, rather than irritating, I find it charming. There's so much more behind his conceited mask. The butterflies in my stomach flutter with impatient wings. He presses his body to mine to keep us connected as we turn swiftly, and all I want is to draw even closer to him.

I remind myself that I'm here on a mission, that I can't let my emotions get in the way, but every moment in his company makes it harder to deny the fire brimming under the surface. The way his hand feels on the small of my back, the way his eyes sparkle in the candlelight—it's all too much. I need to keep my distance.

Yet here I am, dancing with him, as if my entire reason for being here tonight isn't to steal from him. To make him Talentless.

The music winds down, the valse coming to an end. "If you'll excuse me." I curtsy again, eager to leave, but he grabs my hand.

"That wasn't a full dance," he says.

The orchestra starts playing again, but this time the tempo is faster. Around us, the couples all bow to each other once more before leaping into a lively polka—combining the rotation of the valse with the driving gliding steps of the galop. The last time I attempted it, I was a child. There were no chandeliers above my head, or polished wood under my heels. My dress was but a nightgown, and my dancing partner was Father. There wasn't even any music, only Mother's enthusiastic clapping as we twirled around, hopping with the imagined beat. But this is not my old house—this is a ballroom. And the man before me is not Father.

"I insist." Nuriel bows again.

I can sense the blush blooming on my cheeks, the pleasant warmth that spreads in my stomach from knowing he enjoys my company. Perhaps even desires me. Yet the very same thought twists me from within. I shouldn't care about him. I shouldn't feel that rush of energy at his touch or have my heart skip at his gaze. *I am a thief* . . .

"I haven't practiced these steps in a while," I mumble.

But Nuriel takes my hand. "Just follow my lead."

My legs feel like wooden logs as I join in time for the first skip. Then we are twirling around the dance floor. I hop and turn and glide, unaware if any of it is in the right order or if I'm making a fool of myself. The music is driven, pushing the couples to spin rapidly and give in to the exhilarating tune. I can see Pauline among them, dancing now with a different man in a blue mask. We pass José and Lady Arnould, and Véronique and the marquis's son.

With each turn, my heart beats faster and faster, the euphoria of the dance sneaking into my bones and banishing all thoughts. The ballroom around me is a blur of colors, the other couples fading into the background, the music brimming from within as if playing through my blood. There is nothing but the movement, but the dance, and Nuriel's firm grip, sending tingles through my limbs.

As we spin, a flash of color catches my eye—a shade of magenta so vivid it cuts through the whirl in my mind. The sight of it is quickly swallowed by the many other dancers. I throw my head back to spot it, but the dance is too fast. I hop with the beat, allowing Nuriel to guide us around the dance floor, when I see it again. Just by the stairs, a lady in a rich, flamboyant dress is watching, holding a silver mask up to her face on a slender wand.

I try to keep my eyes on her as we turn, taking in more of her appearance with each spin. The satin bows and pleated trimmings. The delicate puffs of tulle on her sleeves. The way her shiny locks fall on her shoulders. We spin one more time and she moves her hand, dropping the mask for just a moment. But that's all it takes for my heart to seize, and for my count to falter.

I misstep, not following Nuriel's lead. My heel catches on the train of my skirt. I stumble and yelp, but the vicomte's arms stop me from hitting the floor. Another couple nearly crashes into us, and Nuriel yanks me out of the way at the last second.

"Let me guess . . ." He pants. "You blame the dress."

But my focus is elsewhere, my eyes searching the crowd for the magenta gown.

My sister is here.

Dahlia was right. Anaella did come around; she just needed time to wrap her head around it all. To understand that everything I'm doing is for her, for us. And now she's here, taking her first steps into our shared future. This ball is the perfect opportunity to present her to society—the sister who came from the countryside to live with her successful, well-established older sibling.

"Cleodora?" Nuriel—no, *the vicomte*—shakes my shoulder. I really shouldn't allow myself to get so comfortable with him.

"I'm sorry," I say, taking a step back.

"Are you not feeling well? Do you wish to sit down?"

"No . . . I'm—"

"Cleo?" My sister's voice is like a ray of sunlight.

I spin on my heel to find Anaella standing right behind me, holding her mask up to her eyes. She looks radiant, the vivid gown complementing the healthy blush on her cheeks. Opals dangle from her ears, matching her Talent ring. Dahlia clearly did not spare any expense.

"Ann . . . you came!"

"I did."

I want to jump and hug her, but with the vicomte standing right next to me, I have to be restrained, respectable.

"Will you introduce me?" Anaella's eyes sweep over the vicomte.

"Of course." I glance between them. If things were as they used to be, my sister would have heard all about Nuriel by now. She'd have known about our outing in the botanical garden, about the way his mesmerizing eyes captivate mine, about how we almost kissed. But as it is, she has never even heard his name. Perhaps for once it's better this way . . . she doesn't need to know how complicated my emotions toward my target have become.

"Ann, this is Vicomte Lenoir. He's the host of tonight's ball. And, my lord, this is Lady Anaella—"

"Finley. Anaella Finley," my sister says before I can finish.

Finley. Our father's name.

Why did she stop me from introducing her as *Adley*? How am I supposed to explain that she's my sister now? This is supposed to be my opportunity to present her to society, to start our new life. Anaella knows that. That's the reason she came here. Isn't it?

When I look at my sister's face, I'm not so sure. I thought she'd be content. I imagined a smile on her lips, maybe an excited spark in her eyes. But all I see is tension in her jaw, and coldness in her gaze.

If she isn't here to accept Dahlia's offer, why did she come at all?

"A pleasure, Lady Finley." The vicomte kisses the back of her hand. "Though I must confess, your name is not familiar. Did you travel far?"

"Not too far, my lord," Anaella says. "In fact, I—"

"I do feel a bit light-headed." I cut her off before she can say more and turn to the vicomte. "Would you mind getting me a drink? Something without alcohol?"

His eyebrow cocks up, and for a moment I'm sure he's going to refuse. It wouldn't be out of character for him. But then he nods, striding away without a word.

At once I grab Anaella's arm. "What are you doing?" I whisper. "You can't use *that name* here."

"Why not?" She lifts up her chin. "You should be proud of it."

I glance around, but nobody is paying us any attention. I've already made one enemy in Véronique. Her plan to use the coachman to find my secrets might have been foiled by his death, but if she somehow catches our conversation and learns my real name, that will be the end of me.

"Did you come here just to ruin my plans?" I whisper urgently.

"I came here to convince you to stop this madness," she whispers back at me. "When that *Dahlia* woman sent me the dress, I knew this was my only chance to stop you before you do something you will regret. Please, Cleo." She begs me. "Don't do this."

My heart sinks all the way down to my stomach. This is not how seeing her again was supposed to go.

"But Ann, look around you! Look at *yourself*." I hasten the words, drawing so close to her that my lips are next to her ear. I need her to see, to understand. "We were starving, Ann, and you were dying. You're healthy again! We're together, wearing these marvelous dresses like the ones Father used to make. This could be our life. This *will* be our life. We can still fix this. We can say that you used a different name tonight as a part of the masquerade ball, just as a game. We can still introduce you to society. I just need to find the vicomte's gem, and all of this will be ours."

"Do you even hear yourself?" She takes my hand in hers as she lowers her mask, revealing the pain written in every line of her face. "I don't want to take another name. All of this—" She gestures to the hall around us. "None of it matters. You're not a thief. Cleo, just come home with me. I know you will never hurt anyone. It's not who you are!"

But she's wrong. She has no idea what I've already done. How I stole the vicomte's blood—made the choice to hand the drenched cloth to Dahlia. How I fired the coachman—how his body was thrown in the river because of me. I'm not as pure as she believes me to be. And there's no going back now.

"Think about Papa." The lively music swallows her hushed tone, but the urgency in it is gripping. "You took his book with you for a reason. To remind you of who we are! What would he have said—"

"Papa isn't here." I pull away from her hold. "He's dead, Ann. He's been dead for a long time now. We need to move on. It's *my* responsibility to take care of us."

The pain in her eyes is crushing; it's like watching a wounded animal. And it's all my fault. I did all of this for her, for us. Yet I've hurt her in the process. I shouldn't be this harsh with her. I shouldn't throw Father's death in her face.

"Ann . . . forgive me, I didn't mean—"

"A drink for the ladies." The vicomte appears by my side, handing me a glass of what looks like orange juice and offering another to Anaella. How does he even have oranges at this time of year?

I straighten up quickly, realizing how suspicious Anaella and I huddling together so closely must look to anyone watching. Appearances are my only weapon now.

"I was hoping you might accompany me on a small detour, Lady Adley." He continues before I even take a sip. "There is something I'd like to show you."

I drink some of the juice to stall, the sweet-sour taste dancing on my tongue. Anaella only grips her glass far too tightly, the mask once more concealing her face. I've failed to win her over, and that pain will haunt me. But none of that matters right now. With or without my sister's approval, I will see this plan through. She will have to forgive me after the fact. Stealing the Talent is the only way to move forward, and if using the vicomte's affections can help, I won't reject them.

"Certainly. I'd love to." I crack a faint smile.

"It was a pleasure meeting you, Lady Finley." He bows his head to Anaella, but she doesn't return the gesture.

Instead, she grabs at my sleeve when he turns around. "Cleo, please," she whispers.

I shake her off without a word and rush to catch up with the vicomte. I have to force myself to not look back at her. To not let her plea change my mind. I wish I could turn away from it all and do what she asks. I wish I could be the woman she believes I am. I wish I could give her this life some other way. That I could keep my ruby without embracing the monster within . . . But I can't.

The vicomte leads me toward the stairwell, helping himself to a stuffed mushroom from a passing tray before placing my hand in his. I fight against the warmth spreading inside me—this *isn't* a romantic escape. This is just a part of a plan. A way to get to the upper floors of the manor. Soon we are out of the hall and walking down a wide corridor. Massive portraits hang on the walls, eyes seemingly following us as we pass.

"Where are we going?" I ask. "Won't anyone miss you back in the ballroom?"

"Hardly." He chuckles. "It's only expected for couples to sneak away on such a night."

Couple. My mouth turns dry.

But he is not wrong—there are couples sneaking around every-where, sharing forbidden kisses and passionate caresses in hidden and not-so-hidden nooks. I gasp as my eyes fall on a gentleman and two ladies sneaking into a nearby room, their clothes half undone, eager to tear off the rest. Is that what the vicomte has in mind for us? My cheeks burn hotter at the thought.

We turn into another corridor when I notice a couple leaning by an open window. Unlike the others, they don't seem to be in the middle of a passionate interlude just yet. The woman is tall, wearing an exqui-site gown in shades of pink that leaves her shoulders bare along with most of her bosom. I almost turn away when I notice the druzy gem of her necklace. Josephine Garnier is not the person I'd have imagined sneaking away with a man, not when she could be at the center of a large social event. And yet, I hadn't thought she'd be the kind to have a secret passage in her shop, either. I stare shamelessly as we get closer . . . and then I recognize the man by her side.

I nearly stumble again but manage to keep my composure. Henry, one of the guards Dahlia assigned to me, is pressing his body closer to Josephine's.

My gaze darts away from them at once as I hurry to stay close to the vicomte. Is this Henry's way of keeping watch on me? Or is Josephine just a side endeavor for his pleasure? Whatever the answer may be, his presence is a clear assurance that I'm making the right choice by ignor-ing Anaella—a reminder that Dahlia is watching.

I will fulfill my end of the bargain.

The vicomte leads me up another set of stairs to an upper floor that looks abandoned. His Talent must be somewhere inside one of these closed rooms, ready for the taking. Now if I could just find a way to be here alone so I can search for it.

"Here we are." He opens a heavy wooden door, holding it for me to enter first.

The room is dark, lit only by the moonlight coming through a large window overlooking the garden. But the faint silver light is enough to illuminate the mess—books, scrolls, quills, and strange instruments of measurement cover every surface of the cluttered study. My heart slows a little. This isn't a bedroom where one would take a woman for a night of passion. I bite my lip at the strange sinking sensation in my stomach before mentally scolding myself. This isn't something to be disappointed about.

"Why are we here?" I ask.

The vicomte lights a gas lamp and points to the wall behind the main desk. A painting hangs right between the heavy bookcases—a beautiful landscape of sunset over a bay, the water shimmering as if set aflame.

It's feels like a lifetime ago when I saw it at Renee's art exhibition. "Do you think the water is burning?" I asked the vicomte back then.

"You bought it?"

"Indeed. I brought you here to thank you. Without your insight, I might have missed this masterpiece."

We stand in silence as I take the painting in. It is as beautiful and haunting as I remembered it—vast expanses of water that should speak of freedom but instead echo pain, as though there's no escape from the endless flames.

"I thought of placing it in one of the main halls," the vicomte says. "But I've decided I want it all to myself."

"Is this your personal study?"

"The one place in this house that's mine." He sounds almost bitter.

I turn to look at him, watching the shadows cast by the gaslight playing on his sculpted features. I'm not sure if it's a trick of the light or an effect of the mask, but his eyes are a bit glossy, as if clouded by tears. He blinks and the effect is gone, replaced by his usual teasing smile.

"*Ladies* are usually not allowed in here," he says.

"Oh, is that why it's such a mess?"

He laughs, stacking up some of the books on his desk. "You sound like my mother." Turning his back to me, he carries the books toward one of the glass-covered cabinets.

I follow him, glancing at the titles as he replaces them on the shelves. There are books about philosophy, history, mathematics, even strategies of war. Nothing I wouldn't expect. But one title stands out.

"*L'architecture est un art*," I read the title aloud.

"My friend, the architect, gave it to me as a gift," he says, but hurries to put the book away. "I still haven't had time to read it properly."

"Did you manage to get another meeting at the botanical gardens for your friend? The designs you showed me were truly beautiful."

"Not yet."

"I'm sorry."

He raises an eyebrow. "What for?"

"I . . . You just seem to really care about it."

The vicomte turns quiet, all hints of teasing gone as he stares at a wooden box on the top shelf. "If you could choose, would you be a singer?" he asks.

"What?"

"You said you love fashion." He turns to me. "Have you ever tried it? Making clothes on your own?"

I shake my head. "It's not my Talent."

"That's not what I asked."

I press my lips together for a moment, remembering the feeling of holding a small needle between my fingers, of pricking through muslin with Father's warm, guiding hand. The soft touch of a new bolt of velvet and the excitement of a new lace delivery. I can almost see the endless patterns spread on the floor and the rush of fear and delight at cutting through a new fabric to match them.

"I did . . . a long time ago. But that's not what I'm meant for."

The vicomte sighs. "That ruby on your finger doesn't have to determine that. You are more than your Talent."

"What are you . . . ?"

His hand cups my cheek before I can finish my question, and my entire body tingles in response.

"Monsieur le Vicomte," I futilely try to maintain a sort of formality.

"I told you to call me Nuriel."

He's so incredibly close now. How did that even happen? I can feel his heat radiating toward me, my heart racing as I take in every single detail—the way his hair falls across his forehead, the ripple of his muscles as he moves, the subtle scent of his cologne mixing with the natural musk of his skin. He draws closer with a smile and for the first time I notice a very slight crookedness to his upper lip. Somehow, the tiny imperfection only makes him more beautiful.

"Nuriel . . . I . . ."

With a gentle hand, he takes off my mask, his speckled, gem-like eyes staring right into mine. They hold a passion that resonates in every fiber of my being, a desire I desperately wish to kill—for just sensing it brimming inside me is a betrayal.

Yet the intensity of his gaze weakens my resolve. It's as though he's trying to read my thoughts. To see what's in my heart. For a moment, we just stare at each other, the tension between us palpable, almost unbearable.

Then, without warning, his lips find mine.

And I am lost.

His kiss is not at all the same as Dahlia's—while her touch was hungry, almost tinged with pain, there was an endless sense of softness to it. His lips press against mine with ferocity, as though he's been waiting for this since the day we met. The strength of his desire is overpowering, like lightning striking the bare ground. His hands curl into my hair as he pulls me closer, his fingers tangling in the strands as the kiss deepens. It burns through me like flames erupting from within, threatening to consume us.

At that moment, I throw all caution to the wind. I don't care that I shouldn't allow myself to feel for him. That I need to find his Talent.

That I need to steal from him. All I want is to have him closer. To taste the sweetness of his lips and lose myself in him. It's as though the rest of the world has fallen away, and all that exists is the two of us, lost in this firestorm of desire.

I press myself against his firm muscles, my fingers loosening his tie before moving down to unbutton his waistcoat. There is a hint of confusion on his face, his brow rising ever so slightly in response to my boldness. Yet his hands don't need any extra invitation to accept it.

He lets out a low grunt that sends a pleasant shiver through me. Then we're against his desk, books thudding as they hit the floor, swept away in a delirious haze.

"Cleodora." He whispers my name as we part for air, and goosebumps rise on my skin. Then he kisses me again, his teeth biting lightly into my bottom lip, his hands searching for the laces at the back of my gown.

I tug at his collar, begging him for more, begging for our bodies to entwine and succumb to this madness. His lips trail down to my neck, and I let out a soft moan.

That's when a knock comes at the door.

He backs away from me, chest heaving. "Who is it?"

"I'm sorry to interrupt, my lord," a man's voice replies. "Your mother is looking for you."

Nuriel groans, his frustration echoing my own. I need his mouth on mine.

"Tell her you couldn't find me." He leans in again.

"I'm sorry, my lord, but she says it is urgent."

This could be my chance, the only opportunity I'll have to search without prying eyes. Yet all I want is for him to stay, to kiss me more.

"You should go." I force the words out, each one like a rope around my neck, pulling me farther away from what I truly desire.

Nuriel stops a mere inch from my lips and sighs, his warm breath making me shudder. "Wait for me?" he whispers.

I nod, trying to calm my beating heart.

He steals one more kiss, imprinting his taste on my tongue, before heading to the door. The servant on the other side jumps as he walks out without a warning. "Let's make this quick," I hear Nuriel say.

I gasp for air as he closes the door behind him, my heart pushing its way out of my chest. What just happened? I run my palms over my face. I kissed him. I wanted to keep kissing him. I wanted *all* of him.

His taste, his smell, his touch. All of them linger in his wake, making my body hungry for more. How different they all are than Dahlia's delicate sensuality—harsher, more confident. I thought Nuriel was the white rose, and Dahlia the red—perhaps I've got it all wrong.

Seconds tick by and I'm still frozen in place, as if waiting eagerly for his return. Why am I not moving? This is the chance I've been waiting for. Possibly the only chance to find his Talent. I need to stop fantasizing about his hands running through my hair and focus. He could be back any minute, and the longer I wait, the greater is the risk of me losing myself to him completely. I shudder and shake my shoulders.

"Finally," a tiny voice whispers from outside the window. "I thought all this kissing broke you."

I spin around to see Lirone perched on the windowsill, right behind a set of decorative metal bars.

"What are you doing?" I rush to the window and lift it open. "Where have you been? I haven't seen you in days!"

Somehow he looks even skinnier than usual, his oversized clothes hanging loosely on his tiny figure. He always looks so undernourished—where did he get the strength to climb all the way up here? How did no one see him? If it weren't for the ornate bars I'd have already grabbed him and pulled him into the safety of the room, away from the dangerous edge.

"I've been busy," he says. "Now, c'mon. That call from his mother I arranged won't keep him long."

I should have suspected Lirone had a hand in this. The vicomte's leaving was too convenient.

"Where should I start?"

"Isn't it obvious? The box."

"What box?"

Lirone gives me his signature eye roll and I almost smile. "That one!" He points to the wooden box at the top of the cabinet, pushing his tiny arm through the bars. It's the same box Nuriel looked at before asking me about my singing and my love for fashion. How long was Lirone watching us?

"You . . . you think—"

"Obviously," he says.

My legs shake as I walk toward the cabinet. Could his Talent really be there? Just waiting for me to take it? Could it really be this easy?

I reach for the handle and open the glass door with a soft pull. The wooden box has its own shelf, as if placed with respect.

"Please, Cleo. Don't do this." Anaella's voice echoes within me. "I know you will never hurt anyone. It's not who you are!"

With trembling fingers, I touch the smooth wood, noticing the delicate gold frame covering the corners. It's not the marvelous showcase I imagined. It's an intimate display, placed in the room closest to Nuriel's heart. This is the ultimate conclusion to Dahlia's plan. She told me to get close to him, to flirt and win him over. She knew it would lead me straight to his hidden and most treasured possession.

Can I truly do this?

"Hurry up!" Lirone urges.

My heart falters as I lift the heavy lid. Right there on a cushion of red velvet sits a diamond ring. Waves of energy radiate inside it; they are so bright that I wonder how Nuriel can ever bear to be parted from such powerful magic. The pull of it must be so strong in his blood.

I know I'm about to steal it. But just touching it feels like a crime. I draw a shaky breath as I take it in my hand, and its unexpected warmth seeps into my skin. This is it. All I've been working toward is finally in my grasp. It was so simple, elegant even. All I need to do is close the box and give the diamond to Lirone, and the vicomte will be none the wiser. Not until it's too late.

"What are you waiting for? Toss it!"

I turn to look at Lirone, his hand outstretched, ready to take the Talent and disappear into the night. I should just do it. Hand it to him and get it over with. Finish the task. Make Dahlia happy. Give my sister the future she deserves. Keep my ruby.

But all I can see is Nuriel's honest eyes filling my mind, the easy confidence in his smile . . . All I can feel is the warmth of his lips against mine.

I am not Cleodora. I am a thief. The mantra returns, but it has lost all conviction for me.

Steps echo in the corridor outside.

Lirone shoots me a panicked look. "Cleo! Toss it!"

But I can't.

The handle clicks and Lirone curses under his breath before swinging himself away and disappearing.

I only have time to turn before Nuriel opens the door with a breathtaking grin. Then his eyes fall on me, standing frozen with his Talent resting in my hand.

"What are you doing?" The smile evaporates from his face.

CHAPTER TWENTY-SIX

Behind the Mask

I STARE AT Nuriel with my mouth open, but no sound comes out. What can I possibly say to explain?

"Cleodora. *What* are you doing? I won't ask again." His voice is low, brimming with the threat of thunder.

I shake my head. "I was just . . . I was just looking around and—"

"Who gave you permission to do that?" All traces of teasing or smugness are gone, replaced by a glare so sharp I fear it might cut through me. "Is that the reason you came up here? To see my Talent? To check the *worth of your suitor*?" He spits the words.

"No! I came—" To *steal* your Talent. The truth dies on my lips. I cannot say these words. I need to lie. "I was just curious. I'm sorry. It meant nothing."

Nuriel crosses the room with three large strides and grabs my hand forcefully. "Give me that." He snatches the diamond out of my grasp.

"I'm so sorry," I repeat.

But he doesn't turn back to look at me, rolling the Talent between his fingers. "You really had me fooled." He laughs, the sound dark and painful. A chill rolls through my bones as I see the muscles tense in his jaw. He's furious. Hurt. And it's all my fault.

"With your innocent countryside charms and interest in art and fashion, I almost believed you cared about more than just status and *Talents*. But you're just like the rest of them. Was it all a part of your plan to secure a better title, a legacy Talent for your future child? Were you ever interested in me at all?"

A wave of dread pins me down when he finally looks at me. His eyes, warm and inviting only moments before, now bore into my soul like shards of ice. The elegance in his features has disappeared, replaced by a hard and unyielding expression that sends shivers down my spine. The passion that bloomed between us has withered away, replaced by a seething, all-devouring anger. I have lost him.

My heart heaves under the weight of his words. There is so much truth in them, it hurts. I did use him. I only got close to him as part of a plan. A plan to rob him. To betray him. But even amid the guilt and shame, I can't help the shred of self-defense rising within me. He's wrong about my motives; they weren't all shallow. Were they? I did it for Anaella. For her health. For her life. I had no choice.

But do I even believe myself?

The doubts and the accusations of my sister ring in my ears. She didn't believe me. She said I was doing this for selfish reasons. To have a Talent so I can be rich and adored.

Was I?

"Nuriel, I—"

"You don't get to use my *name*." He stuffs the diamond into an inner pocket of his waistcoat, turning his back on me and any remnant of our relationship. Pain stabs my chest, and I put a hand over my dress, rubbing the silk as the throb of emotions travels up my throat and stings my eyes. "Get out," he grunts.

His words are like a bullet through my heart.

I shake my head, a hot tear escaping the corner of my eye. "But I *do* care about you."

I know the words are true as soon as they leave my mouth. It might have started as a calculated game, but it has long since developed into something more. Every moment we've spent together, every smirk and every bit of challenging banter, has woven itself into my heart. My emotions for Nuriel are real, as real as anything I have ever felt. So different from the pull Dahlia has on me, more rooted, less wild and turbulent, but no less powerful.

I didn't freeze for no reason. That's why I couldn't toss the diamond to Lirone.

Anaella was right. She told me I wouldn't be able to go through with this. Her words made me face the guilt and shame I had buried inside. I betrayed Nuriel, but did I ever really want to? I've hated myself ever since I stole his blood at the botanical gardens.

I put a hand on his shoulder, hesitantly, longing for his closeness. He tenses under my touch. I want to tell him the truth. To no longer carry the burden of lying and scheming. To beg for his forgiveness. But would he ever be able to forgive me?

"I kissed you because I've fallen for you," I say, settling for the part of the truth that's harmless.

He sweeps my hand away. "I said, get out."

"You have to believe me. I was only holding it, it meant noth—"

"Damn it!" He bangs his fist on the desk. "You're worse than the entire *lot* of them! Is *every* word that comes out of your mouth a lie? Get out! *Now!*"

I yelp as he swipes his desk clean with a furious motion, scrolls, books, and quills scattering over the soft carpet, only this time from a fit of rage, not passion. He doesn't even turn to look at me as I stumble back toward the door. I don't want to leave him. I want to stay and beg, but the fury in him is all-consuming, radiating off him in terrifying waves.

There is nothing I can do but run. My heart pounds in my chest, my breath coming in ragged gasps as I snatch my long skirts to keep from crashing down. I dash through the empty corridor, the sound of my own footsteps echoing like thunder in my ears. If this were a dream, I would be the princess escaping from her magical ball, but nothing could be farther from the truth. This is a nightmare, one I cannot escape, no matter how hard I try. The weight of my actions crashes down on me, and I can't help but wonder if I'm running away or toward something. All I know is that I have to keep moving, that I can't stop until I'm safe from the consequences of my own choices.

I nearly plummet down the staircase, tears blurring everything around me. What will Dahlia do when she finds out what I've done? I'll never be able to get Nuriel's Talent now. Not after I fully lost his trust. Nor do I want to.

Just ahead, the massive doors to the ballroom stand open, another dreamy valse inviting me into a world made only for beauty. A world I thought I could be a part of. But in reality, my sister was right. Back in the carriage, right after Dahlia brought her to see me sing, Anaella said I wasn't a lady. Not a real one. I could dress the part. Act the part. Even change my name. But under it all, I'm nothing but a thief.

I rush down another set of stairs toward the main entrance. A weary footman stands up as I approach, clearly startled to see anyone leaving this early.

"My lady, should I get your coat?" he asks. But I can't even speak— can't wait even one more second. "My lady!" he calls after me as I sprint out into the cool night air.

The bright lights from the manor spill out through the massive windows, illuminating my path as I plunge deep into the garden. With fall fast approaching, the chill of the night's air makes goosebumps rise on my skin. I don't have a plan; I have nowhere to escape. But the thought of going back inside makes my stomach churn.

Just ahead, a bench stands among the meticulously trimmed flower beds. My legs give way as I stumble over to it, collapsing onto its hard surface. The cold stone is rough against my skin, but I don't care. I need to stop, to rest, to catch my breath. My sobs finally take hold, the rumbling in my chest raging against the lively music and laughter that echo through the night. What am I supposed to do now?

My head snaps up at the sound of approaching steps. One of the servants must have followed me. But the boots sound too heavy to belong to a footman. One of the coachmen or guards, perhaps?

No . . . the looming figure is way too large, too muscular. "Lady Sibille is waiting for you," a raspy voice says as one of Dahlia's henchmen appears behind a large shrub. Father's coat and my purse are in his hands.

A sudden laugh escapes me, mixed with a sob. Of course she is.

He throws the coat to me. "Come."

I take my purse from his grasp before slipping my arms into the warm coat, trying to soak in comfort from it. Dahlia almost terminated our arrangement before she gave it to me—a prize for bringing in Nuriel's blood. A gift that led to our night together, to a new bond between us. But so much has happened since then, and this time I have nothing to give her. Nothing to soothe her anger or make her forgive how I broke her trust. I promised I was *hers*, but my heart betrayed her—yet another shattered pledge. A shudder passes through me. What will she do to me when she learns the truth?

The unfamiliar henchman doesn't wait before turning away, expecting me to follow. But to my surprise he's not heading for the carriages; instead, he's walking deeper into the gardens.

Could Dahlia be out here? Waiting right under everyone's nose for her final delivery? Each step I take is heavier, like a prisoner walking from his cell to receive his sentence. The paths seem endless, a maze of sculpted bushes, sleeping flowers, and rising branches swaying like dancing silhouettes in the moonlight. I'm not even sure how the henchman knows where to go.

I tense at a burst of giggles to my left. In a split second, the henchman's massive body presses against mine, pushing me against the bark of a tall tree trunk.

"What are you—?"

"Shhh!" He puts a hand over my mouth, leaning closer as if about to press his lips to mine. My heart beats against his chest, anxiety building inside me.

The giggles grow louder as a couple enters my vision, stealing kisses as they stroll. The woman halts when she notices us. "Looks like this corner is taken," she whispers to the man before he grabs her hand and pulls her away around another corner, laughing.

The henchman lets me go, and a pent-up breath escapes me. "Keep up," he says, turning away as if nothing happened at all.

Blood pumping in my ears, I push my wobbly feet faster to keep pace with his large strides. Soon the lights of the manor sparkle far behind us. We follow a narrow path covered by arches casting silvery shadows, and even though the henchman doesn't say a word, I know we are close. He walks slower now, his shoulders pushed back. I wipe away leftover tears as I find myself mimicking him.

The path turns, leading to a secluded area shielded by tall green hedges. Even with a delicate gold mask balanced on her face, it's impossible for me not to recognize Dahlia. She's wearing a marvel of cream damask silk and exotic amber brocading. The fabric embraces each of her soft curves lovingly before opening up to an asymmetrical frill at the hem. It's a gown that speaks of purity, almost fragility. But after having run my lips over every inch of her, I know better.

She doesn't turn to us as we approach, fully concentrating on the plump man beside her. "Adolphe, you never disappoint me," she purrs, staring at a large sunstone gem resting in her hand.

Adolphe Dugléré, the owner of Café Anglais. Apparently, he came through for her tonight. Unlike me.

"It's my pleasure," he says, nearly groveling, before offering an awkward bow and walking away backwards, as though she's royalty. He turns only after he almost bumps into me. "Sorry," he mutters as he stumbles back toward the manor.

"Cleodora." Dahlia's voice is soft, barely more than a whisper. "I wanted to believe Lirone's information was false. But looking at your face, I understand I harbored false hope."

In the shadows behind her, Lirone's tiny frame shuffles, his eyes not meeting mine. He ran straight to Dahlia, not even taking a moment to consider or give me a chance to explain. I knew he was loyal to her, but I had thought, after everything we'd been through—music lessons, hiding the truth about the coachman—we'd formed a bond. Yet he was so quick to dismiss it, to act as if I was nothing but a task for him—someone he had to report on.

I take a shallow breath, but my chest feels hollow, a sense of loneliness settling inside me.

Dahlia wraps the sunstone in silk, giving it to the henchman who led me here. "Eight more to collect. Go."

Eight more . . . How many Talents exactly is she stealing tonight?

The henchman turns at once at her command, and she waits for him to disappear around the corner before bringing her attention back to me.

"How . . . disappointing."

Disappointing.

If only she'd shout at me, it would be less painful. Her dark eyes are misty, full of sadness. Have I caused that? An invisible hand clutches my chest as if squeezing my heart. I have to fight the urge to rush to her side and brush the tears away. How could I have been so stupid? I should never have allowed anything to stop me from completing my mission. If only I'd tossed the diamond, Dahlia would be smiling now.

"I . . . I'm so sorry. I will fix it."

"Will you?" She bats her eyes at me, closing the distance between us. I shiver as she traces her fingers over my cheek. "I need that Talent."

"I will get it," I say, even though I have no idea how. "I was distracted. Nuriel is now carrying it, but maybe—"

"*Nuriel?*" A chill runs through me at the way she says his name, her voice suddenly sharp. The tears all but evaporate from her eyes, replaced by a sudden flame. "Did you develop feelings for the little puppet?" Disdain drips from her words like venom, and I shudder.

I shake my head, eager to deny it. But the truth of my betrayal is written on my face—a betrayal so profound, my failure almost seems inconsequential in comparison.

Dahlia presses her thumb to my trembling lip with a slight tilt of her chin. "My poor little nightingale. I'm sorry too." Her whisper is urgent, raw. I search for her gaze just as footsteps approach behind me. "Finally." She breaks away, her expression a perfectly emotionless mask once more. "Our guest is here."

A small group walks toward us, at least three men, carrying something I can't see in the dark. But at the head of the group is a petite woman in a forest-green gown I know too well.

"Pauline." My voice trembles as I look at Dahlia. "She had nothing to do with this. Please let her go—she's just my maid."

Dahlia laughs.

"Sorry it took so long, Lady Sibille," Pauline says. "She was feisty."

"What . . . You two know each other?" I look between them, trying to understand.

Pauline ignores me as she bows her head to Dahlia.

"Oh my, is that why you needed three of my men?" Dahlia muses. "So glad I can always count on you, my dear."

My jaw drops as Dahlia caresses Pauline's fiery hair, the realization dawning on me. Lirone and my personal guards weren't the only ones keeping tabs on me. Pauline, my own maid, a girl I considered a friend, was just another thread in the tapestry Dahlia wove around me.

"You lied to me," I say.

Dahlia raises her perfect brow. "I *never* lie."

"You . . . you didn't tell me—"

"Ah, but that is not a lie." She shakes her finger at me, as though I'm a naughty child who needs to be educated. "I never told you anything about your maid."

"*My lady,* thank you for the dress." Pauline curtsies to me, but the usual timidity and friendly demeanor are gone. I feel sick to my stomach.

She's no longer the sixteen-year-old girl with freckles who brushed my hair, picked my dresses, and comforted me. That girl never existed.

It was all an act.

"But why?" I ask.

"Think of me as a contingency plan." Pauline's lips turn upward in a smirk. The expression looks so alien on her delicate face. "One that was clearly necessary. Bring her over here, boys!"

The henchmen move out of the shadows, and I recognize Henry among them. Seems like his dalliance with Josephine didn't take him too long. Two of the men are carrying something in their arms. Not something. *Someone.*

My heart races as they place the limp body on the ground at Pauline's feet.

Please no. Please. Please. Don't let it be—

Anaella.

"No." The word escapes me, ice spreading through my veins as I fall to the ground at my sister's side, not caring for Pauline's looming shadow. *Please be alive.* She has to be. I run my hands over my sister's still body; her skin is cold to my touch. But then I notice the soft rise and fall of her chest and a sob bursts from my lips. Thank the heavens. Relief floods through me, but it's quickly replaced by a sickening wave of guilt. How did we get here? All of this was supposed to keep her safe, to heal her. Instead, I've been a greater threat to her life than the winter fever ever was.

Her head rests in a strange angle on the grass, her beautiful gown now partly torn, a cut screaming red on her cheek. I trace the line with a trembling finger. It will leave a scar, forever marking the darkness I brought on her. I want her to wake up and giggle, to say that this is all a joke. But her eyes remain closed, twitching sparingly, as if she's dreaming. Perhaps it's best that she remains unconscious for now.

Reality is not a place I want her to witness.

This is what happens when you cross Dahlia.

The demon has emerged to replace the angel.

How could she have done this to me? After everything she told me of her own loss, I thought she understood my pain—shared in it. I believed that she cared for me, that our connection meant something to her. How could she just blink it all away, flicking off her emotions like extinguishing a matchstick?

"What have you done to her?" My voice is stronger than I thought it would be.

"She refused to come quietly," Pauline says.

When I look at her, she's still smiling, not showing a hint of remorse. Did she *enjoy* hurting my sister? Rage makes my vision blur as I lash out at her, wanting with all my heart to strangle her delicate, dainty neck. "How could you?!"

Rough hands grab me, pulling me back before I can lay a finger on Pauline.

"Let me go!" I shout, and a hand lands on my mouth.

"Quiet now." Dahlia leans down and brushes a dark lock from Anaella's face. "Such a waste of beauty." She sighs. "I truly didn't want it to come to this, Cleodora."

I try to fight against the man's grip on me, but it's useless. He's too big. Too strong. His hold on me is like heavy metal claws pinning me down.

Desperation clings to my bones, making me tremble. My mouth is suddenly dry. I'm helpless. A pincushion for Dahlia and Pauline to stab over and over again.

"Lirone, dear," Dahlia calls.

I've forgotten he's still here, sticking to the shadows and watching the horror unfold. His eyes are wide as he steps forward, his gaze glued to my unconscious sister. The fear on his face is heart-wrenching—like watching another piece of his innocence getting stolen.

"Tell me again why Cleodora failed to deliver my Talent."

He hesitates, his gaze jumping to me for a mere second. Does he feel bad for what happened? Is he looking to me for support? "She and the vicomte were . . . *kissing*. After he left, she found the diamond . . ."

"Yes?" Dahlia says.

"I . . . I was waiting at the window. She just needed to toss it over, but—" He freezes as his eyes meet mine. I beg him silently not to say the truth, to come up with some excuse that will still allow me to protest my innocence. I can see the debate behind his unblinking stare, the understanding that his next words will determine my fate. It shouldn't be this way. He's just a kid. A kid who at that moment turns to look at Dahlia with the loving eyes of a son.

And right then, I know it's hopeless.

"But she didn't." Lirone stares at Dahlia. "The vicomte returned, and I ran to you, Lady Sibille."

I want to be angry, to lash out and fight. But it's not Lirone's fault. He's captivated by Dahlia, and I can't blame him for it. If our roles were reversed, I cannot be sure I wouldn't have done the same. My body resigns as I stop fighting against the henchman's hold and close my eyes.

No way out.

This is the end.

"Thank you, my love." Dahlia takes him in her arms, pulling him into an unexpectedly intimate embrace, like a mother holding her child. It's full of the softness I know so well, but now I can see something else underneath it. Something twisted, cruel—her struggles, her pain, the parts of her life that echo my own, have poisoned her heart. "Well, I suppose that settles it." She sighs. "I have no other choice."

She waves, and Henry steps forward, a gun in his hand. A glinting jade gem adorns its grip, but its presence only makes it more menacing. Is that his Talent? One meant for violence?

A shiver chills my entire body.

No. No. No.

This can't be happening.

She wouldn't.

And yet . . .

"Take care of this," Dahlia says.

He aims the gun at my sister's head.

My heart stops. This is all wrong. This is all *my* fault. I was meant to protect her.

I have to do something. I have to stop this.

Without thinking, I use all my strength to bite the palm of the guard muffling me. He curses as he drops his hand, his hold on me faltering.

"You little viper!" the man calls.

I dash forward, a cry escaping my lips. "Stop!" I position myself in front of Anaella, trying to block the gun, but the man has already recovered. He grabs me, his hands wrapping tightly around my waist as he pulls back. "Please. I'll do anything!" I struggle against him. But he's just too strong. I can't possibly escape.

Then Dahlia raises her hand, and the world freezes for a second.

He lets me go.

Henry lowers the gun.

"Anything?" Dahlia says.

"Anything." I'm shaking, tears streaming down my face. "Please. I beg you."

She starts pacing silently, and in the silver glow of the moon she truly does look like some divine being—only now I'm certain it's a demon. Her porcelain skin glowing, her raven hair shimmering. She is the perfect monster, one who doesn't even need to hunt for her prey.

Her beauty lures it for her.

"Don't think I enjoy this, Cleodora." She stops to look at me, the endless black pools of her eyes drawing me in from underneath her mask. "I wanted us to be together. For you to be *mine* . . . But I'm no longer sure that's possible."

Her words pull at my heart, the unexplained urge to please her fighting to pierce through my fear.

"Please." I stagger toward her, taking her hand in mine. She doesn't pull away. Even though she's moments from ending my life, I can't help the spark igniting at the touch of her smooth skin. If she ever cared for me at all, she won't do this. "Don't hurt my sister. Please, just give me one more chance."

I squeeze her hand, wishing for the softness she once shared with me to return.

Dahlia studies me for a moment that feels like eternity. "As you wish," she finally says.

I gasp in relief. "Thank you!"

"Since the vicomte is keeping his gem on his person, your opportunity tonight is lost. But you will bring me his Talent in one week."

"What?"

My heart drops again. She cannot mean that. That's too soon. Especially come morning, when the police realize what happened here tonight. This party was the one perfect event to steal a multitude of Elite Talents—a calculated carefully crafted plan. Dahlia's operation should be lying low after this. Why give me another chance at all if she's sending me on a doomed mission?

"The opera premiere will be your last chance. Your sister will stay with me as . . . motivation." Dahlia strides away from me and waves to Henry. He lifts Anaella off the ground as if she's no more than a sack of flour. I want to scream at him to put her down, but the risk of having Dahlia change her mind is too great. "Don't disappoint me again."

I nod, but my entire body is shaking.

"Lady Sibille?" Pauline says. "What about the boy? He should have stopped her from her foolishness long before it came to this. He should be punished as well."

But Dahlia seems uninterested, already walking away. "As you see fit, dear."

A wicked grin spreads across Pauline's face as she looks at Lirone, revealing the true evil behind her mask. Too late, I see her grab the gun from Henry's hand. The world slows as she cocks it and aims.

I scream, the gunshot piercing my ears.

CHAPTER TWENTY-SEVEN

Torn Apart

LIRONE'S TINY BODY falls to the ground like a puppet that's lost its strings.

"No!" I dash forward, but hands reach out to restrain me.

The henchman grabs me by my coat sleeve and yanks me back. I pull away harder, so hard that the seams rip and the coat slips away from my frame, leaving me free with only a single sleeve hanging on my arm.

I fall to my knees at Lirone's side. "Please. Please." He's just a kid. He doesn't deserve this. My nostrils fill with a metallic scent that sends my gut lurching. Blood gushes from the bullet hole in his stomach, pulsing with the beat of his failing heart. "Lirone," I whisper, but he doesn't reply. He's losing too much blood. I press my hands over his wound, trying to force the stream to stop as it oozes under my palm.

Strong arms grab me again, the henchman relinquishing the torn coat in order to pull me away from Lirone's still body.

"Let me go!" I cry. "He needs help!" But the henchman is relentless, ripping me away and dragging me back.

A whistle echoes through the night, and the man curses.

"We have no time," Pauline says. "Leave her."

"But Lady Sibille said—".

"Lady Sibille didn't say to get caught," she hisses.

Gun still in her hand, she throws another glance my way and sneers.

How could I have been so blind? Was she always this cruel, this cold? I can still see her soft smile in my mind, her bewilderment when I had her fitted for the gown, the awe on her face just earlier this evening when we stepped into the ballroom. This couldn't have all been a lie.

But then I remember something else—her eagerness for social events. The hunger in her eyes as she held my ruby in her hands. She was starved for this world, just like me. Dahlia was her way in. Just as she was mine.

Am I staring at my own future? Willing to lie, cheat, and even kill to get what I desire?

No. Not my future. A *reflection*. I've already done all those things myself.

I lied to my sister. Tricked and cheated Nuriel. Caused the coachman's death. I'm no better than the monstrous version of Pauline that stands before me.

A call comes from behind the massive green hedge. "Who's there?"

The henchman lets me go, cursing again under his breath. Then he and Pauline dart into the shadows, disappearing into the garden's maze to follow Dahlia, Henry, and my sister.

Lirone's tiny body is lying limp on the grass. I don't even know if he's still alive. I want to drop by his side again, sob, cry, stop the bleeding. But he needs medical help I can't provide . . . and if I get caught, my sister will face the same fate.

"Over there!" Another call comes, followed by resounding footsteps.

"I'm so sorry," I whisper into the night, though I know Lirone can't hear me. The steps are getting closer, but I'm already picking up Father's torn coat and my purse from the ground and staggering backward. I turn another corner and start running when I hear the shouts.

"Here! Get help! He's been shot!"

At least the guards can give him the care I can't. They might have never expected to be actually needed tonight, but I'll bet the Lenoir family secured the best personal guards money could buy, all boasting medical expertise. Maybe they can save him.

They *will* save him.

I need to believe he'll live, or else I'll break.

I push my legs faster, tears blurring my vision. I have no idea where I'm going; the road ahead is nothing but a dark haze. All I know is that I cannot get caught. I have to get away from the guards if I want a chance to fix any of it.

I've really done it—I've ruined absolutely everything.

I disappointed my sister. Put her in danger instead of protecting her. Caused the coachman's death. Failed to steal the Talent. Hurt Nuriel. Enraged Dahlia. And possibly cost Lirone his life.

All for what?

The tears come stronger, streaming down my face as if bleeding my soul out through my eyes. I tremble in the cold breeze, pressing Father's ripped coat to my chest as I force air into my lungs. My mind is fractured. My heart shattered. As if, like the coat, I too was torn at the seams—destroyed by brutal hands.

My foot catches on a paving stone and I stumble to the ground, cutting my hands on hard gravel. I wince in pain, a sob escaping me. I have no strength to push myself back up. To go on.

What if Lirone *is* dead?

Just like the coachman . . . If the guards had not appeared after hearing the gunshot, would the henchman have thrown his body in the river, too?

I shudder, another sob wracking me. I need to keep quiet, but the pain is too strong to hold in.

It's all my fault.

I was supposed to be the responsible one, taking charge after our parents passed. But I've made all the wrong choices.

"Think about Papa. What would he have said?" Anaella's voice echoes in my head. I hushed her. Ignored her words. But I know the answer.

Father would've been ashamed.

If he were alive and standing before me, I wouldn't be able to look him in the eye. He raised me to be kind, caring, honest, hardworking. Yet everything I've done in the past months has gone against his legacy.

I don't deserve to wear his coat. I don't deserve to carry his book with me. I'm nothing like the daughter he created it for.

I told myself I was doing it only for my sister. That I agreed to Dahlia's deal because I needed to pay for a doctor. But that wasn't the only thing that made me say yes.

It was the ruby.

The beautiful ruby, sitting on my finger.

It was all I ever wanted. To have a Talent, to be respected and adored. I longed for the acceptance of society, the sense of worth. The ruby provided all of that and more.

But at what cost?

I want to tear it off and toss it far away, never to see it again. But that won't get rid of the magic embedded in my blood. The only way to do that is for me to relinquish the gem to someone else, or die and take the Talent to the grave with me. Like Father did when he drowned.

I finally push myself up from the ground, whimpering in pain at the cuts on my hands. Blood covers my palms, both mine and Lirone's combined together in shades of red and dry brown. I look down, noticing the crimson spots on my ripped and wrinkled skirt.

What am I supposed to do? How am I supposed to fix this?

Dahlia has my sister.

I need to get her back.

But I cannot steal Nuriel's Talent to do so. I cannot keep going down the same wretched road I've taken up until now. I must do this the right way. The way Anaella would want me to. The way Father would've wanted me to. And that means only one thing.

I need to bring Dahlia down.

It's an insane thought. A terrifying one. Just playing with it in my mind feels like jumping off a cliff, as though Dahlia might be listening to my thoughts.

Weakness enters my limbs at the thought of her dark eyes. There was softness in them when she looked at me, something caring . . . loving. She shared parts of herself that resonated so deeply with my soul, and in those rare moments I was certain she felt the same. Was any of it real?

I got swept up in fantasies and dreams, and I trusted her blindly; I gave myself to her, even though I knew how dangerous she was. Lirone clearly thought of her as a mother, yet she turned her back on him without a second thought, as though, by sheer will, she'd turned her heart to stone. She walked away. She didn't even care what punishment Pauline would choose.

Perhaps he and I have both been fools.

Still, my heart clenches at the thought of betraying Dahlia, rejecting the idea violently. But in my head, I know there is no other way. She will never let my sister go without the vicomte's gem. And even if I did manage to bring it to her, I would forever be under her control. The only way to free myself is to ruin her operation. To make sure she can never cast her spell on me—or anyone else—again.

I let out a shaky breath as I wipe away tears with the back of my hand.

The garden is quiet, no evidence of guards nearby. Water cascades down the three round tiers of a small fountain in a steady, calm flow. The sweet scent of flowers stands in the air, replacing the memory of the metallic smells of blood and gunpowder. The manor is far behind me, its windows twinkling in the distance. I must have reached the far edge of the gardens.

Soon enough, I'll have to turn back. But I cannot return without a plan.

Dahlia's influence is endless; her spies are everywhere. I have no information about Dahlia's operation, no idea how it works or where she is based. And I can't go to the police. When the dust settles after tonight, they will be on high alert. The entire city will be thrown into chaos. Not to mention that Dahlia might as well have policemen in her pocket. If I make one wrong move, take any direct action, it could all backfire on my sister. That's a risk I'm not willing to take.

Fear grips my insides. It's practically a suicide mission.

I cannot do this alone.

I need help.

And I cannot keep lying.

To fix this, I need to untangle everything I've twisted. To come clean about all I've done and ask for forgiveness from those I've hurt. To do that, I must start with the one person I've deceived more than anyone else.

Nuriel.

I stare back at the manor, thinking of the rage that twisted his face. He won't want to talk to me, but I'll have to make him listen. He deserves the truth.

The resolve quiets my trembling body, settling on me like a layer of fog. The trickling fountain lures me in, its soft ripples twinkling as they reflect the darkened skies. I take a deep breath as my hands pierce through the calm surface, allowing the water to wash off the blood. The pain. The anger. The betrayal. Soon the only evidence left of the horror is the raw scratches marking my palms in faded pink.

That will have to do.

I pick the pieces of Father's torn coat from the ground and string my purse back to my wrist. This is the first decision I've made that Father would be proud of. The thought fills me with strength as I turn back toward the manor.

The walk back feels shorter somehow. One moment I'm washing my hands in the fountain and the next I'm already right under the windows of the ballroom, with music and laughter echoing from above. I hurry along the narrow path toward the entrance, but before I get there a personal guard blocks my way.

"Stop right there," he orders.

I halt, my heart beating faster. I must look a mess—puffy eyes, hair tangled from the fall, not to mention the bloodstains on my skirt. I lower my arms, letting father's coat hide the crimson spots. "Is everything alright?" I ask, my voice only slightly trembling.

"I'm so sorry to bother you, my lady." The guard bows, averting his gaze respectfully. "You should go back inside. It is not safe to walk alone at night."

I clear my throat. "I was heading back for another glass of champagne anyway." I hope my tone is as light and entitled as I intend it to be.

"Let me escort you, my lady."

I nod, allowing him to lead the way. As soon as he turns, I try to smooth out my skirt and run a hand over my hair, tucking the stray strands behind my ears. The warm light of the entrance spills out on the front stairs, coloring them in gold hues. Here there are more guards, but they are no longer standing at ease. Instead, they are walking in and out of the main doors with determined strides.

I hold on to Father's coat more tightly. "Did something happen?" I ask, feigning innocence.

"Nothing you need to worry yourself with, my lady." The guard accompanies me up the stairs, only turning to me when I'm safely inside. He pauses, finally looking at my face. I hold my breath. Can he read the guilt written on it? Can he see the traces of tears and pain? "Enjoy your evening," he finally says.

I let out a silent sigh of relief as he leaves me and joins another group of men. But I cannot let my defenses down just yet. The entrance to the manor is not as quiet as when I left it. Guards, servants, and even a few guests have gathered in the foyer. In all the commotion, no footman even approaches to take my coat.

"Baron Laurent said he heard it himself. He thinks it was a duel," a lady in a lacy black gown says to her friend in a hushed tone.

"And you listen to that drunk? Didn't he also say he thinks he dropped his gem in the fountain?" her friend answers.

How typical of them to dismiss what's right before their eyes—too busy drinking, dancing, and gossiping to realize the truth. By the time they sober up, their gems will be long gone.

"But I'm telling you," the woman continues, "one of the guards mentioned that they found a child."

"Why would a child be out here on his own? And what monster would shoot a kid?"

A crippling sensation runs down my spine.

"Poor thing," the other lady says, pressing a gloved hand to her chest. "They say he bled to death."

No.

I stagger backwards, crashing right into a passing gentleman. "My lady, I'm so sorry," the man says.

But I don't care. My mind is spiraling out of control. Lirone is dead because of me. The image of his tiny body lying on the grass fills my mind—the blood dripping from his wound, coating my hands. The sneer on Pauline's face as she looked at me, showing no hint of remorse. The anguish crashes down on me, making my head spin. I cannot breathe.

"My lady!" The man's voice rises, his words tinged with alarm. "Someone get her a chair."

Hands lead me through the crowd, pushing me down to sit. Someone offers me a glass of water, while another tries to get me to talk. But their words are an incoherent buzzing in my mind.

I washed away all traces of it in the fountain, but Lirone's blood is on my hands.

"What is going on here?" a voice calls over the men. "Cleodora?"

I blink through my shock. Nuriel is standing right before me, his face an empty mask.

"Everything is fine over here, gentlemen," he says, and even though his voice is cold, his familiarity is a welcome relief. "I'll take care of the lady myself."

The men bow and leave, but there is still a crowd watching us. My lower lip is trembling, my chest gushing with suppressed sobs that wish to tear it open. I cannot let Nuriel see any of it. I need to get a hold of myself. To tell him the truth.

"Nuriel, I—"

"I told you not to use my name," he hisses under his breath. "I thought you left. Come, I'll get you a carriage." He grabs me by my arm and pulls me up, not caring for the muttering crowd.

"You're hurting me," I say, trying to get out of his grasp. He tries to pull me forward, but I refuse to budge. "I need to tell you something. It's important."

"I don't have time for any more of your lies right now," he says. "You need to go."

"But—"

He grunts before suddenly lifting me up in his arms. I yelp as he presses me to his broad chest, carrying me outside, to the astonishment of the gawking crowd. I'm too stunned to even fight him.

My arm flails as he walks down the wide entrance stairs, and my purse threatens to fly off my wrist again. I try to grab it when I notice a giant bloodstain on its side. Panicked, I manage to stuff it under the coat, doing my best to cover it, along with my bloodied skirt.

His arms are strong, sure, warm. For just a second while he holds me, I almost manage to forget that he hates me.

"Get Lady Adley's carriage," Nuriel orders, whistling to a waiting coachman. "She's unwell."

"Let me down," I manage to say, but there's no conviction in my words. "Please. I need to tell you the truth. I—"

"Nuriel!"

I turn my head to see Madame and Renée walking toward us, no longer wearing their masks. They hold their long skirts up as they hurry down the stairs.

"What is going on?" Renée's eyes dart between us.

"Stay out of this, Renée," Nuriel says, but he finally puts me down. I stumble, my legs weak.

This is all too much.

"Watch your mouth, young man," Madame snaps back.

"It's fine, chère." Renée puts a hand on Madame's shoulder. "Nuriel, what is all this about people hearing shots in the garden?"

Another stab of pain pierces my chest. I cannot bear to listen to the news of Lirone's death again.

Nuriel takes his hands off me. "A boy was found shot, and I need to get my bearings and go to the Hôtel-Dieu. So, if you'll excuse me."

"The hospital?" I say before he can leave. "Is the boy . . . is he alive?" My heart is rushing in my chest. Could it be?

"The guards found him in time." He sighs and turns away from me, striding back toward the manor. But I don't care that I didn't get to tell him the truth yet.

Lirone is alive.

CHAPTER TWENTY-EIGHT

Cleodora Finley

"MY LADY, YOUR carriage is here," a coachman says.

I snap out of my thoughts, turning to look at the waiting horses. "Good. I need to get to the Hôtel-Dieu."

Madame blocks my way. "Cleodora, what are you talking about? You can't go to the hospital alone at this hour."

"I have to." I try to push past her. "You wouldn't understand."

"Enlighten me, then." She stares me down, folding her arms across her chest.

I bite into my lip but say nothing.

"Chère, don't pressure her." Renée joins Madame's side. "Are you not feeling well, dear? You look pale."

I start shaking my head but stop. "I am a little faint."

Madame huffs. "Well, in that case, I'm definitely not letting you go on your own."

"Certainly not," Renée says. "We'll go with you."

Before I can protest, Madame turns to the carriage and climbs inside, not waiting for the coachman's help. "Come on, then, we don't have all night!"

Renée puts a gentle hand on my shoulder as we follow her.

"To the Hôtel-Dieu," I say to the coachman. "And hurry."

"Certainly, my lady," the man says.

With both Madame and Renée inside, the carriage feels cramped, our large ball gown dresses dominating the space. They sit close together on the bench opposite mine, their fingers intertwined. Yet while Renée is staring out the window into the night, Madame's eyes rest on me, as if trying to pry the truth out of my lips.

"You didn't have to leave the ball for my sake," I mumble as the carriage shakes under us.

"That party was a bore." Madame brushes me off. "The only interesting thing about this evening was the dramatic ending. And since I don't believe we're truly going to the hospital for you to see a doctor, I have a feeling we'll learn a lot more about it by accompanying you."

"Hélène!" Renée hits Madame's shoulder gently, but she can't fully hide the interest on her face, either.

I should tell them the truth. After all, that was the decision I made— come clean, stop lying. But I also need to be smart. I don't know if the coachman can hear us, and after tonight I don't know who I can trust. If Dahlia finds out . . .

No. I can't even think about that.

I tear my gaze away from Madame and Renée and turn to look out the window, the silver shadows rolling on the dark road as the horses trudge forward. The Hôtel-Dieu is the largest hospital in the city, situated right in the center of L'Île de Lutèce.

Last time I was there, I was called in to identify Father's body. I remember walking down the grim corridors, looking out through the scratched windows at the lashing river that stole his life.

I don't want to relive that. I never want to set foot in that place again.

But Lirone is there, lying in one of those hard beds, facing unimaginable pain. Alone. Scared. Hurt.

I cannot leave him.

A dull ache builds in my chest as the tall buildings of Lutèce close in around us. Soon we are across the river, the massive cathedral towering above as we circle around toward the hospital. The carriage comes to a stop by the wide stairs leading up to the arched entrance.

The coachman opens the door for us, and I take in the large, U-shaped building. A long courtyard runs along the middle, surrounded on both sides by rounded windows and stone archways. In the darkness, the walls seem black, as though stained by the sickness lying within. I should walk straight inside, yet I'm frozen in place, remembering once more Anaella's small hand grabbing mine as we stood at this exact spot, an officer waiting for us to go inside.

"Cleodora?" Madame says.

I push away the image, a stray tear escaping. "I'm okay," I say as I wipe it away with the back of my hand.

Madame's eyes grow wide, and she grabs my wrist before I can bring my arm down. "What happened to your hand?" Her voice is sharp as she stares at the fresh cuts.

I pull my hand away from her, trying to hide it under Father's coat. But that only encourages her. With one strong tug, she pulls the coat away, revealing not only my hand, but the bloodstains and tears on my skirt. Her jaw drops in obvious shock.

"I fell," I say, offering only the half-truth, as I grab my coat back to hide the horror behind it.

Madame and Renée exchange looks but say nothing. Keeping my lips pressed tight, I stride toward the nearest door, both of them following closely behind.

A tired nurse in a white uniform looks up as we enter, blinking rapidly as she takes in our fancy gowns and sparkly jewelry.

"May I help you?"

"I hope so," I say, forcing my voice to remain calm. "A boy was brought here from the Lenoir Manor. I need to see him."

Behind me, Madame and Renée tense, but I don't care. Lirone is all that matters right now.

The nurse checks through a stack of papers on her desk, narrowing her eyes in the dim light of her gas lamp. She stops on a page, running her finger down the lines, and my heart quickens. This must be it. But then she keeps flipping through, wasting my time.

My leg jitters under my skirt. "Well?"

The nurse looks up at me, her watery blue eyes unimpressed by the vision of the entitled lady before her. "Are you related to the boy?"

"Not exactly . . . But I'm the closest thing to a family he has."

"Patient 1002." She sighs. "Gunshot wound to the abdomen. The bullet was extracted successfully by guards on site, and he has already been moved to the recovery ward. No essential organs damaged."

I close my eyes for a second, tears threatening to overflow once again. This time I won't be visiting the morgue. He is going to be okay.

"Can I see him?" My voice trembles.

The nurse's lips press into a hard line. "He needs rest." She turns away from us, walking toward a nearby door.

But I can't accept that.

I reach for her hand before she can leave. "Please."

Her eyes find mine, softening for the first time, as if she finally sees the person behind the mask of glamour. "Do you know his name?" she asks. "We have nothing on the record."

"Lirone," I say. "His name is Lirone."

She nods and I let her hand go. "Follow me."

Our heels echo on the stone floors as we walk along the wide main corridor. Even though it's the middle of the night, the hospital is not quiet. Nurses and doctors enter and leave closed rooms, while patients in thin robes fail to sleep through various pains.

I try to keep my eyes ahead and not let them stray. I do not need to see any more horrors tonight. A movement from a room to my left grabs my attention, but I immediately regret following the instinct to look. A man lies on a hard bed, writhing in pain as a doctor examines a bloody gash on his chest. I shiver, shifting my gaze back to the nurse.

I focus on her short frame, her high blond bun. The way her shoulders rise and fall with each step. But nothing will keep the image of Lirone's wounded body from my mind. The way he fell. His blood dripping onto the grass. The way his closed eyes twitched in pain.

"Would you like us to wait outside?" Madame asks, drawing my attention.

I didn't even realize we'd stopped walking. The nurse stands by a closed door, waiting impatiently. I know Madame and Renée would respect my decision if I asked them to wait for me, even though their curious faces make it clear they wouldn't like that. But this is a chance to tell them the truth . . . and their presence is comforting. I don't want to face this alone.

"No," I say. "Please come with me."

"He might be sleeping," the nurse says. "If he is, don't wake him."

I nod, taking a deep breath as she pushes open the door.

The room is small, overlooking the darkened river from its single window. But this time there's no dead body awaiting me. Just a hard metal bed with a thin mattress. And upon the white sheets is Lirone. Somehow he looks even smaller, younger. Too young to experience such pain.

I take a hesitant step toward him. I just want to see his face, to see his features resting in sweet sleep and not twisted in agonized torment. But as I lean over, he turns, round eyes staring right at me. I jump.

"What are you doing here?" he asks. Though his voice is weak, his glare is as sharp as ever. Accusing.

"I needed to see if you were okay."

"Well, I am. You can leave now." The hurt is written on his face, the sense of betrayal. I'm the reason this happened to him, even if I wasn't the one who pulled the trigger.

"I'm not leaving you." I shake my head. "I'm not like *her*."

His lip quivers before he turns his head the other way, refusing to look at me.

"Cleodora." Madame's voice reaches me as if from afar. "How do you know this child?"

I turn back, taking in her wide-eyed stare. How do I even begin to explain it all?

"Lirone is—"

"What in the devil's name are you doing here?" The door is flung open, and I jump.

Nuriel stares at us in bewilderment. He's still wearing his silver waistcoat, but now it's paired with a long jacket, and his bow tie is undone. His hair is messy, and there are drops of sweat on his forehead as if he's been running.

"I could ask you the same thing," I say, lifting up my chin.

"I told you I was heading here," he snaps. "I *also* told you to go home."

"Will you both shut up?" Lirone groans, the sound weak and painful. "You're giving me a headache."

Nuriel closes his mouth.

"Cleodora knows the child, Nuriel," Renée says softly.

"Don't believe a word that comes out of her mouth." He sneers. "She's a liar."

I flinch at his words, shame and pain hitting me like arrows.

"Stop this." Renée glares at him. "I don't know what went on between you two, but whatever it is, you have to put it aside. This child is more important, and he has already confirmed that he knows Cleodora."

"How?" Nuriel narrows his eyes.

"She was just about to explain when you burst through the door."

Nuriel's face is radiating anger, hate. Receiving his forgiveness might not even be possible. But I have to try. This is my chance.

"Close the window," I say, lowering my voice. "And make sure there's no one outside in the hall."

They seem confused by my orders but follow them anyway. When the room is secured from any prying eyes or ears, I sit down on the edge of Lirone's bed. He shifts, pulling his leg away from me, but, to my relief, doesn't reject my presence.

"I need you to promise me something," I whisper to him. "You cannot run back and tell her anything about me anymore. I need to be able to trust you."

Renée tries to intervene, "Cleodora, the child clearly—"

"Lirone?" I say, ignoring her.

This is too important.

I take a deep breath and close my eyes for just a moment. "Please, Lirone. I cannot keep working for her. Not after tonight . . . You shouldn't return to her either."

Lirone tenses. I'm not sure if he even knows anything other than life under Dahlia's rule. Did he ever have a family that cared for him? Was there anyone who showed him what family should look like? Unconditional love, safety, warmth?

The tension in the room is so heavy, I feel like I'm suffocating. Then Lirone gives the tiniest nod of agreement. I let out a sigh.

"I'm going to tell you everything," I say, looking straight at Nuriel. "I'm not proud of it, but I beg you to listen until the end before you make any judgment."

"We will," Madame says.

But it's Nuriel's confirmation I'm looking for. "*My lord?*"

"I make no promises."

I force down the lump rising in my throat. This is not the assurance I wanted, but it will have to do.

I start slowly, telling them about Anaella's sickness, about how we didn't have money. I tell them about Father's Talent, and how it was lost when he fell into the river. About his shop, here in the city. I see their confusion. The way the wheels spin in their heads as I reveal my real name. Father's name. Then I take them back to the first time I saw Lady Adley. I explain how I tried to steal from her, and how I was caught. From there it's a whirlwind of lies, deception, and death, all connected to the woman who has set my world aflame—Dahlia, Lady Sibille, the leader of the illicit trade in Talents. Their faces grow dark, their stares hardening. I can see the shock, the disgust, the pity, the fear.

Lirone stays silent as I talk, but he's no longer turned away from me; he's drinking my words in with the rest of them. It's as though hearing our shared tale somehow brings him strength.

"I'm not sure how many Talents were taken tonight . . . I was only meant to steal yours." I look at Nuriel, and the words are like hot coals on my tongue. "That's why I had your diamond in my hand. But I couldn't do it. I couldn't betray you. And Lirone paid the price." I choke for a moment, fighting back tears. "Pauline, my maid, shot him as punishment."

"Pauline?" Madame speaks for the first time, breaking the flow of my story. "She seemed like such a lovely girl . . ."

"She works for Dahlia." I force the words out. "She hurt my sister, and now they're holding Anaella as collateral. She was the girl you saw me with at the ball, my lord. They were going to kill her, but I convinced Dahlia to give me one last chance."

"What does that mean?" Nuriel's voice is low, almost inaudible, his bright eyes boring into me. I long to see some softness in his gaze, a hint that he understands, even if he might never forgive me. But there is nothing.

I bite my lips before speaking my final words. "I have until the opera premiere to bring her your Talent, or my sister dies."

I expect them to shout at me, to storm out and never want to see me again, but instead they all just stare at me, unmoving, waiting for me to go on.

"Umm . . . that's all of it," I mumble. "I never wanted to hurt any of you . . . I . . . I'm sorry."

"You're *sorry*?" Nuriel lets out a breathy laugh and pushes up from his chair. "You're a bloody criminal, and if what you're saying is true, there was an entire lot of them under *my roof* tonight."

"Nuriel, calm down." Renée puts a hand on his shoulder. "I'm not sure any of us would have made a different choice in Cleodora's situation."

"*You* did," he shoots back.

"I had luck." Renée squeezes Madame's hand. "Clearly, Cleodora had none."

I have no idea what they are talking about but, to my surprise, Nuriel relaxes back into his seat. For just a second, the fire in his eyes recedes.

"So you are truly the daughter of Camille Finley?" Madame asks. "He was such a Talented tailor, an artist."

I've never heard Madame praise anyone so freely.

"Yes," I say, my voice ringing strong. And as I say the word, I feel taller, filled with pride. Warmth spreads inside me. Father's work spoke for him—each gown he made was a combination of hard labor and heart. It wasn't just skill or magic that made him the perfect dressmaker. He had vision, and so much love to share through his creations. Yet the memory of him was washed away quickly, just like his gem—borne away by the river, never to be seen again.

I should never have forsaken Father's name. I should have held on to it, fought to keep it alive, not cast it aside.

Sour guilt rises up my throat. I will never make that mistake again.

"Well . . . *Miss Finley*." Madame nods to me in acknowledgment. "What is your plan now? Why come clean?"

I take a deep breath, the weight of my next words pressing on me. Yet, as insane as my plan may be, I have no other choice. "I have no intention of stealing your Talent, Vicomte Lenoir. I need to take Dahlia's operation down."

"Have you gone mad?" Lirone bursts out, wincing as he tries to push himself higher up the bed. His blanket moves, revealing bloodied bandages and sickly pale skin.

Before I can cover him, Renée shoots forward to his side. She tucks his covers with gentle hands, finishing with a stroke of his messy hair.

Lirone opens and closes his mouth as he stares at her with

unblinking eyes. Then he shakes his head and says, "Lady Sibille's operation is too big to mess with. Not to mention she has eyes and ears everywhere. I should know . . . I was one of them."

"Everyone has a weak spot . . ." I say.

"Not Lady Sibille." Lirone shakes his head and winces again. "She knows exactly how to use *your* weaknesses, but you can never find hers. If you want your sister safe, you can't go against her."

"But—"

"There's no 'but,' Cleo. Even *I* don't know most of her methods."

"But you do know some?" Nuriel asks quietly from his chair.

Lirone looks at him with narrowing eyes. "Yes."

"Like what?"

"Like, names of some of her Talent suppliers. Shipment methods. Some guards." Lirone lists them on his fingers. "Dahlia has been working on this operation for years. She has clients overseas. Her men were supposed to collect twenty-three Talents tonight, including yours."

Twenty-three.

I have to applaud Dahlia's initiative. It was the perfect plan—so elegant, so simple. With years between her last heist and this one, society has become complacent. One by one, the Elites dropped their guard, daring to flaunt their gems again like no one could harm them. They danced in the ballroom, laughed and drank, snuck away to the gardens for passionate caresses, suspecting nothing while their gems were stolen under the cover of the most lavish of parties. In one fell swoop Dahlia bested them all. By the time everyone realizes what has happened she'll be long gone, back to her lair of luxury and shadows. I can almost see the perfect smile blooming on her lips as she revels in the chaos left in her wake.

Another image enters my mind. An unlikely couple, standing close together in a dark corridor.

"Miss Garnier." Her name slips off my lips. "She's working for her too, isn't she?"

It makes such perfect sense, I don't know how I didn't see it before. Her strange behavior. Her avid interest in social events. The secret passage in her store. Her rise from unknown modiste to household name within mere months.

I remember the newspapers claiming that she inherited her Talent from a long-lost aunt across the sea. I never had any reason to doubt it. But now I know better.

There was never an aunt. Just Dahlia.

Lirone nods. "Yes."

Renée puts a hand on her chest. "Oh my . . ."

"I always loathed that woman." Madame grabs Renée's shoulders.

That's when I remember the conversation I overheard in their salon. Renée and Josephine used to be lovers. But that's not all that was said that evening. The women also spoke about an expansion plan for Josephine's business. Something about overseas shipments.

"I don't think Miss Garnier is *stealing* Talents . . ." My voice sounds hollow as the realization dawns on me. "I think she's *shipping* them."

Lirone's body stiffens beside me, and that's all the confirmation I need. "You know something." I glare at him.

"Cleo . . . I can't . . ."

"Dahlia walked away from you! She let Pauline shoot you!"

"But . . ." There are tears in his eyes. And for once, he finally looks like the lost child he is. A child who just lost the only motherly figure he's ever known. "You really shouldn't," he mumbles.

"You need not be afraid." Nuriel's voice is softer. "You were found on my grounds, which puts you under my protection. I will place guards outside this room to make sure no harm comes your way."

But Lirone is still looking only at me, unblinking eyes searching mine.

"Please." I rest a hand on his leg. "Tell me."

He puffs his cheeks and blows air before rolling his eyes. The familiar gesture is so welcome, I have to stop myself from kissing his head.

"The modiste's store is a front," he says. "Chances are Anaella will be held there too. The shipment is going out in a week. And Vicomte Lenoir's Talent needs to be in it."

Nuriel quiets, his face blank as he reaches for his waistcoat and presses a hand against his chest, marking the spot where his diamond still lies in hiding. "All for this." His voice is charged, strained.

"Your gem won't be there, but as I mentioned . . . she does have your blood already," I say, remorse rippling within me. "But this shipment could be a chance to catch Dahlia in action. If I can somehow get the police to intercept it—"

"And what about your sister?" Nuriel asks.

My eyes shoot up to his, and for a moment I see no anger in them. His stare is intense, but soft, almost resembling the way he looked at me before our kiss. It makes me want to close the distance between us once more, to gather him into my arms, to angle my face up to his. But then he breaks his gaze, shattering the dream.

"If twenty-two Elite Talents were stolen tonight, the police will want to keep this quiet for as long as possible," he says. "Another widespread panic like last time will not make their job any easier. Once the gossip gets started, it will be hard to keep it in check. At least, the fact that it all happened under my roof is in our favor. My family and I will have a fair bit of control over the narrative; and they will do everything to detach themselves from rumors." He is calm, collected, authoritative. It's a side of him I've never seen before. "As for Cleodora's sister, I'm very familiar with the type of building Josephine's shop is located in. If she's there, she'll be held in one of the cellars. We'll need the police—"

"You can't just go to the nearby station," Lirone says, groaning again as he shakes his head. "Dahlia has eyes everywhere. A whisper of any of this and Anaella is as good as dead."

Nuriel nods. "I have some connections I can trust. We'll need officers to go along if we want to contain this. But we'll have to break your sister out before the police raid the operation, or she might get caught in the crossfire."

"I might be able to help with that," Renée says. "Josephine still has a soft spot for me."

Madame stands as well. "I'm not letting you do this without me."

"You . . . you want to help me?" My voice is barely above a whisper.

Renée exchanges a look with Madame before reaching for my hand. "That ruby on your finger might not genuinely be yours." She circles the Talent with her thumb. "But my gem . . . is not even magical."

"Renée . . ." There's a warning in Nuriel's tone.

She ignores him and takes off her moonstone brooch. "It's just a rock."

My jaw drops as she rests it in my palm. She's not lying . . . It sits inert, not pulsing with any magic. I've seen her wear it every single time we met—how could I have missed it? The gem never glowed, of course, but I thought nothing of it since I never actually saw her painting. I just assumed it was her Talent.

"But how—?"

"I was lucky enough to have Hélène's faith in me." Renée smiles at Madame. "And even luckier that Nuriel fell in love with my paintings. I faked inheriting a Talent and Nuriel spread the word by purchasing my art. The moment people believed I had a Talent, things started falling into place. They were seeing what they wanted to see, and I painted only in the privacy of my studio." She stares at the moonstone with a mixture of love and deep sadness. "I know what it feels like to have no magic. I only wish people could see the value of my work without it."

It all makes sense now—the fact that Renée was older when she started painting, how protective of her Madame seems, her close bond with Nuriel . . . Renée's natural gift is clearly special to have fooled so many. If only her gem had been obtained back when the mines were magical, she could have fed it with her blood, actively endowing it with her own skills and creating a new Talent that could be passed and honed through the generations—just like the original singer who held my ruby. Instead, like me, she was forced to live on the outskirts of society until she found how to cheat her way in.

"I . . . I don't know what to say . . ." My bottom lip starts trembling.

Renée just smiles, wrapping her hands around me in a warm embrace. "I'm sorry you didn't have my luck."

I let myself sink into the protection of her touch, pieces of the weight on my chest lifting with each stroke of her hand on my back. For once, I don't feel so alone.

"From now on, your luck is about to change," Madame says.

"Yes . . ." Nuriel's voice doesn't sound as convinced, but the resolve in his eyes is undeniable. "So let's start planning how we are going to free your sister. Will you help?" he asks Lirone.

Lirone sighs. "I'll . . . tell you what I know."

Renée pulls back from her embrace. "Good. Let's end this nightmare you've been living in. We believe you, Cleodora Finley."

CHAPTER TWENTY-NINE

A Flower in Bloom

DAWN PAINTS THE sky in soft pastel hues as the sun opens up like a flower on the horizon. The river sparkles in the golden light, its surface glistening as though speckled with gemstones. I take a deep breath, allowing the crisp morning air to envelop me as I walk the city streets.

The buildings around me are quiet, laced with sleep, blissfully unaware of the horrors of the night just past. I wonder how long their innocence will remain.

My legs are tired, but I don't mind. I snuck away from the hospital, leaving my carriage behind. I'm not ready to go back to the estate. Not yet. I need to relish this sense of freedom just a little longer before I go back to being Lady Adley.

The world can wait for just a moment more.

They all agreed to help me—Nuriel, Madame, Renée . . . Lirone. After everything I've done, their trust in me is more than I deserve. I never thought they could forgive me. But they all promised to keep my secret.

I pray that the plan will work. That the press will stay in the dark long enough. That Nuriel's connections in the police will collaborate. That the panic won't spread. But even if all goes perfectly, there are still a few key points missing. For one, I need to figure out how to sneak away unnoticed from the opera premiere.

We're close; I can sense it. With everyone's help, it no longer feels like an impossible task.

But the risk is real. I need to be careful. Keeping the perfect mask for another week, convincing Dahlia I'm still working on stealing the Talent—it won't be easy. Even now, as I cross the massive bridge, I know I'm being followed. A shadow has loomed in the dark since the moment I left the hospital.

In truth, I'm not sure why no henchman has stopped me until now. It's that same level of confidence that baffled me when Dahlia shared information in front of Anaella back during our carriage ride—a complete and total disregard for any danger. Is it because she is so used to having the upper hand that she can't imagine anyone would possibly dare defy her? Maybe she simply thinks this is all a part of me getting back in the vicomte's good graces. Or perhaps . . . after everything that happened tonight, she just expects me to be an emotional wreck. Visiting Lirone or walking on my own might not concern her at all since she believes she has me right where she wants me.

Whatever the reason, I'm certain that if Dahlia suspected my motives I wouldn't be walking free right now.

I turn toward the maze of streets hiding my old home, my new sense of conviction burning within me. Dahlia intended her actions to shock me and force me to take action—and they have. Just not the actions she's hoping for.

I let my feet lead me down the familiar route. I haven't been in these alleys since I left home months ago. Somehow, the gray stones and crumbling rooftops don't look as dreary as I remember. There is something comforting about them, as though each crack is a proof of life. *My life.* My identity. I was never quite sure of what it was before.

The faded sign above our shop is tilted as if threatening to fall. My heart aches at the sight of it. I've missed my home. I've missed feeling like myself. I want to jump for joy, dash forward, and throw open the door. I can almost hear Anaella's laughter and the sound of Father's sewing machine whirring softly.

But Father's sewing machine has been silent for far too long. And my sister isn't waiting for me inside.

There is no home in this place. Not without them.

I press Father's torn coat closer to my heart, my hand stiff as I turn the handle. The door is unlocked and creaks in complaint when I push it open. I blink, letting my eyes adjust to the darkness inside. Everything is just as I remember: the tall shelves, the wooden counter, the cash register . . . It's as if no time has passed. Yet the place is cleaner than when I left it.

Almost *too* clean.

I trail my finger over the counter. Not a single speck of dust. This must be the work of the nurse Dahlia hired. Nurse Dupont must have left when my sister decided to go to the ball; after all, her services were no longer needed. Though after tonight, I'm certain Anaella will need medical attention.

I close my eyes, fighting to keep myself collected. I cannot allow myself to think of what Anaella is going through right now. The thought of her stuck in some cellar, confused, hurt, and alone is too much to bear.

The room spins around me. I stumble toward the sink and grab a glass from a nearby shelf. Opening the tap, I allow the water to flow for a few seconds to get most of the murkiness out. But the water is clear— not even a hint of grayness. How did Dahlia get this done?

The lengths she's gone to are astonishing. She has kept her end of the deal completely, even beyond my wildest expectations. The doctor, the nurse, the house, the food, the dresses . . . She was going to make my sister into a famous designer. She is indeed a woman of her word.

A ruthless, calculated, sensual beast.

She might be honest, but her truth is only partial, her promises intoxicating until they turn to poison.

I take a long sip of water and the emptiness of the store presses in around me. I'm so tired my eyelids are closing on their own.

With a sigh, I drag my feet toward the back room. Perhaps I can lie down for a few minutes, pretend I'm just a kid going to sleep without a care in the world. The two beds are made, new sheets covering the old mattresses. I sit down on the edge of my bed, finally letting Father's coat and my purse drop down beside me.

I've been grabbing onto them like a lifeline all night long, feeling the weight of Father's book, digging my fingers into the velvety coat as if it could soothe my soul with its softness. These are the only things I have left of him, and now the coat is ripped and the book is sitting in a purse covered in blood.

The pressure on my chest grows, exhaustion taking hold in my bones. I'm about to close my eyes to rest when my gaze falls on the desk by the wall. My sister's sketches are stacked in neat piles to one side, while a new watercolor set and brushes sit right in the middle. The bright shades are so vibrant, they almost manage to bring a smile to my lips. I can imagine Anaella's delighted laughter, the spark of joy in her eyes when she saw them. If only I'd been here to give them to her myself.

There are new sketches at the top of the pile: fantastic designs of feminine, pink, frilly skirts, coral corsets, silk layers, sheer sleeves. Her gowns are like an array of radiant jewels and blooming flowers, each one more captivating than the last. Every color stroke reflects my sister's soul, her art. I flip through the pages, tracing the delicate lines and scribbled notes. I'm turning over another page when I see it.

It's the same design Anaella was working on the day I was captured by Dahlia. The gown is even more stunning than I remembered—the velvet petals, the sparkling beads, the sweeping skirt. She has altered the color scheme, finally adjusting the design to her original vision. Shades of ivory and champagne transform the dress from a colorful garden into a sea of lilies, giving the gown a delicate feeling. Yet the textures add richness to it, something passionate. No, these aren't innocent lilies. These are the petals of white roses.

Compared to it, the extravagant gown I'm wearing seems inadequate. Anaella's design showcases the kind of dress that demands recognition. It's a dress that deserves to be seen on stage.

I gasp, almost dropping the entire stack of sketches.

This dress is the embodiment of Nova—The Enchantress. Her hunger for life. Her beauty. Her redemption. This is the dress our director has been waiting for.

And it might also be a solution to one of my problems. This dress might be the key to sneaking away unnoticed after the premiere.

The wheels in my brain start turning, banishing the webs of sleep. It's an elegant plan. Simple, yet insane. I don't even know if it's possible, if I'm skilled enough. Maybe I'm just delusional. And it would require cooperation from someone who has no interest in helping me. Not unless I offer something undeniable in return . . .

But in my mind I can already see it working, and I know I have to try.

I rush to the front of the store and stand on my tiptoes to reach a leftover bolt of muslin. The rough fabric is dusty and a bit damp, but just holding it in my hands makes my heart quicken with excitement.

Using the money I have access to as Lady Adley to buy proper materials will be easy, and there is a sewing machine back at the estate that I'm certain I can move into my room. The servants will find it curious, but ladies have taken up stranger hobbies than sewing. I can make Dahlia believe that this is all a part of my plan to get closer again to Nuriel—she'll be reassured if I seem to be moving forward with a scheme. One week is not a lot of time to sew a dress, especially with rehearsals; even Father would have struggled with such a deadline. But if I work through the nights, I just might be able to get it done.

I spread the fabric on the floor and reach up to the counter where we store our chalk. But something is still missing.

My body is shaking as I head to the back room and pick up the bloodied purse. But this time, the tremors are not purely of fear. A few crimson spots have sneaked their way through the fabric and stained the pages, but other than that, Father's book lies perfectly in my hands, finally back in its rightful home. The patterns for my sister's new design will not be in it, but Father's knowledge is. His essence, his tutelage, his guidance.

I place it on the floor right next to the waiting fabric and reach again for the chalk. My fingers tingle in anticipation as I pick it up, energy pumping through my veins.

Only this time it's not with magic.

<hr />

I'm not sure how time can both move at a frightening speed and slowly stretch out forever, all at once. Yet somehow all the rehearsals and sleepless nights of finalizing the plan and sewing are racing past in such a blur that it makes me breathless. While, at the same time, each day of listening to false rumors and sensing Dahlia's men watching from the shadows passes with agonizing slowness.

Over the last week there hasn't been a single person in the city who hasn't heard some form of gossip about what happened at the masquerade ball and the reason officers started roaming the streets—a violent gang on the loose, a mysterious mob-lord gone into hiding, even tales of an entire network of child slaves being exposed. At least the sheer absurdity of the rumors means they are far from the truth, which serves not only to keep Dahlia appeased, but to keep my plans on track.

Still, by the end of the week every cell in my body is taut with tension.

The opera house is a whirlwind of movement. The excitement and pressure of opening night is so high it's like a physical wave of energy pumping through the halls. The busy stage workers, the stretching ballerinas, the stern orchestra members, the anxious singers warming up with vocal acrobatics—I've never seen or heard such commotion, not even before the gala.

But the adrenaline isn't only because of the upcoming performance. The police are in the halls, desperate both to secure the house from a possible grand theft and to keep their real mission a secret from the public. To me, though, they are a reminder that time is running out, that after tonight everything is going to change.

There are so many things that can go wrong. One misstep and everything will fall apart, resulting in scenarios too horrible to imagine.

I stare at the array of chocolates and flowers strewn upon my vanity, my stomach tense. The ruby pulses with anticipation. I draw in a long, deep breath, closing my palm over Father's ring. All I can do is go forward with the plan. Which means that for the next few hours, my focus needs to be on the stage.

"Almost done, my lady." A timid maid fixes my hair with yet another pin, averting her gaze when our eyes meet in the large mirror of my dressing room.

I haven't seen Pauline since the ball, and my household has been rippling with gossip, since none of the servants has been brave enough to broach the subject with me directly.

Her absence feels strange. She was the one constant in this new life—the person I saw every morning and night. Something in me misses the ease of her presence, the familiarity and comfort of it. A part of me even longs to hear her wishing me luck, as she always did before each rehearsal or performance.

But then I remember the coldness with which she held that gun. The way she smiled at the pain she inflicted.

I'm not sure why Dahlia decided to keep her away from me. Perhaps she needs her to play some other role in her operation. Or maybe . . . just maybe, she knows it would be too painful for me. Perhaps she still cares.

I'm almost ashamed that I want the second option to be true.

"Are you ready for your costume, my lady?" the maid asks.

My body tenses.

I haven't told anyone in the production about my gown; the surprise of it is key to my plan's success. They all expect me to wear Josephine's latest, forgettable design. After the director rejected, vociferously, her "evil queen" costume, he and Josephine reluctantly settled on a rounded shoulder line, tulle-layered gown in shades of brown that makes me look like a chocolate cupcake. It's as though with each new attempt the dresses became worse.

If I walked out on stage in that gown, no one would remember it by the time the curtains fall. Leaving an imprint on the minds of the audience is crucial.

The maid reaches for the crisp white apparel box on the table, and my heart quickens. I switched the gown inside when I arrived and stuffed the horrid brown dress behind the couch. But was that a mistake? What if my own dress is even worse? I only managed to sew on the last of the beadings late last night, and I was so tired, I'm certain it came out sloppy. Besides, some of my stitches are too tight. Father would have made me redo them.

Panic seizes me and I jump out of my seat, pushing the lid of the box down before she can open it. "I think we should wait a bit longer. I need another vocal warm-up!"

"But my lady, there's not much time." She fidgets. "Perhaps you can warm up again after I finish dressing you."

"But—"

"There's no reason to be nervous, my lady. This is a big night for you, but you have nothing to fear with such a bright Talent."

But that's just it. I don't have a Talent. Why did I think I could make such a complicated gown without one?

My heart beats frantically as the maid opens the box, her eyes widening, her lips parting. She hates it. This plan will never work.

"It's beautiful, my lady," she whispers.

Beautiful.

And for just a moment I'm floating, all worries and nerves banished by that wonderful word. Tears spring to my eyes and I blink them away. Could it be real? Or am I dreaming? But the reverent way in which the maid touches the fabric is undeniable. I've done it. Even with all its faults, I truly have created something beautiful.

The maid pulls the dress out of the box, allowing the sweeping skirt to drape over the table. I can't deny the pinch of pride that takes hold of me as light shatters over the sparkling beads. I've brought my sister's vision to life.

All without a Talent.

Anaella was right all along . . . If only she could see it for herself.

The maid helps me out of my robes and into the gown. Unlike all of Josephine's dresses, the bodice fits me perfectly without squeezing the air out of my lungs. The length of the skirt touches the ground without me fearing I'll step on it and fall. Father taught me well.

And as I stare at myself in the mirror, my fears are gone.

It's the perfect dress for my plan.

I trace my fingers over the velvety petals as I spin around. The excess fabric fans out, making it look like a flower mid bloom.

The maid claps in delight. "You look like an Enchantress. Miss Garnier truly outdid herself!"

The fall back to reality is harsh, cruel. Josephine doesn't deserve the credit for this.

I open my mouth to say as much when a knock comes at the door. "Maestro Mette is calling everyone to the stage," a man dressed all in black says.

I force myself to breathe as I follow him out of the room. The reactions of the maid instilled confidence in me, but I still need to see the reaction of one specific person. Only then will I know if my plan can actually work.

José's warm voice reaches me before he appears around the corner, openly vocalizing outside his dressing room. He stops mid phrase.

"Ma chérie!" he cries dramatically, pressing a hand to his chest. "You are like a goddess among mortals!"

"Don't exaggerate!" I chuckle, but inside my heart soars.

"What happened to the . . . *cupcake extravaganza?*" He whispers the last two words as if speaking them might somehow make the dress reappear.

"Better not to mention it."

"Well, in that case," he interlaces his arm with mine, "let's just call it a miracle!"

It feels so natural. Walking toward the stage. Joking around. Humming softly to make sure my voice stays warm. Enjoying the pulse of magic from my ruby. As I let out a laugh and allow José to lead me down the corridor, it feels as though none of this will ever change. Yet the sight of the policeman by the stage is enough to shatter that dream.

José eyes the man suspiciously before pulling the heavy curtain to the stage wings, gesturing like a proper gentleman for me to walk ahead of him.

I straighten my back, holding my head high as I pass the policeman and step onto the stage. Over the last few days it has been transformed completely—the wide black floors now rise and fall with small slopes to mimic the opening scene of the battlefield, while the background features a stunningly accurate representation of a burning land. I watched in awe at the switch of sets through our final run-throughs, each piece of scenery more stunning than the last. Yet seeing it now in front of me, knowing that soon the massive red curtains will rise and reveal it to the awaiting audience, is almost unreal.

My astonishment is cut short by a wave of welcoming gasps.

"Oh my!" Lady Arnould calls.

But it is the look of shock and jealousy that spreads on Véronique's face that I was counting on. The seething hate in her eyes makes me want to jump with joy.

She will be only too happy to hear what I have to say after this.

"*What* is this?" A shout breaks the moment.

Josephine Garnier stands by the director's side, a vein on her forehead bulging with fury as she takes in my dress. After discovering the truth about her part in Dahlia's operation, I like her even less than before. But I can't show any sign of that. Not yet, anyway.

"This is not the garment I created for you! What is the meaning of this?"

I ignore Josephine's shrieking as I stare right at our stage director. It's him I need to impress, and given the fact he hasn't screamed at me yet, I know I've succeeded. He puts a hand on Josephine's shoulder, hushing her.

"A blooming flower." His lips stretch into a look that I can only interpret as a smile, even though it looks rather painful. "Magnifique!"

Josephine fumes, resting angry fists on her waist. "Mr. Agard, you can't possibly—"

"You see? You loud, impossible woman!" He throws the words at Josephine. "This is *art*!"

Josephine's face contorts as though he's just slapped her. And I cannot deny the sweet satisfaction that spreads within me as she storms out. No one rushes after her this time.

The stage director steps forward, taking my hand. "You are truly the embodiment of The Enchantress." His eyes travel up and down my body. "Who created this masterpiece?"

My heart hums as if wanting to burst into song, proclaiming the dress as my own. But I need to keep up my role for one more night. I cannot confess to being the daughter of a great modiste. What I *can* do is bring honor back to Father's name.

"It was created by the House of Finley," I say, my voice brimming with pride.

"Finley?" The director squeezes his brow. "I will have to meet the artist."

"Indeed." Maestro Mette joins in, already wearing his sleek tailcoat, ready to take the conductor's podium. "But as much as we'd like to marvel over the costume change, we don't have the time. I'm sure you've all noticed that we have some guests with us backstage tonight." The group grows silent as the cast throws sideway glances at the waiting policemen. "Rest assured, there's nothing you need to concern yourself with. The police are here only as a precautionary measure. The performance will go as planned, uninterrupted."

I hear a scoff from behind me. Clearly rumors have spread far too wide for everyone to accept this fictive explanation.

"The doors will open soon for the audience," the Maestro continues. "I want to take a moment to thank you all for your hard work. I'm very proud to stand here with you today and open a new season for Le Nouvel Opéra de Lutèce. I trust this production will be a huge success. So have fun, and let your Talents shine."

"Toi toi toi!" José calls, and soon the entire cast echoes him.

"Now, go! We have only a few minutes." Maestro Mette pats the stage director's shoulder as they walk away toward the orchestra pit.

"I don't buy a word of that," one of the ballerinas says. "I heard they were considering canceling the performances. They say there's a gang on the loose."

"*I* heard something happened at the masquerade ball," her friend answers. "My uncle locked himself inside the house all week. I think . . ." She drops her voice to a whisper. "They won't tell me anything, but I think his Talent was *stolen*."

The ballerina's eyes grow round.

"Nonsense." Véronique barges in. "If that were true, the Lenoir family would be the first to know, and they'd never have brought their Talents out in public. Yet I know for a fact that they are here with a full display, as is proper for such an event."

I almost smile. They're all acting exactly as Nuriel said they would. The whispers, the police, his family, all trying to create an air of assurance. To stop the chaos from erupting. It won't last—not after what we have planned for tonight. But for now, all I need is a few more hours.

I position myself close to Véronique. "Do you have a theory of your own?"

Her exasperated sigh is the exact response I hoped for.

"Not one I'd share with you." She turns her back to me, striding backstage.

I hasten to follow her. I don't have much time before the performance starts. "Can we talk for a minute?"

She pauses, lifting an eyebrow. "I have nothing to say to you."

"Don't be so sour, Véronique." José grabs both her shoulders from behind, making her jump. "Just because the opera is overrun by police and Cleodora is about to steal what is ridiculously rumored to be our one and only show, doesn't mean you can't try to bury the hatchet." He winks at me, chuckling at his own joke.

"Actually," I say, "can I talk to *both* of you? Privately?"

The smile fades from José's face as they both stare at me, but they don't argue. I lead them to the closest free room, earning a glance from yet another policeman before shutting the door behind us.

"I have something to ask you both," I say, taking in the empty violin cases around us. This area is clearly assigned to the orchestra members.

"And why would I do anything for you?" Véronique flips her hair back.

I have to force down my anger. I'm counting on her hatred for me tonight. "Because it will give you what you want—the upper hand."

She narrows her eyes silently, allowing me to talk.

"After the show tonight, I have some . . . family business to attend to."

"That's not suspicious at all," Véronique muses. "Running from the police, are we?"

"Not funny, Véronique." José presses his lips tight.

I ignore them both. "I'll need to leave discreetly, and I cannot afford to have the press or any fans following me."

Véronique snorts. "That will be impossible after they see you on that stage."

"Which is why I need help from both of you."

"What can we do?" José asks.

I take a deep breath. "I need Véronique to wear my dress after the performance. You'll pretend to be me, and together, as the two stars of the show, you'll sneak into a carriage and lead the press away."

"So you think I'll agree to this just for the chance to wear that gown?" She lets out a laugh. "You're delusional."

"No." I shake my head. This is it. The words that will change everything, that will truly set the plan in motion. "You'll help me, because if you do, I'm willing to give you the one thing you want most."

"Cleodora?" José takes a step toward me.

"I will quit the opera house. The role of The Enchantress and any that follow will be yours."

José gasps, but Véronique only smiles. "You will simply give it all up? What could possibly be so important to you?"

"Wouldn't you love to know?" I force a smile back at her, knowing the mystery will only draw her in further. If only her plan with the coachman had worked, she'd already have her answers. But instead, the coachman suffered the consequences of her meddling. "None of that matters. My offer stands—lead the press away so I can sneak out. And I'll quit."

"Cleodora, you can't!" José grabs my hand. "What is this really about? Are you in danger?"

"How do I know you'll keep your word?" Véronique cares nothing for my safety. Only for her role.

"When the press finally catches up to you, make the announcement that you will be singing the lead as Nova in all future performances. With you in the dress and me nowhere to be found, not even Maestro Mette could change the published narrative."

A spark ignites in her eyes as she twirls a strand of hair. "Deal," she says before heading out the door without a second glance.

It's done.

In the background, I can hear waves of sound as the audience fills the hall, excited chatter ringing above the tuning orchestra. The ruby on my finger reacts at once, the magic so strong it's almost painful, demanding that I sing.

This will be the last time I listen to its pull.

"Cleodora . . ." José urges. "You can still stop this. Your Talent is too great—"

"My Talent isn't worth the sacrifices I've made for it," I say, looking straight into his kind eyes. "I promise it will all be clear to you soon, but please trust me. You've been a true friend, José. And I am proud to share the stage with you one last time."

"I do trust you," he says, kissing the back of my hand. "And if this shall be your last performance, we'll make sure it will be remembered for the ages."

A call comes from outside the room. "Five minutes to curtain!"

"Thank you," I say.

"Come on." José pushes his shoulders back, bracing himself. "Time for Lutèce's Nightingale to sing."

CHAPTER THIRTY

One Last Song

THE EDGES OF my mind blur as I make my way to the stage. It's as if I'm passing through a tunnel whose walls block the noise and nerves, leaving a place only for what's right ahead.

The lead oboist plays the official tuning note, announcing the start of the concert and hushing the audience. A cascading effect of strings follows him, playing a floaty and open A string, then the D and E strings. Soon the rest of the orchestra joins, the different instruments fusing together to create perfect harmonies. I take a deep breath as they quiet, giving way to a wave of applause that announces the appearance of Maestro Mette at the podium.

For a moment there is nothing but silence—the world perfectly still in anticipation.

Then the massive red curtains rise, the overture taking over as dancers flood onto the stage.

The familiar harmonies wash over me. My heart beats fast against my rib cage as my ruby sends a wave of magic through my blood. From the stage wings, I can see the crowd in the darkened hall. It's a full house—each pair of glinting eyes mesmerized by the gliding ballerinas who echo the haunting melody with every move.

The footlights cast menacing shadows over the small slopes the dancers twirl around, making the battlefield come alive. Goosebumps rise on my skin. I just want to stand and stare at the beauty unfolding before me, to merge with the crowd and enjoy this wonder.

But I can't. My entrance is almost here.

The magic surges inside me, wilder than ever before.

This is the ruby's true purpose. It pulls with invisible strings, as if the magic is an entity of its own, yearning for the music, for the adoration of the crowd. The power of it is frightening, undeniable.

I need to give in to it. I need to let the magic take over and sing.

And yet I'm frozen.

After tonight, I will never let the notes fly out of my mouth again. Each precious melody will be my last. And though I know I've made the right choice, my throat clenches.

José's singing spirals around me, calling me to the stage.

My body moves of its own accord, reacting to the cues I've rehearsed for weeks. A collective gasp echoes through the hall as I emerge—the crowd, taking me in for the first time. My eyes wander over the ballerinas lying on the ground as I move up toward the horizon, The Enchantress searching for her Lover in the face of each member of the audience.

That's when I see him.

Vicomte Lenoir is sitting in the Emperor's Box to my right, his captivating eyes locked on me. Elbows resting on the railing, he leans his chin on his intertwined fingers. And when he shifts, the light dances off his diamond ring.

The music moves into a touching minor key. This is it.

I must sing.

My lips part, but my throat is still clenched. Then Nuriel smiles, and warmth spreads through me, determination and magic mixing together in one final flood of elated inspiration.

The next thing I know, I'm singing.

My feet tremble as I walk, my long skirt swaying with the movement. Against the darkened set of flames and blood, the cream gown transforms me into a ghost roaming the battlefield.

Each lovely note leaves me with a bittersweet taste, a strange mix of melancholy and the promise of freedom. Just like The Enchantress, my own emotions echo the hunger for life, for meaning, for belonging. And the music is the perfect outlet.

My voice takes on a life of its own, soaring and filling the entire house. I let my feelings infuse the phrases, drawing them out of the depths of my soul and presenting them to the audience. The crowd in return gives me strength, replenishing my energy with their adoration. I drink their intoxicating love as if it were rain pouring from the heavens on a scorched land, while they, in turn, feast on my song, only growing hungrier as the music intensifies.

There is something electric in the connection. Something intimate.

I have never experienced anything like this before . . . But I *have* seen it—in those final fittings Father used to have with his clients. Whenever a lady would try on her custom-made gown, created especially to let her true self shine. In those moments, when a woman would look at her reflection, the reaction was always the same: a smile, followed by a look into Father's eyes in the mirror. A silent thank-you, an appreciation of his art.

There was something magical about it. But as I sing, I realize it was never the Talent that created these moments. It was the heart Father poured into his work. And it is the heart I've poured into my gown and the vulnerability I allow now into my singing—that is what is creating this moment.

The woodwinds take over as the scene changes, matching the temperament of the urging percussion. Around me, the dancers spring back to their feet, flowing silk sleeves fluttering behind them in ghostly wisps. They circle the stage in a spiraling tornado, swallowing me inside their wave of movement.

The music grows in a fantastic crescendo, my body tingling with its intensity. Then we are no longer on the battlefield. The stage shifts beneath my feet, spinning to reveal a hut in a quiet forest.

José's strong arms lift me from the ground, placing me on a soft bed, as a detailed painting of a forest is lowered from above, followed by an array of sculpted tree trunks. I catch a glimpse of the vivid foliage before closing my eyes, imagining myself walking into the background scenery.

The orchestra drops to a dreamy pianissimo, moving the plot between visions of the past and present as the story unfolds for the audience. With each scene The Enchantress delves deeper into her memories, forced to face the decisions that led her to The Lover, and filling her with guilt—for The Lover is no longer just a stranger to her, and stealing his life to prolong her own is no longer just a matter of calculated business.

The stage shifts from a forest to a magical library, to a darkened cellar, to a sun-kissed meadow with ballerinas throwing flower petals in graceful arches.

José stands before me—at long last The Lover and The Enchantress face each other without the shadows of their past. The final duet ripples softly, our united voices allowing the truth to finally be revealed. And as I sing those last words, their power echoes in my heart stronger than ever before—the sacrifice is *not* worth it. The dagger falls from my hand, my ruby shining as the warmth of the magic travels through me, as if saying goodbye.

And just like The Enchantress, I feel wholeheartedly that I have made the right choice. I can only hope that my story won't also end with a tragic death.

I watch with wide eyes as The Lover falls to the ground, mortally wounded by his own hand. The stage lights brighten, signaling the surge of power that heals The Enchantress with the breaking of a new day. The orchestra builds up to the conclusion and I turn toward the crowd, allowing the light to wash over me, reflecting off every single bead on my gown—the sparkle every bit as magical as the enchanting harmonies.

Then the music ends.

For a moment, the world stays still as the curtains fall with a whoosh of air. I hold in a tight breath, the dramatic tension pressing on my chest. It's really over.

Riotous applause follows, exploding like fireworks in a roaring wave of clapping and enthusiastic cries of "Bravi!" The ecstatic energies seep into my bones all the way from beyond the curtains, melting the tension in my body.

"Fantastique!" José kisses both my cheeks as the entire cast springs into action, clearing the stage for the bows with wide grins. "Come!" He takes me by the hand, leading me to the stage wings just in time before the curtains rise again.

The crowd is wild, cheering in a standing ovation, waiting for us to execute our final cue for the night. The dancers are first, sinking slowly to the stage with one leg extended in a gesture of reverence. They glide backwards as the stage manager shouts from the wing for the chorus to take their spot. One by one, the singers step to the front, allowing themselves to show thanks to the audience.

Véronique comes forward, her perfect grin shining as she takes in the crowd. Even after performing she hasn't broken a sweat; not a silver-blond hair is out of place. Tomorrow night she'll be in the lead role, allowing her understudy to take her place. I can only imagine the victory she'll celebrate with me finally gone.

Then it's José's turn, and the crowd goes even wilder, whistles echoing through the hall in appreciation of the male lead. He takes them in as he blows kisses to the audience and claps for the orchestra and Maestro Mette.

"Lady Adley! Go!" the stage manager shouts.

I leave the shadows of the wings, the stage lights bright in my eyes. My heart beats so loudly in my ears it almost manages to drown out the crowd. Almost. I don't think anything can fully overpower the thunderous applause.

It's a sound of true adoration, everything I ever dreamed of.

With both hands on my heart, I go into a deep curtsy, taking in their love. I have shared all of myself with them tonight, every nook in my soul exposed and offered through song. They toss flowers to the stage, red roses landing by my feet, their deep color as vibrant as my ruby.

It's the perfect way to say goodbye.

The curtain calls stretch on until my cheeks hurt from smiling, the crowd refusing to relax and let the magical night come to an end. Finally, the clapping dies and the red curtains hide us from the hall, but on the stage the celebration is just beginning. The crew is cheering, hugs and kisses following lively chatter and laughter. Even the police lingering at the stage wings are smiling—the evening has passed without any incident.

So far.

I follow along, faces blurring as people congratulate me, tapping me on my shoulders.

Patrons soon find their way to the stage and I'm surrounded as each of them wants to personally compliment me, kiss my ring, and admire my gown.

"Lady Adley!" Maestro Mette's face is the image of pride. "Brava! You've outdone yourself tonight."

"Thank you, Maestro." I bow my head.

"No, no!" He laughs. "I should be the one bowing to you. This season will be our best yet!"

I smile and nod, but inside, my body tightens. I will not be a part of the season, and I can't stay here much longer.

My sister is waiting, and I cannot let her down.

I don't belong here anymore.

Luckily, I know the celebration is going to move outside soon enough. But not before I complete the next phases of the plan.

"If you'll excuse me." I flash another smile at our conductor.

I bump into the person behind me as I turn.

"Leaving so soon?" Nuriel asks, straightening the ends of his sleeves with a harsh tug. His movements are sharp, precise; somehow, they make me nervous, even though I know his appearance is not as coincidental as he's pretending.

"It was a long night," I say.

"Oh, but it has only begun."

The hidden meaning behind his words is written in every line of his face, from the way his jaw clenches to the slight tension in his brow. He knows what's at stake.

I nod, plastering on a polite smile as he starts walking toward the back of the stage, making me follow him. "Did you enjoy the performance?"

Nuriel lifts one eyebrow. "Do you need my approval?"

"That's not what I—" I bite down on my words.

What was I expecting? Praise? Affection? Or . . . a sign that he still cares? All futile. The only reason the vicomte is still talking to me is so we can take down Dahlia's operation. He wants to shut off the illicit market, to retrieve the stolen Talents. He cares for justice, not for me.

Nuriel nods his head toward one of the watching policemen, stopping right under some of the large set pieces still hovering above. Hanging by massive ropes, the tree trunks of the set are like a floating forest. I gaze up and notice that one of the hollow wooden pieces is swaying—it's almost time.

When I look back at Nuriel, he's staring at me. "It does seem that you were being truthful about your love of fashion. That dress is art."

"I . . . Thank you."

"I'm merely stating a fact," he says, but my heart still races as he takes a step closer to me.

His voice drops to a whisper. "Are you ready?"

"I'm not sure . . ."

Nuriel touches my chin, gently angling my head to face him. "No time for self-doubt."

My eyes meet his, and for a second, the world freezes as I sink into his emerald gaze. There is a hint of softness in it, a glimmer of warmth, of passion. Or perhaps I'm imagining it.

This is all a part of the plan, after all.

But does he need to lean in so close? The warmth of his breath makes me shudder as our lips almost touch.

Above, the wooden piece starts shaking.

His body stiffens, his eyes hardening. At once I'm pulled away from the fantasy.

"Don't let it hit me," he whispers, just as a massive crack reverberates overhead.

A scream.

A shove.

A crash.

I heave as we hit the ground, my body pressing against Nuriel's as he crumples under me. The massive tree trunk that swayed above us is now cracked in its middle, lying right where we stood. I pushed us out of the way just in time. A few seconds later and we both would have been hit. But I have no time to catch my breath. I have only moments to act.

"Are you okay?" I ask, running my hands over Nuriel as if to check that nothing is broken. But I don't wait for his response. My fingers finally make their way over his palm, sensing the warmth of his diamond.

"My lord! Lady Adley! Are you hurt?" The calls come from all around.

Nuriel shifts his focus to the crowd, trying to stand.

This is it.

My hand closes around his as I help pull him up; the ring slips off his finger smoothly and lands in my palm. My hand shakes as I hurry to close my fist around it.

It actually worked.

"I'm fine!" Nuriel says. "Just grateful for Lady Adley and her quick reflexes. But somebody here needs to be fired!"

"Everyone, please take a few steps back!" a policeman yells. "We'll get to the bottom of this!"

"Let's all move away while we make sure the rest of the set is secure," Maestro Mette calls, and the muttering crowd follows, shooting glares at the dangling tree trunks above.

But no other pieces are going to fall tonight.

My grip tightens around the diamond as I spot Madame near the stage ropes, a proud smile on her face. She provided the perfect distraction—allowing my "theft" to take place and giving me a perfect reason to retreat from the crowd.

Nuriel is now surrounded by worried ladies, all fussing around "the poor vicomte." He maintains the troubled facade so well I might have fallen for it myself if I didn't know better.

"Lady Adley, you're so brave," a woman to my right says, and others mutter their agreement.

I smile, but I have no time for their praises. Phase two of the plan is still ahead, and Véronique is already by the door.

"If you'll excuse me, ladies," I say. "I need to go refresh myself. I'm a bit shaken."

Understanding nods follow me as I head backstage, making sure to nudge Véronique with my elbow as I pass her—a gentle reminder of our deal. Then I break away from the stream of people, turning the other way toward my dressing room.

My fist is clenched so tightly over the vicomte's ring that its sharp edges prick my skin. I still don't quite understand why Nuriel agreed to risk his Talent for this. It's one thing to want to help, and another to put your most precious possession in the line of fire. Perhaps the fact that he himself was a target made it all personal for him. In truth, the entire incident was his idea. So were half of the fake rumors circulating in the city, and the offer to collaborate with his private contacts in the police.

I can only hope it was enough to fool Dahlia's men.

Leaning against the door of my dressing room, I let out a pent-up breath. I open my hand slowly and stare at the diamond. It's as beautiful as I remembered, its surface polished and glowing under the dim lights.

Just from touching it I can sense the magic pulsing, confirming the greatness of the Mathematical Talent it hosts—one of the oldest Talents on the entire continent.

This is not how I imagined myself holding it, but the purity of my intentions this time only makes it sweeter.

Still, the fact that everything has gone so smoothly so far only heightens my nerves. Too many things can still go wrong tonight. The most immediate one depends on Véronique.

Will she keep her word and come to take my dress? Her jealousy is just deep enough that I think she might. She wouldn't want to miss her chance to get rid of me. Would she?

I'm biting the inside of my cheek when the door opens, making me close my hand again around the diamond.

"Let's get this over with." Véronique strides into the room. "Why are you still dressed?"

I sigh in relief. "Couldn't really get the dress off on my own. Can you help me?"

Véronique pouts but reaches for the lacing on my back without a word.

I press my lips together tightly as she works, holding up the bodice with closed fists. "You sang beautifully tonight," I offer, trying to break the tense silence.

"Thank you," she says, pulling at the strings with force.

"Careful of the dress," I say just as the gown loosens, kept up only by my tight grip. I'm careful not to open my hand and expose the ring as she helps me out of the dress, leaving me in just my crinoline and linens.

"Now help me," she orders, already turning her back to me.

But the diamond is still in my fist, and I can't undo her dress with only one hand.

"Well?" she snaps.

Without thinking, I stuff the ring into my mouth before she can turn to look at me.

She huffs as I tug at the red velvet string of her bodice. "Can you hurry? A child moves faster than you." Véronique taps her leg as I work, each second stretching. "I don't understand you," she finally says. "You came here out of nowhere, rose to stardom, got everything anyone could ever ask for—Talent, money, romance, adoration. They call you 'Lutèce's Nightingale,' for heaven's sake. And now you're just giving it all up? I don't buy it."

She turns to face me just as her own dress releases. But I cannot reply, the ring still sitting on my tongue.

"You have nothing to say?" She lifts her brow. "Typical." Véronique pushes away from me, managing to slip out of her dress on her own. Still standing inside her crinoline, she reaches for my gown and pulls it over her head. The creamy petals rattle softly as she fans the fabric. "Where did you even get this dress from?"

I shake my head ever so slightly, wishing desperately I could speak as I help her with the beaded bodice.

"Fine, don't tell me anything. But I know you're hiding something. The House of Finley closed down long ago."

I almost swallow the ring from shock. A fit of coughing overtakes me as I cover my mouth with my hand, spitting the diamond right into my fist. "What do you know about that?" I manage.

She narrows her eyes. "Only that that fashion house hasn't made anything worthy since my mother graced this stage."

"Your mother?"

"Mirella Battu, the great soprano. Seriously, have you been living under a rock all this time?"

The memory grabs me. The image of Father holding my hand as we cross the river, carrying a beautiful sky-blue dress. "This garment will be worn at the masquerade ball by the great soprano Mirella," Father said. "In a few years, it will be you who sews her dresses."

The words echo in my mind as Véronique adjusts the corseted-bodice. "Your chest is so small to fit in this," she complains, pulling to loosen the laces in the back.

But I can only smile. Because Father's promise came true. The great Mirella might have retired, but a dress I made is now being worn by her daughter. And even though she won't admit it, admiration is written on her face.

"Do you have a cape?" she asks.

"Umm . . ."

"A cape!" She flips her hair in annoyance. "So I can cover my head when I step outside. You do want them to think I'm you, right?"

"Yes. Of course!" I rush to get my cape from its place on the armchair. "Here you go."

Véronique puts it on, pulling the hood over her head. "I ought to call those policemen downstairs to interrogate you with how sketchy you're acting."

"Why don't you?"

She raises a single perfect eyebrow. "And risk my chance of getting rid of you? Trust me, if my mother could have got rid of your cousin years ago, she'd have done it. The Adleys and Battus have been rehashing the same old pattern for too many years. It's time for the *better* name to win. I must say, though, achieving it this way isn't as fulfilling as I thought it would be. But at least I don't have to dirty my hands anymore."

The reference to the coachman sends a chill down my spine. But what happened to him wasn't her fault. It was mine. Véronique had no idea what she was getting involved in. All she wanted was to reclaim her rightful place at the opera—a place that her mother raised her to assume. She deserves it more than I do.

"I'd say I'll miss you, but that would be a lie," Véronique says, turning away from me toward the door.

"Thank you," I call after her.

She pauses for just a second before striding out of the room.

I have no time to waste, but somehow all I can do is stare at the closed door, the diamond still hidden in my palm. The minutes tick by. Véronique must already be outside. Will she and José pull it off and get into a carriage without her being recognized? Will the street be empty when I sneak out?

Forcing my legs to move, I turn my back to the door. I'm still in my undergarments, and Véronique's costume is on the floor. Picking it up, I carefully place it on the pink couch before swiftly stepping out of my crinoline. I have already selected my escape dress beforehand, the dark navy gown and petticoat waiting for me on the rack. Even though it's not the most inconspicuous of choices the busk at the front of the bodice was the deciding factor—allowing me to put it on with ease.

Soon I'm dressed, wearing my own hooded cloak and clutching my purse as I hurry down the corridor toward the exit. I promised myself this would be the last time Father's book would be away from its rightful place at home. After everything I've gone through with its weight in my hands, facing tonight without it felt wrong. I draw strength from its presence—a reminder of what I'm fighting for.

There are barely any people around, but I keep my head low as I skip down the stairs two at a time. The door stands open, revealing an empty street and cool night air.

It worked!

It really worked.

Except now the riskiest phase of the plan still lies ahead.

I only manage to place one foot on the pavement before a shadow looms over me.

"What took you so long? Lady Sibille is tired of waiting."

CHAPTER THIRTY-ONE

When the Bell Tolls

HENRY IS QUIET inside the carriage as the horses pull us forward through the dark streets. I clench my teeth and stare at my knees, doing my best to avoid his gaze.

Last time I saw him, his callused hands held a gun, his expression unfazed at the thought of murder. The image of his giant arms carrying my unconscious sister before they disappeared into the night is forever branded in my mind.

If Lirone's information is accurate, none of the henchmen are allowed to hurt me. Yet Henry's giant figure still makes me shudder. I press my body to the wall of the carriage, trying to minimize any contact with him.

If all goes according to plan, he should be taking me straight to where I need to go. All I have to do is act shocked when we get there. A dash of scared won't hurt either—though that won't be difficult to achieve, seeing that my heart is already racing.

"Where are we going?" I feign ignorance.

Henry grunts. "If you want to see your sister, keep your mouth shut."

I lower my head, my hand clammy as I tighten it over the diamond. This ring is my only hope to save my sister, the only card I have left to play.

I need it to be enough.

According to Lirone, the shipment of the Talents will happen at midnight, and since the performance ended so late, time is running out. A fact I was counting on. No one, not even Henry, wants to risk Dahlia's wrath if the diamond doesn't make it on time.

Even though Henry keeps the curtains shut, I can tell we are getting closer. I sense the bouncy shift of cobblestones under us, then the smoothness of stones as we cross the river over the bridge, the rushing water barely audible over the sound of turning wheels and clopping hooves.

Soon we slow, the careful pace marking our entrance into the narrow alleys surrounding the main avenue. We must be heading to the storage areas at the back of the fashion house. I'm fidgety, bouncing my leg under my skirt.

What if Dahlia sees through my act?

Fooling her henchmen is one thing, but Dahlia could always read me like an open book. My fears, my needs, my desires, they are all exposed under her gaze. One glance of her dark eyes is enough to awaken the need to please her. And one brush of her cherry lips is all it takes for me to forget myself and want to lay down my life for her. Just thinking about her soft touch makes my head cloud. How am I supposed to hold myself against her?

The carriage comes to a stop and my heart jumps to my throat.

I'm not ready for this.

One wrong move and my sister will pay the price, and the vicomte will never see his Talent again. Air refuses to fill my lungs, leaving me light-headed. The burden is too much. But I cannot turn back.

I have come too far.

Henry grabs me by the arm, dragging me out into the grim street. A single streetlamp twinkles at the far corner of the alley, giving a mellow glow to the gray stone walls. Just ahead, guards load a large wagon covered by a black awning, while more men carry wooden crates from a door to my left. And right there at the threshold, overseeing the work, is Pauline.

I freeze.

Where is Dahlia?

I did not expect to see my treacherous maid. In fact, I hoped I'd never have to see her ever again. Yet here she is, fiery red hair loose around her shoulders and a tight black dress aging her up a few years. My insides quiver, my stomach threatening to empty itself onto the uneven pavement.

"Well, well, well, look who decided to show up." Pauline looks up from the chart in her hand. "You're late."

"Her fault." Henry shoves me forward.

"Of course it is." She sneers. "Where is the Talent?"

"In her hand. I saw her steal it from the idiot myself. He was searching for it like a lost puppy right before we left." Henry barks out a laugh.

"I bet he was." Pauline cracks a smile, the expression resembling the lovely grins I remember, and yet there is something wrong about it—something twisted. "The police won't be able to cover things up much longer. Though I do appreciate the irony of their failed efforts. Chaos is inevitable now."

From the smirk on her face, one might imagine she actually relishes the idea of the panic to come. Years of quiet and safety snatched away in one fell swoop. It makes me sick.

Another man appears from inside the building, followed by a woman in a deep pink coat. "Twenty more crates left," Josephine Garnier says. "I hope the wagon has enough space." She pauses as her gaze falls on me, her eyes narrowing. "What is *she* doing here?"

Her voice is full of disdain. Did she not know I was working for Dahlia this whole time? Or is her anger aimed at the dress I wore today and the humiliation I caused her by outshining her creations?

"What are *you* doing here?" I force the words out, keeping my mask of ignorance intact. "You . . . you work together?"

"Ugh, I have no time for this," Pauline snaps. "I was hoping Henry brought you here so we could throw you in the cellar with the other one. But if you really have the Talent, just give it here so we can get this over with."

I stiffen, lifting up my chin. "My sister first. Or does Dahlia not keep her promises anymore?"

Pauline narrows her eyes, her lips tight.

"Do you want me to take her?" Josephine asks.

"Fine, but be quick and—"

"Miss Garnier!" A man comes rushing out, panting. "The bell on the main floor is ringing."

"At this hour?" Josephine blinks.

"It's some lady. She seems drunk, and . . ." The guard shifts uncomfortably for a second. "She keeps shouting that she made a mistake letting you go."

My body tenses in anticipation of Josephine's reaction. Her cheeks are turning a deeper shade of red. I guess Madame was right about her all along. The one thing Miss Josephine Garnier craves more than anything is praise. That will be her downfall.

"Oh, well, in that case." She pushes her chest out. "I'll go take care of that. Pauline, could you—"

"Go." Pauline sighs. "You," she shoots at me. "Inside, quickly."

I stumble as I chase after her, the darkness of the corridor closing around me. "Where are we? Is this Miss Garnier's fashion house? Where is Dahlia? And where is my sister?" I let the questions spill out, a combination of fake and real ones to keep it all believable.

"Stop talking," Pauline orders. "You're giving me a headache."

I bite my tongue, shoving my rage deep inside. If all goes well, the smug smile will be wiped off her face soon enough. She deserves to pay for everything she's done.

But Dahlia's absence sets my nerves on edge. I search for her around each corner, but she's nowhere to be seen. How am I supposed to bring her down when she's not here?

Pauline leads me to a rusty metal door. A lit candelabra awaits her on a shelf along with a set of keys. Stuffing the key into the keyhole, she turns it and pushes the door, the shriek of metal reverberating.

At once, the familiar sound grabs hold of me and an image flashes in my head. A dark room filled with the heavy scent of mold. A rope cutting into my skin. Dark red marks on a concrete floor. I know the truth before I even glance inside.

This is the same cellar that held me when Dahlia's thugs captured me the first time.

"Who's there?" My sister's voice echoes from within, and that's all it takes for my self-control to falter. I dash forward past Pauline, nearly tripping down the stairs.

"Ann!" I fall on my knees at her side, running my hands over her as if to convince myself that she's real.

"Cleo? Is it really you?" Her voice trembles.

She's sitting on the floor, cramped in one of the corners of the cellar, with a dirty blanket covering her body. Her skin is pale, her eyes red from crying, her curls a mess of tangles. I kiss the top of her head, my fingers tracing the line on her cheek. The deep cut has closed, a faint red line running from just under her eye to her jaw.

"Oh, Ann . . . I'm so sorry." I wrap my arms around her.

"No, *I'm* sorry." She sniffles into my shoulder. "I made everything a million times worse."

"You have nothing to apologize for. I should have listened to you sooner."

A snicker comes from behind me. "How touching," Pauline says. "Now give me the gem."

I turn to face her, wiping the tears from my eyes. "Let my sister go first."

"You really think you are in a position to negotiate?"

"What about Dahlia?" I ask. "Why isn't she here?"

"You like the sound of your own voice too much. Lady Sibille put me in charge. Now give it to me."

I clench my teeth as I stand back up, everything inside urging me to refuse.

I cannot let her have the diamond.

But getting Anaella out safe is all that matters. That's why we didn't have the police burst in here before now. "Will you let Anaella go right away?"

She rolls her eyes, opening her palm.

Acid burns my throat again as I place the ring in her hand.

"Thank you, Cleo." She smiles.

"Now let her go."

"Oh, I don't think so." Pauline examines me like a cat looking at a fat mouse. "You see, I don't think you deserve to keep that Talent of yours, either. And I definitely don't think you can be trusted."

Panic clenches my throat. "What happened to you? I—I thought you were my friend. You and I, we're the same."

"Your friend?" Pauline lets out a laugh. "I was your *maid*. And I hated every minute of it. 'Yes, my lady.' 'No, my lady.' What a bore. And as for us being the same . . . nothing could be further from the truth." She circles her hand over the diamond. "You think that just because we both longed for a Talent we share some sort of kinship? But you only had to be Talentless for, what, a year? I had to live with it my entire life. Your father was a craftsman with a gem. My father was a drunk with seven kids. I've been working for Lady Sibille since I was a child!" Her face is now a mask of rage. "That ruby should've been mine once that stupid old woman tried to back out of her deal!"

"What—what are you talking about?"

"You didn't really think the former Lady Adley *wanted* to retire, did you? No one breaks a deal with Lady Sibille. You only got that Talent because she was an idiot—she grew tired of her missions but she wanted to keep all the perks. When Lady Sibille wanted to send her away, she tried to go to the police instead of accepting her fate. She could have enjoyed her old age by the beach, but instead she ended up getting herself killed. At least she got what she deserved."

I feel sick, hot and cold flashes running through my body.

"And now . . ." She draws a gun from a hidden pocket sewn into the seam of her dress. "It *will* be mine."

Anaella yelps in fear, and I hurry to shield her body with mine. "It's me that you want. Let my sister go and you can have the ruby."

"So she can run to the police?" Pauline shakes her head in amusement. "I don't think so. Lady Sibille ordered us not to hurt you, but if you struggled and I had no choice . . . I'll be her hero." She aims the gun at my leg. "First, we'll need some blood for the ceremony."

"Close your eyes," I say to Anaella just as the gun fires.

My sister screams, and a second later there's a thump as a body hits the ground. I gawk at Madame's tall figure hovering over Pauline's limp body and gripping a fabric beater—the sturdy tool I've seen countless times smoothing out textiles, turned weapon in her hands. Just next to me, dust falls where the bullet dug into the wall.

"Are you girls okay?" Madame asks.

"What . . . ? Who are you?" Anaella trembles.

"I've never been so happy to see you!" I rush to hug Madame. "Is Renée—?"

"She helped me get in, and she's keeping Josephine distracted," she says, clearly forcing the words out. "I hate that the horrid woman still has a soft spot for her."

"I know." I squeeze Madame's hand. "Thank you for coming. You saved us."

She clears her throat. "Yes . . . well. Let's get out of here."

I snatch the diamond back from Pauline's limp hand and stuff it in my purse before helping Anaella up the stairs. "We need to be quiet— there are too many guards around."

"This way," Madame whispers as she leads us down the narrow corridor.

We climb a set of stairs, the floor under our feet soon turning from concrete to carpet. A moment later, Madame pushes open another door and we are in the upper level of the store, a row of fitting rooms stretching out on each side.

I hold Anaella's hand tightly as we tiptoe forward all the way to the main entrance. I pause by the door when I see Madame is stalling. "What are you waiting for? We have to go."

"Not without Renée," she says. "You go. I'll follow."

"What are you talking about?" I whisper. "This isn't part of the plan. You can't stay here on your own."

"I'm not leaving without her."

I bite my lip as I stare at her. But it's clear there's no changing her mind.

"Ann . . . listen to me. I need you to run to the corner of Rue de Legros, by the bakery that used to be on our street. Do you remember the man you met at the ball? He'll be waiting there—Nuriel Lenoir. I need you to tell him your name, and that I'm waiting for him. Do you understand?"

"What?" Anaella shakes her head rapidly, barely keeping herself from crying. "No. Cleo, I can't leave you here. It's too dangerous. You—"

I grab her by her shoulders and look straight into her eyes. "I need you to trust me. Please."

Her entire body is shaking, but she gives me a tiny nod.

"The corner of Rue de Legros, by the bakery," I repeat. "Find Nuriel."

She places her hand on the doorknob, and I feel Madame's body stiffen beside me.

"Wait, the bell!"

But her warning is a fraction too late. As the door swings open, the string hanging above stretches and the bell chimes, shattering the stillness. I flinch, a wave of dread washing over me. That's done it. Our location has been exposed. My heart drops as footsteps echo toward us in the distance.

"Go!" I say, seeing the color draining from Anaella's face.

She runs.

CHAPTER THIRTY-TWO

The Choice

ANAELLA SLIPS AWAY quickly and quietly, but the damage is already done. Everything was going so perfectly until now, I almost believed we could make it, that our plan would work without a flaw.

How naive of me.

Footsteps echo from the upper floor, and a second later Josephine appears at the top of the stairs. Her gaze falls on Madame, and then on me.

"You," she spits.

"Mon amour, where did you . . ." Renée's voice falters when she takes in the scene.

Within a split second, Josephine grabs Renée, pulling out a knife and pressing it to her throat. "You liar! I can't believe I fell for it. Guards!"

I should run, follow my sister and find Nuriel. But I'm frozen. I cannot leave Madame and Renée behind. I cannot just abandon them when the entire reason they are here is to help me. I cannot have any more innocent blood on my hands. Not after the coachman.

"Let go of her, you strumpet!" Madame calls, not bothering to keep her voice down anymore.

"Or what?" Josephine mocks as henchmen flood the room.

I don't even fight when they grab me. There are too many of them, their guns gleaming in the faded lamplight.

Madame is feistier; she's swinging her fabric beater at their heads as they lunge for her. "Rot in hell!" she curses as they snatch her weapon and push her to the ground.

"Silence!" A gunshot pierces the air, and Renée screams.

My breath is so shallow I fear I might faint. But no one falls in a pool of blood before me. The room is as silent as a tomb. I let my eyes wander up, taking in Pauline's tiny figure and the gun still aimed at the ceiling above her head.

Her face is a vicious mask of vengeance, marked by a stain of blood from where Madame's beater struck her. Yet the wound only makes her seem more feral. I quiver at the sight. We should have locked her in the cellar when we had the chance.

"Lady Sibille put me in charge tonight." She bites on each word. "I'll be damned if one more thing goes wrong. Do you all understand?"

The henchmen nod, and the rough hands holding me down grip me even tighter.

"You . . ." Pauline steps slowly down the stairs, her round eyes glued to me. "You thought you could break a contract with Lady Sibille. Free your sister and keep your *boyfriend's* Talent. You make me sick."

She snatches the purse from my grasp and starts digging inside it at once. I flinch as Pauline empties my possessions onto the floor, throwing Father's book down as if it were a dirty rag she didn't want to touch. Her lack of regard for it makes my blood boil.

"You are the one who makes me sick," I say, surprised by how even my voice is.

"I'll take that as a compliment." Pauline's lips curve into the familiar twisted smile as she considers the diamond in her hand. "Take this and store it with the right blood sample," she orders one of the men, handing him the gem along with her gun—no longer needing it with the hoard of henchmen surrounding us. "The shipment should be ready by now."

"Pauline, let's get this done quickly," Josephine urges, her knife still pressed to Renée's throat. "We don't have all night."

"What are you going to do to us?" I ask, trying to get them to talk longer. I need to stall, to buy enough time for Anaella to get to Nuriel and the police. He is our only hope now.

"If you need to ask, you're more daft than I thought." Pauline sneers. "I just wonder where we should toss your bodies."

Josephine chuckles. "How about the river?"

My eyes snap up to hers, but she's not looking at me. Instead, her eyes are glued to Father's book still resting on the floor, something resembling hunger in her gaze. "Having her end up like her father seems like nice symmetry to me."

A shiver runs down my spine, my mind blanking for a second. *What did she just say?*

"You know, I never did like guns much, so impersonal." Pauline grabs my hand before pulling out a knife, but I'm beyond caring.

Josephine *did* recognize the book when I was last here. She knew exactly who I was. Who my father was.

But Father's fall into the river was an accident. A horrible accident that happened because he was desperate. His Talent was lost in the fast-moving river that took his life. The police said so.

Pauline's knife slices into my palm, reopening the scar Dahlia gifted me months ago, with a searing pain that makes me scream. She's forcing the ruby off my finger, but my mind is still spinning.

The report said Father was drunk. I always thought it must have been desperation that drove him to liquor, even though it went against everything I knew about him. Father never drank. The world spins around me and my breathing turns ragged. It can't be true. His fate couldn't possibly have been the same as the coachman's. It simply couldn't. And yet . . .

Pauline leans closer to me, looking right into my eyes as she places the knife on her own palm. "Your Talent is mine," she whispers.

The doors behind me burst open and a crack of gunfire splits the air. Someone screams, and the hands holding me loosen their grip. I cover my head and duck as another bullet strikes the statue in the middle of the room.

"Get them!" The cries of the thugs are now matched by the shouts of policemen.

Stone particles are scattered over the floor where the angel statue's head rolls. I shuffle to my feet, suddenly free of any hold.

Pauline curses and raises her knife. The hate in her eyes is so deep I'm certain she's about to strike me. "You . . ." She draws the word out with loathing. Before I can even react, three policemen grab her and drag her away. "Let me go!" she screeches, elbowing one of them in the face.

I should feel some sort of triumph at her fall, but all I care about now is getting to Josephine.

I need to know the truth about Father.

She is still at the top of the stairs holding Renée as her hostage and taking in the fight with a wide glare. I can see the fear on her face—the debate in her eyes as they linger on the book. Then her gaze meets mine, and her hold on Renée tightens. I know her next move even before it happens.

"No!" I cry just as she pushes Renée down the stairs.

The world slows as her body tumbles down with horrid thuds. Madame's scream cuts through me like a knife as she charges forward, catching Renée just before her head can hit the ground.

But I can't tear my eyes off Josephine as she steps back, trying to sneak away.

I cannot let that happen.

I spring forward, grabbing Father's book from the floor with my good hand and charging up the stairs.

"Running away without your prize, *Mademoiselle Garnier*?" I call after her.

Josephine is almost at the back door leading to her storage area and cellar, but she pauses as she scowls at the book I'm waving over my head.

"This is what you want, isn't it?" My voice is nearly swallowed by the noise of the fighting below. It's a desperate move, trying to lure her to talk instead of fleeing. Yet somehow her hand still hasn't reached for the door handle. "Was ruining my father's business not enough for you?" I take another step toward her.

"Your father was a fool." She spits the words at me.

"Liar! Father was a true artist. Unlike you!"

My skin crawls as she laughs in response, the sound untamed. "One day you'll end up just like him—at the bottom of the river. Right where you both belong. My only regret is that the bastard took his Talent with him."

He took his Talent with him . . .

"You wanted to steal his gem." I know the words are true as they leave my lips. "Did Dahlia put you up to this?"

"Dahlia?" She laughs again. "She couldn't care less about a little fish like your father. But I never quite figured out his methods, no matter how hard I tried." There is a glimpse of madness in her eyes when she stares at the book. "And now you hold the answers I need."

Before I can understand what's happening, she charges toward me. We both crash to the floor as she flings herself on me, her hands grabbing the book. I cry out, but I don't let go.

"Give it to me!" she screams into my ear, aiming a painful jab at my ribs.

I wail in pain, my heart all the way up in my throat. I cannot let her take Father's book. I cannot let this vile woman defile his memory.

A wave of adrenaline runs in my veins as I push against her, and I manage to snatch the book from her grasp. She lunges at me again, eyes full of madness and rage. A second later, I smack the thick cover right into her face with all my strength and feel a crack. She staggers back from shock, blood dripping from her nose.

"You vile creature! I'll get you for this!" she cries.

But now heavy steps echo behind me, and police officers dash forward, grabbing Josephine and pinning her down. Then Nuriel is by my side, his hands helping me up to my feet.

"Let go of me!" Josephine shouts, saliva bubbling at the corners of her mouth. "Do you know who I am?"

"Wait!" I yell at them as they start dragging her away. "I have one more question for her."

They pause, staring at Nuriel as if waiting for his command. He nods.

I look right into Josephine's eyes, ignoring the blood now smearing her lips. "Did you kill my father?"

She spits at my feet. "I wanted nothing more than his Talent. You have no idea what it's like to be gifted magic and still not be the best. But the idiot tried to fight. He died before I had the chance to get my hands on it."

Tears spring to my eyes and my legs buckle under me, but Nuriel's strong arms catch me before I fall.

"Take her away," he orders.

I watch as they carry her, her hot pink coat dragging on the floor behind her. Her shouts echo through the hall like the feral cries of a wounded animal, receding only when they force her outside.

"Are you alright?" Nuriel asks.

"I will be."

"What was all of that about your father?"

"The truth, finally . . ." And even though tears stream down my cheeks, I'm smiling. Father was a hero. He fought for his family, for his Talent. He wasn't a desperate man, or a drunkard. He was a man of honor until his last breath. I hug his book tighter to my chest.

I try to stand on my own, pulling away from Nuriel gently. But his embrace tightens around me instead.

"I swear I'll be fine. You don't need to—"

"I was so worried we were too late." He speaks over me. "When your sister . . ." There is a tremble in his voice that makes me look up at him. His beautiful eyes, full of softness, lock with mine.

"What are you . . . ? We got the Talents, so you don't need to worry anymore."

He shakes his head, stroking a stray curl from my face and tucking it behind my ear. The warmth of his touch calls to me, inviting me to lean in and let it seep into my skin and revive me.

"I wasn't afraid because of the Talents. Did you honestly think I did all this just to help those stuffy Elite snobs keep their gems?"

And though he doesn't say the words, they hang in the air between us: *I did it for you.*

Nuriel's smile brightens as I finally allow myself to sink into his embrace.

"I believe this is yours." He pulls out my ruby. "That maid of yours gave us quite the fight over it. She'll be locked up for a long, long time."

I stare at the ruby, its magic calling me to reunite with it. But something inside me rejects it. This is not who I am. Not anymore.

"I . . . I don't want it."

"What will you do with it, then?"

I place the ring on my finger, the echo of music and the soft humming of a child echoing in my mind. "Give it to someone who deserves it."

He hugs me again, and a policeman appears at the top of the stairs.

"My lord, we need you outside. We believe we found your Talent."

"Your diamond!" I gasp. "The men took it before I could—"

"Don't worry about it." He smiles at me. "I'll be right there," he calls to the policeman before turning back to me. "I honestly hoped they wouldn't find it again."

"What? What do you mean?"

"Haven't you guessed by now?"

I look deep into his eyes; all his guarded secrets and games are finally at an end. The books in his study, the sketches he carried around, his dedication to the greenhouse designs, the ease with which he offered to risk his Talent for this mission.

"You're the architect."

"I am. Just as you are the modiste," he says. "We are quite the pair, aren't we?"

"I guess we are." I can't help but smile at him.

"My lord?" the policeman calls again.

"I'll be back soon." Nuriel cups my cheek warmly. "Cleodora."

I stay in place for a few moments as he walks away, the tension dropping in my body until I nearly fall down again.

Down in the shop, police are swarming, but the fighting is done. Bodies litter the ground, while men in handcuffs sit among the ruins of bloodied dresses, suits, and shards of stone.

Madame and Renée are nowhere to be found, but I'm told they've been taken by the police to get medical care. I should go down and look for my sister, but I can't stop feeling as if something is missing.

Something important.

Someone.

Where is Dahlia?

Why isn't she here? Did she really leave Pauline in charge and stay away? I know she doesn't do any of the dirty work herself, but for her to just disappear . . . She wouldn't leave so many Talents in the hands of a puppet. It makes no sense. My thoughts trail away as I look down the corridor. Right at the end of it is Josephine's private fitting room. The door is slightly open, allowing a sliver of warm candlelight to fall into the carpeted corridor.

My legs start moving before I can think.

My heart hammers in my chest as I slowly push the door, and the familiar scent of jasmine envelops me.

"I've been waiting for you, dear." Dahlia's soft voice cascades over my skin, and I shiver. She looks at me with her beautiful, innocent doe eyes, leaning gently against the desk as if she hasn't a care in the world—as if she is not the shadowy beast I know her to be.

"Dahlia . . ."

I should shout, alert the police, and call for help. But all I can do is stare at her—at the way the crimson fabric hugs her figure just as it did the very first time I saw her. At how her lush, black hair drapes over her back in soft waves. How her perfect lips are slightly parted, as if inviting me in.

"You've surprised me, Cleo," she says. "Not many people manage to do that."

I force myself to swallow as she pushes away from the desk, stepping closer to me.

"It seems as though you have a choice to make."

"I should call the police . . ."

"Yes. You should. But you won't."

"You never cared about me. You don't care about anyone. You had Lirone shot."

"My lovely, if I'd wanted the boy dead, I'd have sent someone to finish the job. I was the one who whistled back in the garden to alert the guards to your location."

My mouth drops. Could she be lying?

No . . . Dahlia never lies.

"I was too lenient with you." She sighs sweetly, that echo of pain lingering in her voice. "I have only myself to blame."

Her gaze is hypnotizing, and it sends electric shocks down my spine.

"What . . . Why . . . How could you do all of this? After everything . . . How do you just shut your emotions off?" A warm tear escapes the corner of my eye. I want to hate her. I want to stop her. But her hold on me is far too great. "Why can't I let you go?" My voice cracks.

"Oh, Cleo, don't you see? I didn't just want you to be mine . . . I wanted to be . . ."

Yours. Was that what she meant to say?

She tilts her head, the sentiment dying on her lips. Instead, all that remains is a glint of longing flickering on her face. "We truly did have something special."

I shake my head as I brace myself, desperately trying to shield my soul from the lure of her sweet words.

"Shhh . . . Don't strain yourself." She presses a finger to my lips. "It's not your fault. This is *my Talent.*" My heart skips a beat as she plants a kiss on my forehead, her lips softer than the flutter of butterfly wings.

But she doesn't say more, doesn't explain.

I don't try to stop her as she strides to the large closet. Pushing the clothes aside, she reveals the secret passage, the one I had only guessed the existence of before. "Goodbye, my lovely nightingale," she whispers before disappearing inside.

CHAPTER THIRTY-THREE

Spread Your Wings

THE SEWING MACHINE whirs happily as I step on the pedal, feeding another seam beneath the needle. The rich velvet is slippery in my grasp, but I keep my grip firm.

"Make sure the tension of the stitches isn't too tight, mon coeur." The memory of Father's voice echoes in my head. "Velvet is a tricky fabric. If you try to tame it, it'll only work against you. You have to give it room to breathe."

I smile as I release the tension of the silk thread. I'm not Father—I don't have his Talent. But I do have his memory and his legacy. Every lesson he taught me, every time he guided my hand as I sewed, every hour we spent studying patterns. Father raised me on the knees of fashion and taught me everything he knew. But he did more than that.

He made sure I fell in love with the art.

Fixing his coat is like sewing my past to my future—the final mark of bringing back the grandeur of the House of Finley.

"Cleo, your guests are here," Anaella calls as she enters the room, her face beaming.

After almost a month, her scar is now a faded white trace. But its presence only adds to the strength of her natural beauty.

"Bring them in. I just have one last stitch." I step on the pedal once more, the needle responding as I push the fabric. I make sure the machine's lever is at the top before removing the coat and cutting the loop thread.

I grab the pen resting on the desk, staring at the open page in Father's book. The sketch of the coat is old and wrinkled, but his writing is still as clear as ever. I press the tip of the pen to the page, scribbling my own note with a steady hand: "*Sep. 21st. Restoration is complete.*"

My heart swells as I flip through the stained and withered pages. Each one of them is a precious memory, and the blank ones at the end await new memories that Anaella and I have already started creating.

"It looks perfect," Anaella says from the doorway. "As good as new."

Madame steps from behind her, entering the room with a quick stride. "We've already established what a gifted modiste Cleodora is. And so have the papers!" She waves a picture frame in front of me as Renée and Lirone join us.

"Hi, Cleo." Lirone smirks.

The color has returned to his face, and he has been gaining weight. The old torn coat he used to wear is nowhere in sight, replaced by a clean jacket that actually fits his size, and new leather shoes. Renée has her good hand resting on his shoulder, while her other one is still braced after her fall.

"We thought it would be nice for you to have the article framed and hanging above your desk," Renée says.

I stare at the headline, forcing my smile to remain intact as I read the words I've already memorized.

Shockwaves hit the city!

Lutèce's Nightingale revealed to be a gifted modiste and a police informant, responsible for the fall of the city's largest illicit market operation.

I have read the article too many times to count. It calls me a brave woman who risked her life to stop the stealing of Talents. The woman who prevented another widespread panic and made sure the lost gems were returned safely to their owners. Of course, there is no mention of me ever being a part of the operation that set out to steal them to begin with. No one even cares that I wasn't really related to Lady Adley.

To the world, I am a hero.

An entire section of the article is dedicated to my dress, my costume for The Enchantress. It's called a masterpiece, a gown that breathes life into whoever wears it, as if it were made of magic. And they call me "The *gifted* modiste without a Talent."

With such high praise, and with Josephine's fashion house closed, it's no wonder people have flooded our shop. Suddenly everyone wants a creation by the House of Finley.

"There was another arrest yesterday, did you hear?" Madame says as she hangs the framed article on a small hook on the wall. "Those thugs are not so loyal after all, it seems. With the right amount of pressure, they all started turning on each other."

"Unfortunately, they're still chasing that Dahlia woman." Renée shakes her head. "I really can't believe she wasn't there when it all happened."

My stomach tenses, and a bitter taste fills my mouth.

She was there.

I let her go.

The lingering connection between us was too much for me to fight. But I could never bring myself to speak that particular truth. Not that it matters. Dahlia's entire network has been exposed and ruined. And with all of society aware of her operation, rebuilding it would be practically impossible.

I shake the thoughts of Dahlia from my head.

All I can do now is focus on the future. On a life without her seductive ways and dark promises. A life of integrity that honors Father's legacy.

This is the reason I had everyone come today.

"We should start, before the shop opens." I clear my throat before turning to Lirone. "Are you sure you're feeling strong enough?"

He gives me his signature eye roll. "I've been all healed up for weeks. You guys are way too worried about it."

"You lost a lot of blood, mon petit monstre." Renée runs a hand through Lirone's thick blond curls, her motherly affections spilling out with each word. "You know we had to wait."

Lirone pouts, but he doesn't try to escape her touch. He has been living at Madame and Renée's home ever since he left the hospital. And I have a strong feeling that the arrangement will be permanent.

"Are *you* sure about this, Cleo?" Anaella takes my hand in hers. "You know that if you want to keep it, I'll support you."

"I don't think there's a soul in the city who wouldn't," Madame says. "Especially after they found out that old Lady Adley used to be one of the thieves. Not to mention that all the legal paperwork names you as the rightful heir."

I shake my head. "It's not my calling. Music isn't in my blood . . . not without the magic. But it is in Lirone's." I reach for the drawer in my desk. The ruby ring pulses when I pick it up, the magic singing in my veins. "Let's do it."

Lirone's eyes light up as he looks at the ring. "I'm ready."

Taking a thin silver knife from the desk, I carefully insert the blade under the prongs holding the gem and twist. The setting loosens without much of a fight. But disassembling the ring is the easy part. With a deep breath, I slice my palm, tracing the same original cut. This scar will stay with me forever, but now I can repurpose its memory. "The shinier the jewel, the bloodier the Talent," I say, echoing the words Dahlia spoke so long ago. But it isn't *my* blood that the stone craves anymore. I close my hand over the gem and the magic reacts at once, the ruby pulsing in time with my heart.

"Let me." Renée takes Lirone's palm in hers gently, and with a steady hand copies the cut I made on mine, only far deeper. He flinches but doesn't cry in pain.

My arm trembles as I pass the ruby to him, and his own blood coats the gem. At once my body quiets down, the static flow of magic evaporating and leaving me with a blessed calm. The absence of magic used to fill me with emptiness, but now I'm simply lighter, freer. I slip Father's empty ring over my finger and smile.

I am myself again.

"How do you feel?" Madame asks Lirone.

"I feel . . . like I want to sing!"

We all laugh.

It's all so right.

Anaella squeezes my good hand and whispers to me, "Father would be so proud. I am too."

A bell rings in the shop, drawing our attention.

"What time is it?" I ask. "My first appointment should be at ten."

"Still a few minutes. They can wait," Anaella says.

"You have so many clients," Madame notes. "You'll need help soon."

"I already have that covered," I say as I wrap a fresh bandage over the cut. Renée does the same for Lirone. "I've sent the doctor to care for Basset's sister. He wrote to me yesterday that she'll be ready to travel in a few weeks."

"Basset? Your old coachman who . . ."

"Died . . . yes." My heart clenches. "He was trying to care for his family. Now I will do that for him. Starting with training his sister—she will have a craft and a future."

Madame rests her hand on my shoulder and gives me a small squeeze. The bell rings again, impatiently.

"Maybe Véronique is early," Anaella says.

"You have Véronique coming in today?" Madame raises her brow. "Who would have thought I'd see the day she came to an establishment famous for its owners' lack of Talent. The world truly has gone wonderfully mad."

I chuckle as I walk to the front, all ready to ask Véronique to wait and then face her "charming" retorts. But it's not the diva standing by the door.

Heat rushes to my cheeks as Vicomte Lenoir walks in, waving a large scroll in his hand. His light forest-green silk vest glints in the morning sun, brightening the color of his eyes and contrasting his perfect, sun-kissed skin. I smile as I take in his messy hair and crooked tie—his disheveled look both familiar and inviting.

"Am I interrupting?" he asks. "I brought the new design ideas for the expansion."

"Perfect timing, actually," I say, as he spreads the paper over the counter, revealing a beautiful sketch of a modern, elegant shop that would put Josephine's store to shame.

"I believe we can remodel the entire building." His voice rings with excitement. "I'm already working on getting the permits." He pauses for a second, hesitant. "I also brought you these."

From behind his back, he pulls a bouquet of white roses, their sweet scent enveloping me.

"They're wonderful!" I say. "Thank you, my lord."

"My lord?" He cocks his eyebrow at me. "I thought I told you to call me Nuriel."

"Ugh, just *kiss* already!" Lirone whines from the back.

Laughter fills the air, but all I can see are Nuriel's magnetic green eyes as he leans in closer.

"Cleo, I think we'd better open. It's almost ten," Anaella says before our lips can meet.

I pull away from Nuriel reluctantly. "I'll be right back."

My smile is unwavering as I turn to the door. And as I flip the "Closed" sign to "Open," I feel as though I could fly.

Acknowledgments

If my heart could sing, *The Kiss of the Nightingale* would probably be its melody. I have spent so many years, and so many tears, working tirelessly to bring my artistic aspiration to fruition that having the opportunity to combine my passions for opera, writing, and magic is truly a dream come true. But this moment would never have arrived if it weren't for some amazing individuals I cannot possibly thank enough.

First, to my parents, who have supported every crazy new passion I brought forward, no matter how odd it seemed at first. Thank you for always believing in me, for always getting on board with my plans, and for helping me strive and reach ever higher in whatever I desire.

To my biggest supporter and the man who sat with me through long nights, reading every single draft of every piece I ever wrote. My dear Yoav, you believed in my ability to craft stories from the start. You helped me brainstorm and encouraged me to keep pushing forward no matter how much I struggled. This book would've never looked the same without you.

To my brilliant agent, Millie Hoskins. I could not be more grateful for the amazing fortune that brought my opening pages to your desk. Thank you for believing in me and my story. Thank you for loving Cleodora, Dahlia, and Nuriel as much as I do. Thank you for making my story stronger with your editorial thoughts and for connecting with my vision in a way that makes me feel seen and so supported. I could not have asked for a better partner and champion to work with. A large thank you also to the foreign rights team at United Agents, especially to Alex Stephens and Jane Willis, for all your faith and for working tirelessly to bring my stories out to the world.

To my editor at Tundra Books, Lynne Missen, and the entire team for welcoming my books and me into your catalog with so much love. Thank you, Lynne, for your brilliant editorial notes and your endless kindness and enthusiasm. Special thanks also to Bharti Bedi for your thoughtful editorial insights, and to Samantha Devotta and Graciela Colin for being the most fantastic publicity and marketing team and for sharing your endless excitement for my story.

To my editor and publisher, Christina Demosthenous, and the entire Dialogue-Renegade family. Your unwavering dedication and belief in my work has been so inspiring. I feel so fortunate to have your insight, patience, and expertise to guide me. Thank you to Eleanor Gaffney and Alexa Allen-Batifoulier for the editorial care, and thank you to Emily Moran and Millie Seaward for your incredible approach to the marketing and publicity, and for making sure my story can find its readers. Another thank you to Carrie Hutchison for bringing my story to life via audiobook.

I could not be more grateful to have such fantastic teams on my side, collaborating to bring *The Kiss of the Nightingale* out into the world.

Another special thanks to Amy Mae Baxter, who read my book and decided to make my dream a reality. Your enthusiasm and clear passion for Cleo's story captured me from our first call. I am forever grateful for the chance we had to work together, and for how you made this story that much stronger and more heart-felt. Thank you for taking a chance on me.

Thank you to Tim Byrne for the most beautiful cover I could have hoped for. Not only is it visually stunning but it embodies the spirit of the story fully. I absolutely adore all the details that you managed to incorporate and how perfectly they work with the themes of the book. It's the type of cover where the more you look the more details you see, and the more you love it.

To my critique partners, beta readers, and writer friends: Allara Mist, Poppi Multz, Jen Ciesla, Athena Balanou, Natasha Tinsley, Sarena Flanigan, Anca Demeter, Taylor Munsell, Ejay Dawson, Alexandra Atman, and Julie Reynolds. This book would've never happened without your constant cheering, invaluable feedback, and unwavering faith. I could not ask for better friends to go through this journey with. Thank you for always being there for me.

To all of my wonderful teachers who helped me discover and develop my singing voice. You helped me find joy within music and instilled such passion in me for the art of singing; your energies and support shaped me into the singer I am today and helped make this book the product of love that it is.

And finally, thank *you*, my dear readers. Thank you for picking up *The Kiss of the Nightingale* and for making my dream of sharing Cleo's story a reality. This book is for you, with all my love and appreciation.